W9-BNI-283
To see a World in a Grain of Sand
And a Heaven in a Wild Flower
Hold Infinity in the palm of your hand
And Eternity in an hour
William Blake
Auguries of Innocence

$2.75

In The Shelter Of The Willow Tree, He Waited For Her

They had been together almost nightly in the past three weeks, and, somewhere along the way, light banter and easy camaraderie had yielded to hungry desire and smoldering passion. Neither knew where their reckless emotions would lead, for there was no thought of tomorrow, only the here and now and the joy of each tender moment.

Gator's heart had won out in debate with his head, and no longer did he worry over the right or wrong of it. Anjele had told him she felt the same, and there was no turning back. All that awaited was the consummation of their hungrily raging bodies.

Also by Patricia Hagan

Midnight Rose

Available from HarperPaperbacks

HEAVEN IN A WILDFLOWER

PATRICIA HAGAN

HarperPaperbacks
A Division of HarperCollins*Publishers*

HarperPaperbacks *A Division of* HarperCollins*Publishers*
10 East 53rd Street, New York, N.Y. 10022

Cover illustration by R.A. Maguire

First printing: March 1992

Printed in the United States of America

❖ 10 9 8 7 6 5 4 3 2 1

CHAPTER 1

New Orleans, Louisiana
Summer, 1858

A WARM BREEZE WAFTED THROUGH THE open French doors leading to the porch. Wearing a thin chemise and pantalets, Anjele stood just inside her room. She was supposed to be taking a nap, or at least lying down, because it was the season of the ague, or yellow fever. People believed resting in the hottest part of the day helped prevent the disease, but going to bed was the last thing she felt like doing in such miserable heat.

The shade of the spreading oaks, dripping with shadowy moss, looked cool and inviting along the avenue leading to the sleepy river beyond. She longed for a swim, but not in the thick, brown waters of the serpentine Mississippi. It was her secret place she yearned for, the hidden freshwater pool she and Simona and Emalee had discovered a few years ago. Hidden in the fringes of Bayou Perot, it was fed by an underground spring that kept the water from becoming stagnant. Best of all, they had never seen a snake or an alligator there.

Sadly, as she stood there enjoying the view, she was struck once more with awareness of how time was running out to enjoy the things she loved on the plantation. Since her sixteenth birthday the month before, when the formal announcement of her engagement to Raymond Duval was made, a feeling of desperation had descended. All her life, she'd been well aware of the pact between their parents, but it wasn't till it became official and a wedding date set for Christmas that the actuality had soaked in. Now, thinking about moving into New Orleans, leaving this beloved place to return only for visits, made her stomach knot with dread.

She had grown up loving to spend as much time as possible traipsing after her father, whom she adored. He had taught her to ride a horse and shoot a gun as well as any man—unknown to her mother, of course, who didn't approve of her learning masculine skills. So it had become a cherished secret between her father and her, only now she had to fit in those times around her music.

Ida Duval, Raymond's mother, insisted Anjele start learning to play the piano, something Anjele had resisted in the past. Miss Ida felt it was a nice touch for a hostess to be able to entertain her guests after dinner and, since Anjele's mother was much too busy to give Anjele lessons, Mrs. Melora Rabine was sent twice a week to teach.

Anjele smiled to think how surprised everyone was to discover she had a natural talent. In no time at all, she was able to play anything by ear, after hearing the melody only once or twice. But Claudia, her adopted sister, had been studying for years and accused her of having been practicing secretly, declaring it was not possible to master the piano so fast. Anjele neither denied nor confirmed. Long ago, she'd learned there was no getting along with Claudia.

Ida also sent someone to instruct in needlework, and Twyla turned a deaf ear to Anjele's protests. Anjele suspected the real reason her mother was going along with everything Ida wanted was to keep her busy so she wouldn't have time to slip away and be with Simona and Emalee. Acadian girls. Her mother didn't approve of them but wasn't as vocal as Claudia, who warned that Ida Duval would have a fit if she knew Anjele socialized with the lower classes.

Anjele was well aware that lots of other people looked down their noses at the Acadians due to the mixed heritage of some, but it didn't matter one bit to her. She felt sorry for the way their ancestors, French Canadians, had been driven from their colony of Acadia by the British, forcing them to find new homes in unfamiliar territories. Many, like the families of Emalee and Simona, had chosen to settle in the fertile bayou lands of southern Louisiana. They lived in small, compact, self-contained communities deep in the swamps. When they sought work, it was in the cane or cotton fields. But, unlike the Negro slaves, the Cajuns were paid wages and free to leave at quitting time to return to their bayou homes.

Anjele envied them their happy, carefree lives as she listened to Emalee and Simona and the other girls describe the merriment that went on in their compounds as they cooked their supper. Cauldrons of turtle soup or crawfish gumbo bubbled deliciously while fiddlers played rousing Cajun tunes in an effort to ease their weary spirits after a hard day. They would sing, and sometimes, on the banks of the shadow-silent waters of the mysterious bayou, and even though she wasn't allowed, Anjele longed to be a part of it all.

Two years ago, Simona had married, when she was only fourteen. But that hadn't stopped her from spending time with Anjele whenever possible. Anjele would slip down to the edge of the cane fields and wait till the overseer wasn't looking, so both Simona and Emalee could dart away. The trio would then disappear into the moss-shrouded forest for a few stolen hours at their secret pool, treasured memories that now filled Anjele with longing on the hot and humid afternoon.

Suddenly she was torn from reverie by the sound of the door from the outside hall opening. She watched as Claudia crept stealthily into the room. Seeing Anjele's empty bed, she glanced about wildly, spotting her at the open French doors."You're supposed to rest until two o'clock, and it's only half past one," she said sharply.

"So are you," Anjele reminded her. Dear Lord, she couldn't remember a time in her life when they weren't sparring. She honestly felt she had tried through the years to get along, but it was a hopeless situation. Claudia despised her and always would.

Claudia's ice blue eyes flashed with defiance as she lifted her chin and smiled gloatingly. "Mother said I could go with her to take tea at Miss Ida's. We're going to be leaving soon." She was also wearing a chemise but several ruffled petticoats covered her pantalets. She crossed the room to a large mahogany armoire and jerked open the mirrored doors.

Anjele, stunned by her nerve, demanded, "What do you think you're doing?"

Claudia ignored her as she pawed impatiently through the gowns hanging inside till she found what she was looking for and yanked it out in triumph. "I'm wearing this. It's cooler than anything I have, and it will look better on me than you, anyway."

Anjele shook her head in firm denial. "I'm wearing that to Rebecca Saunders's birthday ball tonight."

"So? Wear it. We'll be home around five." Draping the garment over her arm, she started out.

Anjele ran to block her path. She hated to have an argument, but every time Claudia borrowed her clothes, they were brought back mussed. And the dress was a favorite for the sweltering weather—a cool, pale green color, fashioned of light lace and chiffon and draped off the shoulder with a scooped bodice.

She knew Claudia was only using the heat as an excuse. The real reason was her larger bosom, which would be more revealing in Anjele's smaller bodice—and all for Raymond's benefit. Claudia had never made a secret of the way she felt about him. Not that Anjele was jealous. Actually, it concerned her that she wasn't.

Anjele repeated her objection, adding, in an effort to pacify, "I'll be glad to let you wear it another time."

Claudia's eyes narrowed. "You'll be sorry."

"You have other dresses." She bit back the impulse to point out that Claudia actually had a much nicer wardrobe than she did. It was merely another way her mother made sure she could not be accused of favoring her natural daughter over the adopted one.

"It's because of Raymond, isn't it?" Claudia challenged. "You're afraid he'll think I'm prettier than you, so you don't want me to look nice."

Quietly, Anjele yielded, "You are prettier than me, Claudia." And she believed that to be so. Anjele envied her cousin's naturally curly golden-blond hair and limpid blue eyes, while thinking her own appearance to be a bit on the plain side. Her mother said it was because she didn't try to be glamorous, which was true. Anjele much preferred her long hair blowing in the breeze when she went riding, and it was too much trouble to sponge her skin with rosewater and lemon juice. She saw nothing wrong with tanned flesh and sunburned cheeks.

Claudia was getting angrier by the minute. "If I'm so pretty, then how come it's you Raymond is going to marry?"

Anjele sighed and shook her head, wondering once more why it had to be this way between them. Claudia knew as well as she how it all came to be but pushed back impatience as she reminded, "Ida and Elton have been friends with Momma and Poppa forever. It was always understood."

"But you don't love him . . . ." Her words trailed off as Jobie, the little servant girl, appeared in the doorway.

Looking fearfully from one to the other, Jobie finally held out the tray she was carrying and said to Anjele, "I got yo' lemonade, missy."

Anjele stepped back long enough to allow her to place it on the table by the window but made sure Claudia did not rush by with the dress.

When they were once more alone, Anjele saw no need to continue the subject of Raymond and tried to end the conversation. She held out her hands to take the garment. "I'm sorry, but I can't let you borrow it, Claudia. Not this time."

Claudia was silent for a moment, then whirled around as she cried, "Very well. But if I can't wear it, neither will you. Not tonight, anyway."

Before Anjele could make a move to stop her, she

ran to where Jobie had left the pitcher of lemonade and quickly snatched it up to pour the liquid on the dress. Horrified, Anjele rushed to yank the garment away from her, at the same time accidentally knocking the pitcher to the floor with a loud crash.

Claudia began to shriek, "You're crazy! Your own dress! I don't believe this, and all because I asked to wear it . . . ."

Anjele realized just what she was up to at the same time her mother, hearing the uproar, came charging into the room. "What in heaven's name . . ." She saw the gown Anjele was holding, the huge, wet stain on the bodice, spreading to the skirt. Crossing the room in quick strides, she jerked it from her and demanded, "What have you done?"

Claudia was not about to allow Anjele to defend herself, and told her hastily conjured lie. With a feigned look of horror and dismay, she wailed, "You can see what she's done—ruined it, that's what, and all because I wanted to wear it this afternoon. She accused me of wanting to look nice for Raymond and said she'd make sure I couldn't wear it."

"Oh, Anjele, how could you?" Twyla Sinclair moaned. "This was a terrible thing for you to do. Why couldn't you let your sister wear it?"

She's not my sister, Anjele silently, furiously, fumed but knew better than to say so out loud. Nothing made her mother madder than to be reminded Claudia was actually her second cousin and not her adopted sister.

"Are you going to answer me?" Twyla asked tightly, evenly.

Claudia positioned herself behind Twyla so she could grin at Anjele in triumph.

Anjele bit her lip thoughtfully. So many times, she'd been through similar scenes, and the outcome was always the same—her mother believed Claudia's side of the story. Not to do so meant calling her adopted daughter a liar, which would make it appear she was favoring her real daughter. Long ago Anjele had stopped defending herself to salvage her pride, and this occasion was no different. With a careless shrug, she responded, "You're going to believe what you want to, Mother. Nothing I say ever makes any difference."

At that, Twyla wailed, "Why do you have to be so difficult? Why do you always make trouble?"

Claudia had to put both hands over her mouth to hold back delicious giggles. About to lose control, she backed out of the room, pausing at the door long enough to stick her tongue out at Anjele before skipping down the hall.

Anjele threw herself, face down, across the bed, preparing for another of her mother's diatribes.

She did not have to wait long.

"Why do you take such malicious pleasure in hurting your sister? I should think you'd take pity on her because she's adopted, Anjele, instead of being bitter about it. What if it had been I who died in childbirth, instead of your father's cousin? What if you had been the pitiful little baby abandoned by your father in his grief, left to be cared for by relatives? Wouldn't you have wanted compassion? Wouldn't you have wanted to be treated like one of the family? Of course you would, yet you seem to go out of your way to antagonize poor Claudia.

"I had hoped your engagement to Raymond would make a difference," Twyla raged on, pacing up and down the huge room, waving her arms in the air. "I thought it would mature you, but it hasn't. You aren't thinking about marrying him. All you seem to care about is annoying your sister. You know she's always hoped by some miracle she'd be the one to marry Raymond, but even if it hadn't all been prearranged, it was you he wanted. So do you have to twist the knife?"

Anjele didn't respond. Experience had taught her it was best to let her mother rave on, even though silence was considered further insolence.

She shut her out by concentrating on the beautiful blue skies beyond, picturing fields of sugarcane dancing in the wind in a rainbow hue blending from near white to yellow and on to green and purple and red and violet, even striped stalks, all nearly six feet high, swaying proudly in the rhythmic breezes. How she longed to be out there amidst it all, and—

She came back to reality with an excited rush, for suddenly her mother had caught her interest.

" . . . and I'll expect you to practice the rest of the afternoon," she was saying, changing her tone from anger to disappointment, which meant the scene was, mercifully, coming to an end. "Miss Melora says the new Beethoven piece needs more work, and she'll expect you to have it mastered by the time she returns. She'll be in Baton Rouge only a week."

So, Miss Melora wasn't coming today. Anjele burrowed her face in the pillow so her happiness wouldn't show. There was absolutely no way she was going to stay indoors if she could help it. This was her first chance to get away for a few hours in so long she couldn't remember.

She was relieved to hear her mother leaving.

Twyla paused at the door to deliver the final punishment. "To teach you a lesson, since you ruined the dress you were planning to wear to Rebecca's party tonight, you won't be going. Raymond can just escort your sister, instead. I'm truly sorry, Anjele, but that's how it must be."

I really don't care, Anjele silently answered, though she knew Raymond wasn't going to like it. He had told her how Claudia made him uncomfortable, fawning over him as she did.

She waited till she saw their carriage leave, then hurried to slip on a light muslin dress. The house was quiet. The servants were, no doubt, out back in the kitchen, preparing supper.

She made her way down the rear stairs but was met by Mammy Kesia as she stepped into the service hallway.

"And where you think you goin'?" the old woman said. "Your momma told me you was to practice the piano till she comes home around five this evenin', and from the way you're sneakin' around with that gleam in your eyes, I'd say abangin' on them keys is the last thing you got in mind."

Anjele thought a moment. Kesia was easily persuaded to look the other way, as long as she didn't get in trouble doing it. Impishly she inquired, "And what might be your plans for the afternoon?"

Kesia knew her for the scamp she was, just as she sympathized for the way Miss Twyla went too far in her determination not to show favoritism between the two girls. Kesia was also well aware of how Miss Claudia was always lying and scheming to cause trouble, only she managed never to get caught. So, feeling sorry for Miss Anjele, Kesia kept her expression stern as she replied, "I'm gonna be in the garden, pickin' peas, that's what I'm gonna be doin', and even though I can't hear you at that piano, I know you gonna be doin' what your momma said for you to do."

With that, she walked away.

"Bless you," Anjele whispered, waiting a moment before also taking her leave.

She headed towards the rear, where the kitchen was separated from the big house because of the danger of fire. The *pigeonniers* and gardeners' sheds were nearby. Then came the long twin lines of slave cabins—the older ones built of brick, the newer constructed of whitewashed wood.

As she passed, Anjele cheerily waved to the young girls busily weaving dried palmetto fronds into fans.

There were many other buildings, as well—icehouse, laundry, smithy, tannery, gristmill, stables, barn, and dairy.

Farther back, to one side, lay the sprawling cotton field sand cotton gin, to the other, the great, flat fields of cane. Intersected by an elaborate grid of canals, the land could drain surplus water into the swamp at the rear of the plantation, where a second levee had been constructed to hold out the backwater. A bucket-wheel, driven by steam, dipped water from inside the levee at the back and poured it into the swamp.

The sugarhouse was situated at a convenient point for transporting cane from the fields and hogsheads of sugar down to the pier at the river, but was now devoid of activity. Harvesting would not begin for several more months.

Anjele knew where to find Emalee and Simona. It was their task to carry jugs of water out in the fields to the hoe gangs. Amidst the glistening waves of cane, their backs bowed to the unmerciful sun, workers moved slowly up and down the rows, chopping away the choking blades of grass.

Not wanting her father to see her, should he be around, she entered the dark bordering forest and suddenly felt swallowed up by the great phantasmal cascades of moss descending from the huge serpentine limbs of the oaks and pines above. She watched every step, lest a deadly water moccasin be in her path. The way was familiar, for she had skirted along the woods at the edge of the cane fields many times.

As she moved along, she peered out now and then through the foliage, finally spotting the girls, together as always. Waiting till they moved in her direction and were only a few feet away, she called softly.

They did not hesitate. Glancing about to make sure they weren't seen by master, overseer, or drivers, they broke into a run and crashed into the woods, giggling and hugging Anjele in their delight.

"Where you been?" Simona wanted to know. "We not see you for many days. Been prettying up for the beau, eh?"

Anjele made a face. "Not hardly. You know how I feel about getting married." She proceeded to confide the latest incident with Claudia and finished with how she'd managed to sneak away for the afternoon in hopes of persuading them to join her for a swim.

Emalee slapped her on the back. "You no gotta ask twice. What for we waiting?"

Anjele loved to hear the Cajuns talk, for they had their own patois, a delightful combination of archaic French forms with idioms taken mostly from their Indian and Negro neighbors.

Emalee turned to lead the way deeper into the woods, but Anjele happened to glance back toward the cane field, and that was when the stranger caught her eye.

His tanned shoulders were incredibly broad. He was bare chested, his skin bronzed from long hours in the sun, and his muscles gleamed like liquid gold. His waist was narrow; his trousers stretched tight across rock-hard thighs.

Slowly, Anjele tore her fascinated gaze from his body to move upward, only to gasp at the realization that he seemed to be looking right at her. But that wasn't possible, was it? She was swallowed up by the dense foliage between, yet there was the play of a knowing smile on his lips. She saw, too, even from her distance, that it was a nice face, boldly masculine but handsome. His sable hair, thick and long, was pulled back behind his neck. Even from so far, she could see the cool arrogance in his dark, smoldering eyes.

Emalee and Simona continued a few feet before Simona realized Anjele was not following and turned to scold, "Hey, what you waiting for? If the driver see us, we get in big trouble, and he might say we can't work no more this season. What you be lookin' at, anyhow?"

Suddenly embarrassed, Anjele hastened to join her, but Simona strained to look past her and promptly teased, "Ah, you be lookin' at Gator," she flashed a knowing smile. "All the girls, they look at Gator. He very fine to look at, too, no?"

"Very fine," Anjele did not hesitate to agree, surprised to realize she'd never so boldly expressed her feelings about a man before, particularly someone she didn't know. "Who is he? I don't think I've ever seen him around here before."

As they followed the path, Simona confided what little she knew about the enigmatic man known only as Gator. "He just come here a few weeks ago. Somebody said his poppa is an overseer in the cotton fields."

Anjele didn't want to appear interested but for some strange reason felt a burning desire to learn more about the intriguing young man. "Why do they call him Gator?"

Emalee proceeded to explain. "I heard some of the menfolks talking, and they said this Gator, he wrestled a bull alligator when he was only sixteen. It happened someplace else, 'cause he ain't from around here. Anyway, he was out in a swamp, huntin' for hides, but this one, it was maybe twenty feet long, biggest ever seen, and it took him by surprise and dragged him down in the waters. You know gators, they do that with their prey, hold on and drag it down and roll it over and over till it drowns."

Anjele shuddered to imagine such horror but urged, "Go on. What happened?

"Well, those watching say that fight went on fifteen, maybe twenty minutes. That gator, he kept draggin' the boy down, and finally, he come up, and the gator, he was dead. Ever since, nobody, they say, ever know Gator by any other name."

Anjele marveled, "It's a wonder he's not scarred."

The Cajun girls giggled, and Simona dared suggest, "Maybe he is—where you no can see."

"But maybe where she would like to see," Emalee teased.

Anjele was used to their good-natured bantering and laughed with them.

They left the main trail into the bayou and skirted a

levee before making their way to the banks of the secret pond. "Nobody ever find it, because no one ever go around the levee," Simona pointed out happily.

As they had done when they were children, they stripped off all their clothes and dove into the cool water. They swam and splashed and laughed and ducked each other and when they were finally exhausted, stretched out on the grassy bank to bask in the late afternoon sunshine.

Conversation eventually turned to Simona's marriage, as she was always eager to talk about her husband.

With a knowing wink at Anjele, Emalee dared to prod Simona, "Tell us something besides how nice he is. We want to hear how good."

Anjele chimed in to urge her on, and Simona audaciously obliged, describing her personal life in detail.

Anjele listened, entranced, but not without a cold ripple of apprehension moving down her spine as she thought of doing those things with Raymond. To have him touch her that way, and to do that to her body, filled her with dread.

Too soon, it was time to leave, and Anjele was secretly glad, because listening to Simona had depressed her. She became even more dispirited when the girls began to talk excitedly of a party that night.

"Crawfish gumbo," Emalee cried, "and a big turtle stew. The menfolk, they got spirits abrewin', and old Sam, he gonna tune his fiddle right."

Simona exulted, "Frank, he know the close dancin' they do in Bayou Teche. He teach me, and, oh! We get as hot as the crawfishes and the turtles boilin' in the pots."

This time, Anjele did not join in the laughter, and when they asked what was wrong, she reminded them how she had to miss the birthday ball, adding, "And I'm not jealous over Raymond escorting Claudia. I wasn't even looking forward to being with him anyway. It was just that I wanted to go to a party and have some fun."

With a sage grin, Simona declared, "You got to learn you got to make the good time yourself. Nobody gon' do it for you, my friend. Say!" She snapped her fingers as the reckless idea struck. "How come you can't come to our party tonight? Who's to know if you sneak out?"

Anjele allowed herself to savor the idea. She might never get another chance, and it wouldn't be the first time she had shimmied down the trellis from her balcony to the terrace below, though not since she was a little girl. Still, she knew she could probably do it and get away with it. Her mother and father would both go to the ball to pay their respects to Rebecca and her family and toast her birthday. The Saunders's plantation was an hour's ride away, at least, so they wouldn't be home till nearly midnight.

Simona and Emalee looked at each other in delight, and then Simona spoke the magic words, "We dare you."

At that, Anjele accepted, silently blaming her inability to resist a challenge.

The possibility of seeing the handsome stranger again had nothing to do with it, she told herself, even if thinking about him did provoke a strange, warm rush inside.

CHAPTER

ELTON *SINCLAIR KNEW SOMETHING WAS* wrong. Twyla had not said a word during the fresh strawberry appetizer. Anjele, also strangely quiet, hardly touched her crawfish bisque. The only one eating with relish and apparently in a good mood was Claudia. Her eyes were glittering, as though she harbored some kind of delicious secret. He hated to ask what was going on. Twyla had a rule against certain subjects at mealtime, and family problems was one of them. Still, the tension was getting the best of him. He held out his glass for a refill of cool muscadine wine as the main course of fried shrimp and collard greens was being brought in, and decided to attempt conversation himself. "Looks like this season's sugar is going to be better than last year's," he announced proudly to no one in particular. "I figure we'll produce over a thousand hogsheads."

Twyla offered a perfunctory smile and murmured tonelessly, "That's nice, dear."

Claudia gasped, "Is that all you've got to say? That it's nice? Mother, each hogshead weighs over a thousand pounds. A thousand hogsheads will be a record for BelleClair."

"I know, I know," Twyla said, adding dully, "I keep the books, Claudia, remember?"

"That's all the more reason for you to be excited." She turned to Elton. "I think it's wonderful, Daddy. Just wonderful."

He glanced uncomfortably at Anjele and realized her mind was a million miles away. What could be preying so heavily? Certainly not romantic woolgathering over Raymond Duval. He suspected she regarded her forthcoming marriage as what it was—the fulfillment of a commitment, as he had done when he married Twyla. But Anjele was still young. She'd settle down, have her own family, and be happy. Whatever was bothering her would smooth itself out.

He tried to concentrate on the food set before him but could not help thinking how he wished Anjele and Raymond would be living at BelleClair after they were married. He'd never had the sons he wanted but was proud of Anjele. A pity her home would be the city, because she'd make a fine planter's wife, like her mother, who found time to be a mother and a hostess, as well as a commander and tutor of the household slaves. She also kept many of his accounts. BelleClair produced hay, beans, Irish potatoes, yams, peas, and raised swine, oxen, horses, mules, sheep, and cattle. Common slaves were involved in sugar making, cobbling, wagon and brick making, along with working the cotton fields. Skilled laborers were abundant—blacksmiths, mechanics, engineers, tanners, cartmen and millers. And Twyla kept up with every bit of it.

It all been started by his father, Leveret Sinclair, who had come to America in the late 1700s to eventually become a prosperous cotton grower. He built the mansion and named it BelleClair.

When Elton had taken over complete control of BelleClair on the death of his father, he shared the philosophy that prime field hands, costing as much as eighteen hundred dollars apiece, should not be committed to the more hazardous tasks. Consequently, he hired Irish immigrant laborers to dig canals and ditches, level forests, and clear wastelands. Finally, it became necessary to hire the Cajuns to help work the fields.

Twyla's father and Leveret had been close friends in Europe. And though Elton had never laid eyes on Twyla till she stepped off the ship in Philadelphia that summer day so long ago, he had fallen in love on sight. Her mother was French, and Twyla, small and dainty, with a radiant smile and dancing brown eyes, charmed everyone she met with her pleasing personality and delightful accent.

All went well, but as the years passed, they experienced a deep void in their lives despite the love growing between them and their life of opulence. They desperately longed for something their love seemed unable to produce, nor wealth able to buy—a child of their own. Elton's two brothers had drowned in a flatboat accident during flood season one year. He and Twyla were both without siblings and found themselves longing for a large family to fill the huge rooms of the great house. But time went by, and they were sadly not blessed in that way.

When Leveret and then Adelia passed away, Elton and Twyla found themselves even lonelier. No matter that they were surrounded by hundred of slaves and

Cajun and Irish workers. They wanted the sound of children's laughter in their world.

Elton glanced at Claudia. Such a pretty girl. So sad she had such a nasty disposition. As a child, she'd had terrible tantrums and would sometimes hold her breath till she passed out. She was demanding, complained constantly, was forever screaming at the servants, and no one liked to be around her. Twyla said Claudia behaved that way because she felt unloved, unwanted, and merely craved attention. Elton disputed that theory as being just the opposite, for it was obvious to everyone around them how Twyla actually deferred to Claudia over her own daughter. And while he would never dare say so, many was the time he wished they had never adopted her. Lord knows, he had tried to love her as his own flesh and blood, and managed to pretend he did, but the harsh reality was—Claudia was just not lovable. But how could they have known such a pernicious disposition existed in an innocent, newborn babe? Their hearts had gone out to the motherless child, and they had been delighted to take her into their home, naming her after her poor, dead mother. Even when they joyfully realized a few months later, after giving up all hope, that their own baby was on the way, they still adored Claudia. It was only when she grew older that she became insufferable.

Elton was well aware Claudia was in love with Raymond and secretly wished she were the one marrying him. At the time the pact had been made between him and Raymond's father, Vinson, a close friend and prominent doctor, Elton had no way of knowing Raymond would ultimately grow up with a disinclination for anything resembling work. Sent to study in

Europe, he couldn't make passing marks and had returned within a year. Confessing he'd never wanted to be a doctor, anyway, Raymond further declared he also had no desire to be a planter. He talked his father into staking him to a stable of purebred racehorses and now spent all his time at the courses or gambling on the riverboats.

A servant brought dessert, a tangy-sweet lemon glacé, but Twyla held up her hand to decline coffee afterwards. "We don't have time." With a nod to Claudia, she prompted, "Better hurry, dear."

Claudia excused herself, but Elton did not miss the gloating smile she flashed at Anjele, who ignored it. He was prompted to ask, "Don't you need to be getting ready, too, Angel?"

Claudia, almost through the door, giggled. "She's no angel, Daddy. That's why she's not going. Just ask Mother."

"What's this?" He looked to Twyla for explanation. "What's going on here?"

Anjele listlessly stabbed at the glacé as she listened to her mother dully repeating Claudia's lies.

"She needs to be punished for doing something like that." Twyla sighed, then continued as though Anjele wasn't there. "Frankly, Elton, their bickering is getting worse, and I can't stand it. I wish we'd set the wedding date sooner. Poor Claudia. It's breaking her heart to see Raymond marry someone besides her, but that's the way it has to be. The sooner it's done and Anjele is out of the house, the quicker she'll start to get over it."

Elton knew, somehow, that it hadn't happened the way Twyla described at all. He could not imagine Anjele being so churlish. Turning to her, he softly commanded,

"Tell me, Angel. Is what your mother says true?"

Before Anjele could respond, Twyla sharply cried, "Of course it's true. I took the dress away from her myself, and it was soaked. Poor Claudia was beside herself."

Anjele had long ago painfully accepted her mother's favoritism for Claudia and stopped trying to defend herself, as it always proved fruitless. But, in this instance, she could not let her father believe she was guilty of doing something so awful. Drawing a deep breath, she looked him straight in the eye and declared firmly, "No, Daddy, it isn't." She hurriedly described how it had really happened.

Twyla shook her head from side. Finally she admonished, "You're only making things worse, Anjele. Now go to your room."

Elton found himself in quite a dilemma. He believed, without a doubt, Anjele was telling the truth, yet to defend her meant taking sides against his wife. Pressing his fingertips against his temples, he desperately wondered how to keep peace and still do what was right.

Anjele relieved him of that decision. She could sense he believed her, which was all that mattered. Reaching to pat his hand, she whispered, "It's okay, Daddy. It doesn't matter. I really didn't want to go, anyway."

Biting back tears, she promptly excused herself.

Anjele thought they would never leave. She stood in the shadows of the veranda waiting for what seemed like forever until, finally, they were on their way.

Without hesitation, she climbed down the trellis at

the end of the porch, trying to be very careful lest she break the wisteria vines. She didn't dare go through the house, for it might not be Kesia on duty but one of the other slaves who couldn't be cajoled into turning her head and not reporting what she saw.

Fireflies flickered in the misty shadows of the oaks. The night was warm, the air thick with a sweet, loamy smell from the fields, for hoe gangs kept the soil around the cotton and cane freshly turned as they chopped daily at the choking weeds. She could smell the river, too, still muddied and swollen from recent rains.

A quarter moon cast enough light to guide Anjele to the woods behind the slave quarters. Simona was waiting there. Familiar with the intricate trails in and out of the bayou, she was able to move by instinct rather than sight.

"I'm so glad you come." Simona gave her a delighted hug. "I start to worry you afraid, but I should know better. My friend, she never turn from a dare."

Anjele knew she would wish she had if she got caught, and said as much, but Simona laughed at her nervousness. "How you get caught? When they come back from party?"

"Midnight. Mother always comes home by midnight."

"No reason to fear. We make it back in time. What you wearing, anyhow?" She stood back to look, only to frown at the peach-colored cotton dress, at the neckline, embroidered with dainty white rosebuds. She gave a low whistle, and Emalee seemed to appear out of nowhere, carrying a bundle of clothes. Simona hastened to explain, "The older among our people, they don' welcome outsiders. They would 'specially not want master's daughter. The young ones, like us, we have tol' you are comin', and they be delighted. But, to keep the old ones from bein' upset, maybe makin' you leave for fear of the master bein' mad, we tellin' them you our cousin from Bayou Teche. So, you put on these clothes, and we quick braid you hair. Say nothin' and nobody know nothin'," she finished with a satisfied grin.

When she was ready, both the Cajun girls clapped their hands in delight, satisfied Anjele could pass for one of their own kind.

With Simona leading the way, they moved into the dark forest and the land of the lonely moss-gloomed bayou. Thick with cypress knees, the banks were pitted by crayfish burrows and fiddler crabs. Above, there seemed to be an umbrella of willows and oaks, with funereal streamers of grey, dolorous membranes of moss.

The scant moonlight struggled to lace the way in a sheen of silver, fighting through the heavy masses of foliage. Somewhere in the distance was heard the baleful growl of a bull alligator seeking his mate amidst the living darkness. A few feet away, the water lapped secretly, almost soundlessly, thick with murky shadow.

"Snakes . . ." Anjele said with a shudder, "I always think about snakes."

Simona sagely said, "And the snake, they think about us, too, and the other way they go . . . most of the time."

"Most of the time," Anjele mumbled under her breath, straining to see the ground.

The flat-bottom boat was right where they had left it, and Anjele balanced in the middle while Simona and Emalee took their places at either end, rhythmically stabbing the water with long poles. They barely made a sound as they moved through the sluggish water. After awhile, perhaps twenty minutes or so, they could hear the sound of music. Fiddles and banjos and accordions, with merry voices singing along.

Excited, Anjele was ready to leap from the boat the instant they glided up onto the bank.

"Remember," Simona gave a last warning, "the old ones not be happy if they find out who you are. It best you stay in the shadows and jus' watch the fun. We bring you stew and drink and we take you home before late."

Anjele could only nod in agreement, all the while longing to move into the circle of things and savor every moment. Already she could see this was a different kind of party than she'd ever been to before. Everyone was relaxed and enjoying themselves, dressed casually and unconcerned about what anyone else thought. No stiffness or formality. But her eyes really widened when she saw the way some of the men and women were dancing. It was not a waltz or a reel but a kind of bouncing jig, up and down, legs kicking, and every so often they would clutch each other by the waist and whirl round and round till they were giggling with dizziness. But it was the occasional slowness of their movements that truly astounded. The music would suddenly change in tempo to a kind of ringing, undulating beat. The dancers would then stand close together, arms on each other's shoulders, moving only from their waists down. The almost hypnotic way they were staring into each other's eyes was absolutely searing.

Anjele remembered the time Simona had confided how it felt the first time she and her husband made love on their wedding night, how he touched her in secret places that made her feel as though she were burning with fever. Her flesh, she'd said, seemed about to burst into flames.

And the way those people were dancing, Anjele realized, she could almost feel the heat emanating from them, as well.

Instructing Anjele to stand at the edge of the clearing, Simona brought her a bowl of turtle stew and a mug of scuppernong wine, then left to go and join her husband Frank. Emalee at last spied her beau—and Anjele found herself all alone.

At first she enjoyed just watching, for it was a treat to witness such revelry. Never again, she realized, would she be satisfied with staid old balls and tea dances, for she was swishing her hips from side to side in time with the music and soon her feet had even picked up the beat of the jigging rhythm. Setting down the bowl and empty mug, she clapped her hands softly, laughing out loud over the way Frank lifted Simona up in the air and whirled her about till they were both dizzy and drunk with merriment.

The evening wore on, and Anjele became apprehensive that maybe Simona was getting drunk on something besides merrymaking. Frank carried a small jug, even as they danced, and both took turns drinking from it. When the two of them at last stumbled over to where Anjele stood watching, she knew her suspicion was confirmed.

"A good time, eh?" Simona laughed, voice slurred. "You maybe like to dance with my man, no? I loan him to you, but only for a little while."

Frank, his arm around his wife, had a lopsided grin on his face. "Sure, why not? We make fun . . . ." He held out his hand to Anjele.

Anjele knew and liked Frank but wasn't about to dance with him, especially when he was well into his cups. "No, but thank you and maybe another time." To Simona, she said anxiously, "It's getting late. I think we'd better start back."

Simona slapped her shoulder good-naturedly and cried, "You don't got to worry. We have you tucked in bed way before you momma and poppa come home."

She threw herself into Frank's arms, and Anjele could only watch helplessly as they danced and drank their way back into the center of the party.

It was late. She could feel it in her apprehensive bones and knew she had to be getting home or risk her mother coming in to check on her and finding her bed empty. There'd be hell to pay then, for sure. Simona was of no help, because Anjele had no intentions of following a drunken guide in the dense, dangerous bayou, much less get into a boat with her.

Frantically Anjele looked around for Emalee and was relieved to spot her dancing with her beau but appearing sober. Pulling her to the side, she told her about Simona and asked hopefully, "You do know the way out, don't you?"

"Sure," Emalee tried to sound confident. Actually, Simona was the one who knew her way around at night. She merely followed Simona. "Tell you what. I ask my Anton to come, too—" She turned and was stunned to find he had disappeared, melding into the crowd. "He go to get more wine. I find him."

She started to move away, but Anjele grasped her arm.

"There's no time. I've got to get back right away. You've been down that path a thousand times, Emalee. You can do it."

But never at night, alone, Emalee cried within, not about to admit out loud. She knew Anjele well enough to know she'd strike out by herself if she didn't guide her. And that would be dangerous. Sucking in a deep breath of determination, Emalee said, "I try. If I find the way is forgotten, we turn back, okay?"

Anjele had no intention of turning back, and cursed herself for coming in the first place. "Let's go. Get me to the other side of the water, and I think I can make it from there."

Emalee was trying not to let her fear show, and as they hurried to where the flatboat had been left on the bank, she continued to dart anxious glances all around, hoping to spot Anton so he could take over.

Anjele helped push off the tiny craft, trying not to think about snakes as the cool, dark water closed about her ankles. There was no time to worry about a wet hem, either. She'd tarried too long and every second counted. "Let's go." She jumped in and grabbed up one of the poles and shoved it down into the muddy bottom to give the boat a forward thrust. "You guide up front, and I'll help all I can. It shouldn't take long to cross. Just don't hit any of those cypress knees sticking up out of the water."

Emalee was too scared to speak. Earlier, it had all been an exciting adventure to be out in the dark, but that was when Simona was along, and Simona was much more adept on the water than she.

They moved slowly and fluidly through the silent water, and Emalee, straining to see any ominous shadows of obstruction, probed ahead with her pole.

Anjele realized the girl was terrified and attempted humor to ease the tension. "Don't be poking any alligators with that thing and get them riled. We don't have your gator killer with us to do battle."

Emalee was concentrating on what she was doing but also wanted to talk to ease the fear in her throat. "Gators not supposed to be here. The menfolk, they try to keep it clear, safe. So many of us go this way to and from work in the fields. As for our gator killer, he stay to himself most of the time. That is why you no see him. The girls, they after him. Even the ones who are married. He don' want trouble, so he never come to make merry when they drinkin' the wine."

"Then he isn't married?" Anjele was careful to keep her tone light. It didn't matter, anyway, and she was actually puzzled by her curiosity.

"I don' think so, but no one really know much about him, except for the story of how he got his name." She gave a soft chuckle, "He is one handsome man, no?"

Anjele wasn't about to agree aloud, even though she did secretly, and instead countered, "Why does he wear his hair that way, pulled back like a horse's tail? It's almost like some Indians wear theirs."

"I hear some fishermen wear hair like that, and somebody say Gator's poppa say his boy been away for a long time whaling."

"Whaling? Then . . ."

She had been about to ask how someone off at sea wound up living in the bayou and working cane fields, when suddenly the boat struck a jutting cypress root Emalee had failed to see. They both screamed as they lost their balance, frantically struggling to right themselves, but Emalee pitched forward into the black water, and the sudden lurch of the boat subsequently tossed Anjele off the side.

The water was not terribly deep but came nearly to their chins. Anjele coughed and spit and clawed at the slime that was clinging to her face. Groping frantically, she tried to find the boat but it had slipped away into the umbra. "Emalee, are you all right?" she called into the night. "Where are you?"

"Here." She was right beside her, voice trembling with hysteria. "The boat . . . can you find the boat?"

Miserably, Anjele said it was gone.

Emalee wailed, "Hurry. We got to get to dry land, and then we try to make our way back to the others. Got to get out of here—fast."

She started to move away, but Anjele reached out to grab her arm and hold her back. "We're turned around. We don't know which way to go. We could head in the opposite direction and hit a deep spot and be in over our heads. Not to mention all the snakes and other creatures in these waters."

Just then, they both heard it—the sound of something moving ominously close through the marsh.

Emalee squealed. "Oh, God, what we gon' do?"

Swallowing against the rising terror, Anjele cried, "Find a cypress knee, quick, and start climbing—"

"Why not just climb in here?"

They both froze at the sound of the slightly mocking voice that came from out of the darkness.

He had glided his boat right up alongside them.

Feeling the strong hand brush against her shoulder, Anjele quickly grabbed it to accept the lift up to safety. Emalee was right behind her.

Anjele was about to thank her rescuer, but before she could speak, he coldly admonished Emalee, "You should have known better. Both times."

"*Both* times?" Emalee echoed, sinking down to huddle in the bottom of the boat.

"Yes. Both times. You knew it was dangerous to go out by yourself into the bayou at night, but you never should have brought her here to start with."

Nervously, Emalee attempted to defend herself, "But she our cousin, from Bayou Teche, and—"

"Don't lie to me. I know who she is." His tone was thick with contempt. "Let her risk her own life if she gets bored with her little rich girls' tea parties. Don't bring her here and jeopardize the jobs of our people."

He stabbed the pole down into the murky waters with almost a vengeance to set his craft in motion.

Though grateful for being rescued, Anjele felt indignation rising and protested, "Wait a minute. I don't know who you are, but you've no right to accuse me of purposely endangering my friend's life. And not that it's any of your business, but I happen to have been invited here tonight." She wished she could see his face, but besides the darkness, he stood at the bow with back turned. She could tell only that he was a large man but was puzzled by the absence of Cajun accent.

Suddenly, Emalee surprised her by saying sharply, "He is right. You don' belong. It is Simona's fault. It was her idea."

Anjele was further astonished at the realization that Emalee sounded as though she were about to cry.

"It doesn't matter whose idea it was," he said brusquely. "Learn your lesson or next time you can both feed the gators. I don't have time to rescue stupid little girls."

"Stupid little girls?" Anjele screeched. "You've no right—"

"No. Say nothing." Emalee clutched her arm. "He tell about this, and I be in big trouble. Please. Forget it all."

Anjele bit down on her lip and clenched her fists and told herself to hold her temper. They went the rest of the way in silence, and the instant the craft touched the bank, she bolted to her feet. Bad enough to have to explain why she was soaking wet if her parents were waiting, without having to endure insults from a stranger. She was trembling with rage and wanted only to get away from both of them as fast as possible.

A firm hand clamped down on her arm.

She tried to yank free, but he held fast, and she furiously cried, "What do you think you're doing? Let me go."

"I'm going to see you as far as the fields to make sure you get out of the woods safely."

She ground out the protest between clenched teeth, "I don't need you."

He ignored her and ordered Emalee, "You stay here. I'll be right back." He stepped onto the bank, jerking Anjele along with him.

He walked with swift, sure steps, and she realized he knew the way well. She was too mad to speak and figured it was just as well because he was obviously also angry over having been so inconvenienced.

They reached the edge of the cotton field. "Go now," he thundered, releasing her and giving her a gentle shove forward. "You can make it the rest of the way."

She whirled about to inform him frostily, "I could've made it all the way, with no help from you . . . ." Her voice trailed off.

The slivered moon suddenly peered out from behind

a cloud to illumine the world around her, but he was already on his way back.

An involuntary shudder rippled down her spine.

In the silvery glow, she could see that his hair, so dark, was pulled back and tied at the nape of his neck.

With shocking clarity, she realized just who had delivered her this night.

CHAPTER

ALL SEEMED QUIET, SO ANJELE CLIMBED quickly back up the trellis to the veranda and into her room. She had just enough time to peel out of her wet clothes before hearing the sounds of a carriage. Fuming to think how she'd been rudely sent on her way without time to retrieve her own clothing, she shoved her Cajun costume behind a chair. She would have to get her things as soon as possible, lest someone find them and eventually trace them to her.

With quick, jerky, movements, she undid her braids and was able to dive beneath the covers just as her mother opened the door to peer inside.

Satisfied all was well, Twyla retreated, and Anjele was left alone in the silent darkness to breathe a momentary sigh of relief.

Sleep eluded her, however, as she reflected on the evening's excitement—and subsequent anger. No doubt the man called Gator had been confident she wouldn't say a word about the rude way he'd spoken to her, but just who did he think he was, anyway, to pass judgment? And she was still baffled over the way Emalee had sided against her. After all, they had been friends for years.

Finally, sleep won out, but it was troubled, as even her subconscious dwelled on the unpleasantness.

"You got company, missy."

Blinking against the assault of midmorning sun when the heavy drapes were drawn open, Anjele sat up to rub her eyes and groggily ask who on earth was calling at such an ungodly hour.

Jobie held out a pink satin robe. "Master Raymond. Calvin told him nobody was up yet, 'ceptin' Master Sinclair, and he was off to the fields since first light, but Master Raymond, he said he needed to see you, and not to even tell your momma he was here.

"And . . ." She giggled. "He said 'specially not to tell Miss Claudia, 'cause—" She fell silent to stare with bulging eyes at Anjele's tangled, matted hair. Stepping closer for a better look, she cried, "Lordy, missy, what did you do to your hair? Did you go to bed with it wet? How come?"

Anjele hurried to the dressing alcove, Jobie right on her heels. One look in the mirror evoked a horrified screech. "Oh, no! I can't let anybody see me like this, Jobie. Take the curling iron to the stove out in the kitchen and heat it up quick, and don't tell anybody why you're doing it."

Jobie rushed to obey, and Anjele picked up a brush and went to work on the tangles. Raymond would have to wait, and she didn't care, because he had no business calling without notice or invitation, anyway. She had to admit being curious, though, as to what brought him so far so early in the day. It was at least an hour's ride into New Orleans, and he and his family lived almost in the heart of the city.

Frustrated, she worked as quickly as her nervous fingers allowed. She had planned, the second she awoke, to run and get her clothes. Now that would have to wait till she got rid of Raymond, which meant chances were increased that a field worker might stumble across them when he went in the bushes to relieve himself. She hadn't hidden them very well, anyway, just crammed them behind a small rock she'd groped for and found in the darkness. After all, she recalled with a frown, she had planned to put them back on before returning to the house. Thanks to the arrogant newcomer, that idea had been dashed.

At last her hair was curled in ringlets even though it smelled vaguely of swamp water despite a generous shower of cologne. She had hastily chosen a plain blue dress but suddenly, on impulse, grabbed up a piece of ribbon and pulled her hair back and tied it at the nape of her neck. Surprisingly, it relieved some of her anxiety as she looked at herself in the mirror and laughed at her fisherman's coif.

Raymond was in the ladies' parlor, impatiently pacing about. The coffee and biscuits Calvin had provided sat on a serving cart, untouched.

When Anjele appeared, he rushed to clasp her hands as he devoured her with eager, anxious eyes. "I'm sorry about the early hour, darling," he apologized hastily. "But after last night, I just had to see you and make sure everything is all right."

Carefully, she withdrew her hands from his tight, almost painful grasp. She could easily see he was upset and was baffled as to why. "Of course I'm all right. Why wouldn't I be?"

"Claudia said—"

"Claudia!" Anjele echoed with a sigh. "I might have

known." She sat down on the sofa and patted the place next to her, inviting him to join her. She reached for the coffee service. Still tired from last night's ordeal, she could barely keep from yawning.

"At the party," he began, sitting down and waving away the offer of coffee for himself, "Claudia said you were being punished for assaulting her and wouldn't give any of the details. When I asked your mother, she said she didn't want to talk about it. The next thing I knew, Claudia was asking me to dance with her, and that's when she said she felt she just had to tell me that the fight was about me."

"About you?" Anjele stopped pouring cream to stare at him incredulously.

He nodded, misery etched on his face. "She said you were saying unkind things about me, that you find me boring, unattractive, and you wouldn't even be marrying me if it weren't for the covenant between our parents. And she said when she tried to take up for me, you got mad and ruined the dress she was planning to wear."

For an instant Anjele merely closed her eyes and sat there, wondering how to respond. The reality was she did find him boring but had never said so out loud to anyone other than Simona and Emalee. But no girl in her right mind could think him unattractive. With curly hair the color of honey and eyes as blue as periwinkles, he was quite good-looking. But how could she explain the emptiness in her heart when she tried to love him, for the last thing she ever wanted to do was hurt him.

Taking her silence for admission, Raymond cried softly, "I know it was all arranged, even before we were born, Anjele, but I'll make you love me. I swear I will."

"You musn't listen to Claudia," she hastened to say. She realized he believed the worst. "It wasn't like she said at all. The argument wasn't about you. It was the dress, and . . ." She shook her head and fell silent. What was the point in going into all the details?

"I'm afraid," she continued delicately, "Claudia sometimes gets things mixed up, but please believe me when I say I've never discussed you with her."

Relief came with a grin. "I should've known better, but I was so upset you weren't there. I wanted to see you, hold you . . . ." His arm snaked out to wrap about her shoulders and draw her closer.

Anjele could smell the whiskey on his breath and knew he had been nipping again from the flask he always carried in his coat pocket. He did that when he was upset about something, a habit she found most disturbing. She moved from his embrace to gingerly remind him, "You know my parents would be very upset to find you here at such an early hour, especially when we aren't chaperoned."

He laughed, reaching for her again. "We're going to be married in a few months, so what difference does it make?"

She set her cup down and quickly stood. "It matters to me," she hedged. "I don't want the servants gossiping."

Raymond thought about how much he wanted, needed, another drink and decided maybe it was best to take his leave. All he had wanted, anyway, was assurance that Claudia was wrong. "Tomorrow," he said, also getting up, "Mother would like for you to come for lunch so the two of you can discuss how you want our rooms decorated."

"How nice," Anjele murmured, unable to display any

enthusiasm. The invitation was a formality, because no one ever discussed anything with Ida Duval. They merely listened to what she'd already decided.

"You see," he went on, when she made no comment on the obvious fact that they would not be moving into his room together after they were married, "Mother says it's proper for us to have separate bedrooms, so she's having a parlor put between the two rooms at the end of the east hallway. But don't worry." He kissed her forehead, "You'll sleep in my arms every night."

Anjele bit back the impulse to ask what business it was of his mother's, anyway. Dear Lord, she cringed to think of living in the same house with that domineering woman. Oh, not that she was ever unkind. Quite the contrary. Ida carried on as though she adored her and couldn't do enough for her. There was no problem there. But it was still Ida's house, and Anjele knew she'd never feel at home there. Besides, she couldn't stand the way Raymond acted like a little boy around his mother, which, Anjele suspected, was one of the reasons he drank so much.

"You really have to go," she said emphatically, leading the way to the front door.

He stepped onto the porch but suddenly put his arms around her and swore, "I don't give a damn who sees us," then claimed her mouth in a bruising kiss.

She tried to return his fervor but could feel no emotion whatsoever. Even when his tongue parted her lips, and she pretended ardency as she clung to him, there was nothing.

"My darling," he whispered shakily, forcing himself to end the wondrous moment. "This is torture."

"Then go." She mustered a cheery lilt to her voice and waved him on his way.

"I love you," he called, hurrying down the steps to where a groomsman waited with his horse.

She blew him a kiss but did not, could not, echo his affirmation with one of her own.

"You're such a hypocrite." Claudia stepped from behind the potted palm in the foyer, where she had been hiding.

Anjele felt her spine tighten with anger but quickly told herself it wasn't worth a confrontation. Instead she turned toward the back of the house without responding.

Claudia was right behind her to grab her shoulder and spin her about. "Why don't you tell him the truth? You don't love him, and you don't want to marry him, and the only reason you're doing it is to hurt me."

Anjele bit back the fury and jerked free to continue on her way.

"Bitch!"

At that, Anjele turned, throwing her resolve to the wind, but Claudia was already running for the stairs.

Maybe, Anjele mused, living with Ida Duval would be paradise compared to enduring Claudia's tantrums, which, she knew, were not motivated solely by her feelings for Raymond. Claudia had always coveted anything Anjele had that she didn't. That sadly included Raymond, who, to her knowledge, had never given Claudia any reason to think he was even remotely interested in her.

She left the house by way of the ballroom, with its mirrored walls and crystal chandeliers. It was on the opposite side of the house from the kitchen and service buildings, so she couldn't be seen by curious servants. Outside, beyond the marble terrace, were the formal gardens. The men working on her mother's prized camellias hardly glanced up as she passed.

Walking by the sundial, she saw it was nearly ten o'clock. It was a standing rule that slaves took a fifteen-minute rest period at that time. All she had to do was stand at the edge of the first cotton field and wait for the bell to ring, and when the workers hastened to a shaded area, she ran quickly toward the dense woods.

The path was worn. She knew exactly how far she had walked before taking the clothes from Simona and changing. She had stepped off to the side and could see the grass and weeds there were mashed down. And, heart leaping with relief, she spotted the rock, then reeled with sudden horror to realize her clothes were not behind it.

Someone had already found them.

For a moment, she could only stand there, wondering what to do. No doubt, whoever found them would see right away they were not the garments of a slave. Not to turn them in would be judged the same as stealing, a serious offense at BelleClair, so they'd be taken to one of the house servants, who would then, of course, present them to her mother. Despite the stifling hot day, that chilling thought evoked a shiver from head to toe.

Wanting to prolong the inevitable, as well as attempt to get her thoughts together, Anjele quickly headed to her private spot on the river.

Above a sloping bank, the draping fronds of a large weeping willow tree offered a secluded umbrella where she could hide from the world and still observe it.

She loved to spend time there daydreaming as she watched the opulent pleasure boats, the river packets loaded with cotton, and the flatboats carrying grain. The nights were best, when she would sneak away from the house after dark to sit for hours in hopes of catching a glimpse of the eerie gleam of a torch flaring on a craft moving silently through the dark waters. She could smell gardenias and jasmine from the gardens behind, and it was here she dreamed the romantic fantasies she did not yet understand, while contemplating the puzzling emotional void that was Raymond.

She sat on the lush grass, drew her knees up to her chest, propped her chin on them, and tried to figure out what she was going to tell her mother about those clothes. As much as she hated to lie, admitting the truth was going to wreak havoc, for sure. Maybe she could get by with saying she'd wanted to go for a walk in the swamps so she'd borrowed some clothes from the Cajun girls to keep from ruining her own. She gave her head a vehement shake. That sounded hollow, even to her. No one would believe it, especially her mother, who would imagine the absolute worst.

Suddenly the draping fronds parted, and a shadow fell across her.

Startled, she leaped to her feet to gasp in recognition of Gator. He further surprised her by tossing a bundle at her feet.

Her missing clothes.

"I thought you might be looking for these."

In mingled astonishment and anger, she asked, "What . . . what are *you* doing with them? How did you find them?" Then, composure returning, she challenged icily, "And how did you know I was here?"

He laughed softly and easily lowered himself to the ground, leaning back against the tree. Bare chested, he crossed his legs as his heavy-lidded gaze moved slowly over her. She was even better looking than he'd thought. Always seeing her from a distance, he had wondered what color her eyes would be and now saw they were a shade of misty emerald green, with tiny flecks of gold. He could also denote a sparkle of rage, which he found enhancing. "Which question do you want me to answer first?"

She bit back a sarcastic retort. Obviously, he wanted to goad. With exaggerated patience, as though speaking to a child, she said, "First, I would like you to tell me how you found my clothes."

He hoped he could keep a straight face, for he was enjoying himself. "Simona told me."

"And why did she tell you?"

"Because I asked her."

Anjele's teeth ground together. She would not let him make her lose her temper. "So why did you take them?"

He yawned, feigning boredom. "So I could bring them to you."

"And how did you know where I was?"

"I was watching, and I followed you."

Exasperated, she sat down beside him, threw up her hands in defeat. "All right. So get to the point. Why are you here? To rail at me all over again for daring to go into the bayou?"

He truly astonished her then as he looked at her and said quietly, "I was wrong. Simona told me the whole story. I realized you were there because you were invited, so I decided to go get your clothes before somebody else found them, to keep you from getting in trouble."

Anjele felt her anger washing away like the crumbling river banks during spring floods. "And you wanted to apologize," she said in wonder.

At that, he threw back his head and laughed. "Not hardly. I said I came to say I was wrong. I didn't say anything about an apology. That would be saying I regret it. And I don't. I'm glad it happened. Maybe it taught you a lesson."

Anjele started seething again, all the while helplessly aware of how ruggedly attractive he was. His arms and chest bulged with muscle, and she tried not to look at the dark mat of hair curling down his lean, flat stomach to disappear below the narrow waistband of his trousers. There was a dark arrogance about him, the rugged contours of his jaw etched with stony determination and unquestionable authority. She wondered how old he was but supposed his years at sea made guessing impossible. There were lines at the corners of his eyes from the wind and sun, which had also left him with a deep, bronze tan. He was, to be sure, a fine figure of a man, and she found him surprisingly appealing. This realization was disconcerting in the wake of rekindled fury. "I don't need you to teach me anything," she said, tightly. "Who are you, anyway? You aren't even called by your Christian name, just some silly sobriquet that means nothing."

"It doesn't?" His brows shot up in mock surprise. "You mean they don't call me Gator for any reason at all?"

She shrugged carelessly. "So you wrestled a big alligator and won. Am I supposed to be impressed?"

Actually, she was, but had no intention of letting him know it.

Solemnly he said, "I didn't ask you to be and don't care whether you are. It suited me fine when folks started calling me Gator, because it gave me an excuse to forget who I really was. I didn't like my self very much back then. So I became someone else."

"Ah, if life were only that simple," she said airily, "everyone would just change his name."

"Have you ever thought about changing yours?"

Later, she would wonder why she had shared such an intimacy when she confided, "My father calls me Angel sometimes. I rather like it."

With a wry grin, he said, "That's not a sobriquet. It's wishful thinking. Anyone with the devil in her eyes is no angel, and you, Miss Sinclair"—he cocked his head and insolently winked—"sure have the devil in yours when you're riled."

She couldn't help laughing because somehow she sensed he really meant no insult. And she was glad she was not sitting any closer to him, for there was something about his nearness that unnerved, but pleasantly so. "What was it about yourself you didn't like?" she asked boldly.

"I did such a good job of putting it all behind me that it's hard to remember. But you've been asking all the questions, and now it's my turn. Tell me. Why did you want to go into the bayou, anyway?"

"I like it there." And it was so. Always she had yearned to experience what it was like deep within the mysterious realm of the swamps but had never ventured there. Perhaps now she dared to find out, knowing in a few months she'd be married and might never have another opportunity. For some reason, however, she wasn't about to divulge that logic.

"Well, I meant what I said." His demeanor became serious once more. "You could've got the girls in trouble. I don't know how much you know about the Acadians' jobs on the plantation, Miss Sinclair, but good ones aren't that easy to come by. BelleClair happens to be one of the best places to work. If your father found out Simona and Emalee took you into the Bayou Perot at night, he'd probably ban them from the fields. They'd be hard-pressed to find work elsewhere, and like the rest of us, they need the money to keep from starving this winter.

"Some of us," he couldn't resist reminding her, "weren't born into a life of wealth and the security that goes with it."

Despite his charm when he wished to display it, she realized he could switch moods without warning. She countered, "You obviously hold that against me."

"When you jeopardize the livelihood of others to satisfy a whim, yes. We won't go into the matter of actually endangering lives, because I have to be getting back to the field now."

He stood, and Anjele was right behind him. "It wasn't that way at all. I've always envied the way Simona and Emalee live such carefree lives. They've told me about the singing and dancing, and I've always wanted to be a part of it."

He raised a mocking brow. "Maybe I'm just a field worker, but I do know a bit about social life among the planters, how some of them keep houses in New Orleans for the opera season, how a few even have steamboats for entertaining on the river. And then there's the horse races and all the fancy parties that go along with them. "So don't expect me to believe you actually have a yen to go into a mosquito-infested swamp to feast on turtle stew and stomp dance to a fiddle," he finished with a sneering chuckle.

Even though he was half a head taller, she met his challenging gaze with one of her own, and her voice did not falter as she pointed out, "You don't know anything about me, Gator, or whatever your name is, and until you do, don't sit in judgment. It just so happens I don't enjoy fancy parties and balls, because I find most of the people stuffy and boring.

"But the last thing I'd ever want to do is jeopardize anybody's livelihood, much less their lives, so you don't have to worry about me bothering you or your people again."

For an endless moment, their gazes locked. Finally, Anjele drew a breath and murmured, "I think you'd better go now. Thank you for bringing my clothes."

He nodded and moved from the caressing web of the willow tree. He took a few steps, then turned to sweep her with a thoughtful gaze, his dark eyes twinkling with secret mirth. "You don't have to cross the bayou off your list of places you'd like to visit, Miss Sinclair. Next time you want to go there, let me know."

He walked up the grassy bank to disappear over the top.

Anjele felt a strange warmth flowing through her veins that was disturbing.

He had not touched her, yet she felt somehow caressed.

It was a feeling she'd never before experienced . . . but one she would long remember.

CHAPTER

THE PEALING OF THE BIG IRON BELL, SIGnaling another day's end at BelleClaire, broke the stillness of the sultry July evening. Slaves and hired hands sighed with relief and began to shuffle from the fields, shoulders stooped in weariness.

Among them was Brett Cody, known only as Gator. As was his way, he walked alone, not joining the grumbling ranks of fellow Cajuns heading for the intricate paths leading into Bayou Perot. He preferred being alone. Companionship led to intimacies he didn't want, questions he wouldn't answer.

Heavy in his thoughts was regret for having left the sea. No matter that New Orleans was a lifetime away from Vicksburg, Mississippi, and his growing-up years in the mysterious Black Bayou. The wild sweetness of the tangled green foliage, combined with the lush fields of cane and cotton and rice, evoked bitter memories he'd thought long buried.

Worse, he mused with furrowed brow, was how his first glimpse of Anjele Sinclair had made him think, for one frozen moment, he was actually looking at Margette. He'd quickly dismissed that painful illusion.

The flame-haired beauty he'd spied among the scrub palmettos bore no resemblance to the petite blond whose memory evoked bitterness, anger. Besides, dainty little Margette would never think of venturing into the wilderness. Hers was a pampered world of luxury wrapped in lace and satin and honeysuckle and magnolias. The only thing about Anjele that reminded him of Margette was the image of yet another wealthy plantation owner's spoiled, bored daughter seeking forbidden excitement.

"Hey, you, Gator."

He glanced around, annoyance mirrored on his sunburned face, but didn't pause, doggedly continuing on his way.

Simona was running between the cane rows to catch up.

"Hey, we got to talk." Panting, she swung into step beside him. "I'm worried about my friend. She not come back to see me."

"Good."

"Hey . . ." Simona dared poke his shoulder, immediately wishing she hadn't as he stopped walking to glare down at her with dark, scathing eyes. Mustering courage to go on, she gave a helpless shrug and pointed out, "You being rude, Gator, not talking to me. All I do is ask about my friend and how come I have not seen her. It been weeks since she was here."

He bit off the reminder, "She doesn't belong here."

"That's not for you to say." Simona was starting to get mad despite the way he was looking at her. "She been my friend all my life, and who is you to come here and tell us what we can and cannot do? Jus' because your poppa is overseer in the cotton fields don' give you no right to tell me and my friends how to do."

He started walking again.

Simona was indignant at the brusque dismissal and yelled after him, "Hey! How come you not go back where you come from? And yo' poppa, too. I hear from my people in the fields he is one mean man, and he beats the slaves and would beat them, too, if he could, but he knows they stick a knife in his ribs if he do. And you just like him, ain't you?"

He shut out the sound of her shouts and quickened his pace, disappearing into the brush. Furious, he plodded onward, not glancing about as he usually did, ever alert for alligators or water moccasins.

But any creature about would, no doubt, have thought twice before venturing to disturb Brett Cody that evening, for his was the face of a man with fury stirred to near menace. He trembled with rage to be likened to his father, because he knew Leo Cody for the cruel, insensitive man he was. Now he was fueled more than ever to return to the sea but sadly knew it wasn't possible till grinding season ended in January, months away. Elton Sinclair had taken one look at his brawn and promptly pulled him to one side and promised top wages, even a bonus, in return for assurance he'd stay the season. Brett agreed, but only because he felt honor bound to pay off the debts from his mother's sickness and burial. He knew his father damn sure wouldn't bother. Leo spent everything he made on gambling, whiskey, and women. Always had and always would.

He reached his isolated pirogue, a dugout he called home. Uncorking a jug of wine, he took a deep swallow, attempting to wash away the bile. But the memories had been ignited, and there was nothing to do but let them play on his mind.

Raggedly, he allowed himself to drift back to the time when he'd left Black Bayou, after Margette Laubache, an older woman of nearly eighteen, had made him the laughingstock of Mississippi. He'd been a fool to ever let himself get involved with her in the first place, but Lord, what a beauty. There wasn't a man alive who wasn't stirred by the sight of her. Yet he'd admired from afar, well aware he was only a poor Cajun field hand, and she was born into a life of privilege. It was only when word spread of his famed battle with the largest alligator ever seen in Mississippi that Margette took notice of him. She sent by a slave that she wanted to meet the young man who'd bested such a savage creature.

Brett had laughed when he heard that. Everyone was making him out to be some kind of gladiator who'd challenged a wild beast in a fight to the death. The actuality was that the damn thing had crept up on him, and he hadn't had time to think about courage or bravery. He was scared to death and fighting to stay alive in the black, cold water. Never would he forget his burning lungs, screaming for air, as he fought to hold off the snapping jaws of death as the gator rolled him over and over, trying to drown him.

He did not, however, share such private thoughts with Margette when he defied all the rules and met her that night in the wisteria-draped gazebo near the river. He hadn't been able to think of anything except how beautiful she was. He remembered what she was wearing—a white lace gown that dipped low to accentuate large and luscious breasts. She smelled of lilacs, and her flaxen hair hung loose about her heart-shaped face.

That night was the beginning. She summoned him again and again, and before long, she was unbuttoning his shirt to dance her fingers across his chest and marvel over his muscular build—all the while teasing his mouth with her lips. He tried, even then, to tell her he shouldn't be there, that they were courting trouble, but she swore her love and demanded avowal of his, and, bewitched, he didn't hesitate to oblige.

Then came the moonless night when there was no turning back. She asked him to come at midnight, when the world around them was sleeping. She wore only a thin nightgown and robe, which she boldly cast aside before lying on the gazebo floor and pulling him down beside her.

Till then, that summer of his sixteenth year, Brett's few sexual encounters had been with cheap prostitutes in Vicksburg, when he ventured into town on Saturday nights with his friends. The episodes were hurried and devoid of emotion. Margette Laubache was a different story. Wild and wanton, she showed him ways of making love he'd never dreamed about, leaving him spent, exhausted—and charged with a feeling he mistook for immortal love.

As weeks turned into months, they met almost every night. Brett was worn out. Toiling all day in the sun, he had only a few hours to nap in the evening before sneaking into the gazebo to remain till nearly dawn.

When grinding season began, he was forced to work eighteen hours a day. Fires under the boilers making sugar never went out, and laborers were assigned shifts, with three quarters of them constantly at their stations. No man got more than six hours of rest out of twenty-four, and Margette demanded those hours be spent with her.

He was exhausted, and it showed. His mother thought he was out carousing with his friends and told him it had to stop. After that, he waited till she and his father were asleep before crawling out a window.

She flew into a rage the night she caught him, screaming, "So! It is true, what I have heard. You are sneaking out to meet that girl.

"Look at you," she wailed, tears shining in the glow of the candle she held in her quivering hand. "Thin like a snake, shadows in your eyes. And I have heard the rumors. I know it is all because of the Laubache slut."

"She's not a slut," he defended.

"Eh?" Her brows snapped together. "What you say? She is no slut? Well, what kind of *lady* sneaks out of her house in the night to meet a man? Slaves gossip, my son, and it is only a matter of time till Laubache hears, as I did. Then there be big trouble, for sure."

Brett decided he might as well tell her. "He's going to hear, anyway, as soon as grinding season is over. That's when she plans to tell him we're going to get married."

At that, she gasped and cried, "You are a bigger fool than I thought if you believe her. Her kind marries her own kind, not a poor boy like you from the gutters of the world."

She began swaying, funny moaning sounds coming from deep in her throat. Afraid she was about to faint, Brett reached out to take the candle as he tried to reassure her, "It will work out. You'll see. She does tell the truth—"

She slapped him, and he cried out, not from pain,

but astonishment. It was the first time in his life she had ever struck him.

"Laubache would see you dead first. Never would he allow his daughter to marry a Cajun!"

"She says it doesn't matter," he dared argue, "She swears nothing is going to stop us."

Mavaline Cody threw up her hands and offered a whispered prayer to God to make her son see that he had surely lost his mind. "Where would you take your bride, my son? Here? In the bayou? You think a girl like her would be happy as a Cajun wife?

"Oh, my son, my son." She cried even harder. "Did I raise you to be so blind and stupid?" She sank to the cot beneath the window, lowered her face to her hands, and began to cry.

He had left her then, knowing he had but a few precious hours to spend with Margette—and also aware nothing he said would make any difference, anyway.

Margette had been angry that he was late. He'd tried to tell her about the ugly scene, wanting assurance his mother was wrong, but Margette didn't want to waste time talking. She stripped him of his clothes and cast aside her own, wild with passion.

As the first fingers of dawn clawed at the eastern horizon, they clung together, bodies slick with perspiration. "I've got to have you all the time," she gasped, her tongue circling his ear as she danced her fingers up and down his belly. "I want you in a house, in a real bed, and where I can have you any time I want you. This meeting in the middle of the night, with the mosquitoes and gnats all around, rolling on these hard planks, is terrible.

"And I can't help thinking," she added huskily, "how much better it'll be somewhere else."

He was used to Margette's rambling on about their future, but this night, needled by his mother's grim foreboding, he found himself on edge, alert for any sign she might be right.

"I think I've finally convinced Daddy to buy a house in town," Margette was saying, "so I can use it for the social season, or shopping trips, and what I can do is just tuck you away there for my very own. Wouldn't that be wonderful? Of course, Mammy Lucy would have to be with me when I stayed there. It wouldn't be proper for folks to think I'd stay there alone, but she won't say a word about you being there, because she knows if she did, I'd have her whipped, so—"

Brett sat up so quickly, she fell away from him with a squeal of protest. Anger rising, he cried, "Wait a minute. You said when grinding season was over, we'd be getting married. What the hell are you talking about?"

She sat up, began pulling on her gown as she petulantly explained, "I have to wait till the time is right. We both know Daddy isn't going to like it, and neither is Mommy, but till I can convince them, you can just stay in town, and I'll take care of you."

"And what happens if they never agree?"

"Oh, well." She picked aimlessly at a strand of hair that had tumbled onto his forehead, "We'll be together, anyway, and that's what counts. I mean, you'll have a good life, Brett, and I'll make sure you always have the best of everything. You'll never have to work or do anything—"

"Except keep you properly fucked," he snapped.

"What's wrong with you? Are you crazy? It's a wonderful arrangement."

"I'm a free man, Margette, not one of your daddy's breeding bucks." He got up and jerked on his trousers.

It was getting light, and besides, all of a sudden he couldn't get away from her fast enough.

"Wait, Brett. Don't go, please." She threw herself against his chest and clung to him, pleading, "Don't you see? This is the only way for us right now. I'll come into town as often as I can. We can make love all the time."

She began to rain tiny kisses over his face, but he stood motionless, his expression granite. When he did not speak, she took the silence for assent, albeit reluctant. Pressing closer, so her breasts rubbed provocatively against him, she whispered huskily "All you'll ever have to do, my darling, is fill me up with your love." Her hand dropped to his crotch.

He pulled from her grasp. "I'm not for sale, Margette, so why don't you just go pick out one of your daddy's slaves, a nice, big buck for your very own?"

For the second time that night, he was slapped.

Face twisted in a furious grimace, she cried, "Who the hell do you think you are, talking to me like that? You should be grateful, damn you! I'm offering you a life of luxury." She raised her hand to hit him again, but he caught her wrist and held it.

"No more, Margette."

"Bastard! You're nothing but a—"

"Cajun, right?" he interjected.

"Exactly," she fired back, "and you should be grateful I'd even consider making you such an offer."

"And flattered you thought I was a good enough stud to keep you serviced in privacy, so you could play the role of vestal virgin for the blue-blooded beaux your family approves of. You never had any intention of marrying me."

Her lips curled back in a snarl of contempt as she pushed her face against his, demanding, "And what else would a dirty Cajun be good for? Do you think I'd actually want to marry a swamp rat? That's all you are, you know, you and all your people. You were run out of your own country, because you weren't wanted, and you've bred with the Negroes and the Indians, and—"

"And hypocritical young girls who masquerade as prim and proper ladies by day and romp like wild, wanton whores by night." Disgusted, he shoved her harder than intended.

She fell, yelping with pain as she hit the floor, scraping her elbows. "You'll be sorry, you dirty bastard!"

Her hysterical cries had rung out in the stillness of the dawn as he ran from the gazebo.

Brett shook his head viciously to clear away the painful cobwebs from the past.

Margette had been right.

He had been sorry.

Very sorry, indeed.

Her screams had brought everyone in the house running to see what was going on. She said he had tried to rape her, and he figured the only thing that had saved him from being hunted down and lynched was the question of what she was doing out in the gazebo at such an hour.

Margette's indiscretion, however, had not excused his daring to cross the invisible, forbidden line.

That same day, Haskill Laubache had sent a foreman to the field to summon both Brett and his father to his office.

Grim-faced and obviously fighting to keep from lunging at Brett, Laubache choked out the edict that if either of them were ever seen on his land again, they'd be shot on sight.

Leo went into a rage, for he'd known nothing of his son's involvement with Haskill's daughter. His job paid more than any he'd ever had before, and the working conditions were superior to other plantations. He begged Haskill to keep him on and make Brett leave, but Haskill stonily refused.

That night, with his mother begging him to stop, Leo had beaten Brett mercilessly.

Brett hadn't lifted a hand to his father, but as he lay on the floor, battered and bloody, he swore out loud he'd never take a licking from him again. "And don't worry," he said spitting blood. "I'm getting out. And I won't be back."

Brett grimaced to think how he'd kept at least a part of his vow. The very next morning, he had left to wander for nearly a year before winding up in Massachusetts to sign on with a whaler ship. Whale oil for lamps was in great demand, and the idea of traveling around the world was intriguing. So, for the next three years he found himself sailing the Pacific and Indian Oceans and on into the Arctic Ocean and Bering Strait.

When at last he had returned to America, he wanted to see his mother. He'd never enjoyed a good relationship with his father, but always, he had loved her.

Making his way back to Mississippi and the Black Bayou, he discovered his parents had moved. He kept on searching and finally traced them to Louisiana and Bayou Perot, just in time for his mother's funeral.

His father had dispassionately described her last months. He had taken her to a hospital in New

Orleans, where they could do nothing to ease her suffering from some strange malady. When she finally died, Leo couldn't even pay for her casket. Brett hadn't saved anything from his earnings at sea. He'd had no reason, instead throwing his money away in every port they came to, on whiskey and women. But he made up his mind to honor his mother's memory by paying all her bills.

He laid aside the jug of wine, too restless to sit still any longer. He wanted to walk the forest as darkness closed in, to try to escape the invisible clutches of the past.

His father liked it at Belleclair and had progressed to become one of the overseers. He assured Brett that Elton Sinclair had his eye on him for the same kind of promotion. But all Brett wanted was to get the bills paid and then move on. Meanwhile, he kept his distance from his father because he despised him.

The sound of a distant whistle and the sight of lights offshore caused him to realize he'd traveled farther than he'd realized in his reverie. He was on the levee, overlooking the river, and not too far away was the huge, draping willow where he'd followed Anjele Sinclair that day.

He smiled to think of the encounter, for his first impression of her had been dashed. Though quite beautiful, she wasn't at all the spoiled rich girl he'd taken her to be. Instead, she seemed possessed of a zest for life, eager to experience everything it offered.

He started to turn back, but a movement caught his eye. A figure emerged from the darkness, skipping merrily across the lawn leading from BelleClair Manse. It was a woman, a girl, he could see now, for her long hair was flowing behind her in the wind, along with the sheer garment she was wearing.

The moon peered out from behind a silver-tinged cloud, and he saw the flaming tresses and knew it could only be Anjele Sinclair.

He watched with interest as she disappeared inside her leafy sanctum.

Something told him to leave, while another part of him reminded he was no longer an innocent boy of sixteen. He was a man. He had been around the world and few things fascinated or frightened him.

So there was no harm, he rationalized, in speaking to Anjele this warm, sweet night.

He headed for the willow tree.

It had been a particularly boring evening for Anjele. Raymond and his parents had been invited for supper, and afterward, his mother had insisted she play the piano. She hadn't wanted to, but polite protests went unheeded. Claudia had stood by glowering but expertly changed her expression to sweetness and light whenever she could catch Raymond's eye.

The men had eventually drifted into the smoking parlor for cigars and brandy, anxious to continue the political discussion they'd been forced to abandon at the dinner table, due to the disapproving glances from their wives. Abraham Lincoln had been chosen by the Republican Party of Illinois to challenge the incumbent Stephen Douglas for the senate. Mr. Lincoln, it seemed, had antagonized many staunch proslavery Democrats from the South when he'd said in his acceptance speech at the convention that he believed the government could not permanently endure if made up of half free states and half slave-holding states.

Anjele would have much preferred to listen to them criticize Mr. Lincoln than hear her mother and future mother-in-law prattle on about wedding plans.

Finally, the evening had ended, with Ida Duval setting a date for yet another party to celebrate the coming wedding. "Christmas isn't that far away," she'd gaily reminded them as they all exchanged good-byes on the porch.

Elton, a twinkle in his eye, had pretended to grumble, "Seems to me you young folks could've set a more convenient wedding date than a busy time like grinding season."

"Oh, listen to him." Twyla laughed. "You'd think there's a time at BelleClair that isn't busy."

"And that's exactly why I'm glad I married a doctor instead of a planter," Ida said. "I much prefer the excitement of New Orleans. But don't you worry, dear." She turned to Anjele. "Soon you can leave all this behind you and move into the city."

Anjele's smile was forced, because thoughts of leaving BelleClair made her sick. The last thing she wanted to do was live in town, but it seemed she had no say in her life anymore, and dismally realized she'd never had.

Finally, she had gone to her room. And once the house was settled and quiet, she had sneaked out and down the trellis to her special place.

Here, at least, she could dream about another kind of existence.

Spying the lights of a passing riverboat, she wondered what it would be like to travel the mighty river north. If she were a man, she knew she'd probably never be able to settle down, wanting, instead, to see as much of the world as possible.

Startled by the sound of movement in the darkness, she called nervously, "Is someone there?"

Brett pulled the draping fronds apart and stepped inside, barely able to make her out in the darkness. "I didn't mean to scare you. I was out walking and saw you come down here. Mind if I join you?"

She was glad to see him. Despite all her resolve, she'd thought of him constantly since their last meeting. "You might as well," she replied, laughing. "But I find it strange after all my years of coming here without anyone knowing, that suddenly my secret is discovered."

"I won't tell anybody." He lowered himself to sit beside her. "I'm surprised nobody noticed before now. Pretty as you are, somebody should watch you all the time."

She felt a warm tremor and instinctively moved a bit away from him, lest he notice the effect he was having. He was shirtless, and she tried not to look at his glorious chest. "So what brings you out this time?" She forced a teasing lilt to her voice. "Have you found more of my clothes?"

"Have you left any hidden about?" he fired right back.

"No, I've been forbidden to go into the bayou, don't you remember?" She feigned mock horror. "And I'd never dare disobey the fearless alligator killer."

He lowered himself further, till he was lying on the ground at her feet. He rolled to his side and propped his head on his hand as he gazed up at her. A snappy breeze was blowing in from the river, sending the willow fronds into a frenzied dance, as well as allowing mellow moonlight to steal inside and illuminate their shelter. "I think you're making fun of me."

"I wouldn't have to, if you'd tell me your real name."

"There's no need."

"It feels kind of strange talking to someone, when I don't know who he really is."

He gave a careless shrug. "It's not like we run into each other every day, though it might be nice," he ventured to add.

Anjele was enjoying the banter, well aware that moments like this in the future would be nonexistent. Marriage. Babies. Tea parties. Church. That would be her world—not slipping away in the night to meet a handsome, exciting man in the cradling arms of a willow tree on the banks of her beloved Mississippi River. Coquettishly she asked, "And what would we do if we did? You say I don't belong in the bayou. Where would you take me?"

"Do you have to be taken somewhere?" Once more, he was impressed by her beauty, her lovely face bathed in silver moonlight, emerald eyes shining with anticipation as she waited for him to weave a world of wonder. "Maybe I can take you there with words," he offered softly. "Where would you like to go?"

She didn't try to contain her excitement. There was no need, for theirs was a budding friendship without pretense. Each knew the other for what they were, and it was a comfortable awareness. "Where have you been?" she wanted to know.

"Everywhere. In three years at sea, I've probably been to almost every major port in the world."

"Tell me what you found the most intriguing," she urged, thinking again what warm, smoldering eyes he had, and wishing there were more light, so she could see the the dimple appear at the corner of his mouth when he smiled.

He said he'd found it all exciting. He described for her the ports of the Pacific, where most American whaling ships were attracted by bowhead whales. He also enjoyed the trips to the Arctic, where the long hours of daylight made it possible to operate around the clock. His job, he said, had been to man one of the light double-ended rowing boats, put off in pursuit with hand harpoons and a coiled line to play the whale, which was then killed with a hand lance when it was sufficiently exhausted.

She drew a sharp breath before venturing to ask, "Was it terribly dangerous?"

"Sperm whales could be real dangerous. I once saw one leap straight up out of the ocean and grab a row-boat in its jaws and bite it in two."

She wrapped her arms about her and shuddered. "I don't blame you for giving it up."

"Oh, I didn't give it up because of danger. I . . ." He paused, and gave himself a mental shake. He had vowed never to let anyone know more about him than was absolutely necessary and he wasn't about to share his real reasons for not returning. Brusquely, he finished, "Maybe one day I'll go back."

"I envy you," she admitted wistfully. "If I could, I'd travel all over the world instead of getting married."

He knew of her engagement. Workers and slaves enjoyed gossiping about what went on in the master's family. "I thought girls wanted to get married," he teased, "especially to rich men."

"Raymond isn't rich. His father is, but Raymond has never hit a lick at a snake in his whole life, as the saying goes. Oh, he's nice enough, kind and sweet, but he's always had anything he wanted, and . . ." she stopped, embarrassed by her own candor. "I'm sorry. My problems aren't yours."

He surprised himself by his own frankness, "A girl as pretty as you shouldn't have any problems, Miss Sinclair, and I figure you've got your pick of beaus, so why marry someone you obviously don't think much of?"

Anjele decided she'd already said too much and decided it didn't matter if she confided further. "I didn't pick Raymond Duval. He was picked for me. By our parents. And that's the way it is."

He nodded, understanding, for he knew it was the way among some of the wealthy planters to arrange marriages for their children. "Well, maybe it will work out," was all he could think of to say.

"Maybe . . ." she lamely echoed.

They sat in silence for a few moments. Anjele thought she couldn't remember having such a nice time with a man, and Brett also mused over how much he was enjoying himself.

Finally, reluctantly, he got to his feet and held out his hand to her, and when she touched him, there was no mistaking the caressing of their fingertips. In the soft glow, their eyes met and held. Anjele was a maelstrom of emotions within, unsure of what to say.

Brett finally cleared his throat, released her and murmured, "I guess it's best we say good-night, Miss Sinclair, before somebody discovers you're missing and sounds an alarm."

"Oh, that wouldn't happen. I do this all the time." Oh, why did she have to rattle on like a ninny, she chided herself, fearing it would sound as if she were inviting yet another clandestine meeting.

And that was, indeed, the meaning he interpreted.

Resisting the sudden urge to crush her in his arms and kiss her till she was breathless, he remarked, "Well, I'm not in the habit of wandering this far from the bayou at night, but it could get to be a habit."

Hc yielded to impulse and softly touched her cheek before disappearing into the night.

Anjele was left shaken by the overwhelming reality that since Gator had walked into her world, nothing was the same.

And the restlessness within burned ever brighter.

CHAPTER

ANJELE COULDN'T STOP THINKING ABOUT him. She told herself it was wrong and crazy to fantasize about what it would be like to have those strong, bronzed arms hold her tightly, his full, sensuous lips pressing against her mouth. But her heart refused to listen to her head, and she found herself obsessed with daydreams and the memories of their time together.

Melora Rabine, seated beside her on the piano bench, gave an exasperated sigh and complained, "No, no, Anjele. Bach intended this piece to be fluid, soft, and you make it sound like a march into war. You just aren't concentrating."

Yes, I am, Anjele silently, mischievously responded, *but not on playing the piano.* Aloud, she lied. "I'm sorry, Miss Melora. I guess I'm just not feeling well today. You know, sometimes a girl has bad days." Darting a sideways glance, she bit back a giggle over the way Miss Rabine blushed.

"Well, then, I suppose we'll make this a short lesson." Melora got up and began to gather her things. "I suggest you have some hot lemonade and lie down."

As soon as Anjele heard the buggy leaving, she

laughed out loud and promptly began to play from memory one of the songs she'd heard in the bayou that night.

At the sound of the lively music, Claudia came running to shriek, "Where on earth did you learn that godless music? You . . . you'll get the piano out of tune," she sputtered.

Anjele ignored her, continuing to play as she swayed back and forth in rhythm.

"I said stop it!"

Claudia charged to the piano, intending to slam down the keyboard cover, but Anjele caught her adopted sister's wrist in time to keep her fingers from being smashed. "What do you think you're doing? You could break my hands."

"If that's all they can play, they deserve to be broken. Now get away from that piano."

Enough was enough. Anjele was sick of yielding. "You don't tell me what to do, Claudia."

Their eyes locked in fiery challenge.

Claudia was shaking, she was so mad. "You're going to be sorry," she whispered between clenched teeth. "You think you're better than me because you aren't adopted, but I'll be the one to inherit BelleClair, wait and see. And one day, I'll have Raymond, too. And you'll have nothing, and . . ."

Anjele had been slowly sliding across the bench away from her to get cautiously to her feet. There was a huge silver candelabra sitting on top of the piano, and she wouldn't put it past Claudia to attempt to hit her with it. While she was used to Claudia's temper and tantrums, never had she seen such a maniacal expression on her face, as though any second she'd go stark, raving mad.

Kesia appeared in the doorway, took one look at the scene, and cried, "You girls stop that fightin' now, you hear me? I'm gonna tell Miz Twyla, and—"

"That won't be necessary, Kesia." Twyla swept by her and into the music room. "I could hear them from my room." With hands on her hips she looked from one to the other. "Well? What's it about this time? I'm sick to death of this bickering."

Kesia discreetly disappeared as Claudia began to wail, "She was ruining my piano, banging on the keys, getting them all out of tune. I asked her to stop, and she wouldn't, and she started calling me names, like always. She said it wasn't my piano—"

"It belongs to both of you." Twyla sighed.

"She said it was hers, that nothing in this house is mine, because I'm adopted, and I haven't got a right to claim anything, that I don't even have the right to be here, anyway, and when you and Daddy are dead, she's going to see to it I'm thrown out. It's not fair. And she's mean and cruel, and I wish I'd never been born . . . ." Pretending to burst into wild, uncontrollable sobs, Claudia rushed out, leaving Anjele to try and dig her way out of the grave of lies.

"How could you be so cruel to your sister? How could you say such hurtful things?"

"I didn't," Anjele denied futilely.

Twyla pressed her fingertips against her throbbing temples. It was never going to end. As long as Anjele lived in the house, it would be this way. Peace would come only when Anjele got married and moved to New Orleans. Claudia, she knew, could be difficult at times, but the poor child had to be going through a terrible time, forced to endure that the man she fancied herself in love with was marrying her sister. "I'm so tired of all this," she began slowly, "and if it doesn't stop, I'm going to have to ask Ida if you can go ahead and move in with her before the wedding."

"No!" Anjele protested. She had to have these last months at BelleClair and also couldn't deny wanting to get to know her new and exciting friend.

She ran to her mother to throw her arms about her. "I'm sorry. It won't happen again. I swear it. Just don't send me to New Orleans. Not now. I wanted one more season here, because once I'm married, nothing will ever be the same. You can't do it, Momma. Please don't send me away."

Twyla sighed again, managed a stiff smile, and gently brushed at her daughter's tears. "All right," she reluctantly conceded, "but another scene, and you leave me no choice.

"Now then." She pushed from Anjele's embrace. "Where is Mrs. Rabine? And what were you playing that upset Claudia so?"

"She left early," Anjele hedged. "And I was playing Cajun music."

"Well, don't play it anymore, if Claudia feels it gets the piano out of tune."

Anjele thought that was the most ridiculous thing she'd ever heard, but wasn't about to say so. She was determined now, more than ever, to avoid any confrontation with Claudia, for she knew her mother did not make idle threats.

She sat back down at the piano and played the Bach piece, and her mother finally left her.

Mercifully, Anjele's thoughts took her away to travel once more to all the exciting places Gator had described so vividly. And she wondered again what had brought Gator to Bayou Perot and BelleClair. Handsome, dashing, obviously intelligent and keen of wit, he was wasted in the fields—as *she* would be, in her new life, married to Raymond. Dear God, there was just so much she wanted to see and do before settling down to marriage.

That evening, she stood on her veranda and willed darkness to descend quickly. From far in the distance came the sound of a riverboat's whistle. A warm breeze drifting up from the river caressed her face as she recalled once more the pleasant evening with Gator.

Yielding to temptation, daring to hope he might come back, she quickly scrambled down the trellis and ran through the night.

But he was not at the willow.

She waited perhaps an hour, feeling more like a fool with each passing moment. Finally she told herself she'd been ridiculous even to want to be with him again. What was the point? They came from two different worlds, and he'd already indicated he didn't think she belonged in his. Obviously he hadn't been serious when he hinted he'd see her again.

So be it.

She went back to the house and climbed into bed, only to stare into the darkness and wonder why, after the scant time they'd been together, he so easily monopolized her thoughts. And all the while, she chided herself and resolved to put him out of her mind.

For the next few days, Anjele did, indeed, manage not to think about him. She spent her time at the piano or reading, but was soon bored to tears. The weather was hot, but lovely, and she couldn't stand being indoors.

One morning she arose at dawn to dress quickly and hurry downstairs. As expected, her father was in the breakfast room, enjoying his usual cup of hot chicory coffee with a platter of eggs, hominy grits, and fried ham.

He was pleasantly surprised to see her. "It's been a long time since you joined me for breakfast, angel. What's the occasion? I haven't forgot my own birthday, have I?" he teased.

"I'm bored." She indicated to Kesia that she'd like juice and toast. "I swear, Poppa, if I have to spend one more day in this house, I'm going to lose my mind. Bad enough, I'll have to move into town once I'm married, so why can't I enjoy what time I've got left here?"

He laughed. "You make it sound like you're dying."

"Maybe I am."

Pity widened his eyes. "Raymond is a fine young man. I'm sure he'll do his best to make you happy."

"Then he should be willing to move to BelleClair. This is the only place I'll ever be happy."

"Your mother doesn't want that, and you know it. She feels it best you move into town and live with Ida and Vinson, for a little while anyway. Long enough to get your marriage off to a good start.

"I shouldn't be talking like this," he continued reluctantly, "but we both know Claudia fancies herself in love with Raymond, and frankly, she might cause problems if you-all moved in here."

"I'm glad you said that," Anjele said gratefully. "It's nice to know you don't share Mother's opinion that I'm always the villain."

"Well, we both know how she is, and she'll never change. Hard as it is, we've got to accept it."

Anjele took advantage of his sympathetic mood to plead, "Can I go with you today? Please? It's been so long since I made the field rounds with you, and it's such a nice day."

"You know your mother wouldn't like it."

"Let her grumble," Anjele said, adding quickly so as not to sound insolent, "Poppa, you just said we had to accept her as she is, and we both know she's going to be upset, no matter what I do. Besides, one day won't matter."

He grinned and threw up his hands in surrender. "Okay. You can go. But don't blame me when your mother gets mad, and another thing—" He reached to catch her hand as she was about to spring from the table. "It's only for a little while. There's not a cloud in the sky today, which means it's going to be blistering hot. After ten, I want you somewhere cool. I heard yesterday that Mrs. Pott's son is down with the ague. It's that time of the year, darlin', and I don't want you afflicted."

She kissed his balding head, assuring him she'd find respite from the heat at the requested hour, then hurried out to the stables to have Sam, the stable boy, saddle her mare. Though her mother usually didn't venture out of her room till nine, it was her routine to have coffee by the window as she went over the day's schedule. Anjele didn't want to risk being seen and forced to go back.

She needn't have worried, for soon they were on their way.

As always, it was with a great sense of pride that she rode beside her father. He sat tall in the saddle astride his magnificent black stallion, and when he paused to speak to overseers or workers, they would remove their straw hats in a gesture of respect.

Anjele knew he was thought of as a kind and fair man, although everyone around was well aware that he could be stern and severe, if need be. And, while a good portion of his life revolved around his position as planter, he was also involved in politics, actively supporting the Democratic Party. She knew this from their talks while riding on days like this, for her mother never allowed such discussions, saying they were of no importance to women. But Anjele loved to listen to him explain the difference in political parties—how many slave owners were urged to support the Democratic party, because it appeared to lean more towards slavery, despite the growing numbers of Northerners opposed. But the Whigs were winning over planters, due to the hope of aid from the North to construct and maintain levees. Her father, however, staunchly asserted that slavery was a Southern issue, and the North should mind its own business.

They rode first by the cotton fields, where Elton stopped to speak with each overseer. Anjele secretly thought his appearance was merely an expected formality, for BelleClair was the epitome of efficiency in all areas. Her father made sure he had capable men in supervisory positions, putting them through an apprenticeship for several years before promoting them to authority.

It was nearly ten o'clock when they reached the last field. As far as the eye could see, the browning plants exploded with white puffs of cotton like baby clouds drifting down from the sky to dot the landscape. The slaves were bent double as they moved doggedly between the rows, huge gathering sacks slung about their shoulders, dragging behind in the dust. Those close by did not glance up at the sound of horses approaching, for they had their day's quota to fill, and few wasted time. It was known far and wide that Elton Sinclair treated his slaves better than any other planter in the labyrinthine riverland. During the grinding season and the most relentless labor of the year, he boosted their morale with generous portions of food, whiskey, coffee, and tobacco.

As a heavyset man stepped among the rows to come toward them, Elton said, "It's nearly time for you to get in out of this heat, angel. Maybe later today we can go for a ride when it's cooler."

Anjele had to admit to herself that she'd been hoping they would reach the cane fields before she had to leave. Foolish though it might be, she'd been hoping to see Gator.

Her father dismounted and went to discuss something with the overseer, and when he returned, she was surprised at his grumbling comment, "I've always tried to have an open mind about the Cajuns, but there's something about that one that bothers me. He's been a good overseer in the past, but I'm starting to suspect he may be mistreating some of the hands, though I can't prove it."

"Wouldn't they tell you?"

"Not if he put a fear into them of what would happen if they did. I'll be keeping an eye on him, though."

Anjele turned to look at the man staring after them. He was not an ugly man. Far from it. In fact, if he were cleaned up, dressed up, he might even be called attractive. Yet there was something about him that evoked a feeling of foreboding. It was, she decided, his eyes, black and cold . . . and mean. Yes, she silently agreed with her father's suspicions, his overseer was probably capable of cruelty. Suddenly she wanted to know, "Why is it you're so tolerant of the Cajuns, while others regard them as *habitans*—poor whites?"

"Well, some of the planters think it's demoralizing to their slaves for the Cajuns to get paid for what they do, but I don't feel that way. If that were the case, they'd have to feel the same towards the Irish, too. I think the discrimination comes from the way they're regarded as vagabonds, having been expelled from their own colony. And they're a bit clannish and keep to themselves.

"Now be off with you," he ordered cheerily, "and get out of this heat." With a wave, he reined his horse about and headed for a pavilion where he could have a few moments in the shade, as well as a dipper of cool water.

Anjele did start back to the house but, on impulse, decided to cut along the levee and skirt the cane fields. There was very little chance she'd see Gator, and she told herself that wasn't the reason she was going that way anyhow, her motive being to delay returning home as long as possible.

In the first field, she was delighted to see Emalee waving excitedly from the edge of a row. Putting aside her mother's edict, Anjele turned her horse in that direction.

"Where you been?" Emalee demanded, wiping perspiration from her sunburned face. "Nobody see you since that night Gator fish us out of water. Next day, he say you get home all right, and we no hear nothing else. We ask, but he just give us that look o' his." She scowled in imitation.

Anjele giggled. "You didn't mock him that night, as I recall. You were scared to death of him."

"Ah, it don't matter." Emalee shrugged. "So, answer me. How come we not see you?"

"Busy with wedding plans." Anjele shaded her eyes with her hand and scanned the waving stalks of cane, but they were nearly six feet tall and it was impossible to see anyone between them. She had only spied Emalee, because she'd been outside.

Suspiciously, Emalee asked, "Who you be lookin' for? Gator? Don' worry. He be in there workin' somewheres. Want me to tell him you out here lookin' for him?"

Anjele was embarrassed, because she had been, but wasn't about to admit it. "Of course not," she said, sharper than intended. "I was looking for Simona."

"Well, she not working. She sick."

"Sick?" she echoed, alarmed, "What's wrong with her?"

Emalee grinned mysteriously. "She have to be the one to tell you."

Anjele seized the excuse to keep from going home yet. She was going to be in trouble, anyway, once her mother discovered she had sneaked off to be with her father, so it didn't matter what time she got back. "I think I'll go see about her. I can find the way if I stay on the path, and there'll be lots of boats tied up on this side." The idea was intriguing, and the path, by day, well defined. She'd gone as far as the swamp with the girls too many times to count, and the distance by boat was a straight course. All she had to do was use a pole to push the craft along, steering among the swollen, waterlogged trunks of the cypress.

Emalee didn't mirror her optimism. "It not good idea. You maybe get lost."

"Nonsense. The other night, it was pitch dark, and you hit something in the water that flipped us over. Otherwise we'd have been fine.

"Besides, it won't be long before I won't have a chance like this to go into the bayou, or do anything adventuresome or daring, for that matter."

"Ah, Anjele." Emalee swung her head from side to side in sympathy, "When I see you so unhappy, it makes me glad I am just a *habitan*."

And sometimes I wish I were, too, Anjele silently lamented, although she knew it was only the mood she was in for the moment.

She rode to the edge of the dense forest. Making sure no one was about, she dismounted and led the mare to a shady spot beneath an oak and tied her there. Riding her along the path would be dangerous, for the horse might be spooked by the strange smells and noises of swamp creatures and run away, or, worse, rear and make her fall.

Picking her way along the shrub-lined trail, Anjele marveled as always at the trees towering above—stands of pine, oak, red buckeye, and magnolia. Ever alert for snakes or alligators, she hurried to the edge of the swamp and its covering of golden club, swollen bladderwort, and clumps of pitcher plants.

She chose the first boat she came to, carefully stepped in, and picked up the long pole, stabbing down into water lilies the size of dinner plates. The thick, brackish water barely rippled as the craft moved along.

She delighted at the variety of wildlife—long-legged

cranes, great blue herons, and a red-tailed hawk, which swooped down to take a cursory inspection of the intruder into his domain.

Lost in the ethereal beauty and the tranquil peace, Anjele did not notice when the little boat began to glide off course. No longer was she poling it along in a straight line, for after each sweeping thrust, it was cutting closer and closer to the edge with its dense undergrowth of saw palmetto. She didn't realize what had happened until a sharp blades lapped her across her eyes. Stumbling backwards, she lost her balance and fell down into the boat. The impact of her weight sent it skidding sharply into a blowup, where gas had forced clumps of decayed peat and roots to the surface.

Anjele, flesh smarting from the palmetto's assault, thought she had reached land, albeit overgrown and barely passable. With her dress soaked from the water standing in the bottom of the boat, and mosquitos attacking, she decided to abandon water travel and instead follow along the edge. It couldn't be much farther to the little village, she figured, even though she had foolishly lost her concentration.

Just as she was about to step out onto what she thought was solid ground, a sharp, masculine voice boomed out in the stillness, "Don't! That's quicksand."

With a ripple of terror, she whipped about to see Gator gliding silently up behind her in his boat.

"Didn't I tell you to let me know the next time you wanted to come in here?" His voice was stern, but as he drew closer, she could see the amused twinkle in his dark eyes.

"It was a whim." She hoped he couldn't hear the pounding of her heart. She accepted his hand to step into his boat. Unable to resist, she coquettishly pointed out, "But you always seem to be following me, anyway."

"Somebody needs to. As it happened, I was coming out to get water when I saw you walking away from Emalee, heading for the woods. She said you were going to visit Simona, so I figured you were heading for trouble—*again*."

She responded by suggesting demurely, "Maybe you'd like to go to work as my bodyguard."

He pretended to be seriously considering the idea, touching fingertips to his chin before finally, firmly shaking his head. "No. I think I like working on the hoe gang better. Less work than trying to keep you out of mischief."

At that, she gave his shoulder a playful tap with her fist and promptly reminded him, "That night beneath the willow, I was no problem."

"No, you weren't," he admitted softly as the image at once came to mind. Her beauty had been ethereal, and it was only with great effort he'd been able to resist gathering her in his arms, and . . . he shook his head to dismiss the vision, all too aware of the sudden warm stirring in his loins.

Anjele was also experiencing strange but delicious twinges of her own, which she tried to dispel with humor. "But you think I'm just a spoiled, rich girl, remember? So what can you expect?"

"I can't be sure about the spoiled part, just yet. Rich, I've no doubt. No." He shook his head again and laughed, "I think I'll stick to the hoe gang." They had reached the Acadian settlement, and he pointed to a path leading off to the left. There were several shacks, built up on stilts to escape the backwater should a spring flood wreak havoc. "You'll find Simona's hut down there, third on the left. I'll wait here to take you back, and I'd appreciate it if you'd hurry. If I'm missed in the fields, I'll be the one in trouble this time."

As she skipped on her way, she lightly called over her shoulder, "That's no real problem, Gator. I hear your father is one of the overseers."

"Not for me," he muttered bitterly under his breath.

Simona shrieked with delight when she saw Anjele. "Oh, it's been too long, my friend. But how you get here? Come inside. I give you wine."

"No, no, I can't stay long. Gator is waiting to take me back. Emalee said you were sick, and I was worried." Curious, she glanced quickly about and tried to hide her revulsion at the poverty in which her friend was forced to live. The rotting boards of the shack were barely hanging together, and there were no windows, only gaping holes chopped through the wood to let in air. The only furnishing was some kind of misshapen pine-straw mattress on the floor, and a table and two benches that looked none too sturdy.

Simona sensed what she was thinking and said stiffly, "I know it isn't much, but Frank, he works very hard, and your father, he promised to pay him extra money at the end of grinding season. We gonna get us another place, bigger, nicer." Her hand instinctively went to her still-flat abdomen and, with a glow of pride, she happily announced, "We gonna need it for the baby."

"Baby?" Anjele echoed, surprised and delighted as she rushed to hug her. "Oh, Simona, that's wonderful. When do you think you'll have it?"

"Maybe early spring. We have lots of time to settle in our new hut. But right now, I throw up a lot, so Frank, he don't want me out in the heat. He say if I eat for two, he work for two." A wide grin spread across her tanned face, then, with sudden, narrowed eyes, suspicion ignited. "Hey, what's this you say about Gator waiting for you? What's goin' on? Last time I talk to him, he plenty mad with you for comin' here. Now you gon' tell me he bring you here?"

They sat down at the rickety table, and Anjele explained how he'd come along just in time to prevent her from stumbling into a bed of quicksand. "I'm lucky he was following me."

"Yeah, but I'm not surprised."

"Why not?"

"Like I tol' Emalee all along, you the first girl Gator ask questions about, and that means he likes you. We never see him with a girl before, and like we tol' you, they all run after him. He is good-looking, all right, but strange, no? He stay to himself all the time.

"But tell me," she rushed on, eyes twinkling, "Is this the first time you see him since that night he fished you and Emalee outta the water?"

Anjele admitted it wasn't and confided how he'd twice shown up at the willow.

Simona clapped her hands together in delight. "See? He does like you." She went to one of the gaping holes and peered out to report, "He down there, all right. And I tell you what. If it weren't for me bein' already married, I'd be one of those girls after him, too."

Anjele didn't say anything, for what could she say? Simona was being ridiculous, and even if what she said were true, what difference did it make? She was not free for any man to court and never had been. From the second she'd drawn her first breath, her fate had been sealed.

Simona pursed her lips thoughtfully. She returned to the table and sat down. "You know," she began in a dreamy voice, "when I knew I was gonna have this baby, I was so happy and proud. To think the beautiful thing me and Frank do together with our bodies could make such a miracle, why, it make me cry with wonder.

"You see, my friend"—she reached to take Anjele's hands in hers and urge her to meet her probing gaze—"when Frank and me lay together naked, we make our bodies sing with the joys of touching and kissing all over. And when he put himself inside me, it's like we become one person. Now we make another person. And it is a perfect thing, a perfect love. One day, you gonna have it that way, too."

Anjele bit down on her lower lip, determined to keep silent. No matter how many times, through all the years they'd known each other, she had shared her hopes and dreams, as well as problems, with both Simona and Emalee, she had promised herself once the engagement had become official not to voice her dismay again. "Perhaps," she finally murmured, then rose to her feet and feebly smiled. "But I guess I'd better be going now. Gator said he'd be in a lot of trouble if he's missed."

"Ha! Who'd dare say anything to him? Everyone scared, for he look so big and mean." She also stood.

"Mean? I don't understand why they'd think that. Granted, he's well built and certainly not the kind you'd want to have trouble with, but I find he's warm and sensitive, and he's also witty and charming, and . . ." Her voice trailed off as she saw the way Simona was looking at her, as if she were trying to keep from bursting into gales of laughter. Annoyed, she demanded, "What's the matter?"

"Nothing." Simona giggled. "Except you sound like a girl falling in love."

"That's the most ridiculous thing I've ever heard. For heaven's sake, I'm getting married in a few months, and—"

"That don't matter," Simona was suddenly serious again. Placing an arm about Anjele's shoulders in a conspiratorial gesture, she said, "You can do nothing about that. That is decided by your family. But the rest of your life, you can do something about. And that includes loving another man if it makes you both happy."

Anjele was only too familiar with the way Simona's blunt honesty could sometimes shock, but this was absurd, and she said as much.

"Okay, okay, you do not agree with me, I know," Simona conceded, "but there be no harm if you and Gator have fun these last few months before you move away. Who's to know? You know Emalee and me would never say nothing. Jus' go your way and have your love, my friend," she urged, "and make beautiful memories to think back on when you have sad times. Gator, he know you gonna marry somebody else, don't he?"

Miserably, Anjele nodded, wishing Simona would stop, because temptation was birthing.

"Then he understand how you only want to have fun, and he not be hurt later. So go to him now. Tell him how you feel. Ask him if he want to help you make these memories."

Anjele laughed, told her she was crazy, and they hugged each other in parting.

She could feel Simona's eyes on her as she hurried to where Gator was waiting.

"One of these days, I'll give you poling lessons," he remarked pleasantly as he helped her into the flat-bottom boat. "Then maybe you can make it through the swamp without turning over or running aground."

Wanting to cast away the depression Simona had evoked, Anjele said cheerily, "Why not now?" She moved to the back of the craft and took up one of the long cane poles.

"All right. I'll cast us off, and then do as I do. Take alternate prods with the pole and push."

When they were on their way, carefully, slowly, gliding through the dark, honeyed water, Anjele asked, "Why do you use the pole? Why not an oar? I've gone fishing with my father on the river, and that's what he used to row us along."

"That was deep water. This is shallow. You've got to not only feel your way along to make sure you aren't about to scrape bottom, but also probe for underwater cypress knees—and alligators.

"Tell me," he went on, "How did you like fishing?"

"I loved it. I think those were some of the nicest times I've ever had." She eagerly described how she and her father would leave the house just before dawn. Kesia would have a basket ready with bread and jam sandwiches and some fruit. They would hurry on their way and by the time the sun burst from the horizon, they'd be in their favorite spot on the river. It was in a fingered cove, shrouded by levees and draping willows and a few banana trees. There they would stay till midafternoon. Sometimes they would sit in the boat, but mostly they sat on the riverbank waiting for the fat catfish to bite the worm and swallow the hook.

"If it hadn't been for all those times, I probably wouldn't know everything I do about BelleClair. Poppa told me everything, but Momma says business shouldn't be discussed around children."

"You're hardly a child, Anjele," he interjected with a sweeping gaze.

Pretending not to notice, she continued, "Poppa doesn't feel that way, and he's told me all about how BelleClair got started in the first place, and how cotton gets to market, and how sugar is made. Everything. I know how many acres he owns and what every inch of it is used for. Why, I'll bet if I had to, I could run the whole place by myself, and . . ." She realized she'd gotten carried away. "I'm sorry. I didn't mean to run on so."

"I was enjoying it. Go on, please."

And she did, glad to share the pleasant reverie. She related how they'd fry the fish to a golden brown in a cauldron of lard. Kesia, or one of the other servants, would spread a tablecloth under one of the big old oaks, and they'd sit right down on the ground and eat. "Of course, Claudia complained about the gnats and flies and mosquitoes, and finally she and Mother would get up and go in the house, but Poppa and I would sit right there and eat ourselves sick and then lie down and look up at the stars, and he'd tell me more stories, and I loved every second of it." She was embarrassed to blink away tears of sadness over the good times ending.

Brett sensed what she was feeling and asked, "Why

don't you ever go fishing with him anymore?"

"Because I grew older, and Momma said it wasn't ladylike. And besides, with the wedding and all, I guess I should be concentrating on other things now, anyway, instead of pining over childish memories."

"Well, I don't think it's childish, and frankly, I don't see anything wrong with it." He thought a moment, then yielded to impulse. "How would you like to show me your secret fishing hole? I might be able to slip away one morning. Those cane rows are getting awfully tall, and it's hard to count heads and discover somebody's missing."

Anjele wondered if she dared, but Simona's plea began to echo, how she should make beautiful memories to think about when the bad times came. She reasoned Simona was right in saying Gator knew she was engaged. There'd be no misunderstanding. She made sure by forcing a casual tone to remark, "Well, if you don't mind sneaking around. I mean, I do have a fiancé, and although you and I know we're just friends, having a good time, we wouldn't want him or anyone else to get the wrong idea."

He drew in his breath, let it out slowly before nodding, "Sure. I understand. Besides . . ." Suddenly, he couldn't resist adding bitterly, "I doubt your father would want you having anything to do with a Cajun, anyway."

"No," she regretted having to concede, "I don't suppose he would."

They moved on in silence, for suddenly there seemed nothing more to be said.

Finally, they reached the place where she'd left her horse.

Tension hung like an invisible shroud.

"Thank you," she offered with a shy smile, "for coming to my rescue—again."

"My pleasure, *ma chère*." His joviality was forced. "One of these days we'll have that fishing trip."

She felt a disappointed stab. Back there, in the bayou, he'd made it sound like an invitation. Now it seemed like idle conversation, insincere and soon to be forgotten. "Sure," she tried to sound flip, uncaring. "I'd best get home."

Brett knew he had to get away at once, or he was going to do what he'd been aching to do all afternoon, which was grab her and hold her and kiss her till they were both out of breath. "Yeah, I guess you do. Goodbye . . . Angel." He grinned and used the nickname he teased her about.

Anjele was disappointmented. Perhaps, she told herself, it was best if they didn't meet again, even though Simona's advice needled.

"How about tomorrow?"

"Wh . . what?" Her heart began to pound.

"Tomorrow," he repeated. "Would you like to go fishing tomorrow?"

It was all she could do to keep from shouting with joy. Struggling to maintain her composure, she explained, "But I won't be able to get out at dawn. It would be closer to noon. I could meet you at the willow. Nobody's around that time of day. Poppa lets everyone break an hour for dinner because of the heat. The fish might not be biting then, but . . ." She gasped, embarrassed at how she'd once again gone on. But he didn't seem to mind, because he was looking at her in a special way, as though he liked what he was seeing and hearing.

Brett opened and closed his hands at his sides with the aching desire to touch her, hold her. He could tell she sincerely wanted to go with him and, while he longed to be with her, he experienced also a flash of pity. Exuberant, filled with life, she was the most spirited girl he'd ever met, and it was cruel for circumstances to keep her harnessed. Yielding to impulse, he asked bluntly, "How old are you, Anjele?"

"Sixteen."

He nodded, reminded of how guileless he'd been at that age. No wonder she looked at the world with dewy-eyed innocence. Born into wealth and all that implied, she hadn't been exposed to stark reality. He'd be doing her a favor, he told himself, to befriend her, and firmly, almost angrily, he promised himself that was as far as their relationship would ever go. "I'll be there at noon," he finally told her, then hurried on his way, before they were seen by some of the field hands.

Anjele allowed the mare full rein, galloping all the way home, hair flying in the breeze wildly, happily, in rhythm with her heart.

CHAPTER

ANJELE AWAKENED TO THE SOUND OF HER mother's excited voice right outside her bedroom. Curious, she scrambled out of bed and went to stand by the door and listen.

"Elton, this is wonderful." Her mother was exuberant. "We haven't seen Delilah and Stephen in years. You know, he's about the same age as the girls. A few months older, I think. I wonder if he turned into a handsome man. Unattractive little boys often do," she added optimistically.

"You can never tell," her father responded. "but what bothers me is whether you can be ready for them by tomorrow. Her letter took so long to get here. Knowing Delilah, she'll be upset to find out she arrived almost unannounced."

"We won't tell her. What's to be done, anyway? She can have the guest rooms on the west corner, and Stephen can have one of the *garçonnières*. Having them here a whole month is going to be wonderful. I'll get started making plans right away."

They went on down the stairs, and Anjele hugged herself with delight. House guests! And for a whole month! And, unless she missed her guess, Delilah Pardee's motive in coming was to try and find a wife for Stephen. Even in a place as large as Atlanta, Anjele sadly supposed it would be difficult to find a girl interested in someone so homely, for she didn't share her mother's optimism that Stephen had drastically changed. Of course, if the Pardees had been rich, there wouldn't be a problem, but they weren't. Her father and Wilbur Pardee had known each other as boys and stayed in touch when the Pardees moved to Georgia. Wilbur had his own feed store there, but she'd heard her father say he made only a modest living.

But Anjele didn't care why Miss Delilah was coming. Exultation came over knowing her mother would be busy, while Claudia, since she didn't have a beau, would be expected to entertain Stephen.

Sure enough, no one noticed when Anjele quietly left the house just before lunch. Her mother was so busy making up menus and invitation lists she had a tray sent to her room, and Claudia joined her, also caught up in the whirl of planning.

Gator wasn't there when Anjele arrived at the willow tree, and she felt a stab of disappointment, but a few moments later, he came walking up the bank from where he'd left his boat tied below.

"Okay," he greeted her, "let's see if you can fish any better than you can swim in quicksand."

She wrinkled her nose in feigned annoyance and joined him to run into the warm summer day.

Soon, they were in the isolated cove, and Anjele surprised him by placing the squiggling worm on a hook herself. Seeing his look of astonishment, she laughed.

"What's the matter? Haven't you ever seen a girl who wasn't afraid of worms?"

Brett knew he'd never seen a girl like her, period, and damn well liked everything he saw. "No, I guess I haven't, but frankly, I was starting to think you're completely worthless."

"Oh, I'm so glad," she said with exaggerated pleasure. "I was really starting to worry about your opinion of me, kind sir, especially after you saved me not only from drowning but from quicksand as well."

"You weren't going to drown. Snakebite, maybe, or lose a leg to a hungry gator. And I've poked that quicksand bed. It's not deep. You'd have been stuck till somebody, or some*thing* came along, but if you want to be eternally grateful, it's okay by me." His dark eyes shone, for he enjoyed the easy banter between them.

Anjele continued to astound. In a short while, she managed to haul several large catfish up and into the boat, while Brett sat glumly without so much as a nibble on his line. Still, he couldn't remember a more enjoyable time. But all too soon, time slipped by, and reluctantly he said he had to get back to the field.

"Do you want these fish?" she offered, a bit embarrassed to have bested him. She needn't have been, for although Anjele did not know it yet, Brett Cody was too sure of himself to ever feel threatened in any way, by anyone.

He accepted her offer and, even though it was a futile gesture, impulsively asked if she'd like to come to his pirogue later to share them.

"I really wish I could," she said sincerely but explained that Raymond had been invited for dinner. To soothe his disappointment, even though he was acting as if it didn't matter, she rushed to share the news of their expected houseguests and how she'd have more free time with her mother and Claudia so busy.

"Anjele, I can't sneak out of the field very often," he reminded her soberly, "but we've still got the evenings, if you can manage to get away."

"But it's hard for me to sneak out till after everyone's gone to bed, and that can be terribly late sometimes, especially with all the entertainment Mother is planning for the next month."

"Well, we'll work it out." He reached to squeeze her hand. "I said I'd show you a good time this summer, and I will. I don't mind waiting at the willow, as long as I know you'll try to be there."

"I'll do my best. I promise."

Their eyes met and held. In that frozen instant, Brett was again waging an inner battle, for he desperately wanted to hold her, kiss her, while Anjele dared to wonder what it would be like if he did.

His line gave a jerk, but the wily catfish got away before he could yank him in. Still, Brett was grateful for the diversion, which allowed the tension to melt away.

Dinner-table conversation centered on the expected arrival of their guests the next morning. Even Claudia was caught up in the excitement and didn't behave as she usually did when Raymond was present by hanging onto his every word while gazing at him adoringly. He seemed more relaxed and at ease and even volunteered to help entertain the Pardees by hosting a visit to a horse race when he returned from a planned trip to Kentucky.

"Is this a business trip?" Elton was quick to inquire.

He was not impressed with the young man's preoccupation with having a good time rather than establishing himself in some kind of respectable business. Elton held to the conviction that it didn't matter how much money a man had, he needed to work at something productive.

Raymond didn't notice Elton's disapproving frown as he explained he was going to buy horses and would be away nearly a month. "There are several farms I plan to visit. It's beautiful country up there, and this is a wonderful time to visit."

"I wouldn't know," Elton remarked tightly. "I have to work."

Raymond shrugged, unmoved by the barb. He was used to the planters looking down on him, and it didn't bother him a bit.

Anjele surprised everyone by unexpectedly pointing out, "If you were willing to live here, Raymond, you could keep your horses here, instead of boarding them at the racetracks."

"Mother would have a fit, and besides, I don't want to *live* with my horses, for heaven's sake. I just want to visit them once in awhile. I'm afraid I'd never be happy anywhere but in the heart of a city."

But it doesn't matter how *I* feel, Anjele silently, sadly, cried.

She could feel her father looking at her and turned to see the sympathy mirrored on his face. He reached to pat her hand, and for an instant, she was reminded of how he always seemed to understand what she was feeling, and how very much she loved him for it.

* * *

The house was spotless, with vases of freshly picked flowers in every room. Twyla had instructed Anjele and Claudia to wear their Sunday best. Lemonade and fig cake were ready to be served. Even the household servants were wearing special uniforms.

It was nearly noon when Claudia, having kept a vigil at the front of the house since early morning, frantically called, "They're here. I can see the carriage coming up the road."

Anjele, reading in the parlor, grimaced as she glanced at the clock. If Gator had been able to get away for a little while that morning, no doubt he'd given up waiting for her to meet him. But she hadn't dared duck out, knowing her presence was required for the arrival of their guests.

Little William, Kesia's son, wearing a red velvet coat Anjele knew had to be terribly hot, stood obediently waiting to take the reins of the team of horses when they were handed to him for looping into the hitching-post ring.

Malcolm, the butler, also resplendent in velvet, opened the carriage door, while the accompanying footmen scrambled in readiness for any orders given.

Delilah Pardee, Anjele decided at once, was nearly three times larger than she remembered—in all directions. Her face was a mass of fleshy jowls, and when she waved at Twyla, who was waiting on the porch, her flabby arms jiggled from shoulder to wrist.

Behind her followed the young man Anjele had known as a child. The only change was that he'd grown taller. His ears were still large, and his nose was even more hooked, but he had a warm and friendly smile.

She recognized Claudia's wide grin as what it was—forced and artificial. No doubt, she'd been telling herself, after all these years Stephen would've changed from ugly duckling to swan and her own Prince Charming would be stepping out of the carriage. But at least she was going to put up a front, and Anjele silently commended her. It would have been just like her to groan in disgust and rudely turn away.

Spotting Anjele, Delilah gave a mock wail of disappointment and whined, "Oh, you had to go and get yourself engaged, you little dickens. Didn't you know I've been saving Stephen just for you?"

"Now, now." Twyla's laugh was stilted. "You've always known Anjele was promised to Ida and Vinson's boy, but we've still got our Claudia."

Anjele bit back a sympathetic groan. Stephen, poor thing, didn't deserve such a fate. No man did.

That night, with her parents engrossed in conversation with their guests, and Claudia surprisingly hovering around Stephen, no one seemed to mind when Anjele announced she had a headache and excused herself for the evening. She didn't even have to crawl down the trellis, but simply walked out the front door and headed straight to the willow tree.

"You did make it." Brett got to his feet, trying to keep the eagerness from his voice.

"Have you been waiting long?"

"No," he lied, not about to admit he'd been there since before sundown.

"We . . . we have guests," she reminded him, all of a sudden unnerved by his nearness.

"I know." He wasn't feeling too comfortable himself, as he thought of what he'd rather be doing besides making small talk. He also knew he had to get them out of there, and fast, for the temptation to hold her in his arms was needling. Suddenly, almost sharply, he asked, "Have you ever seen a raccoon?"

She laughed, "No, but I've heard—"

"Come on." He grabbed her hand and pulled her along, and she ran with him, her long hair flowing as freely as her spirit on that warm, star-dazzled night.

He led her into the forest, picking his way along in the light of a full moon. "You're going to have to be real quiet," he said as they came up to a small pond edged with logs and cypress knees. "They're used to me, but you're a stranger." He pointed to a large tree which had fallen to form a natural bridge over the water.

Anjele could not suppress her gasp of delight to see the brown, furry creatures perched in the middle. One of them turned at the sound, and she bit back yet another cry to see the black mask covering the upper part of his face.

They watched in silent fascination as the larger of the raccoons abruptly thrust his paw down into the water and came up with a small bream.

"Amazing," she said breathlessly. "I can't believe I'm really seeing this."

"Come on. I've lots more to show you."

Anjele lost all track of time, as he led her to his favorite observation points. She was thrilled to catch a glimpse of a doe, a red fox, and a mother possum with two babies clinging to her back.

"How do you find all these wonderful creatures?" she whispered in awe as a bobcat screamed from his perch high in a pine.

"I wander around a lot at night. I guess it's because I view sleep as a waste of time. When my life is over, I don't want to think I spent a third of it asleep. So instead I explore the world by night."

"I envy you. I could never do things like this by myself, and I hope you know how much I appreciate your sharing it all with me." Impulsively she added, "And I don't care what Simona and Emalee say about everyone being afraid of you. I think you're nice, Gator—or whatever your name is—and I like having you for my friend."

He felt awkward, not used to having anyone talk to him in such a way. Finally, he mumbled that he liked being friends with her, too, then said what had been on his mind all evening. "Your fiancé wouldn't like it. Neither would your parents."

"They won't find out," she said with a determined lift of her chin. "It's our secret."

"Have you said anything to Simona and Emalee?"

She shook her head. "I haven't seen them, but when I do, I won't say anything, though I don't think they'd tell. I just don't want to get them involved. It's none of their business."

Unable to hold back the bitterness, Brett said, "Yeah, when you're doing something you're ashamed of, I guess it's best to keep it to yourself. After all, it sure wouldn't do for folks to find out Elton Sinclair's daughter is sneaking out at night to meet a *Cajun*."

Moved by his stinging comment, Anjele said tremulously, "I wish things were different, Gator. I really do. If it were up to me, why, I'd be willing to tell the whole world we're friends. I'd want you to come visit me, right out in the open, for everybody to see. I'm not like my family. I don't even like slavery, and—" She shook her head briskly and threw up her hands to cry, "Oh, what difference does it make, anyway? We've got this summer, and that's it. I'll be married in a few months and will have to live in New Orleans, and if Claudia can find somebody who'll have her, she'll take over BelleClair and run it right into the ground once Daddy is gone. And you'll stay in the swamps and keep working the fields till you're an old man, and human beings will be continue to be bought and sold like cattle.

"So why did we have to start talking like this?" she finished by demanding, tears she could not hold back streaming down her cheeks. "We were having a wonderful evening."

Moonlight glinted in the golden-red threads of her hair as it cascaded over her shoulders, and her tears were tiny drops of silver on her cheeks. Brett brushed at them with gentle fingertips. "I guess it needed saying, Angel. I guess it was inside both of us, and we were trying to ignore it.

"But you don't have to worry about me growing old in the fields." He laughed. "I've got my reasons for hanging around here for a while, but then I'm striking out again."

Though she knew it shouldn't make any difference, because they'd never see each other again after this summer, anyway, Anjele was still struck by disappointment to think of him leaving. "But why? Where would you go? Gator, I was listening to you while you were talking tonight and telling me about the beauty of the bayou, but something else struck me, the pride and love I could hear in your voice. You love this land. Why would you want to leave it?"

He wasn't about to confide he now had another reason besides escaping the cane fields—and she was it.

Being with her, aware they were courting trouble with the intense feelings growing between them, was torture.

She was waiting for an answer he had no intention of giving, and he took her hand and reminded her, "It's late. We've got to be getting back."

But Anjele was not to be put off. "If we're going to be friends, I'd like to know more about you, Gator. So tell me, why are you going to leave a place you obviously like?"

He shook his head and kept on walking, and Anjele, bewildered, could only join him, hating that a wonderful night should end so tensely.

When they reached the edge of the woods, the fields of cotton looked ghostly in the shimmering moonlight. Beyond stretched the land of the dancing, clattering sugarcane stalks. The river snaked in the distance, a black ribbon in the dark landscape. In the middle of it all and towering above like a grandiose castle was the mansion, pitch dark and frozen in sleep.

Stiffly, for she had become miffed by his silence, Anjele said, "You don't have to walk me any farther." Still, she was reluctant to leave him. The only other times she could remember being so enjoyable were those spent with her father. But her experiences with Gator were special in a different kind of way, because it was nice to have a man friend.

He was standing there, waiting for her to leave him, and despite her annoyance over his behavior, Anjele couldn't bear the thought of parting without knowing if she'd see him again. "We're having a barbecue on the front lawn tomorrow evening and lots of people are coming. I might not be able to get away till real late."

His breezy response banished the hopeful smile from

her face. "Well, I guess I need to get some rest anyway. We're working pretty hard in the fields these days. It's hard to get away."

Anjele bit down on her lower lip and silently swore that if she started crying again, she'd throw herself in the river. It was time she started facing reality. He was obviously letting her know he didn't want to risk seeing her again, and she couldn't help wondering why either of them should bother anyway. What was the point? After all, it seemed ridiculous to take such chances for one summer of sunny memories to store up for a rainy day in the future?

Why, indeed, her heart screamed. She knew the answer, just as she was well aware of the risks involved. Without giving herself a chance to change her mind, she blurted out, "I've never had so much fun as I did tonight, Gator. When can we meet again?"

He sighed, ran his fingers through his hair, and looked away. He was trying to grasp his thoughts to express them in a way she'd understand without letting her know how goddamn much he cared, how dangerously close he was to crossing the line of no return.

She sensed he was upset and took a step closer. Gently, she reached to touch his shoulder and whispered, "If you're really afraid of getting in trouble, I understand, and I'm sorry if I've been a pest, and—"

"To hell with it." Brett swore. "I'll be here tomorrow night." He reached for her, unable to hold back any longer.

Anjele felt a jolt slamming throughout her body as his mouth moved on hers to possessively and thoroughly explore and savor. The wonder of it all was overwhelming, staggering, and she swayed against him.

Though her experience in kissing was scant, nothing could compare to this, the wild pounding of her heart, the overwhelming need to part her lips beneath his sweet assault and accept his tongue seeking entrance. Unfamiliar sensations began to wrap about her like a spider's silken web as heated passion aroused to intoxicate.

His mouth was increasingly demanding, tongue seeking and tasting as he pulled her yet closer against him. He felt the swell of her breasts pressed to his chest, felt her trembling in his arms. His fingers moved from her face and with a will of their own, boldly traveled downward to cup each breast in turn.

Moaning beneath the luscious, sensual assault, Anjele clung to him in that breathless moment when time stood still. It was only when she felt his swollen manhood that she came out of the pleasured stupor.

Brett realized that in another instant, there would be no turning back, not on his part, anyway, because the lion of desire was hungrily screaming to be fed. He released her so abruptly, she stumbled backwards. "This time," he declared raggedly, "I'm not going to say I was wrong."

She could see his devil-may-care grin in the moonlight, and boldly matched it with one of her own. "This time," she murmured, "I don't want you to."

CHAPTER

CLAUDIA LOOKED IN THE MIRROR AND liked what she saw—a young woman undeniably beautiful. Golden hair in ringlets cascading about a flawless face. Wide, dusty blue eyes fringed with incredibly long, silky lashes. Flawless ivory skin. A lush, curvaceous body beneath the elegant costume she wore.

The earbobs, borrowed from her adoptive mother, were shimmering pearls to match the crusted neckline of the lavender silk gown. She had opted not to wear a necklace, having no intention of detracting from the cleavage she was so proud of, well defined in the plunging bodice.

Claudia smiled at her reflection. There was no way Stephen Pardee could resist her charms this night. For the past three weeks, she'd been leading up to this time, spending every possible moment with him. At every function, she was at his side. Speculation had begun, she knew, that a romance was budding, but if all went according to plan, there would be no more wondering. She intended to wind up his visit with a formal engagement party. The fact that she didn't love him and never would gave no cause for concern, for she'd reached the conclusion that if she couldn't have Raymond, she would just forget about love and concentrate instead on manipulating her adoptive father into leaving control of the plantation to her and not to Anjele. And it didn't matter that a woman's land and money were the property of her husband. Claudia planned to control Stephen, who would grovel at her feet in gratitude for such a beauteous wife, and of course he would have no qualms about leaving Atlanta to enjoy a life of luxury as her husband.

Secretly she was already grooming herself to take over after Twyla and Elton were dead. She pored through the journals and ledgers every chance she got. Once she understood the operations, competent overseers were all she'd need.

She figured on having two children, with luck boys, spaced two years apart. Having to do *that* with Stephen in order to make those babies was not something she looked forward to, but of course there would be handsome paramours at her beck and call for the real pleasures of the flesh. She knew about *that*, too, having had a few secret trysts now and then.

It still galled, however, to think how she had to marry someone like Stephen to get what was rightfully hers. If Twyla and Elton Sinclair had really and truly thought of her as their daughter, which they should have everyone believe, then they would have kept their original covenant with Ida and Vinson Duval for their firstborn children of the opposite sex to marry each other.

"And here I am," she said aloud to the scowling face in the mirror, "Theoretically, their firstborn."

But the truth was, Claudia angrily brooded, her so-called mother was nothing but a hypocrite. How she liked to boast of loving both her daughters so equally she could never remember which one was adopted. And no matter how Twyla privately bent over backwards to keep from showing favoritism to Anjele, Claudia didn't care. She hated Anjele, because it wasn't right for her to be the one to marry Raymond.

But what also concerned her was the possibility of Anjele having a baby right away, particularly a boy. Elton might decide to leave BelleClair in trust to his grandchild.

She couldn't let that happen, and it was her fervid plan to beat Anjele to the cradle, confident that her baby, growing up at BelleClair, would naturally be closer to Twyla and Elton than one Anjele would be raising in New Orleans. And ultimately there would be no way they would do anything that would mean, upon their deaths, that she and Stephen and their offspring would be forced to move out.

Otherwise, she supposed, she'd wind up with nothing, so her only hope was to marry Stephen.

True, she'd thought of looking to the eligible young men in her social circle, but most of them were already set to inherit farms and plantations of their own. To marry one of them would require moving in with *their* families, and, no doubt, force her to be as subservient as their slaves. Besides, the few she had dallied with were so domineering they couldn't bear the thought of a wife who'd dare stand on her own two feet and not take their every word as gospel. Accordingly, word had spread of her independence, and invisible weeds had quickly sprouted in the courting path to her doorstep.

Stephen Pardee had been the answer to her dilemma,

but Claudia was frankly puzzled over his lack of enthusiasm. She'd let it be known in subtle ways that she was his for the taking, but obviously he was not used to being around girls and didn't know how to react. At times she suspected he was actually avoiding her but credited that to shyness. Still, he came out of his shell whenever Anjele was around, and the two of them chatted and laughed like old friends—which was infuriating. Well, it was all going to change. After tonight, he'd be fluttering around her like butterflies on daisies.

With a pinch to her cheeks for rosiness, she hurried downstairs to where guests were already gathered on the terrace for yet another of her mother's sumptuous buffets. Eating was Delilah Pardee's favorite pastime, as evidenced by her huge size, and as long as food was around, she was happy.

Tables covered in white linen offered an array of spit-roasted turkey and crab-stuffed flounder and dozens of other delicacies. Claudia spotted Delilah, greedily sucking pralines. Asked if she'd seen Stephen, Delilah, mouth full, could only point to the lawn beyond.

Claudia hurried to find him, for it was the opportunity she'd been waiting for, to catch him alone in the moonlight, and—she stopped short.

He was in the moonlight, all right, but he wasn't alone. He was grinning down at Anjele, happy as a child on Christmas morning.

Claudia stalked right over and made no pretense of hiding her jealousy. "Well," she began in a furious huff as they both stared at her curiously, expectantly. "It's a damn good thing Raymond will be back in another week, before you get desperate and start chasing after the bucks in the field."

Anjele blanched and glanced quickly at Stephen to see his eyes bulging with disbelief.

Hands on her hips, Claudia snapped, "So what are you standing here for? You aren't getting Stephen!"

If it hadn't been for Stephen, Anjele would have already been in retreat. She had been even more careful to avoid arguments with Claudia since her mother's threat to send her to live with the Duvals. But she could not allow this kind of humiliation. She met Claudia's icy glare with one of her own. "Apologize, Claudia. You know you're wrong to say such things."

With a haughty toss of golden ringlets, Claudia laughed. "I'll do no such thing. What other reason would you have for being out here in the dark with him, if you weren't throwing yourself at him like a strumpet?"

Anjele resisted the impulse to slap her, grateful that Stephen suddenly came alive to intervene.

"You've gone too far, Claudia. You've no right to talk to Anjele that way. We weren't doing anything wrong, but the fact that we're out here together is none of your business, anyway."

Claudia gasped. She hadn't expected him to come to Anjele's defense.

He held out his arm to Anjele and managed a reassuring smile as he led her back to the party.

Claudia stared after them. Later, she decided, she would find a way to get him off by himself and explain why she'd been so upset. Because she loved him, she would lie, and seeing him with another woman was more than she could bear, and she hadn't known it till that very instant, which made her realize beyond all doubt how very much he meant to her.

Why, it was even better it turned out this way, she cheered herself. Later on, after a few glasses of champagne, music, and merriment, he'd be in a better mood. And Anjele would retire early, as she always did. Claudia was confident before the night was over her engagement to Mr. Stephen Pardee of Atlanta would be official.

"I'm so sorry, Stephen," Anjele said, attempting to gloss over the ugly episode. "Sometimes Claudia gets upset and says things she doesn't mean, and I hope you won't think badly of her for what happened."

"We both know she's a haughty, hateful shrew and God help the man who winds up with her for a wife. These past weeks have been a nightmare. I have to admit, when Mother suggested we pay you-all a visit, with the idea of pairing me off with Claudia, I dared to think she'd changed from the snotty little brat I remembered. From the first day, I knew it could never work out.

"A pity," he went on to say, looking down at her in wistful adoration, "that you've always been promised to Raymond. I think I've always loved you, Anjele."

"Oh, Stephen. You're such a dear to say that," she whispered, touching his cheek in a gesture of tender compassion.

He caught her fingertips, pressed them against his lips. "Some things aren't meant to be. But remember I'll always be your friend, and I only want you to be happy."

Claudia's lips curled back in a snarl of silent rage as she watched them from a distance.

Somehow, some way, she vowed to find a way to

banish Anjele from BelleClair forever.

By God, she wasn't going to let Anjele stand in the way of claiming what was rightfully hers.

It was nearly ten o'clock, and the guests had long ago moved inside to the ballroom for dancing. Anjele knew Gator would have been waiting at the willow for an hour by now, but she'd been unable to get away. Stephen, trying to avoid Claudia, hovered about, and while she wanted to help him, she was desperate to escape.

At last, she had her chance. Delilah wanted to dance with Stephen, and when he excused himself, saying he'd be right back, Anjele was quick to say, "It's all right, Stephen. Enjoy yourself. I'm so tired I'm going to bed. See you at breakfast." And she rushed out before he could protest.

The foyer, for the moment, was empty, so she skirted around the stairs and went out by the rear of the house. Keeping to the shadows, she lifted her skirts and broke into a run.

She was not aware that Claudia had seen her.

Claudia had been watching all evening, anxious for Anjele to leave Stephen's side. When she'd seen her heading for the stairway, Claudia had discreetly followed to make sure she was, indeed, retiring for the evening.

How surprised she'd been to see her sneak out the back way. Any other time, she'd have followed, but this night was dedicated to another cause. Anjele was obviously into some sort of mischief, and Claudia wagered it had something to do with a man. There would be ample time to find out later, she promised herself, turning back to the ballroom—and Stephen Pardee.

* * *

He was waiting.

The instant he heard Anjele approaching, he was out from beneath the sheltering willow to open his arms to her. "God, how I've missed you," he whispered fiercely, crushing her against him.

Standing on tiptoe, her hands clutched his shoulders as she searched for his face in the darkness. "Oh, my darling, I've lived for this moment." Then she boldly kissed him, her tongue melding against his as their bodies clung together.

They had been together almost nightly in the past three weeks, and somewhere along the way, light banter and easy camaraderie had yielded to hungry desire and smoldering passion. Neither knew where their reckless emotions would lead, for there was no thought of tomorrow, only the here and now and the joy of each tender moment.

He drew her back beneath the caressing fronds and gently to the ground. His hands had a mind of their own, quickly manipulating her warm, full breasts from the bodice of her gown. His tongue explored the sweet recesses of her mouth, pausing ever so often to nibble at her lips as he told her over and over again how much he wanted her, needed her, how it was hell not being with her.

Brett's heart had won out in debate with his head, and he no longer worried over the right or wrong of it. She'd told him she felt the same, and there was no turning back. All that awaited was the consummation of their hungrily raging bodies, but he'd made up his mind not to force it. When it happened, it had to be because she wanted it as much as he did, so there'd be no blame or regrets.

He lowered his mouth to her breast, began to suckle, feeling her throaty gasp as his teeth gently held her nipple while his tongue assaulted, sweetly torturing. She clutched his head, fingers twisting gently in his hair to urge him yet closer.

He moved on top of her, and she spread her legs for him to lie between. Deftly, he pulled up her skirt and petticoats, so she could feel his hardness against her.

Anjele moaned softly, arching her back. This was the way it was supposed to be, she told her feverish, throbbing brain, the way Simona had described it between her and her husband—hunger that made her crazy, delicious tremors in her belly, and the feeling that if she didn't have him deep inside her, she'd surely die.

Each time they were together, they'd gone farther and farther, and always she'd managed to resist. Never did he protest or try to cajole or persuade. He would look at her in anguish and say huskily, "Come to me only when you're ready, Angel. It's beautiful only when both want it."

She did want it—with a gnawing, grinding ache which haunted the hours after they parted. Night after night, she lay awake till nearly dawn, reliving every kiss, every caress, savoring his words of adoration. And while the glory and delight made her tremble with rapture, the agony was in wondering where it would all lead.

She felt his hand slipping downwards inside the waistband of her pantalets.

A ripple of honeyed joy spread within, and she was dizzily aware that in a few more seconds there'd be no way she could stop him—or herself. The future she was so afraid of would suddenly be upon them, and there had to be a reckoning, a decision as to what to do about their feelings for each other. Anjele knew beyond all doubt that once he took her, wholly and completely, she'd never be able to marry Raymond or any other man. She would always belong to Gator.

It was only with every fiber of inner strength she possessed that she was able to finally twist away and cry, "No, I can't. Please, let me go."

With a muttered oath, Brett abruptly released her. Leaping to his feet, he tore from beneath the willow to plunge into the sweet river air and drink deeply, filling his lungs in an attempt to cool his heated blood.

Anjele lay where she was a moment, biting back tears born of her own hunger. Finally, she got up and went to stand behind him. Wrapping her arms about his waist, she leaned her head against his strong back and whispered, "You know I want to, Gator, but—"

He patted her hands, unwound himself from her embrace and turned to drink in the beloved sight of her in the dazzling moonlight. "I know you do, Angel, but you've got to be ready with your mind, as well as your body.

"There's something you've got to know, *ma chère,*" he said impulsively. "I'm in love with you. I didn't mean for it to happen. I kept telling myself it couldn't, because we come from two different worlds, and soon you'll be leaving the part of yours that touches mine. But I couldn't help it. You don't know the times I've fought to keep from coming to you but couldn't stay away. And now it's happened, and I've got to deal with the pain."

She startled him by blurting out, "It doesn't have to hurt, Gator. It doesn't have to. We can find a way to be together. I know we can. And now that I know you love me, I'm not afraid anymore."

His eyes searched hers in desperation, for assurance she wasn't lying, and what he saw mirrored there was the adoration reflected in his own.

With a soft groan deep in his throat, he pulled her against him.

But the sound of voices made them spring apart.

Brett pressed a gentle hand to her lips as indication to be silent, then drew her away from the willow and on toward the shadows of the woods. From there, they could see a couple walking along the riverbank.

"It's Claudia." Anjele whispered in surprise. "And that's our guest, Stephen Pardee."

They didn't speak for several moments, watching as Claudia and Stephen walked out to the pier jutting into the river and sat down on the wooden bench there.

Finally, reluctantly, Anjele said she'd have to go. "There's no telling how long they're going to sit there, and if I leave now, I can blend back into the party and not get caught out here."

He understood. He didn't want her to go, but he knew it was dangerous for her to tarry. "Tomorrow night," he vowed, bruising her with a last kiss of parting. "I'll show you how much I love you, Angel, and then nothing will keep us apart."

Believing with all her heart they'd truly find a way to walk together into the future, Anjele ran into the night.

Stephen was terribly uncomfortable. When Claudia had asked him, right in front of her parents and his mother, to take her for a walk down by the river, there had been no way he could politely decline. She hadn't mentioned her earlier behavior, and rattled on about nonsensical things. But he was getting edgy. He didn't like being out here alone with her. Couples didn't pair off this way in the night without chaperones unless they were engaged, and something was starting to needle. He found himself wondering if this was the way a black widow's mate felt as he crawled into her web.

She was chattering about what a shame it was his family had ever moved from Louisiana, because she was sure he'd like living here, rather than in Atlanta. "I just don't like big cities," she lied. "Not even New Orleans. Oh, I love to go to the opera and concerts and go shopping, of course, but give me the peace and quiet of the country and the river anytime, don't you agree, Stephen, dear?"

He swallowed hard, gave his collar a tug, as it suddenly seemed to be choking. "Yeah, sure, but right now we need to be getting back. It's late."

He started to rise, but she reached out and caught his arm and held him firm. Her tone became suddenly desperate. "I asked you to go for a walk with me so we could talk, Stephen, and we haven't talked . . ."

"All you've done is talk," he said, hating to be rude, but he was really getting nervous.

"But not about important things. Like us."

He swallowed again, this time feeling a knot in his throat. "What . . . what do you mean?" he managed to croak.

Giggling, she snuggled closer. "Everybody's talking about us, Stephen. Don't pretend you haven't noticed."

"No . . . I haven't." He wriggled on the bench, managed to scoot a few inches away from her, but she continued to hold onto his arm.

"Of course you have." Another giggle. "Everybody is wondering when we're going to announce our engagement, and I was thinking we could go ahead and tell my parents and your mother tomorrow, so we can get started planning the party. You-all are leaving in a week. That's hardly enough time, but we can do it, and—"

"No!" Yanking from her grasp, he leaped to his feet to cry furiously, "No, Claudia. We're not getting married. Whatever gave you such a crazy idea?"

"Crazy idea?" She felt as though she'd been dashed in the face with a pail ful of cold water. Slowly she got to her feet. "Why, Stephen Pardee, you know you and your momma came to Louisiana to find you a bride, and you should be grateful I'm willing to marry you, because it's obvious no belles in Georgia will have you."

It wasn't really that bad, he reflected miserably. The girls his mother had sent him to court were all rich and wanted no part of someone from a mediocre background like his. He wouldn't let himself think his homeliness had anything to do with how he'd been rejected, for he'd tried to make up for his unattractiveness by cultivating a pleasant, cheerful personality. But he wasn't about to defend himself against Claudia's cruelty, and snapped, "Well, that's none of your concern, and even if I had thought about courting you, I would've surely changed my mind when I got here to find out you're the same haughty, sharp-tongued little girl I remember.

"Now I'm going back to the house," he told her firmly, turning on his heel, "and because I'm a gentleman, I'm going to forget we had this conversation."

"Goddamn you!" she bit out savagely, eyes glittering with rage.

He turned slowly, dazed by her venom.

"It's because of Anjele, isn't it? You're too blind to realize what you can have by marrying me, because she's got you bewitched. You've sneaked in her room at night, haven't you? And I'll bet the two of you rutted till dawn like animals. That's why you're in a hurry now, to get to her and do it, you filthy bastard!"

"Claudia, that's enough!" He was horrified, for he found himself looking at a stranger, a maniacal stranger to be suddenly feared. He began backing away from her, off the pier, stepping to the river bank. "You're crazy. To say such things about your sister, about me, you've got to be crazy. Mother and I are leaving this house first thing tomorrow. I won't stay here around you and your filthy mind."

She watched him run away, darkness quickly devouring him.

"So be it," she called hoarsely after him. "I don't want to marry an ugly toad like you, anyway."

Maybe I failed, she fumed, doggedly heading towards the house, but Anjele will be the one to suffer.

CHAPTER

ANJELE HAD MADE UP HER MIND. GATOR had sworn he loved her, and she had no doubts as to her own feelings. Somehow they were going to find a way to be together the rest of their lives. To marry Raymond now was unthinkable. Never had she dreamed she could feel about any man the way she felt about her beloved Cajun. And after tonight, that love would be avowed for all times, and nothing could stand in their way. Sooner or later her parents would have to accept it, but until, and unless, that day came, she would live with him in the bayou. Together, they would face the future.

It was early, a Sunday morning, and everyone seemed to be still sleeping, for she'd not heard a sound from anywhere in the house. She'd been up since first light, quietly stepping onto the veranda to sit in a cushioned wicker chair and dreamily gaze towards Bayou Perot. He was there, she knew, for no one worked the fields at BelleClaire on the Sabbath. But on this day, she wished they did, for she longed to walk by in hopes of catching a glimpse of him. It seemed forever till night and the hour when, at last, she'd be in his arms.

Anjele jumped, startled, at the sound of voices coming from around the corner of the house. Getting up to look around to where the porch ran all the way down the side, she saw Miss Delilah and Stephen.

Not wanting to eavesdrop, Anjele began backing towards her room but couldn't resist hesitating as she heard Claudia's name mentioned.

"Mother, I can't help it. I just can't stand it any longer," Stephen was saying, exasperated. "She's all over me. Everywhere I go. I can't get away from her. Last night was the final straw. She had me in a very compromising situation out there. What if she tells her father I was trying to seduce her, for heavens sake? He'll march me to the altar with a gun in my back, and frankly, I'd rather die than marry Claudia Sinclair."

Delilah told him to keep his voice down before chiding, "I really think you're overreacting, dear. Perhaps Claudia genuinely loves you, the poor little thing. Just make sure you don't do anything to encourage her."

"I told you. I want to leave. Today."

"That's out of the question. What would Twyla and Elton think? They have something planned for every night next week. If we announce we're leaving, they'll know something is wrong. It'd be terribly embarrassing.

"No," she said firmly, finally, "we're not leaving till we'd planned to—next Friday."

At that, Stephen said, "Well, I won't stay here, and you can't make me, and I don't care what anybody thinks. I'm going into New Orleans to a hotel. I'll wait for you there."

"Oh, dear," Delilah wailed, "we can't have that. Give me time to think. You woke me up with this, and I'm still groggy. I'll think of something, I promise, but don't you go and do something foolish, you hear?"

Her voice faded, and Anjele peered through the spiky leaves of a potted palm to see them disappear through the French doors leading to Delilah's room. What on earth, she wondered, had happened on the pier? Surely he wasn't all that upset over the scene in the oak grove.

She turned to go back into her room, and that's when she saw Claudia watching her from the other end of the veranda and wondered how long she'd been standing there.

Claudia stuck out her tongue and went back inside.

By the time Anjele bathed and dressed and went downstairs, she found her parents in the morning room with Delilah, and the atmosphere was one of excitement.

"Anjele, come in, dear," Twyla called gaily, "Delilah has a wonderful idea. We're going to live on a riverboat for a week. Won't that be delightful?"

Anjele blinked, shook her head, sure she'd heard wrong. Then, remembering Stephen's outburst and Delilah's subsequent promise to rectify the situation, she quickly said, "I don't see how. Don't you have parties and things planned every night this week, since they're leaving Friday?"

She directed the last to Delilah, who promptly, cheerily, countered, "I've thought of that. We've been over the schedule, and everything is small and intimate, so we're going to send word to everyone to meet us at the boat. Your father has already sent a messenger to New Orleans to take care of everything."

Turning to Stephen for reassurance that he approved, she continued, "We just thought it'd be nice to sail around and enjoy the river breezes. It's so terribly hot. Don't you agree, Stephen?"

He was standing at the window but turned to agree dully, "Yes, Mother. I'm looking forward to it."

And Anjele knew why. It was a compromise. His mother would be spared having to come up with a plausible reason for cutting their visit short, and on a riverboat, there'd be little chance for Claudia to get Stephen off to herself. But where did all of this leave her, she wondered frantically and ventured to suggest, "It's a lovely idea, but if nobody minds, I'd rather stay here. I don't care much for being on the river, and—"

"Of course somebody minds!" Stephen practically shouted, desperation ringing in his voice, "We all mind, for goodness' sake. Why, what a boring week it'd be without you, Anjele."

"He's right," Twyla chimed in. "We wouldn't think of leaving either you or Claudia behind."

At that, Stephen frowned and turned back to his unseeing vigil at the window.

Engrossed in the newspaper he was reading, Elton was unconcerned with what was going on around him. Mr. Lincoln and Mr. Douglas were going to engage in a series of seven debates, and Elton was interested in anything to do with Mr. Lincoln. Mr. Lincoln's strong stand against slavery was getting people stirred, while Mr. Douglas was defending not slavery, per se, but the right of Americans to vote their preference. And Elton sure as hell went along with that.

Twyla took note of her husband's preoccupation and gently scolded, "Please, dear. Can't your paper wait?

We have guests, you know."

Managing a contrite smile as he laid the newspaper aside, he thought how glad he would be when they left. Delilah's incessant chattering and the way she stuffed herself was getting on his nerves. Twyla had confided she thought Claudia was hearing wedding bells with Stephen, but Elton hoped she was wrong. God help him if Delilah made her visits a habit. Even if this season's hogsheads set a record, he'd wind up in the poorhouse trying to keep that woman fed.

Claudia breezed into the room, looked around and sensed something was going on. "What have I missed?" She cooed, at once going to stand possessively beside Stephen. "Has something happened?"

Twyla told her of the change in plans.

Claudia forced a smile. Inside, she was bristling. "How nice," she looked at Anjele. "And whose idea was this?"

Don't look at me, Anjele felt like screaming but didn't say a word. The last thing she wanted to do was move onto a riverboat for a week. And how was she going to get word to Gator? She didn't dare try to go into the bayou by herself, not on a Sunday. The slaves walked about the plantation freely. Some of them even took their food and had a little picnic on the riverbank. Her father was very lenient and tolerant of their Sunday activities.

Twyla said they needed to be getting ready in order to leave for New Orleans right after lunch. Anjele felt like crying and went out on the terrace to try to figure out a way to get a message to Gator.

Stephen was right behind her. "I hope you're going to help me out on the boat." He told her what had happened, finally throwing up his hands in defeat to explain, "So you see? I had no choice. I can't risk her getting me into a compromising situation this week. There won't be an opportunity on the boat, if you'll spend every minute outside my cabin with me."

Anjele agreed. After all, she reasoned dismally, no need for him to be miserable, too. And Gator would understand when she explained.

The week passed with agonizing slowness.

Once Claudia realized what Stephen was up to, and how Anjele was conspiring to keep her from being able to get him off by himself, she retired furiously to her cabin and stayed there. Twyla fretted she might be sick, then decided she was pouting about something and left her alone.

Finally, it was over. Stephen and his mother said their good-byes, gushing with gratitude over a splendid visit. Anjele was shaking with anticipation to be on the way back to BelleClair.

Claudia noticed Anjele's nervousness, and, as they rode home in the carriage, started thinking about her behavior lately. Despite her jealousy, Claudia knew Anjele really had no romantic interest in Stephen and was merely being obnoxious. She thought about last Sunday morning, how she'd seen Anjele on the veranda, all moony eyes and staring out into space. But why? She wasn't missing Raymond. For that matter, she hadn't said a word about him all the while they were on the riverboat. She hadn't even mentioned that he was due home the first part of the week. It was as if he didn't even exist, yet something surely had Anjele stirred up.

Something . . . or someone.

Claudia thought about the last night at home, when she'd spied Anjele sneaking out the back way. At first, she had thought Anjele and Stephen were planning to meet outside, but as she had hovered at his side, Claudia hadn't noticed any anxiety on his part to indicate he was supposed to be anywhere else. So, if Anjele's bizarre behavior wasn't caused by Stephen, or Raymond—then who?

As she watched Anjele practically wriggling in her seat with anticipation to get home, Claudia made a silent vow to find out what was going on.

Lightning stabbed the night with iridescent forks, and thunder crashed and rolled in the heavens.

As Anjele stared from the open French doors, she knew it could start pouring any time. The last few days had been swelteringly hot. Everyone had been saying it was time for a real Louisiana frog strangler. The thought of going to the willow with a storm about to explode was disconcerting, but she'd been waiting a week for this time. If he wasn't there, she'd be disappointed but not surprised. After all, he'd had no way of knowing why she hadn't shown up for a week and might be angry. But if he wasn't there, she vowed with jaw firmly set, fists clenched at her sides, she'd go to the fields tomorrow and find him and explain what happened.

Her father had been too busy to join them on the riverboat, so he and her mother had retired to their suite right after dinner to catch up on news between them. Claudia had said she was tired and likewise called it a day. An hour had passed, and Anjele could wait no longer.

The wind was screaming as she stepped onto the veranda, carefully closing the doors behind her lest it rain in. Her hair was blowing about her face as wildly as the fronds of the potted palms along the porch.

The sky was split by a fiery streak of white, and she stared at the trellis. It was a precarious climb in such weather but her only chance without the risk of being seen sneaking out. Thoughts of Gator and how she loved him inspired the courage to climb down.

Lifting her skirts above her ankles, she ran as fast as her legs would carry her. Leaves torn from wildly tossing branches slapped against her face, but she kept on going. Bursting to the top of the riverbank just as lightning once more set the sky ablaze, she could see the willows in a macabre dance of protest against the assault of nature gone mad.

He wasn't there.

She told herself it was crazy to think he would be in such horrible weather. Even the river was rolling with waves crashing against the banks. It was a dangerous time, and there was nothing for her to do but turn back.

And then she heard it.

The sound of her name above the roar of the wind. With pounding heart, she turned to see him coming towards her.

She ran to meet him, and he gathered her in his arms and swung her round and round, showering her face with kisses.

"God, I can't believe you're really here," he cried. "I've been here every night, waiting, hoping, and I told myself there's no way you'd come tonight, but I dared to hope . . . ."

She started telling him what had happened, and before she finished, he was laughing and kissing her and telling her how he'd thought she'd been too scared to come back.

"Oh, no," she whispered, reaching to cup his dear face in her hands as she drank in the blessed sight of him. "I've thought of nothing but this time. Day and night."

He lifted her in his arms. "We can't stay here."

Once more the sky lit up and the outline of the sugarhouse could be seen. Holding her tightly, he ran for it.

Inside, the air was pungent with the sweet smells of last season's grinding. In the intermittent flashes of the storm, Brett found a stack of mats and laid her down. Stretching out beside her, he murmured, "God, I love you, Anjele. I kept telling myself you weren't lying to me, that you really do feel the same for me."

"I do." She slipped a hand to the back of his neck to urge him yet closer. "Believe me, I do."

Suddenly, almost roughly, his hold upon her tightened as he warned, "Never lie to me, Anjele, because if this is all just a game to you, if you're only using me for a lark, say so now, before it's too late."

"You've nothing to fear, my darling." He relaxed his hold and she snuggled closer to tease, "And you *are* a lark—but a lifetime lark. I want to be with you forever."

"We'll find a way," he vowed, mouth claiming hers. "Right now, *ma jolie*, I want you."

And tempest-tossed like the river beyond, so, also, was their passion rampant and beyond control.

Anjele lips parted to welcome the thrusting invasion of his tongue. His hands tore at her gown, and she helped him, lest it tear, rendering herself naked to him.

His hands moved possessively over her, trailing down her back, her sides, finally claiming her breasts as he tore his lips from hers to lower and devour each nipple in turn.

Her own exploring fingers moved to cup his buttocks and pull him closer, moaning in her throat as she felt the thrusting hardness of his manhood crushing against her. Deftly, he released himself, and the pulsating was instantly against her bare flesh. Blood turned to fire as he guided himself to touch the core of her feminine being, teasing, tormenting as flames licked into her belly.

She was gasping, sobbing, wanting him to take her, possess her, never let her go. Nothing else mattered or ever would. At that very moment, she knew she could go away with him and never return, for thoughts of being without him seemed akin to the breath of life denied.

He rolled to his back, taking her with him. "I don't want to hurt you."

She straddled him, dizzily stunned by how inhibitions were tossed like the frenzied winds beyond in the wake of furious intent to consummate their love.

He grasped her waist to guide her slowly onto him, urging her to set the pace.

She bit back a gasp of pain, for it did hurt. All Simona's descriptions of lovemaking had not prepared her for this part. There was one sharp stab of agony, and she did cry out, and he pulled her down against his massive chest and rained kisses, whispering, "It's all right. It won't hurt anymore."

Gently, he thrust his hips upwards, filling her, but she wanted him above her, in total possession. They moved to the side, and instinctively she pressed her thighs against her chest in ecstatic surrender to his assault.

In a sudden flash of light, she could see his face, and in that frozen moment sought her own reassurance and commanded, "Tell me you do love me, Gator. Tell me you want me as much as I want you, forever and always."

"Always," he obliged tersely, for he was struggling to hold back his own cresting pleasure in deference to her own.

He did not have long to wait.

The feeling spread like hot lava. Anjele cried out, but only with the shock of pleasure never dreamed of. And as the throes of joy rolled over her entire body, Brett took himself to the pinnacle of his own release.

He did not let her go. For long moments, they clung together in silence, each too mesmerized by the wonder of it all to speak.

But slowly, Anjele was sinking back to reality, and where liquid fire had replaced blood flowing through her body, now it was as though ice water had quenched those flames. Dear God, what had she done? If he really didn't love her, if she, in fact were only a lark to him, she couldn't bear it.

He felt her tension and dared to ask, "Having regrets, Anjele?" He moved to lie beside her, his fingertips gently moving up and down her arm in a gentle caress.

She bit her lip and nodded, though he couldn't see the gesture in the darkness. In the wake of passion spent, the obstacles between their two worlds became as starkly clear as the momentary stabs of clarifying lightning.

"What is it?" He probed, alarmed. Maybe he was wrong, and she was merely having a good time this summer before settling down to be another man's wife. Try as he might, Brett still couldn't shake the cobwebs of his past and how he'd so foolishly dared believe another rich planter's daughter.

In a small, timorous voice, Anjele offered, "Can we make it happen? Can we tear down the barriers of the invisible walls that separate us and make our world one?"

"Only if we want to." He raised himself up on his elbow, wished he could see her eyes and find love and determination mirrored. "It won't be easy, sneaking around like this. There'll be hell to pay if we get caught."

She felt a wave of panic as a roll of distant thunder echoed the sickness of her heart. What if they did? Would he stand up to her father and demand to marry her, or would he run farther back into the bayou and forget she'd ever existed? She'd gambled everything on this night of passion, and now, in the sobering afterglow, she was terrified to think of the possible consequences.

Suddenly she knew she had to get away and think things out. She leaped to her feet and began fumbling in the darkness for her clothes.

Brett made no move to stop her. If she *was* having doubts, she had to work them out herself. He had been about to explain why he was staying around these parts, how he planned to leave as soon as grinding season was over. As for the future, he wouldn't try to talk her into leaving but intended to let her know he'd take her with him if she wanted to go. But it had to be her decision.

Anjele groped her way to the door. He was not following her. Uneasily, she spoke into the brooding darkness. "I'd best be going. It hasn't started raining yet, and I can make it back without getting wet."

He got up then and came to stand behind her, wrapping muscular arms about her and pulling her back against him. With her head tucked under his chin, he said softly, "I'll be at the willow tomorrow night."

She turned and raised her lips for his kiss, then forced herself to pull away and run into the night.

Dimly, she was aware of the first raindrops, cool against her feverish skin. What was he keeping from her? What deep, dark secret made him reluctant to tell her his real name? Was there a wife somewhere? Or a lover no one knew about? And what a fool she felt like to recall how she'd thought they'd be making plans to run away together, instead of merely discussing sneaking around in hope of not getting caught. If he really loved her, wouldn't he have been as anxious as she to make immediate plans for the future?

So many questions nagged, and of only one thing was Anjele sure—tomorrow night, and every night, she would find a way to be with him. And, somewhere along the way, everything would be resolved.

She knew she was young and naive in many ways, yet dared believe when she loved him with every beat of her heart, he just had to love her back.

Brett wondered if he'd made a mistake. A fatal mistake. Maybe he should have kept his feelings under control awhile longer. Anjele was a baby when it came to the ways of love, and he couldn't be sure what she expected from him. And as he watched her run away, he felt a cold chill of foreboding.

She was spooked.

No doubt about it, he'd scared her.

He only hoped once she calmed down, thought about it, everything would be all right. It wouldn't do for her parents to notice anything wrong.

He walked out into the rain, now coming down in stinging torrents.

For sure, he silently vowed, tomorrow night he'd tell her everything, and while he'd try not to influence her final decision, he'd ask if she loved him enough to go away with him once his debt was paid.

Claudia was drenched, but not from the rain, for long before it had begun to fall, she'd broken out in a cold sweat. Watching them in the throes of animal passion, illuminated by the interspersing slashes of light, she'd felt awash with her own burning fever.

She had slipped in, unnoticed, through the back doors to stand not over twenty feet away. She recognized the man. A Cajun. And quite handsome. One day when she'd been out riding, she'd seen him and dared stop to chat. There had been times in the past she'd had dalliances with a few of the white workers and had been in the mood to take on another. But he'd been cold as ice, and she'd felt humiliated by his rejection. Now, to see him pumping away at Anjele made her quiver with anger. She hadn't been good enough for him, and once more Anjele had stolen a man from her.

It was only when they'd both left the sugarhouse that she began to laugh, and the laughter continued till her sides were hurting.

What a fool Anjele was, for she'd played right into her hands. Once Raymond found out she'd been coupling with a field hand, like a bitch in heat, he'd never marry her. Claudia would have him eating out of her hand.

But first things first, she decided as she ducked her head and ran out into the blinding storm.

First, she'd tell Twyla, and then everything else would fall into place.

CHAPTER 9

Twyla stared at Claudia in horror and disbelief.

Well, she knew Claudia exaggerated at times when it came to telling on Anjele. It was something she'd dealt with since they were children. But this tale could not be an embellishment—it had to be an out-and-out lie, and Twyla dared say as much. Mustering patience, she began gently, "Dear, I know you're disappointed Stephen didn't ask you to marry him, but Anjele had nothing to do with it. He knew she was engaged before he got here, and I saw her do nothing to undermine your interest, and—"

Claudia stamped her foot in exasperation. They were in Twyla's room, and Twyla was propped up in bed on satin pillows having morning coffee. Claudia had hardly slept a wink all night in anticipation of telling her what she'd seen in the sugarhouse. "This hasn't got anything to do with Stephen," she said furiously. "I'm trying to tell you what I saw her doing in that sugarhouse, but you won't listen."

"I am listening," Twyla was starting to tremble. "I'm just praying there's a mistake, dear, that you didn't see what you thought you saw, or it was somebody besides Anjele, and—"

"Go and look in her room. I'm sure you'll find her wet clothes. It was pouring by the time she got back to the house. I know, because I was right behind her, and my clothes are still wet this morning. It was her, all right, and I know what I saw. Good heavens, Mother"—she threw her arms up in dramatic gesture, eyes widening in feigned disgust—"I've seen animals doing it, so I know what I saw her doing with that filthy Cajun field hand. Every time lightning flashed, I could see them clear as day. She was naked and had her legs wrapped around him, and he was on top of her grunting, and . . . "

She managed a convincing shudder of revulsion. "It was disgusting. I wanted to run away, but I was afraid they'd hear me and know I was there and saw it, and I don't want anyone ever to know I was witness to such filth. I lay awake all night gathering the nerve to come to you, because I thought you should know." Claudia was so proud of herself—she was even able to muster a few tears.

Twyla quickly set aside her tray, threw back the coverlet, and rushed to gather Claudia in her arms. "Oh, my poor dear," she whispered above the hysteria welling from deep within. "You should have come and told me when you saw her leaving. I know it must have been terrible for you." She held the girl as she cried, all the while frantically wondering what to do.

When Claudia seemed to calm down, Twyla drew her to sit beside her on the bed. Holding her hand, Twyla urged gently, "Now, tell me. Do you think this was the first time she's met this man?"

Claudia shook her head and said quickly, "Oh, no. I think she's been meeting him for some time now. Don't you remember before we went on the riverboat, how she'd excuse herself early every night and go to her room?"

Twyla nodded. She hadn't thought anything about it at the time, but now she began to wonder.

"And I saw her sneak out the last time we had a party, the night before we went on the boat." Claudia frowned to recall the ugly scene on the dock with Stephen but pushed it aside in favor of the present subject, which she was enjoying immensely. "I imagine she met him that night, too. I think she's probably been sneaking off with him for a long, long time. They surely acted like they knew each other real well," she added with a sneer.

"Would you know this man if you saw him again? We have so many Acadians working here."

Claudia seized the chance for revenge over Gator's so cooly spurning her and lied, "I'm afraid so, Mother. One day when I was riding near the fields, he . . ." She pretended she could not go on.

Twyla gasped. "He didn't try to touch you, did he?"

"No. But it was the way he looked at me, and he said something to one of the other men, something I couldn't hear, but it had to be nasty, because they were both laughing."

"You should have reported him."

"For what? Talking? Laughing? He would've said it had nothing to do with me. But anyway, I know who he is."

"You know his name?" Twyla turned to clutch her shoulders, gave her a gentle shake. "Tell me."

"I don't know his real name. The Cajuns call him Gator, because of some big fight he once had with an alligator. Somebody said his father is one of the overseers in the cotton fields. I think his name is Leo."

Twyla drew a sharp breath. She knew exactly who Leo was, for Elton had confided his fear that the man was being unnecessarily cruel to some of the slaves. She wasn't surprised he'd have an equally despicable son. "Now, listen to me," she said, still holding onto Claudia, forcing her to meet her steady, burning gaze. "You aren't to say a word to anyone about this, do you hear me?"

Claudia continued her pretense of being embarrassed. "You don't think I want this to spread, do you? I'm so ashamed. If this gets out, no man from a decent family would court me. And what about Raymond?" She pretended to think of him for the first time. "If he hears about this—"

"He won't," Twyla said quickly. "And no one else will, either. I'll take care of it. You just go on as though nothing has happened. And listen to me, Claudia." Her eyes narrowed in warning. "I don't care how angry you get with your sister, you are not to let her know you saw her. Understand? Now, promise me."

Claudia didn't hesitate at another lie. "Believe me, Mother, that's what I want to do more than anything else in this world." She closed her eyes as though to shut out the dreadful image. "Of course I promise. But what do you intend to do?"

Twyla got up and steered her gently to the door. "You let me worry about it, and you go on as though nothing has happened."

When she was alone, Twyla began to pace up and down her room. Why? Why in the name of God had Anjele done such a thing? What had led her to such sin and degradation—and mere months before she was to be a bride?

Think, she commanded her burning brain. Think of what must be done to avoid scandal. Worst of all, what if Anjele fancied herself in love with the Acadian and was planning on running away with him? It had to be stopped, quickly and discreetly.

As always, Elton had left early that morning to make his rounds but was expected for lunch. Instructing Kesia to send him straight to her, Twyla remained in her quarters, not wanting to encounter Anjele lest she lose her temper and ruin her plan. Oh, she was furious! The child had always been willful and stubborn, but Elton had defended her, claiming she was merely independent and spirited.

To move up the wedding date was out of the question, because Twyla now had to face the reality that it was not the time for Anjele to marry anyone. She needed rigid training in obedience to tame that wild, reckless spirit. Otherwise she might be an unfaithful wife, and if gossips found it out, the good name of Sinclair would be ruined.

With a ragged sigh, Twyla acknowledged the only reasonable solution was to send Anjele to a strict girls' boarding school, all the way to England. It wasn't unusual for upper-class families to send their children abroad to study, she reasoned, and though a few eyebrows would be raised over postponement of the wedding, Twyla would merely state a desire for Anjele to be properly educated in order to make the best possible wife for Raymond. She was only sixteen after all.

But first things first, Twyla brooded as she heard the sounds of Elton's footsteps coming down the hall.

Elton listened, face stricken and paling with each word she spoke. When she'd finished, he collapsed in a chair and whispered hoarsely, "I don't believe it. Claudia is lying."

"I thought she might be exaggerating," Twyla admitted, "but I now believe every word was gospel. She was devastated, poor dear. Seeing her sister . . ." She gave her head a violent shake, refusing to envision such a loathsome sight.

Elton's hurt and horror was rapidly being replaced by a white-hot anger that made him start to tremble all over. His hands gripped the chair so tightly his knuckles whitened, and his teeth clamped together till his jaw began to ache.

Twyla told him of her plan, explaining, "I haven't seen her this morning. She doesn't know she's been found out. I was waiting till I talked to you.

"We have to be careful," she went on, starting to pace about the room again. "First of all, if she does indeed fancy herself in love with this man, and he also cares for her, we can't have the two of them pining for each other, or they'll try to find a way to get together.

"No," she vehemently struck at the air with her fist, "They must despise each other."

Elton slowly nodded, livid. To think of that man, whoever he was, ravishing his beloved daughter . . . He clenched his fists. Dear God, he could so easily kill him with his bare hands. "You know who he was?" he asked.

"Claudia said his father is one of the overseers. The

father's name is Leo."

"Leo!" He made a hissing sound. "I'd about made up my mind to get rid of him, and this does it. I'm going to run him off, and—"

He was getting to his feet, about to burst from the room, but Twyla rushed to push him back down in the chair and kneel before him. Taking his hands in hers and squeezing, she reminded him of her plan. "We can't do something rash out of anger, Elton. Now, listen to me. We're going to make this man think Anjele came to us in hysterics last night, saying he'd raped her."

His gaze snapped to her face, and Twyla recoiled from the scorching fury in his eyes. "Was it?" he challenged, "because I'll kill the bastard, so help me . . . ."

"No, no, it wasn't rape, but frankly, I wish it had been. It'd be less painful if she hadn't done it out of her own free will, but Claudia said she wasn't forced. But you've got to tell Leo that Anjele claimed she was, so his son will hate her for lying. Don't you understand what I'm trying to do?"

He nodded miserably.

"And I'll arrange for Anjele to think she was merely another of his conquests. I'll make up something for her to hear from"—she hesitated, thinking, then snapped her fingers—"those Acadian girls. Simona and Emalee. I'll persuade them to say something about him she'll believe."

"Go to Simona," he advised. "She's in a family way. I've promised her husband a bonus at the end of the season so they can move to a larger place. Tell her if she doesn't cooperate, not only will they not get the money, but I'll run them both out of the bayou. Leave

Emalee to her. She'll see she goes along with it.

"And I'll rip that goddamned trellis down with my bare hands," he finished with a roar, leaping to his feet so suddenly Twyla fell backwards.

Righting herself, she was up and after him to block his exit. "You can't do that. We can't let Anjele know we know till after you get rid of that man. Don't you see? She has to slip out to meet him and be hurt not to find him waiting. We let her go a few nights and then let her know we've discovered she's sneaking out. We'll pretend not to know anything else. By that time, she'll be so brokenhearted and devastated over what she's learned from those girls, we'll have no difficulty in spiriting her away to Europe. And when she does return, she'll have grown into a young lady who can appreciate a fine husband like Raymond."

Later, Elton knew he'd no doubt regret agreeing to send his beloved daughter away but realized there was nothing else to do. "Very well. I'll take care of getting rid of that bastard, and you take care of making Anjele believe it wasn't all a scheme to separate them."

Leo Cody had run all the way to the office when he got the message Master Sinclair wanted to see him at once. Maybe, he'd dared hope as he hurried along in the stifling afternoon heat, he was going to be taken out of the cotton fields, at last, and promoted to the easier job of overseeing the cane harvest.

But the second he walked in, he knew the purpose for summoning him was anything but good news.

Elton was waiting in his private office and had dismissed the other workers so they would be alone.

Harshly, coldly, he demanded verification. "You have a son, don't you? A cane worker?"

Leo was bewildered. He seldom saw Brett, or Gator, as he was now called. They'd never been close, anyway, and since he'd come back from sea to find his mother dead, he seemed to blame him, and the gap between them had grown wider. Yet he'd always been a good worker, and Leo couldn't figure out what was going on but knew that whatever it was, Master Sinclair was mighty riled. "Yes sir," he finally admitted, absently drifting back into the Cajun dialect he'd tried to forget, "I got a son. He never give no one no trouble, so why you upset?"

Elton brought his fists down on the desk so hard it bounced. The cords stood out on his neck, and his eyes threatened to bulge from their sockets. "My daughter said he raped her. Last night. At the sugarhouse. She came home with her clothes in shreds, bruised all over. She says your son did it."

Instinctively, Leo began backing away, twisting his hat in his shaking hands as he swung his head from side to side in panic and denial. "No sir. No sir. Not my boy. He be a good boy. He never do nothin' like that. Not my boy."

"He did!" Elton slammed the desk again and came around it to tower above Leo. "I'll kill him if I see him, Leo. You make sure I don't. The only reason the son of a bitch isn't already hanging from one of those oaks out there is that I want to keep this quiet to protect what's left of my daughter's virtue. I want you to know I thought about hanging you, too, for siring such a rogue."

Leo shrank farther away, but Elton was right on him.

"Yes, Leo, I might kill you, too, and none of the slaves would say a word about it. I've heard stories about your mistreatment of them, and I'm surprised you haven't wound up as gator bait in the swamps before now, despised as you are. Never let me see your face on my land again."

He suddenly grabbed Leo by his shirt and sent him across the room to bounce off the wall and sprawl to the floor. "And you tell your mangy son if he's not out of Bayou Perot by dawn, he's a dead man."

Leo crossed his arms across his face and withered to tears of pleading. "Yes . . . yes sir, I tell him, all right, but you got no cause to be mad at me—"

Elton grabbed him and gave him a shove that sent him stumbling towards the door. He was right behind him to give him a swift kick that tossed him outside and into the dirt. Whipping out the pistol he always carried, he promised grimly, "If I see you again, or if I hear you've breathed one word of this to anybody else, you're dead, Leo."

Leo crawled, scrambled, stumbled to his feet and broke into a run as fast as his shaking legs would carry him. It was only when he reached the sanctuary of the swamps that he dared slow down. His breathing was ragged, his chest pounding in agony, but no longer from fear. Fear had been replaced by cold rage. Elton Sinclair had no right to take it out on him, by God. He couldn't help what Gator had done.

Damnit, Leo knew he had worked hard to get where he was. And so what if he'd had to drag a few slaves into the bushes and teach them a lesson? At least he hadn't used the cat-o'-nine-tails across their backs, like they deserved, but only because that would leave a scar. Instead, he'd beaten them with his fists, and who could see a bruise on their black skin, anyhow?

No sir. Sinclair had no right to treat him like he did and run him off.

And oh, Lord, he fumed, was he mad at Gator. The job at BelleClair was the best thing that had ever happened to him, and by God, Gator was going to pay for making him lose it.

He kept on going till he reached the shack he shared with a fat woman named Adele. She wasn't much to look at but a fine cook and never refused him in bed. Made a good wine, too, he remembered, taking a jug from the shelf and throwing the cork away as he hooked his thumb around the neck and hoisted it up to his shoulder.

Leo fed his anger with drink, and as soon as he'd dulled a bit of the pain, he was looking forward to retribution. First, he'd take care of Gator, and then he'd get his stuff and get out of the bayou. No need hanging around asking for trouble. But Elton Sinclair, he vowed, would rue the day he'd treated him worse than he'd treat a slave. He'd pay, all right. Someday and somehow, the uppity son of a bitch would pay.

He took his jug and headed for Gator's pirogue to wait for quitting time in the cane fields. He supposed he should have gone straight to get him, but frankly didn't give a damn if Sinclair had seen him and made good his threat. It would save him the trouble of beating Gator to a pulp. But he'd been too scared, himself, and the wine was starting to work its magic.

He could wait.

The clanging of the bell echoed throughout the steaming plantation. Weary, soaked in sweat, the slaves and

Cajun workers gratefully made their way toward home.

For Brett, the day had seemed interminably long. He'd found himself wishing for a fine pocket watch, like rich folks carried, so he could see how many hours were left before he'd see Anjele. Instead, he'd had to content himself with watching the blazing sun, calculating the time, reminding himself it really didn't matter. Quitting time wouldn't be till shadows made it almost impossible to see his hand in front of his face.

By the time he got to his pirogue, it was so dark he had to light a fire to see his way to get around. Stripping off his filthy clothes, he climbed into the barrel where he caught rainwater for bathing. A quick washing, clean clothes, and he would be on his way.

His stomach rumbled with hunger, but he wasn't about to take time to fix something to eat. All he had on his mind was holding Anjele in his arms and telling her all there was to know, so there'd be no ghosts. It was the only way he knew to make her believe he loved her. He'd bare his soul and give her his heart.

Frankly, it worried him how she had rushed out into the night. But, after all, it had been her first time with a man, and no doubt she was nervous, frightened. Tonight, however, he intended to make her see she had no reason to be afraid of him, or the future.

He stepped out of the barrel and was reaching for a towel when suddenly the air was split by the crack of leather.

The whip wrapped around his torso in a blinding flash of pain, and he fell to his knees. Before he could react, the whip was jerked back, raking flesh, then popped again—once, twice, crisscrossing his back, the cuts deep and bloody.

It was only on the fourth blow Brett was able to fight his way from the cocoon of agony. He caught the end of the leather thong with his hands, felt flesh painfully splitting but held on and gave a mighty yank. His attacker cried out and tumbled forward into the firelight.

"Poppa, you!" Brett towered over him. "What the hell is going on?"

Leo got to his feet before roaring, "You goddamn fool, have you lost your mind? Raping Sinclair's daughter? I ought to kill you and save him the trouble."

Brett reeled before the astonishing charges. For the moment, pain was forgotten as he grabbed his father and slammed him against the nearest tree. "Talk, damn it! You tell me what this is all about, and do it fast."

Leo repeated everything Sinclair had said, then warned, "You'd best get out of the bayou, or I might get so drunk one night I *will* kill you. You cost me the best job I ever had, all because you couldn't keep that thing in your pants." Catching Brett off guard, Leo brought his knee up to smash into his son's crotch.

Brett staggered backwards, and Leo grabbed the whip and started to strike again. Brett rolled away just in time as leather slapped the ground inches from his face. He kicked out, and the old man fell.

Despite the agony ripping through his loins, Brett managed to stand, and in a rasping voice alien even to his own ears, warned, "I don't want to kill you, but if you hit me again, I will." Turning his back, he staggered to where he'd left his clean trousers.

"You better get the hell out," Leo shrieked from where he lay, knowing he was too drunk to defend himself. "I'm tellin' you, you're a dead man."

Brett snatched up a few belongings. His shotgun. Clothes. A side of bacon. A bag of chicory. He stuffed them all into a knapsack. It was pitch-dark, and he was exhausted from working all day and felt as if he were going to throw up from the pain between his legs. But he knew he had to leave—and fast.

He wasn't worried about his father trying to beat him again.

Neither was he worried about Elton Sinclair.

The fact was, he was leaving because he feared what he might do if he laid eyes on Anjele. It was all becoming clear now. When the passion died down, she'd been scared of what she'd done. Probably she had been caught sneaking back into the house. Everything blew up at once, and she had yelled rape to protect herself.

The bitch! He cursed, thinking how he hated her, but hated himself even more for being such a goddamned fool—again. He headed deeper into the bayou with no fear of the night.

His rage would light the way.

Anjele sat beneath the willow, knees hugged against her chest. At first, she had passed the time by thinking of all kinds of reasons Gator was late, but finally she had to face the painful reality that he wasn't coming. There was nothing to do but go home, crawl up the trellis, sneak in her room, and hope for a reasonable explanation later. She didn't dare go into the bayou in search of him, for that would not only be foolish—but also humiliating.

She got up and headed up the gently sloping riverbank, shoulders stooped with disappointment, chin quivering as she tried not to cry.

CHAPTER 10

EMALEE WAS HOLDING OUT A DIPPER OF cool water to one of the hoe gang when Simona jerked her sleeve and leaned to whisper, "Who's that woman on the white horse over yonder by that pecan tree?"

Simona shaded her eyes with her hand and strained to see in the glaring early morning sun. "Why, I believe that be Miss Twyla."

"Well, how come she out here? I never see her out much in the summer."

Simona shrugged. "I don't know, but we soon gon' find out, 'cause she waving at us to go there."

They were at the edge of a cane row and set their buckets and dippers down, should a thirsty worker seek water. It was a scorching day, and in the few hours they'd been in the fields, already they'd made four trips to the big water barrel for refills.

Twyla dismounted to stand in the shade. She returned neither their smiles nor polite greetings. Crisply she addressed Simona. "I understand you're in the family way."

Simona swallowed hard and nodded. She felt the first ripples of foreboding needling at her spine.

"My husband has been very pleased with your husband's work, Simona. I believe he promised him a bonus after grinding season."

Again, Simona nodded. She was really starting to worry, because Miss Twyla looked terribly mad about something, and she couldn't think of anything she'd done. She hadn't seen Anjele in weeks and didn't think Emalee had, either.

Twyla looked at Emalee. "I understand you have two brothers who work for BelleClair, along with your mother and father."

Emalee fearfully admitted that was so.

Twyla coolly glanced from one to the other as they watched and waited nervously. "I'm afraid I have bad news for you, Simona," she began with an imperious lift of her chin. "There won't be any bonus for your husband. As a matter of fact, you may tell him to stop by the overseer's office this afternoon and draw his final pay. And yours, as well. You two won't be working at BelleClair any longer.

"You, too, Emalee," she concluded. "And your family."

Emalee stuffed her fist in her mouth to hold back the bubbling sobs, but Simona, lips quivering, dared reach out and clutch Twyla's sleeve in pleading desperation. "But why? Why you do this to us? What we do to you? We know you never like us to be around Anjele, and we have not seen her in long time. Please, whatever we do, let us undo it . . . have a second chance."

Her reaction was exactly as Twyla had expected. Coldly, she removed Simona's hand. Pursing her lips, as though reconsidering her orders, she finally asked, "Maybe there is something you can do. Tell me. What do you know about one of your people called Gator?"

Now Simona was really confused but quickly replied, "Nothin'. Nobody know nothin' about Gator. He keep to hisself. Somebody say he not show up for work this mornin'. But what's he got to do with us, Miss Twyla? How come you doin' this to us?" Her hands went to her slightly rounded belly, as though to protect the now insecure future of the baby growing inside.

"You didn't know he and Anjele have been secretly seeing each other?"

"Oh, no ma'am!" Simona swung her head wildly from side to side, and Emalee chimed in to assure she didn't know anything, either.

Twyla was surprised but sensed they spoke the truth and decided it was time to get right to the point. "If the two of you cooperate with me, you may continue to work at BelleClair, and so can your families. If you refuse . . ." She let her voice trail off for effect.

"We do it," Simona cried, willing to do anything, for well she knew it would be impossible for Frank and her to find comparable pay working anywhere else in the Delta.

Emalee likewise assured cooperation.

So Twyla proceeded to tell them, in no uncertain terms, exactly what she wanted from them. "And you'd better be very convincing," she warned. "Anjele must not suspect anything."

Simona and Emalee exchanged nervous glances, then Emalee dared wonder aloud, "What about Gator? What if he tells her we lyin'? He gon' deny it all when he hears, for sure."

"For sure, he won't," Twyla flashed a gloating smile.

"He doesn't dare show his face either at BelleClair or Bayou Perot, ever again. You need not concern yourself with him, or his father, whom I understand has also found it to his best interest to leave.

"So," she finished, satisfied with their response, "do I have your word you will do as I've told you?"

"Yes," Simona said stiffly, "but I don' like doin' it. Anjele, she my friend. I don' like lyin' to a friend."

Timorously Emalee admitted, "I don' like it, neither."

For the first time, Twyla's haughtiness and anger melted as she said compassionately, "You girls must believe me. It's for her own good. No one else knows. No one must ever know." She had been holding her handkerchief in one hand and opened it to reveal a large roll of bills. She handed it to Simona, who was blinking with renewed bafflement. "Here. Take this as a token of my appreciation. But promise me one more thing."

Simona had never seen so much money in her life and instantly agreed, "Anything."

"If this Gator shows up, if you hear of him anywhere around, you must get word to me or Master Sinclair immediately. Understand? And you must not say anything to him about what you've done."

Simona knew that was the last thing she'd ever do, and a quick glance at Emalee confirmed she, too, had no intention of telling Gator or anyone else about the scheme. To soothe her conscience, Simona told herself Miss Twyla was right. They were doing Anjele a favor to end her illicit romance with Gator.

Without another word spoken, they watched Twyla mount and ride away, and only then did Emalee say fearfully, "I don' know, Simona. I don' know if I can do it. Anjele, she gon' know I'm lyin', for sure."

Simona stared at the money. "Well, I can. For this much money, for my baby's future, I can do anythin'. And you know I'll share it with you. So when the time comes, you jus' let me do the talkin', and all you gotta do is agree with everythin' I say. You can do that, can't you?"

Emalee nodded. After all, her welfare, as well as her family's, was at stake. "Sure, I do it. I don' like it, but I do it."

Anjele returned to the willow the next night, and when Gator again did not appear, she knew with heavy heart something had to be wrong. She tried to remember every word spoken, searching for some hidden nuance to indicate his insincerity. But she could recall nothing. Their times together had been wondrous and happy. Desire hadn't been the total sum of their pleasure when together. Each time there was sufficient moonlight, he'd introduced her to yet more of the enchantment that was the bayou. Many evenings, they'd merely sat beneath the willow and talked of the world and all its splendor, and Gator would again tell her of his exciting travels on the high seas.

Above and beyond anything else, Anjele had felt that a warm, lasting friendship existed between them. Never would he just walk away without explanation, especially after the last night they were together, when she'd given him all a woman has to give the man she loves.

Dejected, forlorn, miserable, Anjele knew there was no need to wait any longer. He wasn't coming this night. Something told her he wouldn't be there the next, or the next, but by God, she was determined to find out what was wrong and tomorrow morning, she promised herself, she'd go to him in the cane field and get some answers.

She dreaded going back to the house, knowing sleep wouldn't come as she tossed and turned all night, restless and worried. It was going to be difficult to slip away in the morning, for Raymond was to have returned to New Orleans tonight and would no doubt be arriving early to call. He'd been away nearly a month, and she hadn't missed him at all. How could she, when she was obsessed with another man?

Anjele was also curious as to why Claudia was behaving so mysteriously—ignoring her, except to smirk now and then, eyes dancing as though she knew some deep, dark secret. And her mother wasn't herself, either, or her father. Both seemed to be avoiding her, and at the dinner table, tension hovered like stillness before a storm. She was puzzled by it all, but didn't dwell on it since she was far too preoccupied with her personal concerns.

She'd been out of the house for perhaps two hours when she returned to climb up the trellis.

But the trellis, she realized with a stab of horror, wasn't there. It had been removed, and before she had time to wonder what was going on, Twyla stepped out from behind a hydrangea bush.

"Mother?" Anjele saw her stricken face in the scant moonlight. "What . . . what are you doing here?" she stammered, swept with chilling dread.

"I might ask you the same thing, dear." Twyla was wearing a light silk robe over her gown, her long, dark hair pulled back and tied at the nape of her neck. When Claudia reported that Anjele had once again climbed down the trellis, Elton had had one of the gardeners take it down. Twyla had then taken up vigil in a rocker on the side porch till she saw Anjele coming across the lawn. "I think," she said slowly, evenly, "we should go inside and talk about this. Your father is waiting in his study."

Now Anjele knew, with startling clarity, the reason for everyone's mysterious behavior—especially Claudia who, no doubt had seen her leaving, and tattled. There was nothing to do now but follow her mother and face the inevitable.

Her father sat behind his desk, fingers templed as he silently struggled to hold his temper. He waited till both Anjele and Twyla were seated before taking a deep breath and quietly asking, "Where did you go tonight, Anjele?"

She told herself it wasn't really a lie. "For a walk."

"You climbed down the trellis to go for a walk? Why couldn't you just go down the stairs?" Not giving her a chance either to confirm or deny, he half rose from his chair to yell, "I'll tell you why—you met a man, didn't you?"

He sat again, stealing a glance at Twyla, who gave a slight nod of approval. He was following the planned scenario perfectly.

Anjele stared down at her hands and nervously twisted them in her lap. Not about to admit the truth, she murmured, "It's like I told you. I wanted to go for a walk, and I knew if you-all heard me going down the stairs, you wouldn't let me go, because it was so late."

He glanced at Twyla again, gratefully indicating it was her turn. Dear Lord, he hated this.

Twyla began gingerly, "Anjele, we don't believe you, and we don't think you realize what a serious thing you've done. If Raymond ever found out, he'd never marry you, and neither would any decent man. You must tell us who you were meeting, so your father can ensure he never says anything about it."

Anjele was silent.

With an exaggerated sigh, Twyla turned to Elton. "Well, when she stops meeting him, he'll realize she got caught and no doubt be afraid to say a word. There might be hope no one finds out." She turned to Anjele with genuine tears and cried, "How could you do this to us? How could you shame your family this way? You're a sinful, willful girl, Anjele, and you've broken our hearts." She lowered her face to her hands.

"I'm sorry," Anjele whispered—and truly was. "I never meant to hurt you."

At that, Elton roared, "And what were your plans if you hadn't been found out, for Christ's sake, girl? Are you such a trollop you'd cavort right up to the eve of your wedding?"

Anjele saw no need to confide how she'd fallen in love and dared to dream of a future with her Cajun. Her world had just collapsed around her, and she desperately needed time to think. As long as they didn't know who he was, he was safe, at least, but adding to the nightmare of the moment was the wonder and worry over why he hadn't appeared the past two nights. "How long have you known?" she asked bluntly, something needling inside. Perhaps it was all a trick, and they knew who she'd been meeting and had gone to him and warned him to stay away.

Twyla had been waiting for doubt to surface and was ready to exclaim, "Why, this very night, of course. Do you really think we would've known such a thing and allowed it to continue?"

Elton angrily chimed in. "I wish, by God, I had known. I wish I'd been there to see you crawling down that trellis, because I'd have been right behind you with a gun to shoot the low-life bastard who'd entice you to meet him in the shadows like some whore!"

"Elton!" Twyla gasped.

"It's what it looks like," he said savagely.

"Why did you do it?" Twyla asked. "Whatever enticed you to do such a wicked, wicked thing?"

Miserable and ashamed, Anjele could think of no response.

Twyla rose to cross to where her daughter sat and knelt before her. Clasping Anjele's cold, shaking hands, she told her, "Your father and I had a talk while we were waiting for you to come back, and we've reached a decision."

Warily, Anjele lifted sad eyes to meet her probing gaze.

"We've seen no enthusiasm in you for your wedding, and frankly, we've sensed rebellion growing since the engagement was made formal. You've treated Claudia terribly. You're obviously unhappy. So your father and I think it would be in your best interest to send you away for a while."

"No!" Anjele cried, jerking her hands away. No matter that she was in deep trouble, her own anger boiled over. "I don't want to go and live with Ida Duval. Not now. Maybe I don't have a say after I'm married, but for God's sake, don't make the misery begin a day sooner than necessary."

"We aren't talking about sending you to Ida's."

Anjele looked at her father, but he would not meet her tormented eyes. She turned once more to her mother in bewilderment. "Then where—"

"England. To a nice girls' school outside London. You'll be well educated, and you'll mature into a fine young woman, and when you come back, all this will be forgotten.

"And don't worry about Raymond," Twyla managed an encouraging smile. "I'm sure he'll be pleased to think of having a wife so gloriously learned. And he can go abroad to visit you. It'll be an adventure. Meanwhile, there will be no shame or scandal involving the family name."

Fiercely Anjele shook her head. "No. I won't go. And you can't make me. I'll run away. Tonight, if need be." She stood, trembling from head to toe, hysteria rising. Later, she'd deal with the situation, but for the moment, nothing else mattered except to find out what had happened to Gator. She'd believed him when he professed to love her, and only something terrible would keep him away. Why, he'd gone to the willow tree every night she was on the riverboat, hoping she'd be there. If he hadn't given up on her then, she told herself she owed him the same trust.

They had anticipated such a reaction, and Elton was ready with the concession, "Very well. We'll talk tomorrow. Everyone is upset right now. Go to your room, Anjele."

She ran all the way upstairs, not at all surprised to see Claudia standing at the landing, eavesdroping.

Her expression one of gloating triumph, Claudia giggled, "Well, well. Looks like Daddy's little angel turned out to be daddy's little whore. I don't know why they're so surprised. I knew it all along." With a haughty flounce, she whipped about and retreated to her room.

Anjele didn't care what she said. She didn't care what anybody said. All she wanted was for daylight to come quickly so she could slip out of the house and find Gator.

Sleep eluded her till just before dawn, and Anjele was so exhausted she didn't awake till midmorning. In a panic, she leaped out of bed to dress quickly, all the while wondering how she could get out of the house without her mother seeing and asking where she was going.

She needn't have worried.

When she went downstairs, Kesia told her Twyla and Claudia had left earlier to go into New Orleans to welcome Master Raymond home. "Don' know why they was in such a hurry. Seems to me, he'd a' been headin' out this way, first light, but they was already on the road for town."

Anjele knew the reason. Her mother was afraid Raymond would sense something was wrong and wanted more time for things to calm down before allowing him to see her. Good. That meant she could be on her way to the cane fields.

Emalee spotted her first. They were standing at the edge of the fields, next to the large water barrel, where they'd been since morning. Workers were grumbling about having to come up to get their water, but they weren't about to let Anjele slip up on them unnoticed.

"Here she comes," Emalee whispered. "She's getting off her horse now."

"Keep your back turned," Simona snapped. "Pretend to be filling the pails. Follow my lead. Agree with everything I say."

"I'm so scared she'll know we're lying," Emalee fretted. "Oh, I wish we didn't have to do this."

"It's like Miss Twyla said, it's for her own good. She should've known better than to get involved with him in the first place."

Simona braced herself, then began in a loud voice, "That Gator, I swear, he fool us all, no? And so stupid, he was, to go messin' with another man's wife. It's like every unwed girl in the bayou wasn't enough for him. I guess he have to be greedy and sample them all, eh?" She forced a raucous laugh.

Emalee's giggle sounded hollow and false even to her own ears, but there was no time to worry about it, because Anjele was upon them.

Simona whirled about, pretending surprise. "Why, hello, my friend, I can't believe it is you. It has been so long." She was surprised at her successfully cheerful tone. Giving her friend a quick embrace, she knew Anjcle had heard, all right, for she was stiff, cold, and the look in her emerald eyes mirrored the confusion within.

"We jus' talkin' about the Gator," Simona dared continue. "You remember him?"

Emalee, feeling a bit braver, decided she needed to add something to the conversation, "You know. He pull us from the water."

"And he bring you to see me. Ah!" She slapped her forehead with her hand, as though forgetting her advice till now. "I hope you did not listen to my foolish tongue that day, when I tell you to go and make merry with him. But you a smart girl. I bet you saw him for what he was from the start."

"I don't know what you're talking about." Anjele

tried to appear indifferent. "We were just friends, that's all. I haven't seen him in a long time. I thought I'd come by and say hello to all of you. Is he working close by?"

"Gator? Here?" Simona guffawed, slapped her knee. "Why, he probably miles away by now, as fast as he left with the bullets flyin' over his head."

Anjele, jolted, asked, "What are you talking about? Who was shooting at him?" Dear God, she screamed within, surely her father couldn't have found out who he was.

"Carl Norville, 'cause he found him in bed with his wife." Simona pretended to be suddenly concerned, "Hey, somethin' wrong? How come you look so funny? Face all white. It don' be the first time a man tries to kill a man he finds with his wife. Won't be the last. Gator, he was just lucky he got away, but he sure left lots of cryin' women behind. Now that he's gone, it all comes out. Boss Farrand, he told Frank, Gator stayed out every night, and by day, he'd almost always catch him in the woods ruttin' with some girl."

Anjele swayed, and Emalee, afraid she was about to faint, clutched her arm and advised, "Maybe you better sit down a spell in the shade."

"No. No, I'm fine." Anjele vehemently shook her head and held up her arms to ward off any consoling gestures, knowing she had to get hold of herself lest suspicion be aroused. So far nobody knew what a fool she was. Her parents only knew she'd been with a man, and that's all they were going to know.

She started toward her horse.

"Hey, come back," Simona called. "You jus' got here. Stay and visit a spell . . . ."

But she kept on running. Then, quickly mounting, she gave the mare the reins and rode away.

They stared after her, and finally Emalee lamented, "I still say it's a shame. I was watchin' her face, and I could tell she loved that man. Where he go, anyway?"

Simona said she didn't know. Nobody did. Both the enigmatic Gator and his loathsome father had not been seen since the day before yesterday. She lifted the water pail, at last ready to head into the rows of tall, bushy cane stalks. "It don't matter, Emalee," she murmured. "It wasn't meant to be, and we gotta forget it ever was."

Emalee doggedly nodded and fell into step behind her.

Anjele was lying across her bed when she heard her mother come upstairs. She waited a moment, then got up and went and knocked on the door.

"Yes, who is it?" came Twyla's apprehensive voice, for unknown to Anjele, she was expecting the visit.

Anjele opened the door and stepped inside.

Twyla saw the misery etched on her daughter's face and knew the ploy had worked but wanted to ease the tension and offered, "Claudia and I went to visit Raymond this morning, to keep him from coming here, because I was afraid you weren't up to facing him just yet. But he's so anxious to see you, he insists on coming for tea this afternoon. If you don't feel you're ready, I can make your excuses when he gets here."

"No, that won't be necessary," Anjele said with resolve. "I'd like to see him. I need to explain about the wedding being postponed."

Twyla held her breath.

Anjele closed her eyes momentarily, then opened them to reflect inner anguish as she declared in a tone of calm finality, "I've decided I want to go to school in

England, and the sooner I can leave, the better."

Twyla's breath caught in her throat. It was what she had prayed to hear but, in that moment, realized she felt no joy in triumph, though Anjele would never know of the deception. At that very moment, Elton was busy getting rid of Simona and Emalee, along with their families. He would see to it they were quickly and securely ensconced on the plantation of a friend of his, all the way in Alabama. It was the only way to ensure there'd be no one around to remember, or reveal, what had really happened.

Now, however, seeing the anguish and heartbreak mirrored on her beloved daughter's face was almost more than Twyla could bear and, for one frozen instant, felt the impulse to confess all. But she dared not, instead yielding to the overwhelming rush of love and the need to comfort as best she could.

Quickly rising from the bed, she went to fold Anjele into her arms. "Oh, my darling, I'll miss you terribly, but it's all for the best, you'll see."

Anjele succumbed to the tears she'd been fighting against, and, responding to her mother's embrace, clung to her and whispered hoarsely, "I love you, Momma."

Twyla stepped away but drew her to the bed to sit down beside her. Then, holding both of Anjele's hands in her own, she felt the need to assure, "Even though you might not think so at times, you're my first love. Sometimes, I know it appears I favor Claudia, and maybe I do, because I've felt so sorry for her, and—"

"There's no need, Momma," Anjele interrupted. "I understand, though it's been hard at times, but I've never doubted your love for me. I wish . . . " She paused to swallow past the lump in her throat, "I wish all this hadn't happened."

Twyla reached to tenderly brush a wisp of hair from Anjele's forehead, then slipped an arm about her to pull her close once again. "You're going to find as you grow older there will be lots of things in your past you wish hadn't happened. It's part of life. Just remember to look forward and never back, and one day, you'll forget all about this unhappy time."

"And always remember," Twyla concluded with a firm hug as she attempted to blink away her own tears, "God loves you, and so do I."

And, as her mother held her tightly, Anjele silently avowed, "Wherever you are, Gator, I hope you can feel how much I love you."

Brett felt a stabbing chill. He shook himself, thought it ridiculous to be cold on the sultry August day, and figured it was some kind of reaction to the wounds on his back. Some of them were deep and would be awhile healing.

He went to the railing and stared out at the muddy, rolling river. How like his own life, he thought. Recklessly going along, dirtied by stupid mistakes. Like falling in love. Never again, he vowed for maybe the thousandth time since that fateful night. He'd make no promise to a woman beyond pleasuring her in bed. Where love was concerned, his heart had turned to stone.

Another passenger on the packet stepped up to the railing. Amiably, he asked, "Where you be headed, friend?"

Brett mumbled he wasn't sure.

The stranger placed his hand on Brett's shoulder in a friendly gesture but withdrew it when Brett shot him an icy glare. "Well, I was wondering," he said, "if you might be looking for a job."

Brett shrugged. He figured he'd wind up going back to sea.

The stranger persisted. "This job would pay well. Allow me to introduce myself. Gilbert Samuels. St. Louis."

He held out his hand. Brett merely nodded. He was about to walk away.

"I work for a company that's starting up a stagecoach line to take mail out west. From Missouri all the way to California. It's going to be rugged and dangerous, and that's why we're paying top wages. You look like a strong and courageous man, and you might be just what we're looking for."

Brett felt a spark of interest. Missouri to California. Virgin country. Rough and wild. A challenge. Good pay. But, most of all, a chance to forget while trying to stay alive. What more could he ask for at such a miserable time in his life? With a crooked smile, he suggested, "Let's have a drink and talk about it, mister."

He headed for the saloon, the stranger eagerly following on his heels.

CHAPTER 11

England
1862

MISS DEAGON WALKED INTO THE ROOM. She was holding an envelope, which she kept pressed to her bosom as she took her place behind the walnut desk.

Anjele had been dreading the meeting with the headmistress. Swallowing hard, she began, "Miss Deagon, I want to apologize for what happened. I know I wasn't supposed to be in the kitchen after hours, but some of us were hungry, and it was just a lark, really. And I had no idea that cake was for your tea this afternoon. I thought it was leftover. Seems I'm always in trouble, and I'm truly sorry. I only have a few months left here, and—"

"You may have longer than that." Miss Deagon fingered the envelope thoughtfully.

Anjele was stunned she could even consider such a horrible possibility. "What are you talking about? I'm going home in a few months. It's understood. My parents are expecting me. Surely you won't try to keep me here as punishment. They'd never allow it." She leaned forward to clutch the edge of the desk.

Miss Deagon sighed and turned in her chair to gaze out the window at the gray, depressing day. The very last thing she wanted to do was keep Anjele Sinclair at her school one hour more than necessary. Already, the girl had been in her charge longer than was customary, but her parents were quite wealthy and had been willing to pay the price to board her. Still, Miss Deagon had been counting the days till it was time for her to leave. Anjele's independence undermined the school's strict code of decorum. Her indomitable spirit served as a beacon of inspiration to other girls to resist obedience.

Yes, she had been truly looking forward to her departure. Still, she did not like having to be the one to break the terrible news. Wanting to ease into it, she began by reminding the girl, "There is a terrible war going on in your country."

"Yes, but what does that have to do with your implying I have to stay here?"

Miss Deagon continued to hedge. "The latest I heard was that it's feared New Orleans may be attacked."

"My father wrote me about that," Anjele said stiffly. "He said President Davis is worried because the Yankees are now on an island off the coast of Mississippi, and there's talk they might attack either New Orleans or Mobile, but we've got troops ready to defend both places, and I'm not really worried. In fact, I'm anxious to get home and be with my family and help fight for BelleClair, if need be."

Miss Deagon winced at the disgusting thought of

one of her young ladies engaged in combat with anyone for any reason.

"Queen Victoria has said our country will maintain neutrality," she remarked. Anything to stall, while she carefully framed what needed to be said.

Anjele knew all that. Probably she knew more about the war than Miss Deagon, because her father wrote often. Exasperated, she pressed, "Would you please tell me what's going on here?"

With a resigned sigh, the headmistress turned to face her once more, "Yes, I—"

"Miss Deagon." The door opened and Miss Maples apologetically peered in to interrupt, "I am so very sorry, but there's a matter that needs your attention. One of the cooks has cut her hand rather badly in the kitchen, and the other workers are hysterical. Can you come, please?"

"Oh, for heaven's sake!" Miss Deagon rose and rushed out.

Wearily, Anjele slumped back in the chair, with no choice but to wait longer to hear what her fate would be. But if Miss Deagon thought she was going to punish her by keeping her here, she was wrong. Anjele knew she'd run away if need be.

She thought back to last year, when her parents had come to England for a brief visit. Her father had described how all of New Orleans was reverberating with the question uppermost in all Americans' minds—whether Southern states would secede from the Union. And he, like all the other planters, as well as brokers, debated as to whether they should sell their crops immediately at a good profit or hold cotton and sugarcane for the higher prices they would surely command in the future.

Shortly after they'd returned home, secession did indeed begin, with Louisiana the sixth state to pull out in January, 1861. Her father wrote he'd been involved in helping to secure all United States property, and, by spring, the city of New Orleans was like a garrison. Encampments appeared, and the air was one of martial splendor and holiday festivities. Yet, despite all the preparations, and even after the firing on Fort Sumter, he felt war was still far away.

Then came his letter telling how Ship Island, Mississippi, had been seized by the Union navy, which meant the blockade of Southern ports was tightening. However, blockade runners, he said, still managed to sail into the crescent city about once a week, and when one was sighted, everyone crowded the levees to see what had been smuggled in. And even though prices were exorbitant, her mother wrote she didn't hesitate to pay them for a new pair of soft leather slippers from France or fine silk for a dress.

As for food, there was no real shortage yet, but other items like glass canning jars were impossible to find. Supplies from Northern factories had been cut off and none were being made in the South.

In the last communication received from her father, written in early February, he'd reported that things were becoming increasingly tense. Some slave owners reported rumblings of discontent and threats of revolt by various groups of slaves, especially among those who'd been volunteered by their masters to work on fortifications. Some had even run away. But he was proud to report BelleClair's slaves were content to stay right where they were. While some probably did dream of freedom, they feared the unknown as opposed to the security they now enjoyed.

Anjele wasn't the least bit afraid to return with the war moving ever closer to her homeland. There was nothing she could do, but at least she'd be there in case there was. Most of all, she was more than ready to leave her depressing surroundings.

On a positive note, she was pleased to reflect on how she wouldn't be going back to marry Raymond Duval. The apologetic letter came from her mother only a few months after Anjele's arrival in England. Raymond and Claudia had been quietly married in New Orleans and were living with his family. Twyla hoped Anjele would not be bitter. Claudia had always loved him, she'd written, and Raymond had obviously realized he also loved her.

Anjele had laughed over such a ludicrous theory. Claudia had no doubt wasted little time in relating the scandalous story of Anjele's escapades to Raymond. And of course, he was hurt and angry and allowed himself to be cajoled and manipulated into marrying her.

God help him, Anjele thought. He'd done nothing to deserve such a fate.

Her mother had urged her to encourage the attention of other young men. Miss Deagon was always hosting tea dances to expose her girls to social situations with the opposite sex. Twyla had said both she and Elton would be pleased if Anjele married a distinguished European, but Anjele scoffed at such an idea. Her dream was not to marry but to return to BelleClair.

The door opened, and Miss Deagon re-entered her office, the envelope still in her hand. Anjele watched expectantly as she settled into her chair and adjusted her glasses. Carefully, slowly, she took a piece of paper out of the envelope and unfolded it.

Anjele recognized her father's handwriting. "That's from my father. Why are you keeping it from me?"

She leaped to her feet and held out her hand, but Miss Deagon drew back with a frown. "It was sent to me, Anjele, not you. And if you want to know what he said, sit down and be quiet."

With legs beginning to tremble, she sank to the chair.

"It's unfortunate to have to tell you this now, because the purpose of this meeting was to discuss your inexcusable behavior—"

"I know that, Miss Deagon," Anjele interrupted, "but will you please tell me what is in that letter? You're being unnecessarily cruel."

Miss Deagon felt a flash of annoyance. To think of having to endure another year of Anjele's insubordination was almost more than she could bear. "Very well," she said with a curt nod. Dismissing any feeling of compunction, she told her bluntly, "Your mother is dead."

From somewhere far, far away, Miss Deagon's voice droned on, reading that it was sudden, pneumonia, the doctor thought. It was over quickly. She didn't suffer. But then through the great roaring within, Anjele heard something else—cold, frightening words that brought her up out of the drowning pit of sorrow.

" . . . and regretfully," Miss Deagon was reading aloud from the letter, "I feel it is best that my daughter remain in your charge until such time as it is deemed prudent for her to return home. She is safer where she is than here, in a country rife with war. Please convey to her my love and tell her I will write to her quite soon."

Anjele swallowed against the cry of protest. Through lowered lashes, she could tell Miss Deagon was watching for her reaction. In the bowels of the monastic building, there was a chamber reserved for girls who, Miss Deagon felt, needed time alone to meditate. It was known as "The Pit" and was actually the cruel and unjust punishment of solitary confinement. Anjele had spent many days there, and knew now if she weren't careful, would find herself an inhabitant again. All she had to do was indicate, in any way, that she was not in compliance with her father's request.

"Yes," she finally mustered her voice to whisper, as though talking to herself, "he's right. It's not safe over there, and I need time for grieving."

Miss Deagon smiled with pleasure. Perhaps this was what was needed all along to break the girl's spirit, the harsh reality of realizing that nothing in life is forever. "You have the sympathy of everyone here, Anjele. Losing one's mother is a tragedy, and I think you'll honor her memory by future obedience to our rules here."

The other girls politely left her alone, and Anjele succumbed to tears till there were none left—only the empty, aching pain of realizing she'd never again see her beloved mother.

Finally, with cold, chilling resolve, she began to make her plans to run away. Her father was the only person left in this world she truly loved, and nothing was going to keep her from being with him to share his grief.

She was going to need money for passage across the Atlantic, which was a problem, because she didn't have any. She had never had an allowance, since all her needs were taken care of. Her father paid tuition and board directly to Miss Deagon.

Suddenly she remembered the jewelry she'd worn recently to the opera and leaped up to rush to her dresser and make sure the gold and pearl tiara and earbobs were still tucked into the top drawer. Miss Deagon demanded that all the girls keep their jewels locked away in her safe and dispensed them when needed, but had not yet had Anjele's collected. The pieces were not nearly as valuable as others on deposit, but surely they'd bring enough to pay for passage home.

The day passed slowly, and Anjele's heart was heavy as she dwelled on her loss. Finally night came, and she joined the other girls in the dining room. As she accepted their condolences, she said a silent good-bye to each. They didn't know it, but this was to be her last night behind the cold, gray walls.

All was quiet as Anjele slipped out of bed at dawn and quickly dressed. Not wanting to be hindered by carrying a large bag, she resolved to worry later about a change of clothing.

With the jewels tucked into her velvet purse, Anjele picked up her kid gloves and headed for the curving stone steps to the main floor. The case clock at the end of the hall struck six times.

It was nearly midafternoon when Anjele found herself standing outside the steps leading to Byron Rozelle's flat. She had met him the first year she had arrived in England, at one of Miss Deagon's well-chaperoned tea dances. And, despite the way they were constantly observed, Byron had made no secret of his desire to court her. But even though she had finally made him realize she had no romantic interest in him, or any other young man, they had become friends, and she was confident he would help her now.

It had begun to rain, a cold, steady drizzle, and she was soaking wet, chilled, and hungry.

Byron came to his door almost immediately, took one look at her, and burst out laughing, "My word, where's the cat who dragged you in, my dear?" He stepped back, pulling her with him, "Come in and get warm by the fire. I'll get you a brandy, and you can tell me all about it."

Warily, Anjele allowed him to take the wet cloak and stepped eagerly to the hearth, where a delicious fire was crackling in the grate. Byron disappeared behind a curtain to one side, and she glanced about at the furnishings. They were sparse, but what was there was luxurious and of good taste.

Soon Anjele was feeling better, for the brandy was doing exactly what it was supposed to, making her feel relaxed and soothed. She was able to tell Byron, without bursting into tears, of her mother's death and her subsequent decision to return to America despite her father's wishes.

Byron listened quietly, except to offer clucking noises of sympathy now and then.

"You probably think I've got a nerve asking you to help me," she said finally, "but there's no one else I can turn to."

"Oh, my dear, dear, Anjele." He bestowed a tender

smile as he brushed the damp tendrils of golden-red hair back from her forehead. "'Tis a pity, indeed, you'll never know how happy I could've made you as my wife, and I suppose . . ." He gave an exaggerated sigh. "Persuading you to go to bed with me for a sample is out of the question, but I can bestow a sample of my generosity. You're not to worry. I'll take care of everything. Within a few days, you'll be on a ship bound for the colonies."

"Colonies." Despite herself, she had to giggle. "We won the war, Byron, remember?"

"Ah, yes, you did, but I still can't see why you prefer returning to that dreadful place in the midst of yet another war, when you could stay here and marry me."

Drily she responded, "I'll probably never forgive myself."

"Probably not." He winked at her.

She took the tiara and earbobs from her bag and offered, "Take them. They should bring a fair price. You'll be reimbursed."

He dismissed the notion with an airy wave. "Keep them. Think of me when you wear them. I can take some solace in knowing you won't forget me."

Anjele was touched and could assure him he would always be fondly, and gratefully, remembered.

CHAPTER 12

ELTON SINCLAIR STARED IMPASSIVELY AT the cast-iron fence bordering the stately tomb. He didn't know who was buried there, nor did he care. The only reason he had come to the St. Louis cemetery on Basin Street was to see an example of George Masson's work.

Beside him, George wanted to know, "Well, what do you think, Mr. Sinclair?" He opened the gate with its twining patterns of flowers and oak leaves, waving him to follow with the rolled-up drawings he held. "I've got a nice design worked out for your wife's grave.

"You know yourself," he went on, "I made good machinery for your sugarhouse, and I knew when decorative ironwork came in demand, I could make a little on it as a sideline. Didn't know it would become such a big business. I was getting orders from all over before the war started."

Made of imported marble, the tomb Elton had built for his beloved wife at BelleClair resembled a small cathedral, with stained glass windows and a large mahogany door. Now he wanted to make the site even more elaborate by installing an ornate fence.

"The most popular color now is a light green, like this." George gestured to his newest creation.

"I like green," Elton murmured tonelessly, "and I like this one." He pointed to a sketch of cane stalks with magnolias intertwined. Swallowing against the rising lump in his throat, he said, "Make it five feet high, and I'll want grids at the windows and across the door. If the damn Yankees do make it to BelleClair, the bastards probably won't blink an eye at grave robbing."

George bit back a gleeful smile to think of what the cost would be, for he knew money was of no consequence to Elton Sinclair. Not for a while, anyway. Everybody was dubious about the financial future due to the ever-tightening blockade. Nowadays the levees were almost deserted. Everything was scarce, and if he hadn't hoarded a stockpile of metal in his basement, he wouldn't still be in business himself. The Confederacy would be plenty mad to know he hadn't turned it in for making weapons, but George reasoned he had to think of supporting his family first. "I'll get right on it, Mr. Sinclair," he assured, scribbling notes on thc paper.

"Good. That's good." Elton's head bobbed up and down as he began to shuffle away. "The sooner the better."

George shook his head in pity. Mr. Sinclair had obviously taken his wife's passing real hard, and lots of folks were saying it was as if a part of him had died, too.

He rolled up his drawings. Yes, he felt real sorry for the man—but not enough to cut his price on the ironwork.

He noticed that Sinclair was taking the long way out of the cemetery, walking aimlessly and in no hurry. George took the shortest path. Cemeteries made him nervous, especially those with the tombs above ground with bushes growing out of them. The idea of roots wrapping around a corpse was creepy, and he shuddered and quickened his pace.

Elton was tired. It was as though he'd aged twenty years since Twyla died. He sank down on a bench next to a tomb, absently thinking that whoever was inside wouldn't mind if he sat a spell. Staring up at the bare limbs of the twisted oak, he could see the first buds, a sign of spring. He didn't care. Nothing mattered anymore. At least Anjele was safe, and his one hope now was that she'd find a good man to marry and take care of her and just stay over there, by God, because Louisiana was going to hell with the rest of the South in the infernal war, and—

"Elton, you're a hard man to catch up with."

He looked up into the bearded face of Millard DuBose, his lawyer and lifelong acquaintance.

Elton stiffened. "Who's looking for me?"

Millard sat down, instinctively glancing about to ensure there was no one to overhear. It was a gray, overcast day, and few chose to visit the cemetery, so he felt safe in continuing. "We all are, Elton. We need to know you're still one of us."

At that, Elton flared, "Good Lord, man, I just lost my wife a few weeks ago. I'm in mourning. I'm not thinking about fighting Yankees. Let the young ones march off to war."

"We're fighting a private war, Elton, and you know it. We talked about it at our first meeting at your place nearly three years ago, remember?"

Elton sighed. "I remember."

"You, me and Doc Duval," Millard droned on, "and Seth White and Hardy Maxwell and Tobias Radford and Whitley Coombs. All of us agreed there are ways we can fight the Yankees other than taking up arms. And we've done pretty well, too. We led the takeovers—the Paymaster's Office and the Branch Mint and the Customs House."

"A lot of good it did," Elton said. "I heard at the market a little while ago that Farragut has left Ship Island and headed for Fort St. Philip. If he takes it, along with Fort Jackson, nothing will prevent his sailing all the way up here."

"All the more reason you've got to join us," Millard persisted, placing his hand on Elton's knee for emphasis. "If New Orleans does fall to the enemy, we've got to be organized and ready to work in secret to filter out news to our forces. We can't just surrender to the bastards."

"Like Whitley?" Elton had counted Whitley Coombs among his dearest friends. He also knew it had hurt Whitley when his only son left home to go and fight for the Union but he'd never dreamed Whitley would also turn his back on the South.

Millard frowned. "Yes, that was unfortunate, but when his boy got killed at Manassas, Whitley said he wasn't going to live under the flag that did it."

"He's still a traitor."

"Maybe so, but that's all the more reason the rest of us got to stick together. We can't trust just anybody, so we can't take in new people. That's why you're so important to us. Lord knows, we all grieve with you over Twyla, but you haven't been to any of our meetings since last fall."

"Been busy." Elton looked toward the spire of the cathedral over at Jackson Square as the bells began to peal. He stood in dismissal.

Millard also rose, his mouth a thin, tight line of annoyance. Losing patience, he snapped, "It wasn't an accident I met you here. I was following you. I was told to find you and tell you there's a meeting tonight, here, as a matter of fact, and the others are going to be very upset if you don't come."

"*Here?*" Elton blinked, glancing around at the imposing graves and tombs. "Why here of all places?"

"Nobody will see us, and with the Yankees pressing closer, we can't take any chances, because the minute they enter the city, there're going to be traitors who'll rush to their side, and we don't want anybody to be able to tell about us. We can't meet at saloons or cafés anymore, and we don't want to involve our families by meeting at each other's houses. The cemetery is the logical place. We can leave our buggies and horses at Jackson Square and walk here. We're going to meet at the Tutwiler tomb. It's the largest after you enter the east gate, three rows in. I was the administrator for the Tutwiler estate, and since they've all died out, I happened to wind up with the key to the mausoleum. It's large enough for all of us to gather in it. Mrs. Tutwiler planned it that way so she could sit and meditate next to her husband's coffin. There's even a rocking chair in there"—he paused to laugh—"but old man Tutwiler outlived her, and I never knew him to visit once. It's perfect for us."

Elton said they were wise to be careful but added, "I've nothing to contribute to your meeting, Millard. Now, if you'll excuse me, I'll bid you good day."

"Wish you'd reconsider, Elton," George called after him, exasperated. "If everybody has your attitude, we might as well go ahead and surrender!"

Elton kept on going. It wasn't that he didn't care. He did. Very much. When talk of secession began, he'd been among the most vocal in favor. He had even traveled to Baton Rouge to the Secession Convention to lobby, calling in every favor owed him through the years. And when Louisiana became the sixth Southern state to declare itself independent of the Union, he'd been so ecstatic he'd joined other zealots in securing all United States property.

And that, he recalled with furrowed brow, was when he'd found himself involved deeper than he'd intended.

It had happened when they took over the Branch Mint and Customs House. He had been in the process of counting paper money, so they would know exactly how much they were accountable for, when he noticed a set of strange looking engraving plates. Examining them closer and reading the accompanying print order, he realized the Federal government had been planning to make new paper money printed in green ink, instead of gold. No doubt, they were doing so at other locations, as well.

At once, he had realized the value of the plates to the Confederacy, for they could be used to print counterfeit Federal money, which could be used to purchase desperately needed supplies, like food and medicine.

After first glancing about to make sure no one else was in the room, Elton had slipped the plates inside his coat. Lately he had begun to have doubts about the true loyalty of some of his fellow vigilantes and, until he knew who could and couldn't be trusted, he was not taking any chances. He'd say nothing, hide them away, and when the time was right, he'd present them to the right people.

As far as he knew, it had not been discovered that the plates were even missing. The vigilantes had banished the Federal loyalists working at the Mint, who had hightailed it up North, and no one familiar with the workings of the Mint had been inside to take inventory. That was over a year ago. Elton had said nothing to anyone. And the plates were hidden where no one would ever think to look for them.

Elton considered himself a staunch supporter of the Confederacy, and not solely because of the slavery issue. By God, he considered the whole damn war an issue of states' rights. Northerners had no business coming down South and telling folks how to live. He felt it should be left up to the voters in each state whether or not they wanted to allow slavery. As far as he was concerned, he'd be willing to pay wages to his Negroes, but then he wouldn't be able to provide free housing, food, clothes, and medical care. They were better off as they were, and they knew it. He'd had no trouble at BelleClair. Never had, and never would—if the Yankees would mind their own damn business, he silently grumbled.

But in the past months, he'd backed away from involvement in clandestine activities due to his suspicions of a turncoat among their group. Someone he'd always loved and admired. Elton could only hope he was wrong about the man. Time would tell. Meanwhile, he intended to keep his possession of the valuable plates a secret.

He walked on into the gray and gloomy day, anxious to be done with his business in the city so he could get home before dark and visit Twyla's tomb. 'Twas precious little comfort, to be sure, but it was all he had. How he wished he could bring Anjele home, for he missed her terribly and longed to share his grief with her. But it wasn't safe. Not now. She was better off where she was.

He hurried from the cemetery and headed toward Jackson Square.

He did not notice the bedraggled man slumped next to the brick gatepost. There were many beggars around town, most of them hopeless drunks. He avoided their outstretched hands. But this one, Elton failed to observe, did not reach out to him. And had he seen the flash of furious recognition on the man's face, he'd have been chilled to the bone.

Leo Cody stared at the stoop-shouldered man's back and gave a low, ominous snarl. Reaching into the pocket of his worn denim coat, he quickly uncapped the bottle of whiskey and turned it up to take a big swallow. "Son of a bitch," he savagely whispered. If he'd had the strength to stand, Leo would've leaped to his feet and run after him to grab him and choke him to death, but Leo had been wallowing too long in the gutter of despair. Drunk, he could barely stand, so he contented himself with hurling epithets and threats which Elton Sinclair did not hear.

It was all Sinclair's fault, Leo brooded, that he'd wound up in the gutters of New Orleans. Nobody would hire him except to do a slave's work in the fields. He'd gone to other planters seeking an overseer's position, but once they contacted Sinclair, who refused to recommend him, he was never hired. So he worked odd jobs, or begged for money to buy whiskey, and thanks to Sinclair, he was a drunken bum.

"Gonna get you one day, you uppity bastard!" He threw the empty bottle to smash in the cobblestone street. "You'll pay for what you did to Leo Cody. You'll see."

Elton heard the distant sound of breaking glass but didn't turn around. He was far too absorbed in his grief and misery to notice anything going on around him.

But Millard DuBose saw and heard everything. He shook his head and kept on going, anxious to report to the others that they could no longer count on Sinclair to help in the cause.

CHAPTER 13

AS THE STAGECOACH ROUNDED THE curve, Brett saw the man standing in the middle of the road waving his arms. With a quick glance to assure himself that his rifle was at his feet, he began to slow the team of horses. He didn't like picking up passengers along the way. It wasn't safe. He'd heard of too many wagons being ambushed. He was especially wary since he was making the run alone. When he had left San Francisco, Seth Barlow, who was supposed to be riding shotgun, hadn't showed. Somebody said he was laid up drunk somewhere, with a woman. There wasn't time to look for him. Brett had to stick to his schedule. Unable to find a replacement at the last minute, he'd loaded the passengers and popped leather.

As he drew closer, he quickly surveyed the barren landscape for any sign of danger. Other than low-growing scrubs, there wasn't anything to conceal waiting bandits.

One of the passengers stuck his head out the window to demand to know why he was slowing down, at the same time seeing the waiting man. "Hey," he was quick to protest, "there's no more room in here. We can't hardly move now."

Brett ignored him. The new passenger would ride up above with him, but he didn't feel he owed anyone an explanation. The people on board this trip were irritating, anyway. Usually he'd have one whiner, but all six, four men and two women, had complained since leaving San Francisco. The way stops were primitive, they griped. Food was terrible. He didn't stop for rest and water as often as they wanted. And did he deliberately hit the potholes and rough spots? From sounds drifting up to him, he knew they'd started arguing among themselves, and he was relieved, for they had finally stopped nagging at him.

The instant he reined the horses in, they all began to scramble out to stretch their legs and, of course, to scrutinize the new addition to their group. Before Brett could even climb down, Alton Jacobs, the man who hadn't wanted to stop, began firing questions at the stranger.

"What's your name? What are you doing out here, miles from any town? We're particular about who we take on, mister."

Brett shoved him aside and saw at once the man was no threat. He couldn't be much older than forty, but he had the eyes of a man whose spirit had died. He had big, muscular arms, obviously a hard worker. Yet he seemed old somehow, and his voice, when he spoke, was frail.

"Name's Adam Barnes. Need to get to St. Louis. I got the money to pay for it."

Taking his worn bag, Brett tossed it up with the others. "Climb aboard. We've got to keep moving."

One of the women, Florence Isadore, came up to Brett and said, "Do we have to go right this minute, Mr. Cody? I swear, if I have to keep sitting with my knees pressed against a man's much longer, I'm going to scream."

"Have Mrs. Turnbow change places," he snapped, not looking at her. He'd learned at their first way stop Florence was trouble. He'd been sleeping in the barn, and she'd boldly sneaked out during the night to lie down beside him and tell him exactly what she wanted. When he'd refused to oblige, she had been furious and gone out of her way to be obnoxious since.

"Well, I'll still have men's thighs pressing against me on each side," she wailed.

He bit back the impulse to say she ought to like that, instead ordering, "Everybody back on. This isn't a scheduled stop."

Once on the way, Brett told Barnes what the fare would be but made no attempt at further conversation. He didn't like talking to passengers. Talk led to questions, and he saw no reason to share any part of himself with anybody. The women who came and went in his life quickly learned he never promised anything beyond satisfaction in bed. Companionship wasn't in his nature, and forget about love.

At first, Brett wasn't even aware the man had spoken till he repeated his question.

"Heard any war news?" he asked timorously, as though he really hoped Brett hadn't.

Brett shook his head. He tried not to think about it, because he wasn't sure which side he was on. After what had happened four years ago in Louisiana, he couldn't muster any affinity for the South, yet because he was raised there, he couldn't see himself taking up arms against it. Better, he figured, to stay right where he was, making runs back and forth between San Francisco and St. Louis. When the pony express had operated between April of 1860 and the end of last year, he'd been one of the hardest riders. Indians and outlaws didn't cause him to fret, and he reckoned he'd killed his share of both. But when telegraph lines were connected all the way from the Atlantic to the Pacific coast, he'd gone right back to work for the Overland Stage. A long time ago, he'd thought about going back to sea but the West had got in his blood.

"I'm goin' to get my boy and bring him home," Adam Barnes said, staring at the seemingly endless road ahead. "Ever hear of a place called Pittsburgh Landing, in Tennessee?"

Brett shook his head.

"Battle of Shiloh, they call it. Real bloody. My boy . . ." His voice cracked. "He was fightin' with General Grant. When I went into town for supplies yesterday, there was a telegram waitin' for me, sayin' my boy was killed. I'm goin' to go get him and dig him up from wherever they buried him and bring him home and bury him next to his momma." He pulled a rag from his pocket and blew his nose and apologized. "Sorry. Don't mean to cry like a woman, but he was all I had after his mother died. The three of us, we come out here to prospect for gold, but Martha, she died right off, couldn't take the heat, and Leroy, he never liked it much. Said we'd never make a strike. He took off when the war broke out, and I stayed on. Good thing I did."

He looked at Brett, a sudden lilt to his voice and briefly seeming to come out of his stupor of grief.

"Can't tell you nothin' else, 'cause I got to stake my claim, but the very day before I got that telegraph, I hit a vein with a streak o' gold as big around as my arm." He held it up for emphasis.

Brett broke his silence to point out, "You should've gone to the claims office before leaving Colorado. Somebody might jump it before you get back."

Adam shook his head with confidence. "Nobody will ever find it. I wouldn't know how to get back to it myself if I hadn't drawn me a map."

Brett said nothing. He didn't care about the man or his gold. The fact was, he didn't care much about anything, just took one day at a time.

Adam continued to talk as they rode, ignoring Brett's quiet indifference. Once, he did provoke brief conversation by inquiring as to Brett's stand on the war.

"I don't have one."

"But surely you care who wins," Adam said, incredulous. "Where you from, anyway?"

Brett was puzzled by his own candid response, but there was something about the man he found himself liking. Maybe it was the man's profound honesty about who he was, what he was. "Cajun country," he said . . ."Mississippi and . . . Louisiana," he added reluctantly. There was nothing in that state he ever wanted to remember.

"Southern states. I reckon you'd go with them, if pressed to fight."

Brett shrugged. "It's a senseless war. The North knew it would have to physically invade from the start, and all the South has to do is hang on."

Adam was quick to point out, "They're finding that's not going to be easy to do. The blockade is working. The South is starting to choke."

"But the South's morale is higher. They feel they're defending hearth and home against an invading oppressor. And don't forget, as a whole, the farm boys can ride and shoot a hell of a lot better than the Yankee city boys."

"Last I heard, New Orleans was gonna be attacked any time. A naval fleet was headed there to take over. That'll cripple the South, for sure."

Brett told himself he should feel guilty for not caring, but the truth was, he didn't. In fact, he hoped when federal forces invaded, they stopped off first at BelleClair and drove Elton Sinclair and his whole family back into the bayou they'd forced him to leave.

Adam saw how Cody tensed and worried he might have made him mad by predicting the South's doom. "Hey, don't pay no mind to me. What do I know?" He attempted to smooth things over. "I'm just an old desert rat listening to drunken gossip when I go into civilization for supplies. Probably not a word of truth in any of it."

But Brett no longer heard, for the memories had been triggered, and he was once more plummeted into sad, bitter reverie.

Adam, grateful Cody hadn't gone into a rage, for he sensed he was not a man to be trifled with, instinctively slid as far from him as possible on the bench and made no further attempt to converse.

Days passed as they traveled from dawn to dusk, spacing stops along the way for food and nature's call. They spent nights at way stations, where they enjoyed their one big meal of the day and a break from the constant jarring of the stage.

They were but four days out of St. Louis when a

way-station manager drew Brett to one side to warn him of some particularly unsavory horsemen he'd encountered that morning. "There was six of 'em. I think they were Reb deserters, driftin' around and lookin' for trouble. They said they didn't have much money, and I figured from the looks of 'em, I'd best not get 'em riled, so my missus gave 'em all they wanted to eat, and I bedded 'em down and told 'em I'd only charge half my regular rate. But they sneaked out just before dawn without payin' nothin', and I'm just thankful they didn't slit my throat and rob me. So you keep an eye out."

Brett assured the man he would, although he always tried to be ready for trouble.

It came early the next day.

They had been traveling only a few hours when Adam pointed to what looked like a body straight ahead in the middle of the road and yelled, loud enough for those riding inside to hear, "Jesus! Look at that. Is he dead?"

Brett had already seen and was picking up his rifle with one hand while he pulled back on the reins only slightly with his other. He wasn't about to stop till he could be sure it wasn't an ambush, because it was a good place for bandits to be hiding. Large rocks were on each side of the trail, with lots of scrub brush for camouflage.

"Stop!" A passenger was frantically yelling out a window. "He needs help."

Brett wasn't so sure. For one thing, he didn't see any vultures circling overhead, and in this heat, it wouldn't take long for them to get a whiff of death. The body couldn't have been there long, which meant whoever was responsible wasn't far away. He reined the horses to a sharp left, intending to go around and stop farther down the road. He could come back, gun ready, and check it out himself without endangering the passengers, giving Adam orders to ride like hell if he heard shooting.

He heard Florence's hysterical shriek, "You bastard! Stop! He might be alive!"

Adam nervously watched him out of the corner of his eye, wondering why he wasn't slowing down. And then he was hanging onto the bench with both hands, trying not to be tossed off the side as the wagon sharply lurched to the left just before it would have run over the man. The man, however, suddenly came to life and rolled to the side at the same time the first shots rang out.

Brett ducked, feeling the bullet whiz overhead. Curses and screams of terror exploded from below as he threw the reins to Adam and ordered, "Take 'em and move out!"

Turning, he aimed in the direction the gunfire was coming from—but never got off the first shot.

The impact of the bullet tearing into his shoulder sent him tumbling off the top of the stagecoach and into an abyss of oblivion.

From somewhere far, far away, Brett could hear the evil laughter of the outlaws. The pain in his shoulder was excruciating, but he was about to attempt movement when he froze to hear one of the men saying, "Are you sure the driver's dead? Maybe you ought to put another bullet in his head to make sure."

"Aw, shit, he was dead 'fore he hit the ground," came a confident response from another. "No need to waste ammunition. They're all dead. Let's go."

Someone hooted, "Good haul. That old biddy had a

diamond brooch that'll keep me in whiskey and whores for a year."

Another snickered. "Yeah, I'll be needin' to find some of both after wastin' my time with the young filly. Hell, she died before I could finish."

"You choked her to death."

"Let's go," came an impatient call from afar. "It's a long way to California, and I want to put as many tracks between me and war as I can."

Someone else laughed. "We gonna all feel real bad about runnin' out on our neighbors if the South wins."

"Hell, California's better'n cotton fields."

They rode away, shrieking and laughing over the carnage.

Brett realized, in a flash of white-hot pain and nausea, that he was unable to move his left arm. Struggling to removehis shirt with only one hand, he gritted his teeth as he pressed it against the wound to try to slow the bleeding. As he did so, he looked around at the scene of massacre.

Florence, stripped naked, limbs grotesquely twisted, stared heavenward with glazed eyes. The other woman lay dead a few feet away. Two of the men had been dragged outside and shot in the head, the others had been murdered in their seats.

There had been six of them. Brett had seen them through half-closed lids. He had no doubt they were the Reb deserters the station manager had warned him about, but it had all happened too fast. He never had a chance. Maybe if Seth had been along, things would have turned out different.

Thinking of Seth caused Brett to remember the man who'd been sitting in his place. Shakily getting to his feet, he walked around the coach. Adam was lying face down, blood oozing from a bullet hole in his back. Brett started to turn away but hesitated when he heard a moan. Moving as fast as pain would allow, he went to kneel beside Adam and roll him over. He was still alive but fading fast.

Brett saw him trying to move his lips. "Don't try to talk," he ordered tersely, "They didn't steal the team. I'll take you with me back to the way station."

He started to move away to get a horse ready to ride, but with startling strength, Adam's hand snaked out to grab his good arm. "No. No time. I'm goin', and I don't mind, 'cause Martha and Leroy are waitin', but you gotta take it. I can tell you're a man in torment. The gold will ease your pain. Might as well take it. I ain't got no use for it where I'm goin'. Streets are already paved in gold. . . . " He attempted a rueful laugh, but began to cough, choking on his own blood, which now bubbled from his lips. With his last shred of strength, he pointed to his feet. "Boots . . . map . . ."

With one last gasp, Adam Barnes died.

Brett got up and staggered toward the nervously pawing horses. He began to unfasten the harness of the one closest to him. Bleeding badly, he wasn't concerned with the man's dying words. It was only when he was about to try and mount the horse that it dawned on him maybe he was a fool to pass up the offer.

Returning, he knelt again. Barnes had pointed at his feet and said "boots." Brett removed the left one, ran his fingers inside, but found nothing. Repeating the slow, torturous movements, for he could only use one hand, he managed to yank off the remaining boot. This time, when he felt inside, he touched paper, drawing it out to unfold and see that it was indeed a crudely drawn map of Adam Barnes's unstaked gold mine. As he'd said, no one would ever stumble across it, for it looked to be well hidden.

One day, Brett halfheartedly promised himself, he'd come back and search for it. But right now, he knew he had to get help or he was going to die like the others.

And he didn't want to die.

Not now.

Because suddenly he had a mission.

He was going to get over his wound and then, by damn, he was going to war.

Maybe, he told himself amidst the blinding sea of anguish, fighting for the Union against the South was the only revenge he'd ever have against the Sinclairs.

Capt. John Drew sighed and looked at the lovely young girl standing next to him at the ship's railing. He saw the heated glow of determination in her fiery green eyes and knew it was hopeless to argue. They'd arrived in Philadelphia the day before, and ever since hearing the news that had everyone on the waterfront excited, he'd been arguing with her to return with him to England.

She lifted her chin in firm resolve. "I've come this far. I can make it the rest of the way on my own, but you did promise Mr. Rozelle you'd help me find passage on to New Orleans."

"I know, I know, and I told you I spoke with a captain last night who's willing to try and get you through the blockade. He says the navy has been somewhat tolerant of fishermen once they search their boat and make sure they're only out for food, and not smuggling goods to the Confederates.

"But that's not the point, Miss Sinclair. I told you. The latest word is that those two forts guarding the mouth of the Mississippi and New Orleans are under heavy bombardment by the Union navy, and once they fall, there's nothing to stop the fleet from taking New Orleans. It's a bad time for you to try and make it there. If you won't go back with me, at least let me settle you into a nice hotel where you can wait till things calm down a bit."

Anjele refused even to consider such a delay. The closer the ship had got to America, the more she'd felt the burning, driving need to get home as fast as possible. If New Orleans, and BelleClair, were destined to fall to the enemy, she wanted to be with her father when it happened. With her mother dead, he had no one, for well she knew Claudia would be no comfort.

She took a deep, resigned breath, looked him squarely in the eye, and fiercely, finally, declared, "I'm going. And you can't stop me."

Captain Drew rolled his eyes, threw up his hands in surrender but could not resist the proclamation, "And God help the Yankees if they dare to try."

CHAPTER 14

LEO *TIPPED THE BOTTLE STRAIGHT UP TO* get the last drop of winc. He was drunk. Otherwise, he would not have let darkness catch him inside the gates of the cemetery. But he'd had to steal the wine, and just as he was slipping it off the store shelf and into his pocket, he was spotted. He took off running and wound up hiding in the cemetery, figuring to lay low awhile till they stopped looking for him. But there was so much turmoil he doubted the storekeeper had reported the theft. So he had made himself comfortable, leaning back against a tombstone, and proceeded to drink the entire bottle. Let the rest of New Orleans get hysterical over the Yankees coming, he laughed to himself more than once. He didn't give a damn, as long as he had something to drink.

Only now he didn't, he brooded, wondcring what to do next. He could hear bells ringing, shouts and screams—the sounds of panic. The sky toward the waterfront was glowing from the fires blazing along the pier. Dizzily, he remembered someone talking about how the Yankees couldn't be stopped, so thousands of bales of cotton had been hauled from warehouses to the levee and set on fire.

Sugar and tobacco warehouses were also ablaze.

Leo didn't care. The whole damn city could burn to the ground for all he cared. He was going to close his eyes in hope the spinning would stop, and maybe he'd fall asleep. When he woke up, he'd go out there, and with everybody in a panic, he could steal some more wine, and nobody would even notice.

Seth White gave the iron door of the tomb a tug, and it opened with only a mild grating sound. From the glow of the crimson sky, he could tell the others were already inside. "It's mass hysteria out there," he said to no one in particular. "New Orleans is a smoking inferno. People have gone crazy."

"Of course they have," Millard DuBose remarked drily. "What do you expect? When Lovell withdrew his troops, it left us defenseless."

Hardy Maxwell said, "Hell, yes, and nearly every Confederate soldier in southern Louisiana and Mississippi was sent off to Virginia last month."

Dr. Vinson Duval, sitting in the rocking chair Alma Tutwiler unfortunately never got to use, surveyed his surroundings as the others raged on about the crisis. Two coffins, set in brick vaults and covered with a large concrete slab, dominated the small, square room. The stained-glass window at the rear and the two rectangular windows set in the iron door provided light by day, but with no ventilation the air was stale, almost fetid. He would much have preferred to meet elsewhere but agreed with the others this was the safest place. Joining his cohorts' conversation, he pointed out, "We knew once the Federal fleet sailed past the forts, New Orleans was doomed, gentlemen, just as we knew General Lovell had been busy making plans to evacuate. He ordered all light artillery and shells to be hauled away, as well as clothing, blankets, medicine, wagons, harnesses, and leather. Dear God." He shook his head in dismay, "He took everything but the heavy guns on the levee, which are useless without shot. There's nothing for New Orleans to do but avoid bloodshed and surrender."

Tobias Radford cried, "Have you been to the levees? Have any of you?" He glanced about wildly in the darkness, straining to see their faces. "It's a howling mob of old men, women, and children, all armed with knives and pistols. They know they haven't got a chance, but it's their way of showing contempt for the goddamned Yankees."

Seth kicked the side of the concrete vault and grimaced with pain but nonetheless raged, "And it's all because of overconfidence, inept military strategy, cowardice, lack of preparation, and Richmond's bullheaded determination to protect Virginia, goddamn it!"

"Well, we can't do anything about any of it now, gentlemen," Millard DuBose calmly interjected, "except to remember why this meeting was called and get to the business at hand so we can finish and get back to try and protect our homes and families, shall we?"

"A hell of a lot of good it's gonna do," Hardy said with a snort. "If we do succeed in setting up communication to get information to the Confederates as to what's going on, what difference will it make?"

Dr. Duval reminded, "We can't be cut off from the rest of the world, Hardy. We've got to let our forces know what's happening here. And I haven't given up hope of an eventual counterattack.

"And Millard is right," he added, "We do need to get to the business at hand. It was dangerous for us to come here tonight. I fear there're going to be turncoats seeking favors from the enemy, who'll be eager to tell them they saw a group of prominent businessmen heading into the St. Louis cemetery after dark. It won't take much of an imagination to figure out what we were doing here."

"Exactly," Seth chimed in to agree, then suddenly remembered, "There was a man slumped against a tombstone as I came in. He appeared to be drunk, passed out, but I find it unusual for a man to come into the cemetery at night to do his drinking. Did anyone else see him?"

Millard spoke up. "Yes, and he's harmless. That's Leo Cody. Several years ago he worked for Elton as an overseer. They had a falling out over something. Elton never said why."

"I remember that," Tobias offered. "He came to me looking for work. I checked with Elton, and he said not to hire him, so I didn't. That was awhile back, come to think of it. Since then, I've noticed him from time to time, usually drunk in a gutter. I don't think he's a spy," he added with a chuckle.

Millard said, "He hates Elton. Remember when I told you-all about following him here to try and get him to come to a meeting? Well, Leo was here that day, too. Elton didn't notice him, but Leo saw him. Cursed him and threw a bottle at him after he'd passed. Maybe it's a good thing Elton didn't come tonight. Leo might have thrown another bottle."

Finally deciding they were safe, the men settled down to business.

Outside, several rows away, Leo had succumbed to drunken slumber. No one else was about, for those who had not evacuated New Orleans were either huddled fearfully in their homes, or had joined the motley crowd at the levees in a futile effort to resist the invaders.

He awoke sometime later with a start. Sitting upright, he glanced about wildly, trying to remember where he was. He ignored the grinding headache as he told himself it had to be a dream—no one had really spoken to him, called him by name. And damn it, he was getting out of here as fast as his trembling legs would carry him.

"Yes, Leo, I'm talking to you."

He'd been about to hit the ground running, but froze. The voice was coming from behind the large tombstone directly in front of him. He couldn't see anything except the ghostly white of the marker framed against the glow coming from the flaming waterfront. Choked by the soot-filled air, he coughed, and begged, "Leave me be. I ain't done nothin'. . . ."

"No one is going to harm you, Leo. Not if you stay where you are and listen. If you run away, I'll find you, and I'll kill you."

Leo was not a superstitious man. He did not believe in ghosts. Still, he didn't like cemeteries, and he particularly didn't like the sound of a voice coming from behind a tombstone, calling him by his name, damn it, and threatening to kill him. And the voice didn't sound mean, either. The tone, he noted through the sickening haze of wine, was cultured, refined, and very matter-of-fact. Yet, Leo sensed, somehow the man behind the voice was quite capable of making good his promise of death.

Swallowing hard, gritting his teeth, Leo warily responded to The Voice. "All right, I'm listenin'. Who the hell are you, and what do you want?"

"It doesn't matter who I am. What does matter is that I've got a job for you."

"A job?" Leo snickered. "New Orleans is on fire. By this time tomorrow, Yankees are gonna be crawling all over the place, and my head is bustin' from too much wine. And I'm supposed to believe a voice from behind a tombstone is gonna give me a job?"

The Voice said, "No harm will come to you if you listen."

"I tell you, I'm listening." Leo turned his head, not wanting to keep staring at the tombstone. If he did, he would start believing it was doing the talking, not a voice from behind, and then he'd surely go stark raving mad.

"You know a man named Elton Sinclair." It was a statement, not a question.

At that, Leo whipped his head about to stare, despite his resolve. "Oh, yes. I sure do. What's that bastard got to do with all this?"

The Voice chuckled. "Well, what does he have to do with your not being able to find decent work since he ran you off his place?"

"He said I beat his slaves and he made sure nobody else would hire me. But like I said, what's he got to do with this job you got for me?"

"I want you to follow him. I want to know every move he makes, but he mustn't know he's being spied on. I want to know everywhere he goes, who he talks to. Day and night."

"I can do that," Leo said cockily, "But why? What's

so important about Sinclair?"

The Voice suddenly changed from cool arrogance to thick annoyance. "That's not your concern. Your job is to watch him, damn it, and report everything to me here, once a week."

Leo thought the whole idea of trailing after Sinclair was ridiculous but wanted to see how far The Voice would go. "How much it is worth for me to tell you these things?"

"Never mind what it's worth to me, you idiot. It can be worth twenty dollars a week to you."

Leo's head was spinning again, but this time, not from too much wine. "Did you say twenty?"

"I did. But don't get any ideas about deceiving me, pretending you're following him when you aren't. I'll know if you lie to me, because I'm familiar with his habits. It's a break in his routine I'm looking for. You're to report here every Sunday at midnight. Go to the Tutwiler tomb, three rows inside the east gate. Stand outside and after you've made sure no one is about, start talking. Don't attempt to enter the tomb."

"Don't worry. That's the last thing I'd ever do . . . unless I had to go looking for my money," he added pointedly.

"That won't be necessary. Your money for the previous week will be on the ledge above the door. If I'm satisfied with what you've reported, you'll be paid the next week, and so on.

"He should be easy to watch," The Voice continued. "Since his wife died, he doesn't go anywhere. Doesn't do anything. You'll be able to spot a break in his routine."

"Didn't know his wife died," Leo mumbled, not really caring, then ventured to ask, "What do I call you, by the way?"

"There's no need for you to call me anything. Now get yourself together and get out to BelleClair tonight. I'll want a report Sunday night."

Leo grinned. He was starting to feel real good. It was going to be nice to have some money, and what could be easier than spying on a man he despised? God, he hoped he caught Sinclair doing something real bad, something that would get him in trouble, maybe even hanged. Excited over the possibility, he wanted a drink to celebrate and was suddenly hungry. Despite the hysteria, there ought to be food available somewhere in the city, for a price. "Hey . . . how about an advance? I ain't got nothin' right now, and I can't remember when I ate last."

Only silence came from the tombstone.

Leo repeated his request.

No sound.

Slowly, cautiously, he moved from where he'd been sitting on the vault and tiptoed to peek around the monument opposite.

No one was there.

The Voice had quietly left the cemetery.

They heard the devastating news long before sailing into the Mississippi Sound. Captain Brannigan had wanted to turn back off the coast of Florida, when they'd been flagged by a passing boat that reported the Confederacy had lost eight ships in a futile attempt to stop Farragut's fleet.

"They're not going to let us through," Captain

Brannigan predicted. "If me and my crew weren't too old and grizzled to fight and also flying a white flag of neutrality, we'd have been blown to bits by now, anyway. We've passed three Federal ships so far."

Not about to be dissuaded, Anjele doggedly said, "You were well paid to try, Captain, and that's all I'm asking you to do—try. But if you're afraid, then put me ashore and I'll make it the rest of the way on my own."

He wasn't about to abandon her, and she knew it. Stiffly he promised, "I'll go as far as I can, but when they turn me back, it's over, missy, and if you want to jump overboard then and swim ashore, that's your privilege."

Anjele knew if it came to that, she probably would but didn't say so.

Finally, the sky ahead became thick with smoke, and they began to smell the acrid odor from the still smoldering fires along the levee. Around them were moored other boats which had dropped anchor, not knowing what to do since they weren't allowed to go any farther. Like Captain Brannigan, the captains were fishermen, not soldiers, wanting no part of the war.

Anjele stood at the helm, her long red hair flowing around her shoulders. Cheeks flushed by the wind, clothes damp from the salt spray, she wasn't thinking of anything except how desperate she was to get home. After all these years, to think of New Orleans falling to the enemy was more than she could bear. And now, more than ever, she wanted, needed, to be with her father.

She jumped at the sound of Captain Brannigan's curses and asked, "What is it? What's wrong?" Following his gaze she muttered an oath of her own. A Federal gunboat was coming toward them.

The wooden paddle steamer had been adapted for war, outfitted against shellfire with a girdle of thick planking.

"Those are Parrott guns," Brannigan observed, "and they can blow this boat right out of the water.

"Drop anchor!" He yelled over his shoulder to no one in particular. "Now!"

Anjele watched as the gunboat drew alongside. When it was close enough for a boarding plank to be placed between the two vessels, an officer and two sailors carrying rifles came aboard.

The officer brusquely introduced himself as Captain Durham and wanted to know what the fishing boat was doing in the waters. "In case you haven't noticed, there's a war going on," he sarcastically addressed Brannigan.

"He's working for me," Anjele stepped forward to give him her name and quickly explain the situation. "So you see," she finished, "we're no threat to anyone, and you have to let us through the blockade, so I can get home."

Captain Durham smiled at such a ludicrous request and with exaggerated patience informed her, "Yesterday our navy either blew up or sank the last defense of New Orleans. Captain Farragut has sent a flagship to the city with a summons to surrender. We've heard the mayor has refused, and we're waiting now to see what will happen next. I'm not about to let this boat go through."

Brannigan spoke up. "I can understand your position, sir, and hearing all this, I don't want to head in there, anyway. But what's going to happen? You aren't going to bombard the city, are you?"

Captain Durham gloated, "It won't be necessary. We

hear when Farragut asked for women and children to be evacuated so they won't be harmed in the fighting, the mayor sent word back he didn't want any shooting, because there wasn't anybody left in the city to fight except those women and children.

"But," he added, "Captain Farragut also sent a message he's getting ready to go in, and if one shot is fired, he will level New Orleans to the ground."

Anjele bristled to think of her beloved city being destroyed. "Damn you!" She ground out the words between clenched teeth, green eyes flashing fire. "Damn every single one of you murdering Yankees!"

Brannigan groaned under his breath and turned away. He had witnessed Anjele Sinclair's temper before, when a crewman was foolish enough to be familiar, and he didn't want the officer thinking he condoned her behavior.

Irately, Captain Durham reminded, "We've lost many good men, Miss Sinclair. Both sides are suffering."

"Then go home!" she raged. "Get the hell out of the South and go back up North and mind your own business. We can solve our problems without your interference. Given enough time, states will vote to do away with slavery. There's no need for this. Oh, what's the use?" She threw up her hands, knew she was only wasting her breath.

With the careful self-control which qualified him to be an officer, Captain Durham addressed Captain Brannigan, coolly ordering, "You will have to turn back. Get out of these waters, sir. You are forbidden to tarry. If this boat is still here by morning, I cannot guarantee your safety."

When they were gone, Captain Brannigan walked

over to where Anjele was standing at the railing, glaring at the Yankees watching from the gunboat. He tried to lighten the tension by saying, "Well, I guess this is where you'll have to jump overboard and swim, if you want to go ashore. Better wait till dark, though. You made some enemies, I'm afraid, and they might just use you for target practice while you're swimming in."

"We aren't beaten yet."

"Oh, yes ma'am, we are." He gave the order to haul anchor.

Anjele clutched his arm as she whispered desperately, "They won't see us at night."

Wearily, he touched his fingers to his brow and absently began to rub. With the patience one uses to address a child, he asked, "And where would you have us go, Miss Anjele?"

Excitedly, she cried, "We don't have to go in by way of New Orleans. You can take me all the way home on the river. It flows right in front of my house, and—"

"No ma'am!" Captain Brannigan vigorously shook his head. "I'm not going up that river. No telling how many federal boats there are up and down there, anticipating folks trying to get in and out that way."

"Then we'll cross the river at Main Pass and go up through Barataria Bay. I know that passageway. Poppa used to pay the riverboats to take us that way sometimes. I'll know exactly where you can drop me off so I'll be just a few miles from where our land borders Bayou Perot, and I can go the rest of the way on foot. Oh, please, Captain Brannigan," she implored, "Don't you see? It's my only chance."

"All right," he gave in, angry with himself for his weakness. "And if they catch us and take away my boat, or blow us up, it'll be my own fault for being such a damned fool."

She stood on tiptoe to kiss his whiskered cheek, and offered a silent prayer for safe passage for all of them.

And soon, she sang to herself over and over, she'd be home.

CHAPTER 15

IT HAD BEEN TWO DAYS, AND CLAUDIA WAS still shaken by the experience of standing on the riverbank watching the Federal fleet heading for New Orleans. To actually see the invading enemy had been terrifying. For weeks, the waterway had been a churning mass of all kinds of crafts carrying away people who had chosen to abandon their homes. Now, with Raymond having just come from the city to report the crushing news of official surrender, hysteria was a choking knot in her throat as she worried over what the future held for BelleClair.

Raymond said she needed to look at the bright side. "Maybe it won't be so bad. Financially, your father is better off than a lot of other planters, because he was smart enough to think about what might happen if the war wasn't over as quick as most folks thought. He started growing more corn for food and thinking about how he'd get his crops out when the blockade tightened. Taking them to Texas proved a lifesaver. He's set now. He can keep his slaves fed and clothed, and because he's always treated them decent, he doesn't have to worry about a rebellion, like so many other slave owners.

"Yes," he lifted his glass of whiskey in salute, "I'd say Elton Sinclair can be proud. All he's got to do is sign an oath of allegiance to the Union, and BelleClair is spared."

Claudia turned on him in disgust. "It's a good thing he did plan ahead, because he's certainly useless now, the way he wallows in self-pity over Twyla dying. And you're no help, either. Look at you. All you do is drink. What's going to happen if the Yankees attack here? What's going to keep me from being ravished?"

"Your mouth." He grinned and hiccupped. "Just nag at them, like you do at me, and they'll run the other way."

"Damn you!" she shrieked, whirling away in a swish of petticoats and silk. "You're nothing but a lazy drunkard, and a coward as well."

He drained his glass before responding, "Lazy, only because there's nothing to do. Drunk, because it's the only way I can stand being around you. As for being a coward . . ." He laughed harshly as he stretched out his leg, wounded in battle at Bull Run the previous summer, leaving him with an awkward limp and unfit for battle. "I didn't get this running away from the fighting, my dear. I was headed straight into it. I can hardly be called a coward."

"You're a coward not to be in New Orleans right now," she lashed out, "trying to hold off the Yankees, like your father is doing, instead of hiding here and drinking yourself into a stupor."

He reached for the bottle and poured himself another drink. "New Orleans is lost. Only a fool would stand and fight now. That's why only women and children are left. The men have taken off to regroup or fight elsewhere. As for my father, he's staying because he declared neutrality a long time ago.

"But you can be sure," he added with a snicker, "He'll be among the first to sign a loyalty oath. Father always thinks of money, first, and he'll want to establish himself as a trust worthy physician for the Union forces and their families, so he won't be relegated to prison duty."

"Well, it's time you started thinking about money, too," Claudia snapped. "The white overseers went off to war, and the Negroes taking their places aren't competent. Elton won't come out of his grief long enough to do anything about it, and I need some help running things."

Suddenly struck by curiosity, Raymond asked, "Why do you never refer to him as your father?"

Coldly she replied, "Because he isn't."

"That's absurd. Both he and Twyla raised you like their own daughter. You were even treated better than Anjele, and you know it."

Claudia bristled in defense, "They promised your parents you could marry their firstborn daughter, and if they'd thought of me that way, I wouldn't have had to chase after you, would I? And the truth is"—she walked over to tower above him, so he could feel her wrath as she glared down at him—"you'd still be pining for her now, if I hadn't told you the truth about what a whore she is. You'd never have married me, would you?"

He saw no reason to lie. Perhaps once upon a time he would have. In those early days, when he'd been so angry to learn of Anjele's immoral behavior he'd allowed himself to be manipulated into marrying Claudia, he would have prevaricated to spare her feelings. But he'd quickly realized the mistake he'd made and discovered she was even a bigger bitch than he'd ever dreamed possible. His had been a miserable existence ever since, and if the truth be known, at the time he'd gone into battle, he really hadn't cared whether he lived or died. "No," he said finally, firmly, matching her contemptuous gaze with one of his own, "I damn sure wouldn't."

In a flash, she snatched the glass from his hand and threw the whiskey in his face. "Bastard! I hate you! Stay here and rot, for all I care."

She fled from the room and ran down the hall, down the curving stairway and all the way into the study where she was surprised to find Elton.

He was leaning back in his chair, staring out the window, lost within himself.

"I'm surprised you aren't at the mausoleum. In fact," she added sarcastically, "I'm surprised you haven't moved in there with her coffin."

Elton ignored her.

Suddenly, she could take no more and slammed her palms down on the desk and unleashed the fury she'd been holding inside, "Listen to me! You've got to stop feeling sorry for yourself. People die. Life goes on. And you've got to come out of this and start helping me look after things around here. New Orleans is falling, and you need to go see whoever is in charge of the Union army and let them know BelleClair stands with them."

He remained silent.

"You don't care, do you?" she accused incredulously. "When Twyla died, you gave up. You don't care about BelleClair, and you don't care about me."

He glanced up at her then, frowning. She was a mean and selfish girl. He'd not seen her shed one tear over Twyla's passing. He felt sorry for Raymond for having married her, and he cursed himself for being so weak as to allow her to move back into the house.

Still, he said nothing.

"Maybe I need to ask Dr. Duval to send you away to an asylum," she threatened coolly. "Maybe you belong in one of those places where they put crazy people, because I think you've lost your mind."

At that, he was driven to defend himself, "I am quite sane, Claudia, but if you want to be close to the Yankees, why don't you move back to New Orleans—if Ida Duval will let you live with her," he added tartly.

"Oh, I'm not going anywhere." She gave her head an insolent toss. "This is my home, whether you like it or not, and I won't see it destroyed because of your weakness."

"There is nothing to be done. What will be, will be. My slaves know they're free to go whenever they choose. They choose to stay, because they know here they'll be fed and clothed and have a roof over their heads. When the Yankees come, I'll assure them we offer no resistance. Now get out of here." He waved her away in disgust. "Go back to New Orleans, or somewhere, but get out of my sight. You're a disgrace to your mother's memory, the way you're treating me."

Claudia breezed out, head held high, waiting till she was in the hallway before calling back, "She wasn't my mother, and you aren't my father!"

Elton wasn't stung by her words and hoped she remembered them after he was gone, so that when the will he had rewritten after Twyla's death was read, Claudia would know why he'd left everything to Anjele.

Anjele.

His heart ached at the thought of the daughter he loved and missed so much. The decision for her to remain in Europe had not come easily. He needed her with him now, more than ever. Never had he felt so alone. But it was best she stay where she was. The future of BelleClair, and Louisiana, and of all the South, for that matter, was unknown.

His face tightened as he thought of the hidden plates that would be quite valuable to the Confederacy. All he had to do was wait till things calmed down a bit after the takeover of New Orleans, and he'd find a way to get the plates to the proper people.

Soon, he mused, templing his fingers and staring through them, he could make his move.

Claudia slumped into a wicker rocker on the front porch. Maybe she should go into New Orleans herself and pledge BelleClair's loyalty. She would have to wait awhile, of course, till things settled down and the Union authorities took complete control.

Long ago she'd decided she really didn't care who won the war, so long as BelleClair survived. If the North won, the slaves would, no doubt, be freed, but they'd have to find work somewhere. She could give them their precious freedom on paper, but if they didn't want to starve, if they wanted a roof over their heads, they'd work for whatever she offered to pay. BelleClair was prosperous. She could afford it.

She had also decided to take over, little by little, even before Elton died. And that, she mused with evil satisfaction, wouldn't be long, the way he was withering away in his grief and misery.

As for Raymond, she vowed he would soon learn his place. No matter she'd realized he was a weakling, she wasn't ready to let him go. For a time, when they had begun to have fights and drift apart, she'd feared he would leave her. But as time passed, it became obvious he was clinging to her for security, because his parents weren't at all happy over the marriage and had let him know he was on his own financially.

They'd moved in with the Duvals after their marriage, but within a week Claudia had insisted they find somewhere else to live. She couldn't stand Ida, and the feeling was mutual.

Twyla wouldn't hear of her moving back home, saying Raymond had made it quite clear he wanted to live in the city, and she should obey her husband's wishes. So she had moved into a hotel and rented an entire floor and charged the bill to his father. Raymond then had to start selling off his valuable horses to support them, and Claudia worried about what would happen when the money ran out. Fortunately, Twyla solved the problem by dying, and Claudia began making plans to move back into the mansion before Twyla was even cold. And now, by God, she swore with gritted teeth, nobody was going to make her leave—even the Yankees, because she intended to make her peace with them as soon as possible.

The sound of horses approaching brought her to her feet. Shielding her eyes with her hand against the glaring late-afternoon sun, she groaned when she recognized Ida Duval's buggy, moving fast. It was obvious something was wrong, and Claudia went back into the house long enough to call to Kesia to go and tell

Master Raymond his mother was coming.

Ben, the Duvals' driver, reined the horses to a stop and leaped down to assist his mistress in alighting. With Ida was her personal maid, Flossie, who began handing bags to Ben.

Claudia stiffened with the realization that it looked as though Ida was moving in. "What do you think you're doing?"

"Yankees!" Ida raced up the stairs, calling for Raymond.

Claudia was right behind her. Who did think she was, showing up this way, uninvited, commanding her servants to bring in her luggage. "Of all the nerve . . . ."

But Ida didn't hear her. Raymond and Elton both appeared at the same time—Elton running from his study, and Raymond hobbling down the stairs with his cane.

"Mother, what is it?" He held her at arm's length, searching her face.

"Yankees!" She repeated and tore from his embrace to breeze into the parlor adjacent to the foyer. Making herself at home by flopping on the sofa, she brusquely ordered Kesia, hovering nearby, to bring her a cool lemonade, and only then did she share her dreadful news. "All over the city. Moving in. Taking over houses. Throwing people out on the streets. Terrible. It's just terrible." She began to fan herself frantically with her lace handkerchief.

Raymond attempted to soothe her, "Mother, we knew this was going to happen. You've got to get hold of yourself."

"I didn't think they'd be throwing people out of their homes," she wailed, leaning back and closing her eyes and moving her lips as though in frenzied prayer, then glanced about wildly and cried, "As I was leaving, I actually saw them raising their flag over City Hall. Can you imagine? And the whole town is in an uproar. Total bedlam. No one knows what's going to happen next. I knew I had to get out of there."

At that, Claudia cried, "Why did you come *here*? We certainly have enough problems of our own without your adding to them."

Raymond winced and whispered, "Claudia, please . . ." Then he limped over to sit beside Ida and ask, "Where's Daddy? Why didn't he come with you?"

With a scathing glance at Claudia, Ida responded to Raymond, "You know your father. He's going to stay in his office, in case he's needed, and goodness knows, he already is. I stopped by to tell him I was leaving to come out here, and he was going mad, treating everyone from looters being shot by storekeepers to women fainting." She looked at Elton, remembering, "He said to tell you if you need him later, you know where he'll be."

Elton knew what Vinson meant, and he had no intention of going to St. Louis cemetery for their clandestine meeting. Not now. Not ever.

Ida talked on about the nightmare situation, and when she was spent, asked Elton, "Which rooms shall I take?"

Before he could respond, Claudia gasped, "Surely you don't think we can allow you to move in here. Why, this isn't a hotel, for heaven's sake. If word gets out we took you-all in, next thing you know, it'll be said BelleClair is offering shelter to those running from the Yankees, and I won't have that. You'll have to leave."

"Why, she'll do nothing of the kind," Raymond was

quick to protest, turning to Elton for support. "Don't you agree, sir? Families need to be together at a time like this."

Elton shrugged. It made no difference to him what any of them did. "I've got to go make my rounds." He walked out, head down, shoulders slumped.

"He hasn't made his rounds in weeks," Claudia sneered. "And if it weren't for the overseers, even unfit as they are, nothing would get done, and who's keeping an eye on them? Certainly not you," she accused Raymond.

He spread his hands in a helpless gesture and said, "I'm no planter, Claudia. You know that." He struggled to stand, leaning on his cane for support. "I'm going to show Mother to her room now."

"I told you, I don't want her here," Claudia frostily repeated. "We aren't taking in fugitives."

Ida wailed in protest. "I'm not a fugitive. I just want to be with my son. What's wrong with that?" Tears began streaming down her cheeks and she hated herself for it. The last thing she wanted was for this hateful, spiteful girl to know she had the power to make her cry.

Raymond was getting madder by the minute. "Claudia, you've no right to act this way. And I'll remind you this is now my home, too, and my mother is welcome here."

Claudia lifted her chin in contempt. "I didn't feel welcome in hers. That's why I left."

"That was your decision. She didn't ask you to leave."

"Didn't ask me to stay, either."

Ida knew she could stand no more. It was bad enough, being in the midst of a war, sharing the grief of friends whose sons had already been killed in battle.

Witnessing the fall of her beloved New Orleans had been heartbreaking. But now, to be treated so rudely by her daughter-in-law was more than she could bear. She forced her trembling legs to stand. "I think I will be getting back . . . ." she began, but Raymond wouldn't hear of it.

"You're staying. And if Daddy doesn't come tonight, I'll ride in tomorrow and see how he is. Now come along. I want you to lie down and rest till supper and stop worrying. Everything is going to be all right. I'll take care of you."

Claudia muttered to hell with both of them and went to the study, closing and locking the door behind her. She knew Elton hadn't gone to make any rounds. He'd headed straight for the mausoleum again, to sit next to Twyla's casket and talk to her as if she could hear him. She had followed him once and stood outside to listen. It had been like hearing the mutterings of a man gone insane, which made her all the more determined to prepare herself to take over BelleClair. He certainly was no longer capable, and this was the only time she was able to go through the journals.

She had not been there long when Raymond pounded on the door, infuriated over how she'd treated his mother and wanting to discuss it. "Go away," she snapped. "I don't care what either one of you do. Just leave me alone. Why don't you go have another drink?" she added tauntingly.

He stood there a moment, then went to do just that.

It was late when Elton finally returned to the house. Reluctantly, and only because Raymond insisted, Ida had come downstairs for supper, and when she saw Elton shuffle through the foyer and continue up the stairs, she nudged Raymond and urged, "Do go try and get him to join us. The man is going to grieve himself to death."

Raymond obliged, but Claudia huffily declared it wouldn't do any good. "You're only coddling him, which is the worst thing you can do. He's only trying to get attention, anyway. Leave him alone, and when he gets hungry, he'll eat."

Raymond ignored her and went upstairs.

Ida stared at her in astonishment.

Claudia noticed and cried, "Why are you looking at me like that?"

Ida drew a deep breath, let it out slowly. Dear Lord, she knew she should keep her mouth shut, but enough was enough. "How can you speak of your father in such a way? You should be ashamed of yourself, Claudia."

"He's not my father."

"He's raised you, taken care of you, loved you . . . "

Claudia sneered, "Oh, what do you know, Ida? You hate me, anyway. If you'd had your way, Raymond would've married Anjele, and you'd have liked that, wouldn't you?"

"Yes." Ida didn't hesitate, now that it was out in the open. "I would have. Anjele is a sweet, sensible girl. She doesn't have a haughty bone in her body."

Claudia glared at her, resisting the impulse to slap her.

Raymond came back in, hung his cane on the back of his chair, and sat down. Sensing something was going on, he looked at each of them in turn before wearily asking, "Well, what is it this time?"

"Your mother was just saying how she wished you'd

married Anjele instead of me," Claudia told him, "but it's no secret. I've always known she felt that way."

Ida shook her head and reached to cover his hand with hers. "It wasn't exactly like that, dear. She asked me, and forgive me if I was wrong to do so, but I told the truth."

He shook his head and reached for the wine decanter to refill his glass.

With a sniff of disdain, Claudia admonished, "You drink more than you eat."

He downed the wine in one swallow, and proceeded to pour another.

Ida, unable to watch, and wishing she'd stayed in New Orleans despite everything, excused herself and left the table.

With Elton no doubt in bed for the night, Claudia knew she could spend the time going over the journals and was about to leave herself, when Kesia came running in to announce, "A rider comin' in hard, Master Raymond."

"Tell me, not him," Claudia snapped, giving the old woman a shove as she got up to rush quickly by her. "He's not in charge here."

Kesia was used to Miss Claudia's temper and abuse and paid her no mind. Instead, she held out Master Raymond's cane and assisted him to his feet.

"Want me to find Master Sinclair?"

"No. I'm sure the overseers heard whoever it is, and they'll be alert to trouble." He hobbled into the foyer and through the front doors Claudia had flung open. He didn't like her standing there, so vulnerable, with trouble all around them and was about to say so, just as he recognized his father's horse and felt a chill of foreboding. In the dusky twilight, Raymond could see by his face that something was terribly wrong.

"Daddy, what is it?" he asked fearfully, limping closer to the edge of the porch. "Are the Yankees on their way here? To BelleClair?"

"Not yet. They've got to secure New Orleans before they start thinking about outlying sugar parishes. That may take weeks, months." He dismounted, tossing the reins to the waiting slave and taking the stairs two at a time, not bothering to tip his hat to Claudia. He despised her and found it quite difficult to be polite even under the best of circumstances, and at a time like this, he wasn't taking the trouble. He put his arm around Raymond's shoulder and urged, "Inside, son. We have to talk. Where's Elton? He needs to hear this, too."

Claudia was having no secrets kept from her and ran after them. "You two wait a minute. I've a right to know what's going on here."

"Later, Claudia," Vinson dismissed her, pushing his son gently into the study and slamming the door in her face.

"Damn you!" she shouted, then, not to be outdone, ran down the hall to the dining room. There was a storage closet for china connecting the two rooms. But once inside, she did not open the door adjoining the study, instead pressed her ear against it to listen.

And what she heard made her blood run cold.

"She's back," Vinson was excitedly telling Raymond. "Anjele is back. Someone who knows me recognized her as they were taking her into City Hall and came and told me. I went over there, but they wouldn't let me see her. We've got to get Elton and go back and see what we can do about getting her out."

"Out?" Raymond echoed, bewildered. "I don't understand."

VinsonElton hesitated, hating to have to be the bearer of such disturbing news but knew there was no easy way to say it. "Anjele is in jail, son. The Yankees are holding her prisoner."

CHAPTER 16

ANJELE SAT WITH HANDS PRIMLY FOLDED in her lap, teeth clamped tightly together in an effort to control her temper. Captain Brannigan had said that if she'd kept her mouth shut when the gunboat caught them sneaking into the Barataria Waterway, they would have been turned back again, instead of being taken into custody. Now, thanks to her, he and his crew were being detained till the Yankees decided whether they were actually Rebels passing themselves off as innocent fishermen. The boat had been confiscated, and Captain Brannigan worried it was gone from him forever, even if they didn't all wind up in a Federal prison.

"And it's your fault, damn you," he'd cursed Anjele. "You just had to say something about their mothers, didn't you?"

Anjele had surprised herself by being so crude, but at the time, with the Yankee soldiers roughly shoving her around, accusing her of being a spy, as well as insinuating she was onboard merely to provide sexual pleasure for the crewman, something had snapped. She had indeed given them a good tongue-lashing, which resulted in handcuffs and a very uncomfortable trip back the way they'd come, except this time they were on board a Federal gunboat, going directly into the port of New Orleans.

It had been late in the day when they'd arrived, and she was relieved when she was finally separated from Captain Brannigan and his crew. She really did feel badly about their plight and tried to tell them, but they furiously refused to listen. So she was glad to escape their angry glares and muttered curses.

In the eerie glow of the still-burning fires on the levees and docks, Anjele was horrified at the scene of chaos and pandemonium. It tore her heart out to see her homeland invaded, and she was struck even harder with the desperate desire to get to BelleClair and find her father and make sure he was all right.

She was taken into City Hall, where a grim-faced Union officer named Major Tyler Hembree listened to her story, then accused her of lying. "I think the men on board are Confederate spies, and you"—he raked her with a contemptuous glare—"are merely a prostitute, traveling with them."

"That is absurd!" Anjele cried indignantly, "and if you will send for my father, he'll verify what I say is true."

"Tomorrow," he'd said, airily waving to a guard to take her away. "It's late. My dinner is waiting."

She'd been locked in a small cell, without privacy from the men on either side, and the night had passed miserably. At dawn, she was taken to a closet where a bucket had been placed for her toilet, then returned to her confinement. Breakfast was a cup of water, a piece of bread, and a chunk of boiled salt pork, which she gladly gave to one of the other prisoners.

It was nearly noon when she had once more been taken

downstairs to wait in the office which had been commandeered by Major Hembree, only she hadn't seen him.

A soldier sitting at a nearby desk leered at her till she couldn't stand it any longer. "Why do you keep staring at me?" she yelled at him. "Haven't you ever seen a woman before, or are all Yankee women as repugnant as you are?"

"Bitch," he muttered, turning away.

A few moments later, he got up and went out, no doubt to report her insolence to Major Hembree. Well, there was a limit to how much she could take, and whatever they planned to do with her, she wished they'd go ahead and do it and get it over with.

Finally the door opened, and Anjele glanced up, expecting to see another blue uniform. Instead, with a joyful lurch of her heart, she saw that it was her father. She leaped into his arms, crying, "Poppa, it's you. It's really you. Oh, thank God, thank God . . ."

"Girl, let me look at you," Elton said, choking on the knot in his throat, his own eyes welling with tears. Smoothing back her mussed hair, he shook his head and pretended to scold, "What do you mean, running away and coming all this way by yourself? Didn't you know the dangers? It's only through God's grace you made it."

"Did you think I could stay away? We need each other, Poppa. With Momma gone, and the war . . ." She blinked furiously, trying to get hold of herself. "I knew I had to come home and be with you."

"And you got yourself in a lot of trouble doing it." He managed a smile, wanting to lighten the mood, reluctant to talk about Twyla right then. "Now will you please tell me why they say those men you were with are spies?

"And we won't go into what they're saying about you," he added angrily. "Any other time, they know a father would shoot a man dead for insinuating such a thing about his daughter, but they're in control now, and they know it."

Anjele repeated her story, and he believed her, saying he felt that between Dr. Duval and him, they could straighten everything out.

"Dr. Duval is here?" Anjele asked, suddenly embarrassed to think of others hearing about this.

"He's the one who came and told me. One of his patients saw you being brought in and ran to tell him. He's outside now, talking to a Major Hembree.

"Vinson," he went on to confide, unable to keep the resentment from his voice, "has decided it's in his best interest to cooperate with the enemy. He has volunteered to provide medical services, which I suppose is preferable to being sent to a Yankee prison for the duration of the war. Claudia feels the same about BelleClair, but we can discuss all that later. The thing to do now is get you out of here and home."

While they waited to learn whether Dr. Duval was successful in his attempt to clear up the matter, Anjele recounted her voyage home.

Elton was astonished, as well as impressed by her courage and determination. "But where did you get the money?"

"I'll tell you all about that later." The door was opening, and she was anxious to hear the verdict but the moment she saw Dr. Duval's smiling face, she knew everything was all right.

Major Hembree was right behind him. Without offering any apology for how she'd been treated, he dismissed her by saying, “You can go.”

Elton grabbed her arm. “Let’s get out of here.”

She jerked free. “No, wait a minute.” Major Hembree had sat down behind his desk, and she walked over to ask, “Is that all you have to say?”

His brows snapped together. “What else needs to be said?”

Elton hurried to reach for her again, but she shrugged him away.

“You know now I was telling the truth, and I think you owe me an apology.”

He leaped up so quickly his chair toppled backward to hit the floor with a loud bang. Instinctively, Anjele pulled back, but he leaned so that his face was mere inches from hers, eyes bulging with fury, nostrils flaring, breath hot against her skin as he roared, “Let me tell you something, Miss Sinclair. You and all the citizens of New Orleans and surrounding parishes are now under the jurisdiction of the Union. We are in control now, and we will tolerate neither insolence or insubordination. I don’t owe you anything. You have been conquered, and you owe me gratitude for not having you hanged because of your disrespectful mouth.

“Now get out of here”—he pointed to the door—“before I change my mind.”

For a moment, Anjele stood there, ignoring the pleas of both her father and Dr. Duval to please come, now, before there was more trouble. Finally, she turned, but at the door turned to say quietly, “I am not conquered, Major Hembree. You can put me in jail, put me in chains, but you’ll never conquer my spirit. Just like you Yankees will never be able to conquer the spirit of the

South. And that's what counts."

"I'll remember you," he shouted as Elton and Dr. Duval pulled her from the room. "When General Butler gets here, you can be sure your name will be at the top of his list of Rebels to keep an eye on . . . ."

No one spoke till they were outside, and then Dr. Duval gave Anjele a belated welcome.

"Thanks for all you did for me." She clasped his hand. "I'm afraid this was a homecoming I wasn't prepared for, and I lost my temper."

"I'll agree on that," he nodded without smiling. He turned to Elton. "I appreciate your taking care of Ida for me. I'll get there as soon as I can, but there's much to be done here. Some of the soldiers are sick, and the fleet is short on doctors, so I'm doing what I can."

Anjele gasped. "Surely you aren't treating Yankees, Dr. Duval."

He regarded her coldly. Once, he had adored Anjele, but the fact was, if she hadn't rushed off to Europe, his son would probably not have married her dreadful sister. He shuddered to think of the distress it had caused Ida and him. The only reason he'd bothered to go fetch Elton to help her was that he knew Ida would want him to, regardless. "I'm a doctor," he crisply reminded her. "I treat anyone who is sick, regardless of which uniform he's wearing."

"I see." Her biting tone, her tightly set lips and flashing eyes, mirrored her disapproval.

Annoyed, Dr. Duval blazed, "It's time you realize how things are, Anjele, and get off your high horse."

"I don't care," Anjele spoke through clenched teeth, ignoring her father's prodding to get in the carriage. "I don't intend to make trouble, but neither will I bow down to those bastards. This is our home. They've no right to be here."

Dr. Duval shook his head. With her attitude, she was headed for trouble, and he was only wasting his time trying to make her realize that. Nodding to Elton, he turned away.

As they rode out of town, Elton urged Anjele to pay no attention to the Yankee soldiers roaming the streets.

She obliged, but with great effort. The scene was deplorable—people being dragged from their houses screaming and begging as Yankee officers moved in. Slaves, now freed, danced in the streets and sang in jubilation. "They won't be so happy when they get hungry and start wondering who's going to feed them," she quietly mused aloud, then, wanting to get her mind away from the present nightmare, asked, "How are things at BelleClair?"

Elton proceeded to tell her that not much had changed. "Our slaves have always been treated well, so I haven't had the problems a lot of the other planters have with belligerents and runaways. We planted full crops, and I'll keep on operating as I have been till we see what happens."

Anjele listened as he droned on, sensing he did not want to talk about her mother. She would wait till he was ready, and only then could the grief and heartache be shared.

They were almost home when Elton reluctantly, quietly, told her, "Claudia is here. She and Raymond moved in after"—he hesitated before murmuring softly—"your mother died. I hope it won't be difficult for you, them being there, I mean."

Anjele squeezed his hand. "Claudia has always been difficult, and if you want to know the truth, I never wanted to marry Raymond, anyway."

"I knew that," he said, flashing her an adoring smile, "and you want to know something else? I'm glad you're back, Angel."

Ida was waiting on the porch. Unlike Vinson, she didn't blame Anjele for Raymond's impulsive marriage. She hadn't liked her leaving as she did, however. Not one little bit. There had been something quite mysterious about her sudden departure, but Twyla always changed the subject whenever she asked questions.

"Thank goodness, you're safe." She threw her arms around Anjele. "We've been so worried."

Arm about her waist as they entered the house, Ida said she'd been waiting for her to get there before leaving.

"You're going back to New Orleans?" Anjele was surprised. "But it's terrible there. You may not have a home to go to, the way the Yankees are confiscating property."

"I know, I know, but Vinson says he doesn't think we have anything to worry about, since he's agreed to treat the soldiers." Not wanting to tell of the ugly scene with Claudia, she instead offered the explanation, "If he's going to be there constantly, my place is with him."

Anjele was greeted warmly by Mammy Kesia and all the household servants. There was no sign of either Claudia or Raymond, and she went slowly from room to room, touching things, evoking quiet nostalgia.

Ida insisted on leaving right away, and Anjele found it strange that Raymond didn't appear to say good-bye but made no comment. Her father said she should get some rest, and he'd talk with her later. She was exhausted and after a quick lunch of Kesia's wonderful crawfish gumbo, climbed the stairs and went to her room.

Claudia was sitting in a chair by the window, pinch faced and hostile. Before Anjele could speak, she lashed out, "Why did you come back?"

"This is my home," Anjele reminded her. "Look, we haven't seen each other in nearly four years. Couldn't we try to get along? Do we have to start sparring with each other the minute I walk through the door?"

"I hate you," Claudia said calmly, "and I don't want you here."

"Well, I'm staying." Anjele began to walk about the room, glad to find everything just as she'd left it.

Claudia waited, watched, then coldly said, "Not for long."

She whirled to stare at Claudia and winced at her expression. It was frightening, but Anjele wasn't about to let her trepidation show. "Mother isn't here to take sides with you now. I think Poppa always saw through your schemes and lies. It won't be as easy for you to make trouble this time, Claudia. Now get out of my room." She went to stand by the door.

Claudia made no move to oblige. "I'm not going anywhere till we settle things where Raymond is concerned."

"What's to settle? The two of you are married. I wish you well. Believe me."

"Believe you? I'd be a fool if I did. After all, there aren't many men around for you to chase after. They've all gone off to war. But don't think you're going to take Raymond away from me. Don't you dare even try!"

Anjele was tempted to say if she didn't want him four years ago, she certainly didn't want him now, but

Claudia might tell him what she said, and there was no need to hurt him further. With great patience, she sought to assure her. "You've nothing to fear, Claudia. Now will you please get out of here?"

Claudia still didn't move. "I think you should get out. I think you should go to New Orleans and move into a hotel. Maybe one of the soldiers can take care of you."

"Oh, for heaven's sake! I'm not listening to any more of this." Anjele walked out and kept on going, right out the front door and into the warm spring afternoon. Something had to be done about Claudia, but dear Lord, she didn't have a solution.

"Hey, Miss Anjele. Is that you?"

She turned in the direction of the voice calling, and though the face was familiar, she couldn't immediately remember the woman's name.

"Don't you remember me? Annabelle." The old woman grinned, walking toward her from where she'd been filling buckets at the well.

She was one of the Acadians, and Anjele recalled seeing her in the cane fields sometimes, carrying water with Simona and Emalee. She'd been old enough to be their grandmother, they hadn't been close, certainly shared no secrets. But Anjele was glad to see her, all the same.

Anjele told her how she'd just returned but quickly turned the conversation to her old friends. "Have you seen them about? Where are they working? I'm dying to talk to them. It's been four years, you know."

"You didn't know? They left years ago."

Anjele felt a wave of disappointment. "Are you sure?"

"Oh, yes. I helped them all pack. They went somewheres in Alabama. I never heard from them again." She shrugged. "But lots of us leave. Even to fight in the war. Those who stay are helping the Rebels in the swamps, 'cause nobody knows the way like our people."

Anjele wasn't really listening as she dwelled on the sad likelihood of never seeing her friends again. She'd deeply looked forward to renewing the friendship.

But then something Annabelle was saying got her attention once more.

"Hey, you remember that one they used to tease you about? The one called Gator? My cousin got wounded and came home, and he say he saw Gator in the battle, in the uniform of a Union soldier. He couldn't believe he would fight for them, but he not have a chance to ask him why."

"I guess not," was all Anjele could think of to say, for she was trying not to show any emotion. She couldn't deny her heart had skipped a beat at the sound of his name, but tenderness was quickly washed away by anger at the memory of how he'd betrayed her, and now betrayed her people as well.

"You take care," Annabelle called as Anjele turned back towards the house.

She didn't want to think of Gator, not now, not ever, because it still hurt deeply.

She didn't see Raymond, didn't know he was anywhere about, as she walked up the porch steps, head down, lost in thought.

"Welcome home."

Anjele looked up into his doleful eyes. For a moment, she couldn't speak. The last time she'd seen him, they had been engaged. Now he was married to another, and suddenly it became an awkward moment.

Forcing a smile, she held out her hand to him in greeting. Noting how he leaned on his cane, she asked, "Does it hurt terribly? Mother wrote me about it, and I was so sorry but relieved to hear you survived."

"No pain now, but it was pretty bad for a while. The ball bent my leg bone, though, leaving it crooked and weak. I get by. It could've been worse." He grinned. "But tell me about you. I hear you made quite an entrance into New Orleans."

She sat down in one of the wicker rockers, and he took the one next to her. Relieved he didn't seem to want to dwell on the past by asking a lot of questions, she eagerly described her so-called capture in detail.

He listened, shaking his head in wonder, finally exclaiming, "You always were one to take a dare, Anjele. If anybody could make it from England to here in the middle of a war, it's you."

They talked and laughed and shared memories. Kesia brought them both glasses of lemonade. There was a soft breeze from the river, and with the air sweetened by the fragrance of the first honeysuckle blossoms, it was a nice afternoon. For a little while, both were able to forget how their world was slowly crashing about them.

Claudia stood inside the parlor window listening and getting angrier by the minute. Anjele had said it wouldn't be easy to best her this time. So be it. If she wanted a war of her own, she would have one.

Brett embraced the woman called Big Ruby. He knew she got the name due to her voluminous breasts. But when he thought of the bigness of her, it was her heart, for she had been the one to nurse him back to health, and he knew he owed her his life.

He had tried to make it back to the way station but passed out from loss of blood. By the time the horse ambled in on his own, Brett was near death. He was taken into the next settlement, but there wasn't a doctor. Big Ruby was the next best thing, and she'd made up her mind he wasn't going to die.

And he hadn't.

Fever had set in. He'd hovered in a kind of netherworld for days, unaware of anything. When he'd finally come out of it, he found himself looking into brown eyes, crying with relief, and smothered by those large, luscious breasts.

Big Ruby wanted him to hang around once he got on his feet, but he'd made up his mind to head back East and join the Union army. Now he was saying good-bye, and she was clinging to him and whispering how she knew he'd never promised anything, but she loved him all the same.

"And in a special way, I love you, too," he said, and meant it, knowing it wasn't the way she wanted it. He meant gratitude, friendship. She wanted the forever kind of love, the kind he knew he could never offer, for he had none left to give.

He mounted the horse, gazed down at her and tipped his hat. "You take care of yourself."

"You, too, soldier"—she forced a brave smile—"and I hope you find that angel you were looking for."

He blinked, puzzled. "What are you talking about?"

She shrugged, as if it didn't matter, knowing all the while it did, and it hurt like hell, too. "I didn't say nothing about it, 'cause I kept hoping you'd wind up staying, but when you were out of your head with the fever, you kept calling somebody, calling them an 'angel.' And if she meant that much, I figure you have to love her. And if you do . . ." she grudgingly conceded, "then I hope you find her."

Brett shook his head, as though he didn't know what she was talking about. With a last wave, he rode away.

Angel, indeed, he bitterly scoffed, spurring the horse into a full gallop, anxious to get to the war. Devil was more like it.

But Big Ruby had been right about one thing.

He did love her.

CHAPTER 17

IN THE WEEKS FOLLOWING ANJELE'S return, it became obvious there were more problems to be dealt with than the war. With each passing day, her father seemed to be drifting farther and farther away from reality. Seldom did he appear at mealtime. He was either locked away in his study or sitting inside her mother's tomb. He drank more than she'd ever known him to. He seemed not to care for anything.

The routine in the fields went unchanged. It was a wait-and-see time for those who hadn't fled, to learn how their lives, their world, would change with the enemy in control. Everyone was also waiting to see what would happen once General Benjamin Butler arrived with his land forces.

Anjele tried to make up for her father's dwindling interest by checking with the overseers daily to make sure all was running smoothly. Claudia made sure she was right beside her, and Anjele worried that she would say or do something to cause them to quit. Overseers were in demand due to the scarcity of able-bodied men in Louisiana. In early April, the Confederate States Congress had passed an act conscripting white men between the ages of eighteen and thirty-five. They permitted one overseer to remain on each plantation per twenty slaves.

Fortunately, as the days grew humid and warm, Claudia resisted leaving the cool and shaded house to follow Anjele. Instead, she began to take her carriage into New Orleans almost daily. At supper, she would report on how things were calming down, bragging about making friends with some of the officers' wives who had arrived to take up residence.

Anjele was appalled, and one night, listening to Claudia glowingly tell of having had tea with Mrs. Elisabeth Hembree, she could be still no longer. "Is her husband a major?"

"Why, yes, he is." Claudia raised an eyebrow. "But how would you know?"

Anjele pushed the bowl of gumbo away, having suddenly lost her appetite. "He was the officer who was so rude when I arrived in the city."

Claudia was quick to say, "No doubt it was your fault if he was. Elisabeth told me how the officers are instructed to treat everyone courteously, but of course we both agreed there's a certain limit to how much they can be expected to tolerate. Frankly, I've been well treated."

"Of course you have," Anjele said, "you kiss their asses."

"Anjele, watch your mouth!" Elton scolded. It was one of his rare appearances at the supper table, and he was stunned to hear such language.

"I'm sorry, Poppa," Anjele apologized for her choice of words, adding, "but I can't think of any other way to describe what she does. Surely you don't approve."

He was tempted to admit he didn't give a damn what

Claudia did and that it would suit him fine if she moved to New Orleans and lived with the blasted Yankees. To keep peace, however, he suggested they change the subject. "Your mother always insisted on keeping conversation pleasant at the table."

"*I* didn't start it," Claudia said, determined to have the last word.

Elton held out his coffee cup to Kesia for a refill, making a face as he took a sip. "I don't know why I bother drinking this horrible brew. I can't remember the last time I had real coffee, or chicory. One of the cooks came up with this concoction made of parched corn, and it tastes terrible."

Claudia gloated. "I had real coffee today, and it was wonderful. A supply ship came in yesterday, and all the wives got a generous supply."

Raymond spoke up to tell Elton, "I can get you some coffee. One of the officers gave Daddy a supply as a token of gratitude for him sitting up all night with his sick wife. I'll bring you some next time I go into New Orleans."

Anjele was aghast and slammed both hands on the table as she cried, "You'll do nothing of the kind. We're not taking anything from the damned Yankees."

Claudia giggled. "Oh, you're being ridiculous. When are you going to grow up and realize you're only cutting off your nose to spite your face?"

Elton cautiously suggested, "Maybe you should be a little more tolerant, Anjele. You've got to think of BelleClair."

Aware that everyone was looking at her in accusation, Anjele stiffened. "What do you mean?"

He seemed uncomfortable to have to explain that

he'd had a visit earlier in the day from John Carraway, a planter from a parish upriver. "He says the slaves in the parishes below New Orleans are getting restless, and the only way owners can hope to maintain discipline is by the nearness of Federal troops."

"I don't see what that has to do with us." Anjele shook her head. "We don't have problems here."

"But we could," Elton said. "Those running away are able to incite others, like ours, who've been complacent in the past. John says large gangs are wandering into the Union army camps seeking freedom, excitement, not wanting to work the fields any longer. The soldiers are having to contend with them."

Anjele challenged, "What did they expect?"

"They weren't prepared . . ." Raymond started to join the conversation, but a frosty glare from Claudia silenced him.

Elton went on to explain, "It's going to be an increasing problem, and the day may come when we'll need to ask for protection from the army. I agreed with John we need to meet with General Butler and let him know we're neutral on the war now. We won't be harboring Confederate soldiers or bushwhackers. In exchange, we'll have their support in time of need."

Anjele stubbornly shook her head. "I won't sign an oath of allegiance to the Union."

"*You* don't have to," he said.

Excitedly, Claudia prodded, "Are you going to? Is that what you're getting at?"

Anjele silently begged her father to tell Claudia she was crazy to think he'd ever do such a thing but knew her hope was short-lived before he even spoke.

"Yes, I think it's best for all of us, and it really makes

no difference. Signing my name to a piece of paper doesn't change the fact that my heart and prayers are still with the Confederacy. They can't take that away from me. I'll just be using the Yankees to help us, don't you see that?" He covered Anjele's hand with his.

She didn't see and never would but was glad he was starting to take an interest. "You do what you feel you must, but I won't sign, Poppa."

"You don't have to," Claudia snapped. "Just keep your mouth shut and don't make trouble. Maybe the Yankees won't even know you're around. Thank goodness you won't be going to the ball to welcome General Butler. You'd be sure to embarrass the family."

Once more, Anjele was shocked. "Claudia! Don't tell me you'd even consider going to a Yankee ball."

"I certainly am. And I'm going to have a new gown, too," she proceeded to boast. "Effie Lauteur, like all the couturieres in New Orleans, took down her sign, swearing she'd never sew for Yankee women. And, since no one confessed to being a dressmaker, all the officers' wives were having a terrible time trying to find someone to make new clothes. They aren't used to this heat, and the wardrobes they brought with them are much too warm.

"So"—she swept them with an exultant smile—"when I told Elisabeth about Effie, she was so grateful she told Effie she had to make something new for me, too."

Anjele was sickened. "Effie will never forgive you, and I don't blame her. How could you betray her?"

"Easy. It not only got me a new dress, but an invitation to the ball, and now all the officers' wives adore me."

Anjele muttered, "Don't be too sure."

Elton hated to do so but felt there wouldn't be a better time to break the rest of his news and told Claudia, "You would have been invited to the ball, anyway." He turned to meet Anjele's questioning stare. "I received an invitation for all of us."

Vehemently, she shook her head. "I've no intention of going to any social for any Yankee."

"Please," Elton surprised everyone by pleading. "I want you to go with me, in your mother's place."

At that, Claudia cried, "I don't want her there. She'll ruin it for me. She'll do something to humiliate all of us. I know she will. General Butler will probably have the whole plantation destroyed, the house burned down. . . ." She melted into furious sobs.

Raymond looked at her in disgust, shook his head, and continued eating.

Anjele said she would think about it, knowing all along she would go, but only because her father had asked her to.

Elton excused himself, after hardly touching his meal, and the instant he was out of the room, Claudia began railing at Anjele. "I warn you, if you do anything at that ball to embarrass me, you'll be sorry. I intend to be a part of the new society of New Orleans, and you better not ruin it for me."

Anjele wasn't about to sit and listen to her. She got up and went out on the veranda. It was a nice evening. The sleepily flowing river glowed in the late afternoon sun; the sky was a limpid blue, tinted with streaks of peach and coral. A gentle breeze brought the fragrance of freshly turned soil as the hoe gang completed their day. It was so tranquil, and she took a deep breath, wanting to drink of the temporary respite from the chaos of her world.

The sound of his cane striking the floor heralded Raymond joining her. Lowering himself into a rocker, he said lightly, "If Kesia weren't such a good cook, I swear I think I'd rather starve than endure another round at the table like that one."

"Poppa was right," Anjele dully told him. "Momma never allowed unpleasantries."

He snickered. "*Everything* is unpleasant when Claudia is around."

Anjele didn't say anything. It made her uncomfortable when he criticized Claudia to her.

"Remember the day you arrived?" he continued, oblivious to her silence. "Did you wonder why I wasn't out here with my mother waiting to greet you? Oh, I wanted to be, all right, but Claudia was so mad when she heard you were back, she ranted and raved and dared me to come out here. I would have, anyway, if Mother hadn't been here, but I didn't want her to have to witness another scene. Claudia had already had a fit when Mother showed up planning to stay with us. I didn't want to put her through another.

"Though heaven knows"—he paused for an exaggerated sigh—"poor mother was certainly well acquainted with Claudia's tantrums. The short while we lived there, those two were at each other's throats constantly. I tried to referee for a while but finally gave up and got out of the way. It was a relief to march off to war, believe me."

Out of the corner of her eye, Anjele caught movement and turned in time to see her father walking through the garden and heading up to the family cemetery. He was paying another visit to the tomb. She hadn't wanted to intrude before but now seized the chance to get away from Raymond. "Please excuse me. I'd like to walk with my father."

She hurried away but not before hearing his despondent sigh. Her heart went out to him, but there was nothing she could do. She had enough problems of her own with Claudia without becoming involved in his.

The rose garden sloped gently up to the highest point of the property, where the cemetery was situated. She could see her father emerging from the other side of the garden, heading up the path. She was about to call out to him to wait for her but was startled to see a man standing at the edge of the woods. He saw her at the precise instant she noticed him and swiftly stepped back to disappear into the foliage.

She had but a glimpse of his face and was nettled by the awareness of having seen him before but couldn't remember who he was. Since he was white but not in uniform, she decided he was probably just one of the Acadians who didn't go off to war and was out for a walk. Hurrying to catch up with her father, she put it out of her mind.

He was unlocking the new cast-iron gate covering the door of the tomb. Turning, his eyes lit up. He was obviously glad for her company. "I'd been wanting to ask if you'd like to come up here with me, but I wasn't sure the time was right."

"And I've been waiting for you to ask me, but I'm here now, and that's all that matters."

He pulled open the gate, then unlocked the metal door. As it swung open, he told her, "I keep these keys hidden. There's a loose brick in the hearth of the fireplace in my study. Third one, second row from the left, should you ever want to come up here and visit her by yourself."

Inside, she was stunned to see how he'd made it resemble a small parlor, with a rocking chair and a rug she recognized as one her mother had crocheted. There was even a small table, with a Bible sitting next to a vase of wilting flowers.

Respectfully, she stood back as he knelt and prayed for a few moments beside the concrete vault which held her mother's coffin. Finally sitting in the rocker, he began to talk. He told her of the last days, how he couldn't believe how quickly her mother died after falling ill. There was nothing Dr. Duval could do. Nothing anyone could do. She took to her bed complaining of headache and chills. Then the fever swept her, and she went into a coma. He did not leave her bedside for three days and three nights, and at dawn on the fourth morning, she breathed her last.

"She loved you," he whispered, caressing her hair as she knelt before him and placed her head on his knee, her own tears flowing. "And she missed you so much. Once the war started, everytime I mentioned your staying in England where you'd be safe, she'd get real quiet and sad. She knew it was best, too, but she wanted you home."

"I'm sorry"—Anjele began and paused to swallow past the constricting lump in her throat—"that I ever went away. I never meant to hurt either of you, believe me."

"It's over. No need to talk about that, except to say Claudia didn't make it any easier. Your mother and I suspected she went to Raymond and upset him so badly he went crazy for a while, and that's how she was able to get him to marry her. But if he was so weak, well, God help him." He shook his head.

They stayed until the sun began going down, and Elton said it was time to be getting home while they could still see their way.

He locked the door and gate, then paused before pointing and crying out in astonishment, "Look! There! Coming out of that crevice. Wildflowers. And your mother's coffin is right on the other side."

Anjele followed his gaze to see tiny flowers in a rainbow of colors, sprouting from the tomb.

He reached out with shaking fingers to lovingly caress the delicate petals. "Don't you see?" he whispered in awe, "It's life, growing out of the very aperture of death."

Leo cautiously approached the crypt. He had just heard the chimes from Jackson Square and knew it was midnight. No one had seen him go into the cemetery. Even the Yankee patrols avoided the place, figuring nobody would want to hang around there. He sure as hell didn't but was eager for his money. He was just reaching above the door to get it when The Voice spoke, startling him, as always. "Shit," he said, as the money slipped from his fingers. He quickly stooped to grope for it in the inky darkness. "Don't scare me like that."

"Have you anything to report?" The sound came, as always, from inside the cold, gray walls.

"Nothing. Sinclair don't do nothing but hang around the house or sit at his wife's tomb. I tell you," he added with a derisive snort, "I'm getting sick of hanging around graves."

"Shut up," The Voice hissed. "You're paid to do whatever's necessary to keep an eye on him. Are you sure he hasn't had any visitors? Talked to anyone?"

Leo related John Carraway's visit but said he had no idea what they had discussed. Carraway didn't stay very long, he recalled.

The Voice didn't find the information important. He knew Carraway, and he would not be the sort to work undercover for the Confederates, so he'd know nothing of the plates, and Elton wouldn't confide in him. "Listen to me," he said then, making his voice harsh, stern. "It's time for you to know that Elton Sinclair has something that belongs to the Federal government. I was in hopes you would see him make contact with someone, passing it along to them, and it could be recovered quietly, discreetly, without a fuss. But from what you've told me, he's done nothing out of the ordinary."

"That's right. Just sits up at that tomb. Either inside or out. Doesn't give a hang about his crops, looks like."

"The time has come for us to move. I want you now to do whatever you have to, to make him talk and find out where the property is hidden."

Leo grinned, excitement building. He'd been waiting for a chance to get rough with Sinclair. "Just tell me what it is you're looking for."

"I don't want any trouble," The Voice emphasized. "I want you to catch him by himself. Be sure to wear a mask so he doesn't recognize you. Tell him you know what he took from the Mint, and one way or another, he's going to give it to you."

"Maybe I'll get him at the tomb."

"I leave the place up to you, but I want it done late Saturday, then bring what he gives you to me."

"And what's that?"

The Voice decided to tell him. He was going to find out,

anyway, when Elton handed them to him. "Engraving plates, used to print money for the Federal government, and if they fall into the hands of the Confederacy, the results could be disastrous."

"Well, I don't give a damn about that." Leo laughed. "Only what you pay me. If I get them plates, you'll pay me extra, right?"

"You'll be rewarded for a job well done. Now go. And don't fail me."

"I won't." Leo stuffed his money in his pocket and broke into a run, anxious to get away from the cemetery.

He had thought about hanging around, hiding, waiting to see the man behind the voice when he emerged from the mausoleum.

But something told him he was better off not knowing.

CHAPTER 18

ANJELE HAD NEVER DREAMED SHE WOULD socialize with Yankees. Had it not been for her father's plea for her to take her mother's place, she would never have consented. And to make matters worse, Claudia's new so-called friend, Elisabeth Hembree, and Anjele's nemesis, Major Hembree, had taken over the home of Drusilla and Hardy Maxwell, close friends of her family.

"Where did Miss Drusilla and Mister Herbert go?" Anjele asked her father between clenched teeth as they made their way up the wide steps to the two-story mansion.

Claudia, behind them, impatiently having to wait for Raymond to maneuver the steps with his cane, spoke up before Elton had a chance. "They live in the basement. Elisabeth let them stay on so Drusilla could be her housekeeper. She doesn't trust Negroes. Hardy, I understand, still works at the bank, only he's handling strictly *Federal* money now," she added, amused by the irony.

Anjele, her hand tucked in the crook of her father's arm, felt him tense. Not only must it be terrible for him to think of lifelong friends being so humiliated as to be relegated to living in the basement of their own home, but the reality of Claudia's obviously moving over to the side of the enemy had to be heartbreaking. Anjele wasn't really surprised.

"We won't stay any longer than necessary," Elton whispered to Anjele. "I heard late this afternoon General Butler won't be here, and frankly I doubt he was ever expected. The Yankees just wanted to humiliate us by forcing us to socialize with them."

"But there are those among us who are tickled to death to be invited." She meant Claudia, and he knew it.

"Well, grit your teeth and don't let them make you mad, Angel." He patted her hand. "That's what they want, to get us riled so they can single out potential troublemakers."

She promised they'd not have the satisfaction.

Major Hembree stood in the receiving line, wearing full dress uniform—dark blue coat, double rows of brass buttons, gold epaulets. His silver scabbard hung on his left side, a red tasseled sash about his waist. The trousers were light blue with gold stripes down the sides.

Anjele tried not to frown as she looked his wife over and recognized Effie Lauteur's work in the elegant white silk taffeta gown.

Anjele, respectfully in mourning despite being obliged to attend a social function, wore a sedate gown of black bombazine. Claudia, however, had rebelliously stated she had no intentions of being so drab and morbid.

Major Hembree recognized Anjele right away. He turned to whisper to his wife, who listened with a frown, then joined him in a scornful glare as he greeted Anjele by remarking, "I *hope* it's nice to see you."

"And I *hope* it's nice to be here," she fired back.

A few moments later, she begged her father, "Can we go now? I can't stand all this."

"I'm afraid not. It would be rude. Let's have some refreshments . . . ." He blanched at the sight of Drusilla Maxwell, in the gray costume of housekeeper, doggedly placing trays of food on a table. "Dear Lord," he said under his breath.

Anjele caught his arm as he started towards her. "Do you think we should? I mean, it might embarrass her if we speak to her."

Just then Drusilla looked up as though she'd been expecting them. After quickly making sure no one was looking, she motioned them to follow her to the service hallway. Tearfully, she hugged them both before urging, "Tell any of our friends you see here they're not to be embarrassed for me, but it might be best if they ignored me. It . . ." She stammered, unnerved, "It makes it harder for me.

"And of course," she added bitterly, "it's what *they* want, to make all of us feel like fools, break our spirits so we'll bow down and accept things and not make any trouble."

"What is really going on?" Elton was anxious to find out. "We stay out of town as much as possible, so we don't get much information."

"Some of the widows worried about losing everything are ingratiating themselves with the officers' wives," she said angrily. "And Hardy was telling me the cane growers are coming in and fraternizing with Federal provost marshals in hopes of getting favors, like help in keeping the slaves under control and working, so they can get this year's crop in. Everybody pretty much believes once

General Butler gets settled, he'll come up with some kind of law that says all the field workers have to be paid wages.

"And"—she paused to shake her head in dismay—"I guess you heard General Butler had that man who yanked down a Union flag hanged."

Not having heard, Anjele gasped in horror, but Elton nodded, "Yes, I'm afraid so."

Drusilla rushed to explain her real reason for drawing them away from the party. "Hardy said if I saw you here, to ask you to please slip down in the basement. He's wanting to talk to you. Says it's important."

Elton sighed and reluctantly agreed. He told Anjele to go back to the party, promising he wouldn't be long. He didn't want to see Hardy but decided to get it over with, worried that if he didn't, Hardy might go to BelleClair, and Elton didn't want that. He intended to mind his own business, in hopes the Yankees would leave him and his plantation alone. It was wishful thinking, but in his misery since Twyla died, it was all he had to hope for. And not merely for his sake, for had Anjele stayed where she was, he wouldn't care what happened anymore. For her sake, he sought survival.

He knew how to get to the cellar, for one of their earlier secret meetings had been held there. Quietly he slipped out the back door, groping his way in the darkness behind thick shrubs to the wooden doors covering narrow steps leading downward. He picked his way carefully.

Hardy heard him coming and was waiting. The air smelled sour, for cellars in New Orleans were a rarity, and those who dared have them knew the consequences of constant dampness. Elton grimaced to think that Hardy had never imagined he'd one day be forced to live in his.

They shook hands, Elton reminding Hardy he didn't have much time.

"This won't take long. I thought you should know they're asking questions about the Mint takeover."

Elton tensed. "Why? They've got control now. What difference does it make who was responsible? Besides, what's there to worry about? We all wore masks, and the officials running the place hightailed it north once we turned them loose. All we did was shut the place down."

"They've taken inventory."

"So? We didn't steal any money," Elton said. "The takeover was merely a statement, a demonstration of secession."

"I know, but they're claiming a set of engraving plates is missing. New ones. If they'd known about it, they wouldn't have printed a hundred and fifty million new greenbacks at another mint. They could have stopped circulation. Now it's too late. If the plates fall into the hands of the Confederacy, it could be economically disastrous."

"Ye Gods, man," Elton roared, "which side are you on?"

Hardy withered before his blazing glare, but only for a moment. Smothered by his surroundings as a reminder of what the war had already cost him, he lashed out, "You aren't living in a cellar, Sinclair. And your wife isn't slaving for the Yankees in her own home. What you and I and the others tried to do all those months in secret meetings didn't work. There's no way we can help the Confederacy now. Like it or not, we're part of the Union again.

"We can't beat them," he went on, lowering his voice as he remembered what was going on right above them. "So we have to find a way to join them, in a way that will still give us our self-respect. Some of the sugar growers are even talking about forming a conservative wing of a Unionist group in an attempt to restore Louisiana to the Union while the war is still going on."

"That's absurd."

"Not when you think about it. They plan to ask for two things—keeping slavery and having representation in the state legislature based on total population, which would, of course, give most of the power to the black-belt parishes—the slaveowners."

"It won't happen," Elton predicted.

"It can, and it will, if they don't consider us Rebels, which they will"—he warned—"if they find out we were part of the takeover of the Mint and one of us did, in fact, steal those plates for the Confederacy."

"I'm no longer a part of any of this. All I want is peace for my family and my plantation. If any of you try to say I was involved in that takeover, I'll deny it."

Hardy sneered. "Nobody is admitting anything. But you don't come to our meetings anymore, and you don't know what's going on. I was stupid enough to think you cared, but you don't."

"That's right. Now if that's all you wanted, I need to be getting back upstairs before I'm missed."

"Yes, that's all," Hardy said in disgust.

Anjele was miserable, but Claudia was happily dancing the night away in the arms of Union soldiers. She felt so sorry for Raymond, who was forced to watch, standing beside her and leaning on his cane.

"See the way those bluebellies keep looking over here and smirking? They figure I got this bad leg from the war, and they're goading me by showing me they can dance with my wife, and I can't."

Anjele soothed, "Don't let them get you riled. That's what they want. Pretend you don't care."

"I don't."

Anjele wasn't surprised but made no comment.

With a catch in his throat, he murmured, "You're the only woman I ever wanted to dance with, the only woman I ever wanted for my wife. I was such a fool. I always took it for granted, 'cause you were promised to me, but I see now I should've tried harder to make you love me as I loved you, and you wouldn't have turned to another, and—"

"Raymond, stop it!" she chided, awash with annoyance, as well as pity for the way he bared his soul. Softening her tone, not wanting to deepen his hurt, she urged, "Let the past be. You can't change it, and neither can I, though God knows I would if I could . . . ."

"Anjele," he said, turning to stare in wonder. "Do you mean to say—"

"No!" She quickly dashed his hopes, "You misunderstand. I'd like to be your friend, but you're making it hard when you say such things. I'm sorry you aren't happy with Claudia, but you shouldn't tell me about it. Don't you see that?" she implored.

Just then her father appeared at her side to say, loud enough for those nearby to overhear, "I'm so sorry about your headache. I can tell you're feeling worse. As much as I hate to leave, I think we'd better."

Anjele grabbed the bait. With fingertips pressed to

her forehead, she murmured, "I know. I feel as if I might swoon any second."

Grasping her arm, motioning to Raymond, Elton led the way to offer apologies to their hostess.

Elisabeth Hembree's dark eyes glittered with suspicion. With feigned compassion, she told Anjele, "I'm so sorry you aren't feeling well. By all means, run along."

"Do invite us again," Anjele went along with the pretense of being cordial. "We had a lovely time. You're a wonderful hostess. We Southerners have much to learn from you Northern ladies."

Their eyes met, held, each aware of the other's contempt.

Raymond had gone to inform Claudia they were leaving, and she ran up breathlessly to protest. "We can't leave now. It would be rude."

"Your sister doesn't feel well," Elisabeth Hembree told her.

"Well, that doesn't mean *we* have to leave, Raymond," Claudia whirled on him. "We can borrow a carriage from your father and go home later."

He tried to sound genuinely disappointed. "I'm afraid it wouldn't be safe for just the two of us to be on the road so late."

Visibly disappointed, Claudia's lower lip began to tremble. Elisabeth promptly intervened by putting a comforting arm about her waist and offering, "You two can stay here tonight."

Claudia clapped her hands together in little-girl fashion, bouncing up and down and exclaiming, "Wonderful. We'd love to, and if you-all will excuse me, Captain Barlow has this dance." She skipped back into the ballroom without a backward glance.

"I can't leave her." Raymond said after Elisabeth left them. "But we won't stay the night here. We'll go to my parents."

Impulsively, for she felt so terribly sorry for him, Anjele kissed his cheek in parting.

Claudia, in the midst of a sweeping waltz, turned just in time to see and drew a sharp breath of anger.

Lulled by the gentle rocking of the carriage, Anjele fell asleep, awakened only by her father's gentle shaking. "We're home, honey," he said.

Wilbur the butler was waiting, as always, for their return. Anjele turned towards the curving stairs and heard her father tell him as he handed over his coat, "I'm going to be in the study for a while, but you can go on out to your cabin now, Wilbur. I won't be needing you."

Anjele turned to say, "It's so late, Poppa. Don't you think you should go to bed?"

He didn't respond, once more lost in his sorrow.

Anjele's heart went out to him, but there was nothing she could do.

He went into his study and sat down behind his desk. Leaning back in his chair and closing his eyes, he let his thoughts drift away to the past once more, reliving the glory days of BelleClair . . . and his beloved Twyla.

Outside, Leo Cody hid among the thick hydrangea bushes framing the side of the house. He had followed the carriage on horseback as the Sinclairs went into New Orleans, then lurked about while they went to some kind of party. He felt it was a waste of time.

How the hell could he be expected to know what was going on inside, who Elton was talking to? But so far The Voice was satisfied with the way he did things, and as long as he got paid, Leo wasn't going to worry about it. After tonight, it didn't matter, anyway, he reminded himself, because he was going to get what he was supposed to, one way or the other. He rejoiced to see that only Elton's daughter had come home with him. Not that he was worried about the gimp-legged son-in-law or the loud-mouthed daughter. It just made things easier to know there was only one other person in the house.

He had seen the old butler leave by the back door and head back to the slave compound, and he'd seen the lantern in the upstairs bedroom extinguished, which meant the daughter had gone to bed. The only light in the house now came from the window of Elton's study. Leo could see him in there, looking as if he were sleeping in his chair, his back to the open window.

Leo took the kerchief from his pocket and stretched it over his nose and across his face, then tied it behind his head. Slowly, soundlessly, he stepped over the window ledge and into the room.

Elton, consumed by his meditation, was oblivious.

Leo took out his knife, and, when he was right up on him, pressed the cold steel against Elton's throat. "Move or make a sound, and you're dead," he said against his ear.

Elton's heart constricted in terror. Barely able to speak with the blade pressing into his flesh, his pleading words were barely audible. "Please, take what you want. Just don't kill me."

"I know you got a safe somewhere, you son of a

bitch." Leo pressed the knife harder, barely slicing into the skin. "Tell me where it is, or I'll cut your head off and rip the place apart and find it myself."

Elton knew he was helpless, and he didn't care about the money and jewelry in the safe. With the knife still pressing, he managed to whisper, "Behind the door. Behind the picture."

"What's the combination?"

Elton told him from memory, silently cursing himself for having given his coat to Wilbur before taking the pistol out of his pocket.

"You better not be lying. Now sit still and don't move." Leo began backing away in the direction of the safe.

"No . . . no, I won't," Elton promised nervously. He could feel blood trickling down his neck but didn't dare touch it. "Please. Just take what you want and go."

Leo took down the picture. Then, holding the knife in his right hand, he used his left to work the combination. All the while, he kept glancing back to make sure Elton wasn't moving.

At last, the door popped open. Leo saw lots of bags inside. He opened one, grinning at the contents—an assortment of earbobs and necklaces, obviously valuable. No harm in an extra bonus, he figured. All The Voice cared about was the plates. He shoved everything aside, papers scattering to the floor, intent on finding what he was after. There'd be time later to gather his treasure.

Elton dared touch his fingers to his throat. It wasn't bleeding badly, probably wasn't deep. He would be all right but couldn't take a chance the intruder might decide to kill him, after all. Moving very slowly so as not to make any noise, he gripped the arms of the chair and eased himself up. He needed a weapon.

His eyes fell on the iron poker propped next to the fireplace. Keeping close watch on the man as he rummaged inside the safe, Elton reached out and grabbed the heavy piece and crept toward him.

Leo cursed, because the safe was now empty, and the plates weren't in there. "Goddamn it, where are they—" He turned just as Elton was about to strike and leaped to the side.

The poker hit the floor with a thud, and Elton lunged for him, grabbing the arm holding the knife with one hand, snatching off the mask with the other. "Leo!" he cried, shock causing him to relax his grip.

Leo stabbed him.

Elton, eyes wide with disbelief and horror, clutched his chest. Blood streaming through his fingers, he slumped to the floor.

Leo dropped beside him. "Tell me where you hid the plates, and I'll get help for you. I swear it."

Elton coughed, blood running from the corners of his mouth as he bit out savagely, "Go to hell . . ."

Anjele sat bolt upright to stare wildly about in the darkness. She had heard something.

She swung her legs off the side of the bed and grabbed her robe, yanking it on as she raced for the door and flung it open. The hallway was dark, but as her eyes adjusted, she could make her way to the stairway and down.

All was quiet as she reached the foyer, but she knew it couldn't have been her imagination, and she wasn't about to go back to bed till she found out what it was.

The door to the study was closed, soft light coming from beneath it. "Poppa, are you all right?"

There was no response.

Slowly she turned the knob and peered inside to see her father lying on the floor, a knife burrowed to the hilt in his chest. "Oh, God, no . . ." she wailed, running to drop to her knees beside him. Her hands clutched her throat in panic, then fluttered to touch his dear face. Paralyzed by horror, she could only stare helplessly, praying he was alive.

He opened pain-filled eyes, tried to focus on her, lips moving as he struggled to speak her name.

"Lie still," she commanded, beginning to come out of her stupor. "I'll get someone. . . ."

She started to rise, but with his last bit of strength, he struggled to plead, "No time. Listen . . ."

She slipped an arm beneath his head, raising him slightly. "Tell me, quickly, so I can get help."

Leo stood behind the door, watching and straining to hear, silently cursing, because he'd thought Sinclair was dead. He'd decided he couldn't take a chance on him telling who had stabbed him. Quickly, he reached down and picked up the poker and crept toward her.

Elton's eyes were rapidly glazing over. He could no longer see her through the descending veil of death. His lips moved, the whispered words disappearing in a froth of blood. She leaned down, turning her ear to his mouth in a frantic effort to hear what he was so desperate to tell her.

She heard the sound faintly but did not understand.

"Wildflowers . . ." Elton wheezed.

And then he was dead.

Before Anjele could grasp either the word or the

actuality of her father's death, she caught a glimpse of movement from the corner of her eye. Terror-stricken, she whipped around to look up into the maniacally grinning face, saw the poker he held in his hand, raising it, about to strike . . . .

Awareness flashed.

He was familiar.

She'd seen him somewhere before, but where, who—

The poker hit the back of her head.

And then there was nothing.

CHAPTER 19

IT WAS NEARLY NINE O'CLOCK WHEN THE Duvals arrived at BelleClair. The slave sent by Kesia to fetch Dr. Duval had ridden into New Orleans at breakneck speed, horse lathered and exhausted from being whipped into a full gallop the entire way.

Vinson was having his breakfast when Hannah, one of the kitchen servants, came to tell them there was someone from BelleClair at the back door, and the man was hysterical. The doctor ran through the house, Ida on his heels, to find the young Negro twisting his hat in trembling hands as he sobbed over and over, "The mastah's dead . . . the mastah's dead . . . ."

Unable to learn any more than that, Vinson ordered a groom to get his carriage ready, then went and grabbed his leather doctor's bag. Ida woke Raymond, who dressed on his way out, stepping into his trousers as he came out the back door.

When they arrived at the house, they saw a somber crowd of overseers and household servants gathered on the front porch. Ida paused to ask Mammy Kesia what on earth had happened, but Vinson swept right by them and into the house, Raymond close behind.

Wilbur was in the foyer, visibly shaken, unable to speak and could only point towards the study. Vinson ran the rest of the way, stopping short in the doorway at the bloody scene before him. The place was a shambles, and he knew, even before forcing hinself to walk over and kneel down beside the body, that Elton was dead. The knife was still imbedded in his chest. Vinson closed the frozen, staring eyes, then leaped to his feet at the sound of Raymond's anguished cry.

"Oh, God, no . . ."

Raymond had spotted Anjele, where she'd been placed on the sofa and was kneeling beside her.

Vinson pushed him away. Her face was covered in blood. "She's alive," he said, after a cursory examination, "but it looks like she's hurt bad."

Raymond, not wanting to look at Elton's body, grabbed an afghan and threw it over him. Sickened, shaken, he didn't know what to do with himself just then and began to pace restlessly about. He saw the open safe, the way the room looked torn apart, and said, "Elton must have surprised the robber, and Anjele heard the noise and came running."

"Let's get her up to her room. If she comes to, I don't want her to see his body."

Raymond, unable to assist due to his bad leg, summoned Wilbur.

As they were carrying Anjele up the stairs, they heard the sounds of more horses. Raymond peered out the open door and groaned. "Union soldiers."

Vinson, annoyed, grumbled, "How did they hear about this? We don't need Yankees swarming all over."

Raymond told him he had sent Hannah to tell

Claudia something had happened to her father and she needed to get home right away. "I figured the Hembrees would send someone with her, but not an entire patrol."

"You had no business leaving her at the Hembrees last night. You should have put your foot down and made her leave when you did."

Harshly, Raymond said, "I've only got one good foot, but it wouldn't matter if I had a dozen. Nobody tells Claudia what to do, but I'm not concerned with her right now. It's Anjele I'm worried about."

"And I've lost my best friend," Vinson snapped. "Maybe it's good the infernal Yankees are here. They can get out and try to find the bastard responsible. I'll talk to them as soon as I see what I can do for her." He instructed Wilbur to send Kesia for water and towels so he could wash off the blood and get a good look at the wound.

A scream ripped through the house.

"Claudia," Raymond dully proclaimed. "I'd better get down there."

When Kesia finally brought the water, Vinson got to work, and at last was able to see the gash. From his bag, he took needle and silk thread and began to stitch, relieved Anjele was still unconscious and couldn't feel the pain. When the sutures were secure, he took a bottle containing a mixture of crushed horseradish leaves and vinegar from his bag. As he packed the solution on the wound, he instructed Kesia to tear the bedsheet into strips for bandages.

Finally, Vinson knew he'd done all he could. "Stay with her. I don't want her left alone for a minute. I'll be downstairs, and if she starts to wake up, come get me."

As he descended the steps, Vinson felt anger at the sight of the crowd gathering in the foyer. Through the still-open door, he could see more horses and wagons coming up the drive. Word of the murder was apparently spreading rapidly.

Spotting Wilbur standing to one side, Vinson took it upon himself to order, "Let's get these people out of here and close that door. We don't need a parade through this house."

"I have business here, Dr. Duval." Major Hembree stepped forward. "A murder has been committed, and I need to ask Miss Sinclair a few questions."

"Miss Sinclair is unconscious. When she awakens, you'll be the first to know. Till then, why don't you send your men out to search for the killer?"

"They're already looking around, but it's rather difficult, when they have no idea who they're looking for."

"Do the best you can," Vinson said, coolly sweeping by and hurrying along in the direction of Claudia's hysterical sobbing.

She was in the study, staring at the afghan-covered body, and Raymond was having no success in getting her to calm down. Vinson sat down beside her, opened his bag, took out a bottle of opium, and forced a dose on her. A few moments later, she became docile, and he breathed a sigh of relief.

Everyone seemed to be wondering what to do next. Ida eagerly took over once Claudia was no longer a distracting problem. Quickly she set up the parlor at the front of the house as a receiving area, briskly instructing the stunned servants to get themselves together and prepare refreshments.

Elisabeth Hembree arrived and insisted on taking

Claudia back to New Orleans with her, and no one protested, not even Raymond. Elisabeth also condescended to say she'd send back a supply of coffee and tea, then stood around waiting for someone to fawn over her for her generosity. When met by only hostile stares from neighbors and friends of Elton Sinclair, she huffily lifted her chin and breezed out of the house, deciding she wouldn't send anything.

Raymond returned to the study and went to the safe. The contents were on the floor. No doubt, after stabbing Elton and attacking Anjele, the villain had left without taking time to gather his loot.

He was picking things up, putting them back, when he saw the envelope marked, Last Will and Testament.

Raymond could not resist and opened it. Scanning the few pages, he smiled.

Ida reluctantly told Vinson it was time to do something with the body. Deep in thought, he nodded absently. She took over, ordering wide-eyed, frightened slaves to come inside and carry it to the laundry house in the rear. There, she supervised the bathing and preparation.

Weary of the way, despite his orders, the house was rapidly filling with people, both the bereaved and the curious, Vinson shut himself up in Anjele's room, keeping vigil at her bedside.

Millard DuBose came to inquire about her, visibly shaken by what had happened. "I wonder what the robber was after," he said.

Vinson shook his head. "Who cares? We've lost a fine man."

The hours passed. Anjele made no move, no sound.

Late in the evening, Major Hembree came to ask if there was any change.

"None," Vinson flatly told him, not wanting to encourage conversation.

Nonetheless, the major proceeded to describe how his men had combed the area all around the plantation as much as possible. "They got one of the slaves to go with them, and they didn't see anybody who doesn't belong here. Nobody suspicious. Nobody saw anything or heard anything. Whoever it was got away, and we've no hope of catching him unless she"—he nodded to Anjele—"can tell us something when she wakes up."

"*If* she wakes up," Vinson corrected.

"You think she'll die?"

"I'm surprised she's still alive. It was apparently a savage blow. All we can do is wait, but I do plan to talk to a few of the other doctors in town and maybe get them to take a look at her, get their opinion."

Hembree turned to go. "Well, send a messenger if she starts to wake up. I've got to get back to town now."

"So do I." Vinson stood, stretched, then turned to Kesia, who was sitting in a corner, ready to do whatever was asked. "I don't want her left alone. Not for a second. If there's any change, any change at all, send someone for me. Otherwise, I'll be back out first thing tomorrow."

Raymond was keeping his own vigil in the hall and protested when his father said he wanted him to go back with him to talk to Claudia about the funeral arrangments."

Raymond winced and looked through the door to where Anjele lay so very still.

Dear God, he prayed, let Elton's funeral be the only one.

* * *

Leo crouched in front of the mausoleum.

Damn it, he hadn't planned for it to turn out as it had, but Sinclair shouldn't have tried to jump him.

Finally, wanting to get it over with, he took a deep breath and hoarsely called, "Hey, it's me. You in there?"

The sound cut through the sepulchral stillness. "Where are the engraving plates?"

Leo ran his fingers through his hair and gritted his teeth. "I couldn't find them. There was an accident. Sinclair jumped me. Yanked my mask off and recognized me. I had to kill him. His daughter came in, and I had to kill her, too. But I couldn't find the plates."

Long moments passed, while Leo waited for reaction. He hesitantly prodded, "Did you hear me?"

"I heard you." The Voice was cold, hard, ringing with searing anger. "Tell me exactly what happened. Everything."

And Leo did, from beginning to end, assuring that he had searched thoroughly for the plates, but they were not in the study, and he couldn't take time to search the whole house.

"Of course you couldn't. You say he wasn't dead when his daughter got there?"

"No. I thought he was, but when she ran in, he started moanin' and trying to tell her something. That's when I decided I had to take care of her, 'cause I couldn't take a chance he was telling her who stabbed him."

At that, The Voice sharply asked, "What was he saying? Could you hear?"

"I don't know. She was having trouble hearing him, herself, 'cause I saw her lean over and put her ear against his mouth."

"You made a mess of things, Leo."

"I know, I know." Leo's head bobbed up and down, and he felt sick to his stomach as he thought once more of all the jewelry he'd had to leave behind. Such a waste.

"The girl isn't dead yet."

Leo's head snapped up as he stared at the tomb and cried, aghast, "That can't be so. I hit her with a poker. I bashed her head."

"I assure you, she is still alive. Someone in her family told me so. How long, is anybody's guess. I understand she's badly hurt."

"Did . . . did she say it was me?" Leo started shaking again.

"She's unconscious. She may die without waking up."

"I hope she does," he cried in a rush. "Then she can't tell about me."

The Voice became angry. "Oh, shut up, you fool. Did you ever stop to think maybe Elton told her in his last breath where the plates were hidden? Or that maybe he'd already told her, and she can lead you to them? Stop worrying about yourself and start worrying about finding those plates, because that's the only way you won't be charged with murder."

Leo cried, "What you talking about?"

"You try to leave town, Leo, and I will see you are charged with Elton Sinclair's murder. He was a prominent man. Not only in his parish but the entire state. His death will be thoroughly investigated by the Union forces responsible for law and order in this area."

Leo bristled. "You aimin' to blackmail me?"

"Quite the contrary. I hired you to do a job, and you

not only failed but also got yourself in a great deal of trouble. I'm offering a chance for you to redeem yourself." The Voice went on to explain his plan. "If Anjele wakes up and doesn't remember you, we'll let her live for the time being. We will also assume there's a chance she does know about the plates. It's a chance we'll have to take, and I'll want you to watch her, just as you did Elton. In time, if she makes no move to retrieve them and get them to the Confederacy, you can force her to tell you where they are."

"Yeah, that sounds fine and dandy," Leo said, "but what happens if she don't know, and all she does when she wakes up is scream it was me who killed her daddy. Where does that leave me?"

"It leaves you with enough money to get out of Louisiana as fast as possible. I will see to it. Otherwise, we both know you're broke, and you don't stand a chance of getting very far."

"You didn't leave me no money tonight. You owe me—"

"I owe you nothing. Because you failed, and this is your chance to make up for it. I want you to come by here every night. I will leave a white glove beneath the fence if I am in here. That will be your signal. And don't get any ideas about trying to learn my identity. I have a gun, and if you try to come inside, I will kill you."

Leo chewed his lower lip nervously. He didn't see where he had any choice, but before he could agree, The Voice made yet another offer.

"If Anjele Sinclair lives, and you do get the plates, I promise to pay you a bonus. One thousand dollars."

At that, Leo's brows lifted, as well as his spirits. "You got a deal, mister."

"Then go now," The Voice sternly commanded, "And keep your mouth shut about what's happened."

"You ain't got to worry about that," Leo cheerily called, already on his way out of the cemetery. "You ain't got to worry about that at all."

CHAPTER 20

CLAUDIA WAS ENJOYING ALL THE ATTENtion. Elisabeth Hembree had insisted she stay with her, much to Raymond's annoyance. Wives of Union officers rallied to offer sympathy, while friends of her father instead gathered at the Duvals', choosing not to call on Claudia where she was.

Raymond had stopped by when he returned from BelleClair to see whether Claudia felt like discussing funeral arrangements. She was lying on the divan in the sunny parlor. Elisabeth had assigned a little Negro girl to make sure she had everything she needed.

Sipping a cool lemonade, she listened as Raymond related Anjele's condition but wasn't really concerned. Actually, she was thinking how much simpler things would be if Anjele died. The way she was being accepted socially by the Yankees, she knew she'd have no trouble getting a patrol assigned to BelleClair to keep things running smoothly. She could go on as though nothing had happened, and when the war was finally over, she'd be among the survivors—a very wealthy survivor, she mused, a confident smile touching her lips.

"I know you don't care what happens to her,"

Raymond suddenly lashed out. "So let's get to the real reason I came here—your father's funeral. Or don't you care about that, either?"

Claudia swept him with a frosty glare. "Watch what you say. Someone might hear you."

His laugh was mocking. "Oh, we wouldn't want that, now would we? I mean, look at you. Your Yankee hostess is treating you like a princess, but then the other women of New Orleans haven't ingratiated themselves as you have. They haven't passed along names of seamstresses and the like, who've gone out of business to keep from serving those people."

"It's for their own good. They need money and the Yankees can well afford to pay them. It's not as if they're ordering them to work for free, Raymond. So just calm down, because I'm not going to stand for your treating me this way."

"What are you going to do? Scream? Ask your all-important hostess to send for soldiers to throw me in jail? I think not." Leaning on his cane for support, Raymond struggled to stand. "I want you to know you're an embarrassment to my family, the way you're acting. Because of Anjele's condition, mourners are gathering at my parents' house, which is where you ought to be. This"—he waved his cane to gesture in disgust—"is an insult to your father's memory."

"You don't know what you're talking about. I know what I'm doing. Now get out of here."

"I came to talk about the funeral."

"Let your family plan it. They seem to be taking over, anyway."

"Somebody has to," he snapped, "So I guess there's nothing to do but take care of things myself. As soon as Daddy gets back with news of Anjele, we'll decide."

"You do that. Maybe you can plan a double funeral."

He blanched to realize she could be so cruel, so cold. Still he made no move to leave.

"Well, what are you waiting for?" Claudia asked impatiently. "It's all settled. You and your family will make funeral arrangements. I'm too distraught," she added.

"I also wanted to take you home with me. I told you—people will be calling to pay their respects."

"They're calling here, too."

"Yankees," he sneered. "Your father's friends won't set foot in this house, and you know it."

She gave her golden curls a haughty toss. "Well, they don't really care about offering condolences to his daughter if they let pride stand in their way, now do they?"

"Pride? You don't know the meaning of the word."

Claudia's eyes narrowed as she warned, "You'd better watch your tongue, Raymond Duval, or you'll be staying with your parents permanently. You won't be living at BelleClair when I go back with Union patrols to ensure things will be run like they always have. I'll be rich, and you, like every other so-called *proud* Southerner, will be dirt poor."

Raymond threw his head back and laughed. "You might be banging on the door begging for me to let you in, Claudia, because Anjele might lock *you* out of BelleClair."

"What are you talking about?" Claudia didn't like the gleam in his eye, as though he knew something she didn't.

"Stupid girl," he scoffed. "Do you really think BelleClair is all yours? That your father would leave it all to you, the way you've treated him?"

Claudia had thought of that possibility but also felt confident if Anjele did indeed recover from her injury, she'd be glad to yield her interest. After all, she would realize Claudia's good relationship with Federal troops would be the key to future prosperity. Besides, Claudia figured she'd eventually drive her away, anyhow.

"I'll work it all out later," she said finally, curtly.

Raymond was enjoying himself, for he couldn't remember ever seeing Claudia unnerved as she was now, despite the way she tried to conceal it. "Maybe Anjele won't want to work anything out. Maybe she'll want to run things herself."

"I'd have a say."

"Not when she's the sole owner."

"Elton would never—"

"Elton *did.*"

Claudia's eyes bulged, and she began to shake her head wildly from side to side. "No. You're lying. You only want to hurt me because you're angry at me for staying here, and you're making this up."

"I saw his will. His *new* will. He left everything to Anjele. You, my dear, get nothing."

Claudia swayed, feeling faint. "I . . . I want to see it for myself. I don't believe you. Not till Lawyer DuBose verifies it."

"He can sure do that. I delivered it to him myself."

Their eyes met, held, in challenge.

Finally Raymond decided he was tired of fencing with her. "I'll be going now. I'll send word when the funeral will be."

He turned to go, just as Elisabeth knocked, opening the door at the same time. "Oh, you're leaving," she said to Raymond with a tight smile. "Good. The parlor downstairs seems to be filling up with ladies calling to pay their respects.

"Claudia has become a dear friend to us, you know," she added, well aware of his hostility.

Politely he responded, "Yes, and at a time like this, friends mean so much."

"Not only now, but later." Elisabeth went to sit beside Claudia. "I want you to know Major Hembree and I had a long talk this morning about your situation, dear, and he asked me to tell you not to worry about a thing. He says you'll have all the assistance you need to keep your plantation operating efficiently. He'll assign troops to keep the Negroes working, and you'll have no problem getting your crops in."

Raymond was moved to say, "There are others involved, too, Mrs. Hembree, like me, and let's certainly not forget Anjele."

She shot him a withering glance. "When you take the loyalty oath to the Union, perhaps you'll be included in the plans for BelleClair, Mr. Duval. As for Anjele, with her attitude, I'm afraid my husband has no regard for her whatsoever."

Ignoring Claudia, who was waving him out in hopes of ending the confrontation, Raymond wasn't about to miss the opportunity to announce, "Well, I'm afraid he'll have to regard her, Mrs. Hembree, since she happens to be the sole heir, according to her father's will."

Elisabeth snickered. "But you're forgetting something, aren't you? It's now up to the Federal government to decide if Southerners get to keep their land." She patted

Claudia's knee, gave her a fond smile, "So I don't think my little friend here has anything to worry about."

Raymond limped out, sick to the pit of his stomach.

Brett held the dying man's hand. There wasn't anything he could do but sit and listen to his last ramblings. His stomach had been ripped open. At least he was in shock and felt no pain.

When Brett had joined the army, he'd remained a loner. Yet Billy Bob Hawley, the soldier staring up at him with rapidly glazing eyes, hadn't been put off by Brett's coldness as other people had. He attached himself, determined to make friends.

Brave and courageous, Billy Bob was a good man to have at his side, Brett decided. Eventually he had warmed, and the two had become close friends.

They had been together through the Battle of McDowell, a major battle of the Shenandoah Valley Campaign. Among the few survivors after General Stonewall Jackson's Confederates nearly wiped out their regiment, Brett and Billy Bob were sent to McClellan's Army of the Potomac. But, enroute to report for duty, they'd run into Reb bushwhackers. Billy Bob got two of them before they got him. Brett had taken care of the other.

"I wish," Billy Bob whispered, "I could be buried back home. . . But I don't reckon they'd want me. . . folks called me a traitor. . . ."

"You're no traitor," Brett attempted to comfort him. "You fought for what you believe in. Same as me."

Billy Bob's attempt to smile was more of a grotesque grimace. "What do I believe in, Cody? Jesus, I don't even know. Father against son. Brother against brother. What's the point in this stupid war, anyhow? What am I dying for?"

"Maybe your God will tell you when you get to heaven," Brett offered. Hell, he didn't know what else to say.

"I reckon he will, if my name's in the Lamb's Book of Life. Otherwise, I reckon it'll be Satan doin' the talkin'."

"I'm sure it'll be there," Brett said, having no idea what he was talking about. His own religious upbringing had been scant.

Suddenly Billy Bob was seized by a coughing spasm, spattering them both with blood, and when he finally caught his breath, he reached out and clutched the front of Brett's shirt, using his last bit of energy to pull him close to plead, "Go home, Cody. Go home now. You don't belong here. Neither do I. It ain't our war. It ain't . . ."

With a final gasp, he relaxed his grip.

For Billy Bob, the war was over.

Brett closed his eyes and bowed his head. But he wasn't praying. He was trying to make some sense out of it all. It was times like this he wished he'd stayed out of it, gone looking for Adam Barnes's gold mine. Maybe he'd be a rich man by now. Maybe he and Ruby might have even settled down together, had a family. But he knew that wasn't likely. Back in '58, he'd sworn never to get seriously tangled up with any woman. So far, he hadn't. He intended to keep it that way.

He took down a blanket, rolled Billy Bob in it, and tied him across the saddle. Then he mounted and headed toward Virginia.

Trying not to dwell on the death of his friend, Brett concentrated on the war. General McClellan was advancing on Richmond, Virginia. Brett hoped to catch up with him before he attacked. Norfolk had been evacuated.

He'd also heard Mississippi was the scene of skirmishes near Corinth. Billy Bob had teased that maybe Brett had a special reason for keeping up with news from there and Louisiana, like maybe a girl he had left behind.

Brett frowned.

No, he hadn't left a girl behind.

He had left his heart.

"Damn it, stop it," he cursed aloud, giving his head a vicious shake as though casting away pesky gnats.

But it was no use. Like a dream her face swam before him. God, she was beautiful. Long, silky hair the color of a bayou sunset. Eyes that could devour a man in their dark emerald fires and smoky shadows.

And never before, nor since, he recalled, swept with a heated rush, had he seen a body so perfect. Firm breasts, almost saucily tipped, long, shapely, tapering legs with delicate, slender ankles. He could remember as though it were only yesterday what it felt like to have those legs wrapped around his back, his hands clutching her tight, yet tender, buttocks.

He had tried to hate her for her weakness and lying, but somewhere along the way, love won out.

Despite everything, Brett knew he loved Anjele Sinclair . . . and always would.

So that was why he kept up with how the war was affecting Louisiana. It worried him to hear New Orleans had fallen, was now occupied by Union forces. He could only hope Anjele was safe but reminded himself she had her father to look after her, as well as a husband, because she had probably married Raymond Duval, maybe even had a baby.

Brett knew he was a fool to allow thoughts of her to consume him, but he'd stopped fighting it. That was the way it was, the way it would be.

It was the price he had paid for being so foolish.

"Anjele, can you hear me?" Vinson Duval smoothed her hair from her forehead, touched his fingertips to each cheek as he asked Kesia, "Are you sure she woke up?"

Hovering nearby, wringing her hands anxiously, Kesia assured him, "Oh, yes sir, Doctor, I'm sure. It was just like I said. I come in here this mornin' and told Missy, the girl who sits with her at night, she could leave, and Missy, she say all night long, Miss Anjele, she moaned a little now and then. So I went ahead and started bathin' her face, and that's when she woke up and called out for her poppa, and she started cryin' and went to sleep again. Lawdy, Lawdy," she wailed, tears glistening on her cheeks, "I felt so sorry for that child. I'm glad she did go back to sleep, 'cause Lord knows, I don't wanna be the one to have to tell her her daddy is dead."

Vinson snapped, "You'd better not. I'll be the one to do that. Now go get me a pan of water, the colder the better, and a rag so I can sponge her."

She hurried to obey, and then he dipped the rag, squeezed it, and began to rub Anjele's face. For a few moments there was no response, and then slowly, ever so slowly, her head began to move from side to side. Again he asked, "Can you hear me, Anjele? It's me, Vinson Duval. I'm here with you. Can you hear me, dear?"

Anjele's lashes fluttered.

"Praise God, she is wakin' up!" Mammy cried, slapping her hands together in delight.

He waved her away. "Get out of here. You'll scare her to death. I'll call you if I need you."

She scurried out of the room, anxious to spread the word to the rest of the servants that Miss Anjele was going to be all right.

"Anjele, speak to me," he continued to coax.

She felt as though she were floating in a world of black velvet, soft, comforting. The opium did not want to let her go, yet something unseen was attempting to pull her away from peace and thrust her into—what? She tried to think, to remember, as bits and pieces, images, danced in and out of her mind to tease and torment. Her father. Something about her father. "Poppa . . ." she whispered, not knowing why she was so desperate to see him, hear him, but it was like a dagger twisting in her soul. "Poppa . . . please . . ."

Vinson caught her hands as her fingers began to creep about, searching for something, someone, to cling to. "Anjele, don't think about that now. Are you hurting anywhere? I want to help you." He had diminished her drug dosage, fearing sedation was retarding her regaining consciousness and now realized he'd been right to do so. Yet he didn't want her in pain.

Anjele could see the blood, like a crimson curtain across her brain. Then the curtain slowly began to open, and she could see her father . . . and knew he was dead.

She began to cry, deep, soul-wrenching tears.

"Cry it all out," Dr. Duval urged, drawing her gently into his arms. "Let it go."

He held her for a long time and would have continued to do so, but suddenly there was a knock on the door at the same instant it opened. Drawing away from her, he looked around sharply to see who had dared intrude.

It was Major Hembree, having heard from Kesia that Anjele had awakened, and he was anxious to find out whether she could tell him anything that might help find her father's murderer.

"Anjele, listen carefully," Dr. Duval said, dabbing at her tears with the wet cloth. "I know you're upset, but you've got to help us. The man who murdered your father hasn't been found. Can you tell us anything? Anything at all?"

"I don't remember anything except the blood," she said. "I wish I could . . . ." She gritted her teeth, trying to remember, the effort making her head throb worse. "I can't . . . I'm sorry."

"Did your father say anything to you, Anjele? I hate to badger you like this, because I can tell you're still in pain, but you've got to try to remember. You were found slumped across your father's body, so evidently he died in your arms. Maybe he said something, the killer's name, anything. Try to remember."

"I can't," she whispered hoarsely. "All I remember is going downstairs and seeing him on the floor, and the blood, and then nothing."

Vinson's shoulders slumped in disappointment. "All right. Maybe you'll remember something later. You go back to sleep now. You need your rest."

"No, I don't want to sleep anymore. I feel like I've been sleeping for days." She struggled to sit up, but the effort made her dizzy. Slumping helplessly against the pillows, she pleaded, "Light a lantern, please. I don't want to lie here in the dark."

Vinson and Major Hembree exchanged alarmed glances.

The hour was near noon. The drapes were open. Sunshine was streaming into the room.

Vinson leaned close, staring into her eyes. She did not blink.

He passed his hand rapidly back and forth. She did not react, continued to stare straight ahead.

He looked at Major Hembree again, this time shaking his head.

Anjele was blind.

CHAPTER 21

CONSULTING WITH OTHER PHYSICIANS IN New Orleans, as well as those arriving with General Butler's troops, Dr. Duval found they were all in agreement that there was no way of knowing whether Anjele's blindness was only a temporary condition. The same was true concerning her inability to remember the last few terrifying seconds before she was injured.

With bandaged head, supported by Raymond on one side, Vinson on the other, Anjele managed to attend her father's funeral. They held her up on her feet, there on the windswept hillock, as his coffin was placed inside the mausoleum with her mother's. Trapped in a black void, she realized that never in her life had she felt so alone.

In the days following, she lost all track of time. A few people called, friends of her father to pay their condolences. They offered sympathy over what they delicately referred to as her *condition*, avoiding direct reference to her blindness. She held her tongue, aching to scream that she didn't want their pity.

Finally everyone drifted away, and she was grateful to be alone with her thoughts. Lying there, swallowed by the stygian abyss, Anjele resolved to adapt to her condition, for if her vision did not return, she would not allow herself to become an invalid.

One evening, when Mammy brought her supper tray, Anjele insisted on feeding herself. It was difficult, groping with the fork, and she could hear Mammy's sighs and knew she was making a mess. "I have to try," she repeated over and over. "I can do it if I try."

Hearing the door open, Anjele lifted her head instinctively, wondering who it was, then felt a wave of disappointment to recognize Claudia's voice.

"Oh, that's disgusting. Mammy, what's wrong with you? Why aren't you feeding her? Food all over the bed, all over her. I ought to have you whipped—"

"Don't you touch her!" Anjele cried, sliding her tray to the side and hearing Claudia curse again as her glass of milk turned over, soaking into the bed. She felt harsh hands pushing against her.

"Don't you dare get up, do you hear me? I can see it's time we got a few things understood around here, such as how you're going to do as you're told and stay out of my way. I've got a plantation to run, and I don't have time to coddle you."

Anjele did not need eyesight to know how Claudia looked as she towered over her ranting and raving. She'd seen the expression too many times to count—eyes bulging, teeth bared, hands twisted into threatening claws slicing through the air. She waited for Claudia to catch her breath, then firmly said, "I don't intend to get in your way. Neither do I intend to be treated like an invalid, locked in this room and spoon fed like an infant. I'm going to learn to take care of myself, and you can't stop me."

"I can do anything I want, Anjele. And *you* can't stop *me*. First of all, you're blind and helpless. And if that's not enough, I'll remind you there's a war going on. Planters are running away in droves, but I'm staying, because I have the promise of troops to keep BelleClair operating, and I intend to do just that."

"Aren't you forgetting something?" Anjele quietly asked. "Like Poppa's will? When Mr. DuBose was here to pay his respects, he said when I felt up to it, he'd go over it with me.

"He told me what was in it," she added.

Claudia sneered, "You don't really think that matters now, do you? Fool! I haven't ingratiated myself with the Yankees for nothing. All I have to do is ask General Butler to officially confiscate BelleClair, and for all intents and purposes, it's mine. I've already signed the loyalty oath, and believe me, I can have anything I want now."

Anjele sank deeper into her world of darkness and despair, for she knew Claudia was right. What difference did her father's will make now? He might as well have deeded BelleClair over to the Union.

Claudia was silent for a long time, wanting to give Anjele sufficient time to ponder her words. Remembering Mammy was still in the room, she dismissed her with a wave.

Anjele heard the door open and close, and, thinking it was Claudia who had gone, whispered brokenly, "What am I going to do, Mammy?"

She jumped at the sound of Claudia's laughter once more.

"You aren't going to do anything but stay out of my way as much as possible. And as soon as Dr. Duval says you're over your injury, you're getting out of here. I don't want you around whining and feeling sorry for yourself. I'm much too busy, and besides, I plan to make BelleClair a delightful retreat for the soldiers. I'm going to have balls and parties and barbecues and picnics, and I don't want you ruining everyone's fun by groping about and staggering into things."

Each cruel, hateful word stung like an angered wasp, but with each venomous injection, Anjele's spine stiffened. "This is still my home," she reminded her sister, "and you can't run me out."

Claudia laughed, "We'll see about that."

After she left, Anjele lay there for a long time, carefully planning how she was going to learn to exist in a world of darkness. First she would memorize her room, which would be easy, for she knew it so well already. Next she would go through the entire house, a room, a hallway at a time. Once she could find her way from top to bottom without difficulty, the grounds would be next. True, she'd have to rely on others, like Mammy Kesia, to help her with certain tasks, but she'd succeed, by God. She would not allow Claudia to run her out of her own home.

This time, Anjele made up her mind to fight back.

In the following weeks, she amazed all the household servants by her dogged determination. Able to find her way about the house with ease, she mastered riding skills next. Admitting to needing a guide, for a horse was a moving object and sometimes unpredictable, she enlisted little William, Kesia's son, to go about with her.

Soon the sight became commonplace—the little black boy riding alongside the white lady. Anyone not knowing them would never have guessed she was blind, for Anjele rode with head high, shoulders straight, serene with confidence.

It was only inside, where no one could see, that she allowed herself sometimes to be frightened.

At first, Claudia had watched, waiting for Anjele to fail, and when she didn't, decided it made no difference. Anjele couldn't stop her from taking control of BelleClair.

Raymond, feeling more useless with each passing day, drank heavily. Most of the time, he was in a stupor, not caring what happened. Claudia had threatened to kick him out if she caught him so much as lifting a little finger to help Anjele, much less spend time with her. And he was terrified at the thought of being banished, for there was nowhere to go. His parents had both signed loyalty oaths to the Union, which he adamantly refused to do, and they were reluctant to have him visit, for fear he'd cause trouble, drunk as he always was. With his game leg, he was unable to fight, unfit for any kind of work. At BelleClair, he was taken care of. And when Elton's supply of whiskey and wine had been depleted, and Claudia had made no effort to persuade her Yankee friends to furnish him with more, he surprised even himself by devising a secret distillery to make a crude kind of rum from molasses. He then made one of the sugarhouses a secret retreat and spent most of his waking hours there.

Meanwhile, with the help of Major Hembree and approval of General Butler, Claudia was able to keep the cane and cotton fields efficiently moving right along, heading for a most successful yield at season's end. She was able to find several competent overseers willing to work for reasonable wages once assured that troops would be around to deal with any slave uprisings. Once everything was under control in that area, she turned her attention to making BelleClair a Union retreat. Officers were invited to stay in luxury indoors, while soldiers camped out on the lawn beneath the great, spreading oaks. No longer did she have to worry about the plantation being ransacked or raided. Woe to any forager who dared disturb the peace.

Anjele hated the Yankees, and when they were about, she refused to leave her room. Mammy would describe the lavish dinner parties, and she knew her father was probably turning over in his grave.

Sleep did not come easily, for she was haunted by memories of that fateful night. She knew there was something important just out of her grasp that desperately had to be recalled. Yet she could force her memory to go no further than kneeling beside her father, sickened and terrified by the blood, the knife sticking out of his chest. It had finally come back to her that, yes, he had said something to her, but it was like feathers in the wind, floating higher, higher, always out of reach, only to swoop and dance and tease as she desperately tried to discover what it was that tortured so.

Eventually she had also been able to dwell on the terrifying glimpse of the poker, slicing through the air. She had seen a man—but who? Always, as his face started to emerge from the wispy clouds of oblivion, the image slipped away, lost in the shadows of her tormented mind.

Anjele found the lack of war news frustrating, for she clung to the hope that Rebel forces would retake New Orleans, but she didn't know what was going on anywhere. Raymond was forbidden to come to her room, and she did not encounter him anywhere in the house. Claudia wouldn't allow her to take her meals downstairs, and she didn't want to, anyway, what with Mammy telling her how the Yankees came and went at leisure. The only information she got was from Dr. Duval, which wasn't often. As time passed, it became obvious there was no need for him to examine her several times a week. The wound to her head healed. He told her over and over how lucky she was. A bit more force, and she would have died. He could give her no words of encouragement that her vision would return. All she could cling to, he regretted having to say, was hope. He only came about every ten days or so.

He had told her about all the fighting going on in Virginia, as Federal forces tried to capture the Confederate capitol at Richmond. And though the final assault went badly for the South, General Robert E. Lee's forces had been able to hold the Union Army of the Potomac at bay. Anjele was saddened to hear of so many casualties after what was being called the Seven Days' Campaign—over twenty thousand Confederates reported dead.

She was further stricken to learn Jamie Rabine was among them and knew Miss Melora would be devastated with grief. However, she was surprised by Dr. Duval's reaction when she remarked she'd like to go into town to pay her respects to her former music teacher.

"No, it's not safe for a young lady. Especially in your . . . condition," he gingerly added.

Anjele did not argue but quietly made her own plans. Two days later, when Mammy Kesia dutifully reported Claudia had left to go into town to spend the day with

Elisabeth Hembree, Anjele ordered her carriage made ready. "You'll go with me," she told Mammy, "and be my eyes. We'll call on Miss Melora and then we'll go for a walk, and you can tell me what you see. I want to know what it's really like in New Orleans now."

Mammy was leery, confiding she'd heard terrible tales.

"Nonsense." Anjele breezily tossed aside her protests. "TheYankees are in control, aren't they? Surely, they won't allow rioting and such. What could happen? We'll be fine."

Mammy described the streets of New Orleans as very crowded, mostly with soldiers, and Anjele could hear the noise. "I do hope Miss Melora's house wasn't stolen like so many others," she remarked.

The carriage slowed, stopped, and Mammy told her, "We'll soon know, 'cause here we is. But maybe we better wait awhile," she added, "some soldiers are comin' down the sidewalk, and they're starin' right at you."

"So? We aren't doing anything wrong. Help me down, William," she called to the boy, unaware he was already standing in front of her till she felt his hand touching hers.

Warily, Mammy followed, opening a parasol to shade Anjele from the sun.

The soldiers reached them. William held back, but Anjele thought he merely underestimated her bravado in darkness. Stepping forward, she bumped right into one of the men.

"Hey, watch it!" he snarled, then, eyes narrowing in suspicion, accused, "You did that on purpose, didn't you? You think 'cause you're a woman, we're supposed to get out of your way, or you'll just run right into us, won't you?"

Anjele did not immediately grasp what was going on, because William, terrified of the ferocious-looking soldiers, dropped her hand and went to cower behind the carriage. Mammy Kesia, also struck with fear, was barely able to whisper, "Soldiers. Just let 'em pass."

To the delight of his companions, the soldier gave Anjele a rough shove that sent her stumbling back against the carriage. "Get out of our way. Show some respect."

Anjele exploded. "What do you think you're doing? You push a woman and dare speak of respect? You damn Yankee . . ."

She had bumped into Mammy and in throwing out her arms for balance, brushed the parasol. Groping for it, she swung out and managed to hit one of the soldiers across his face. Mammy started screaming, and with William right on her heels, took off down the middle of the street.

"Why, you arrogant little bitch," the soldier cried, jerking the parasol out of her hand and breaking it across his knee. "I'll teach you to hit me."

"Yeah," one of the others goaded. "Remember Order 28, Ned. She's nothing but a prostitute. I say we take her in the nearest alley and throw her down and put her to work."

Anjele was too mad to be scared, and as strong hands clamped down on her shoulders, she fought back, slapping, clawing, kicking, as they began dragging her away.

Inside the house, Melora Rabine had heard the commotion. Flinging open the door, she ran down the steps calling, "Stop it, you scalawags. Leave that poor girl alone."

"Stay out of this," one of the soldiers said, "or we'll

have you charged with Order 28, too."

A crowd was gathering in the streets, and Melora was relieved to see other soldiers running toward them to intervene. "You better leave her alone," Melora shrieked, "That poor girl is blind!"

"Blind?" one of the men echoed.

Anjele felt the clutching hands fall away, but still she fought, whirling this way and that, striking out.

Backing away from her, the soldiers stared in astonishment to realize she really could not see them.

Melora ran up and grabbed her. "It's all right. It's me, Melora Rabine. You're all right now. Come with me . . . ." she quickly led Anjele inside the house and closed the door.

Guiding her into the parlor to the sofa, Melora clucked. "Oh, you poor dear. General Butler and his Order Number 28." She gave a disgusted snort. "It's not safe for our women to be out, what with those soldiers having the right to treat them like a prostitute."

Anjele, calming a bit, asked what she was talking about.

"Why, haven't you heard? General Butler said he was tired of his officers and soldiers being subjected to insults from women of New Orleans, and he's issued an order that says they're to be regarded as no better than prostitutes."

"Dear Lord." Anjele shook her head from side to side. She felt like crying but could not, would not, determined to resist weakness of any sort.

Melora left her to make tea. Returning, she mustered courage to speak of that which cut like a knife to her soul. "I know you're here about Jamie, and I want you to know I appreciate it. It's something I'll never get over. I thought when I lost Fred to malaria ten years ago, I knew what heartache was. I was wrong. When a mother loses a child, the pain is indescribable."

Anjele found her hand in the darkness and squeezed. "It hurts to lose your parents, too. All of a sudden, I realize I'm nobody's child."

"And your own tragedy," Melora offered, "So sad—"

"No, please, don't." Anjele was almost harsh in her protest. "Don't feel sorry for me. I can cope with blindness but not pity."

"And you're doing very well, I hear. Ida Duval was telling me just the other day how Vinson is so pleased with how you're managing to get on with your life. Though how you put up with that traitorous sister of yours is beyond me."

"We do what we must and take one day at a time." Anjele reached out and found the tray, felt for the cream pitcher and was grateful Miss Melora was allowing her to fend for herself.

Suddenly there was a loud pounding on the door, and Melora got up to answer. "That must be Mammy Kesia. I saw her run away, but she probably realized by now it's safe to come back."

Anjele frowned. Mammy would never be so rude as to pound on a door like that. Then the sound of angry voices reached her ears, and she knew her suspicions were correct.

Trouble.

She heard Miss Melora say nervously, "Well, she's in here but remember she is blind, and—"

"We'll handle it."

Anjele groaned to recognize Major Hembree's voice. He came right to her and crisply informed her that she had been charged with violation of General Order Number 28. When told she was being taken to Union Headquarters for arraignment, she bit her tongue to keep from screaming in protest. She did not want to upset Miss Melora any more than she already was, and besides, Anjele wasn't about to give the major the pleasure of using force to take her in.

She spoke not a word, but kept her head held high as she endured the humiliation of having to be led away. Though she couldn't see them, Anjele felt the staring eyes as she passed.

General Butler was in a meeting and not immediately available to pass judgment. Placed in a room to wait, she sensed others were around.

Among the adjustments she'd had to make was the feeling of being trapped in a night never ending, for time stood still in her darkness. She had no idea how long she sat there waiting but fiercely made up her mind not to let her anguish show. She sat with chin up, back straight, did not move.

When Major Hembree finally returned, he took one look at her and knew he'd never seen a more stubborn girl in all his life. Lovely, beyond a doubt, and her blindness, a tragedy. Yet it was a blessing the entire Southland wasn't as obdurate or the Union would never have a chance for victory.

Without salutation, he brusquely informed her, "General Butler has left it to me to deal with you."

Anjele had heard his footsteps and was not startled when he spoke. "So deal with me, Major. Tell me," she continued with obvious contempt, "do you really plan to charge me with prostitution in accordance with your general's famous, ridiculous Order Number 28? I should think a blind harlot would be something of a novelty, even for you Yankees."

Major Hembree stiffened but remained composed. Soldiers were about, having been stationed to keep an eye on the prisoner, and he wasn't about to allow them to witness his discomfiture before a woman, especially a Rebel. "I'll ignore your insolence, Miss Sinclair, yielding once again to your disability. But I want you to know it's only because of your sister that I was able to convince General Butler to be lenient. He was unmoved when I told him about your blindness, because he shares my opinion that you use it to your advantage."

"A lie," Anjele had to protest, biting back the tongue-lashing she ached to inflict.

He went on as though she had not spoken. "So I did talk him out of sending you off to prison, which he thought was the best way to handle your situation. He agreed to give you another chance, but you won't be allowed to return to New Orleans. Until further notice, you are not to leave the grounds of BelleClair, understand?"

"That's not fair. For you to tell me where I can and cannot go isn't right."

She heard the sound of snickering and knew her instincts had been right in sensing others were watching.

With a chuckle, Hembree asked, "Do I really need to remind you're a prisoner?"

"It's not my fault your soldiers are rude and disorderly. They cause the trouble, not the women, and—"

"Oh, for heaven's sake, Anjele, just shut up, will you?" Claudia breezed into the room, murmuring a quick apology to Major Hembree for all the trouble before going on to admonish, "I swear, I've never been so embarrassed in my whole life. There I am, having a lovely time with Elisabeth, when soldiers come to tell me you've been arrested. So help me, if I have to lock you in your room, this isn't going to happen again."

Turning to the major, Claudia assured, "I'll make sure all the groomsmen and servants know she's not to leave. I promise she won't cause any more trouble."

"I hope not. General Butler made it clear next time she'll go to prison. He's fed up with his troops being treated disrespectfully."

"They're treated like royalty at BelleClair," Claudia cooed, offering her most dazzling smile. "And you tell General Butler I'm looking forward to having him visit any time he wants to."

Anjele stood, feeling sick to her stomach to hear such fawning.

Claudia grabbed her arm and yanked her along, furiously condemning her behavior and swearing she'd be sorry if she ever caused one more ripple of annoyance to the army.

Anjele was determined to remain silent. It wouldn't do any good to argue. Not now. Till her vision returned, there was little she could do to assert herself. But she could not, would not, allow herself to think her blindness might be permanent. To lose all hope meant she would be at Claudia's mercy.

And God help her if it came to that.

Leo felt his pulse quicken at the sight of the white glove. He glanced about, to reassure himself no one else was in the cemetery. It was midnight, and it was creepy, and every night he had to go there, hating it more and more. "You in there?" he softly, anxiously called.

"I am here," The Voice replied.

At once, Leo wanted to know, "Did she die?"

"She didn't die. She woke up. She will live."

Leo swore, licked his lips nervously, and dared ask, "Did she remember me?"

"It's being said she remembers nothing beyond her father lying on the floor. She's also blind," The Voice added accusingly.

Leo breathed a sigh of relief. "Then I'll be okay." He was grinning.

The Voice went on, ignoring Leo's mutterings. "You will continue to come by here and wait for my signal."

"Signal for what?" Leo yelped. "You just told me she's blind and don't remember nothin', and if she don't remember nothin', what's to worry about?"

"Shut up and listen to me, you damn fool," The Voice exploded in fury. "None of this would've happened if you'd done your job as you were supposed to. And when the time is right, you're going to finish what you started out to do, which is find those goddamn plates. When I give the order, you will use whatever means it takes to make Anjele Sinclair tell where her father hid them. Do you understand?"

Leo grudgingly said he did.

"There's some money above the door. Enough to keep you drunk for a while."

Leo leaped to get it.

Getting drunk was exactly what he intended to do.

Brett sat outside the tent, drenched with sweat. It was the end of June and steamy hot. All around him, other soldiers were sprawled on the ground, not moving in hopes of catching the blessing of even the slightest breeze. They were finally at Harrison's Landing, the Federal supply base on the James River, but getting there hadn't been easy. When word had come that General Lee's army had broken through Federal lines at Gaines' Mill, McClellan had ordered his troops to retire—he didn't like the word retreat. So they had fought their way, engaging in bitter battle at a place called Savage Station on the 29th of June, and Frayser's Farm and White Oak Swamp the next day. The worst had come at Malvern Hill the first day of July, but then they'd reached the protection of a Federal river fleet. The survivors were lucky to be alive, but a pall hung over the camp to know the dream of the North capturing Richmond had failed.

All Brett wanted to do was go to sleep like the other men, but he had been summoned to headquarters and now he waited. Finally, Sergeant-Major Peterson told him he could go in. He got to his feet wearily, brushed at the dust on his blue uniform, and entered the tent, offering a perfunctory salute.

Colonel Drake stood to reach across his desk to shake Brett's hand and smile. "I'm pleased to meet you, Cody. You've made quite a name for yourself." Brett saw the shoulder straps lying on his desk. Two gold bars. Another promotion. He supposed he should feel something, but what? Pride? He was just trying to stay alive in a war he didn't believe in. So upping his rank only meant he'd be drawing seventy dollars a month, an increase of ten dollars.

"Congratulations," the colonel was saying. "You've been promoted to the rank of captain."

Brett offered obligatory words of gratitude.

"But that's not the only reason you're here." He sat down, gestured for Brett to do likewise. "You're being transferred. General Butler in New Orleans reports they believe Confederate spies are slipping in and out through the bayous. I don't have to tell you his men don't dare try to go in after them, so he's asking for scouts who know the area to come in and show them the trails and make maps, so the bayou won't be so inaccessible to our soldiers. We know you're Acadian, and we've heard you used to live in that area, so you'll be familiar with the dangers associated with swamps and bayous. "You're being sent down there to help out," he finished.

Brett scowled. "I don't suppose it makes any difference if I say I don't want to go."

"Not a bit."

Stiffly, angrily, Brett got up to leave.

Colonel Drake reminded him, "Here are your shoulder straps, Captain Cody."

Brett took them and left the tent.

He headed to where he'd left his horse, because there was a bottle of whiskey in the saddlebag, and never had he needed a drink more.

The last place in the world he wanted to go was Louisiana, because the last woman in the world he wanted to see was there.

CHAPTER 22

ANJELE BEGAN SPENDING HER DAYS AT THE cemetery. When it was hot, the sun blazing down, she would sit beneath the shading arms of a leafy magnolia. When rains forced her inside the mausoleum, she didn't mind, for there was no fear, only peace. Hours passed as she thought of the past, when times were happy. Sometimes overcome with loneliness and despair, she could not hold back the tears. Yet being there was preferable to being back at the house where, to avoid Claudia's cruel nagging and the constant intrusion of the Yankees, she had to remain sequestered in her room.

Claudia had also forbidden any of the servants to walk with her on the grounds, much less go riding with her. Mammy Kesia was allowed only to bring her meal trays to her room.

Actually, Anjele was surprised that Claudia didn't object to her daily treks to the cemetery, but so far, nothing had been said.

Using her grandfather's walking stick to poke and prod her way along the path, Anjele would stay until she heard the bell clanging to signal the end of the work day. Only then would she return, entering the house by the rear to climb the back stairs slowly to get to her room.

One day blended into the next. She never heard Raymond's voice anywhere, but Mammy had confided that he also disappeared much of the time, to drink, she suspected. Claudia didn't seem to care what anyone did, so long as the fields were efficiently run by the overseers. Her only interest was entertaining the conquering enemy, and nearly every day officers' wives came for tea, and a lavish dinner party was held almost nightly. Weekends were endless picnics and lawn parties, weather permitting.

Dr. Duval's visits became even more infrequent. There really wasn't anything he could do for her but repeat the prognosis that she might or might not regain her eyesight. The blow had been powerful, and he never failed to emphasize how fortunate she was to be alive.

But secretly, miserably, she was starting to wonder whether the latter was true.

It was strange, Anjele mused, that there were those who thought because a person was blind, she was also deaf. Sometimes, if she dared linger about the house, perhaps to sit on the veranda, Claudia's new friends would discuss her as though she couldn't hear.

"Such a pity," a woman remarked one day, standing, Anjele guessed, perhaps around ten feet away. "Claudia is a saint, caring for her as she does."

Her companion had eagerly agreed. "I know, and it has to be a terrible burden, especially with her attitude. I understand poor Claudia has to watch her constantly. They say she's quite the little rebel. She actually attacked one of our soldiers, you know. General Butler was about to put her in jail . . . ." Their voices faded as they walked away.

Anjele had got up to find her way to the only place she felt at peace these days—the cemetery.

Sometimes, if Anjele had gone to the cemetery early in the day, Mammy would slip away around lunchtime with a small basket of food, then scoot back to the house to serve the ever-present guests.

One day, right after Mammy had come and gone, Anjele was about to bite into a ham biscuit, when she heard a rustling sound. She had never been scared before, even though the cemetery was hidden from view owing to the rise of the land and all the shrubs and flowers her father had planted. Now, however, she was starting to feel uneasy. "Who's there?" she called in a slightly tremulous voice, telling herself it was probably a field hand strayed too far to take care of his personal needs. "Is anyone there?"

She heard it again.

"Please . . ." she implored bravely, "just go away. You've nothing to fear from me."

True panic began to ripple up and down her spine as she heard footsteps slowly coming her way.

Reaching for the cane, she got to her feet, turning toward the noise to say nervously, "Go away. I don't want any trouble—"

She jumped, startled, as a man who suddenly seemed to be standing directly in front of her said in apparent wonder, "Why, you're blind. You can't see me."

She swung her head sharply from side to side, taking small backward steps in retreat. "I told you to go. Get out of here. Leave me alone. I'll scream if you don't—"

"No, Lordy, don't do that," he was quick to plead. "I'll go. I'll go."

She dared to breathe a little easier.

"I didn't mean to scare you," he apologized, rushing to explain, "I just smelled food . . . ham, and I thought maybe you could spare a starvin' Reb a bite, you no doubt bein' Southern, yourself, but I'll be goin', 'cause I can see you're scairt . . . ."

"No, wait." Anjele wasn't about to let a Confederate soldier go hungry. "Please, take this." Poking with her cane, she found the spot where she'd been sitting, touching the basket. "There," she told him. "Ham and lard biscuits, and Mammy usually puts some fruit in, when we have any, which isn't often, I'm afraid. And I think I smelled some muscadines."

"Oh, Lord, yes, grapes!" He cried around a mouthful of ham, because he'd quickly grabbed up the biscuit she'd laid aside. "Good ham, too. Can't remember the last time I had ham, and this is every bit as good as what we had in Mississippi."

"You're from Mississippi," she said, pleased. Gingerly, she lowered herself to sit while he ate and could hear him eagerly devouring the food. "Tell me, please," she urged, "anything you know about the war. No one tells me anything. Are we winning? Will our men come back and run the Yankees out of New Orleans? Is that why you're here?" She was relaxing, grateful for his company.

"I wish it was, but it ain't, and I ain't got time to tell you 'bout that miserable war, 'cause I got to get back to it soon's I can. I got separated from our regiment when they was fightin' at Baton Rouge and been tryin' to find my way back ever since."

"You've been hiding here? At BelleClair?" she asked, astonished. "Why, this place is crawling with Yankees, thanks to my . . . sister." She nearly choked on the word. "She courts them to get protection for BelleClair, and they're everywhere."

"Well, I ain't been hidin' right around here, but close by. I think I've got my sights set now, and I'm ready to head back to our lines, but I was so hungry I knew I couldn't go nowhere till I got somethin' to eat."

"I'm afraid there's not much here. If I'd known about you, I'd have made sure there was more."

"You mean you folks got food to spare?" he asked incredulously. "Lady, not too many people around these parts got enough to eat themselves."

"Yes, we have plenty." She was bitter to think why that was so. "The Yankees use BelleClair as a kind of retreat, and there's lots of everything. I'll be glad to sneak some of it to you, if you aren't leaving right away."

"You'd do that? You'd sneak lots of food out for me?"

"Of course I would."

"When can you bring it? I'll wait for you. I'll stand a better chance of makin' it back if I don't have to forage for food. I can just keep goin' and head straight for Tennessee."

Anjele's heart began to pound. She had felt so useless, unable to fend for herself, much less her beloved Southland. Here at last was a chance to help at least one Confederate soldier. "Come back tomorrow at dawn, just before folks start moving around and getting ready to go into the fields. I'll have everything you need."

"Can you really?" he asked skeptically. "I mean, you bein' blind, you might not know if you're being followed, and if they catch me, they'll shoot me."

"That won't happen. No one will see me, because they'll all be asleep. Besides, I know my way around the house and the kitchen out back. I can gather what you'll need. Flour. Sugar. Coffee. Fatback. Even some ham," she added with a smile.

"You're an angel," he cried, "and I'll be here, for sure. Now I'm gonna take the rest of your food and skeedaddle 'fore somebody comes along."

"Oh, no, please," she protested, "Don't go. You haven't even told me your name . . . ."

"Letchworth. Tom Letchworth."

She could tell he was moving away. "Tom, please," she begged, "Stay awhile longer. I'm so hungry for news of the war, and you don't have to be afraid of anyone coming around. This is the family cemetery, and nobody ever comes here but me, so . . ." She sadly became aware she was once more alone, as the sound of his footsteps faded away.

Suddenly she felt like crying with frustration.

How would she know when it was dawn? For that matter, how would she even know when it was really night? All she had to go on were her instincts, listening for silence that would indicate the nightly parties were over and everyone was sleeping. Only then could she dare make her way out to the kitchen and pack satchels with food. It might mean sitting at the cemetery for hours, for she'd be unsure of exactly when it was time for the soldier to come. But so what, she bitterly asked herself. What else did she have to do? At least, for the first time in a long time, she was doing something worthwhile. And dear Lord, that meant so much.

Time dragged more than ever. When Mammy Kesia brought her supper tray, Anjele knew she wouldn't eat a bite but would save everything for that poor starving soldier. It smelled delicious, too. "Roast chicken?"

"Sho' is," Mammy cheerily confirmed. "And cornbread stuffin' and sweet taters. Got some blackberry cobbler, too."

"Is Claudia having a very large dinner party tonight?"

Mammy snorted. "The usual. 'Bout six o' them fancy-pants officers and only five of 'em got women with 'em. Don't look nice. Not with Mastah Raymond passed out drunk in his room, most likely sleepin' till noon tomorrow. Naw sir." She sniffed. "Don't look nice atall, but Miss Claudia would have my hide fo sayin' so."

Anjele murmured agreement, thinking that if she weren't blind, by God, it wouldn't be going on. Not under her roof. She'd run the hated Yankees off fast, and Claudia with them, if she dared protest. And Raymond would stop going around in a stupor and straighten himself up and get busy and help out, and . . .

She shook her head to dismiss such wishful thinking.

Toying with the idea of asking Mammy to help, Anjele decided against it. If anything were to go wrong, she didn't want her involved.

Mammy hadn't noticed she hadn't left the lunch basket on the table in the service closet. Instead, she'd brought it up to her room, apparently unnoticed by anyone who might have been watching. Carefully she packed her supper inside, then slid it under the bed.

There was nothing left to do but wait.

For a while she dozed, then awoke sometime later with a start. It would have been nice to be able to hear the case clock in the hallway strike the hour, but that was another way Claudia had to bedevil her. She had ordered all the striking clocks in the house stopped so Anjele wouldn't be able to tell time. "What difference does it make?" she had taunted. "For you, it's always nighttime, so why worry about it?"

Counting the memorized number of steps to her bedroom door, Anjele pressed her ear against it but didn't hear anything. Cautiously she turned the knob, then poked her head out into the hall. All seemed quiet.

Retrieving the basket and her cane with a silent prayer for help and guidance, she left the room and felt her way down the hall. At the stairs she moved extra slowly, hand gripping the railing. The farther down she went, the more assured she became that it was actually quite late. She could almost hear the house breathing, as though relieved to be at rest.

Finally she reached the kitchen out back. Using her sense of touch and smell, Anjele was able to find a large slab of ham, a loaf of bread, and a sack of coffee. Gathering what other staples she could locate, she filled the basket to the rim. Though it would be heavy to carry all the way to the cemetery, she had only to think how much it was going to mean to the poor soldier, and she was instantly fired with energy.

Dear Lord, let it still be night and nowhere near dawn, she prayed, moving as fast as she dared back to the house. Mammy had gone with her the first day to the cemetery, and she'd counted steps, so she knew exactly how far it was and the location of every potential spot where she might trip and fall. But counting had to be started from the veranda, not the kitchen building.

It was a long, arduous trek. She could only walk a few steps before having to set the basket down and catch her breath, for she had to tote it with one hand. Her other held the cane, needed for poking the ground to make sure nothing was in her path.

She listened for every sound but heard only the mournful call of a whippoorwill and the whispering breeze rustling through the trees. Moving slowly along, her mind drifted back to the delightful nights when she'd visit her special place on the river bank. And as always when she allowed such thoughts to invade her heart, sadness overwhelmed as she remembered those sweet, wonderful nights when Gator had come to her there. No matter that he'd broken her heart to bits and pieces with his lies. There was no denying he'd given joy beyond belief, and despite everything, the happy memories were cherished and savored. Never would she forget the first, wonderful night in the bayou, when he'd showed her the magic of that ethereal place in a way she'd never dreamed possible—the tiny creatures of the forest, the way the moonlight dappled through the Spanish moss clinging to the branches above, lacing their paths in silver gleaming.

Yes, those were the moments Anjele allowed herself to dwell upon, for they were all she'd ever have. Why throw them away? Instead, why not cast aside the betrayal and think only of the splendor and glory in his arms? For even now, so many years later, he came to her in dreams, and as she gazed lovingly into his warm, caressing eyes, she saw no doubt, no mendacity, only the adoration and devotion promised. And it was these precious thoughts she clung to in the despair her life had become. It didn't really matter anymore that he had lied, had never meant a word of anything he said. He gave her joy for a little while that now, sadly, would have to last a lifetime.

The cane found the iron gate. She set the basket down and maneuvered the latch, then took the food and went the last little way.

The air was cool, a soft wind blowing, and she found her way to her favorite spot beneath the tree and sat down. Gathering her shawl about her, she leaned back, hoping it wasn't too long till dawn, so the soldier would come and go. Then she could breathe easy, for if a Yankee did come by, it would be difficult to explain why she was there at such an hour, especially with such a large quantity of food. It would be obvious what she was up to, and not only would the soldier be captured, but she'd be in serious trouble, as well.

After what seemed forever, Anjele heard sounds coming from the same direction as before. "Tom, I'm here," she softly called, scrambling to her feet and tapping the basket with the cane. "Wait till you see what I've got for you."

"Mighty nice of you," he began, but then abruptly cried, "Oh, shit! You were followed—"

She could hear him running in the opposite direction, and she began to beat at the air with her arms, crying, "Wait! What's wrong? Where are you going? There's no one here but me—" She jumped as a masculine voice boomed out only a short distance away.

"Wrong, Miss Sinclair. In fact, if you could see, you'd realize you've got lots of company."

With a moan, she sank to the ground, then jerked her head up to recognize Claudia's voice as she came running up the path.

"Did you catch him? Did he get away?" She was asking of the man who'd spoken.

"My men will get him, but one Reb doesn't matter. What's important is we know now who's been supplying these bushwhackers with supplies."

"No, no, you're wrong," Anjele protested. "He's no bushwhacker. He's just a hungry soldier who got separated from his regiment, and he's on his way back, and I only gave him food. And it's the first time—"

"And the last," the man snapped. "Take her away."

Anjele felt rough hands grabbing her. She dropped the cane, tried to retrieve it, but they dragged her away, ignoring her pleas.

"Where you're going, you won't need a cane," someone said.

Claudia shrieked, "I won't help you this time, Anjele. You had your chance. I just hope General Butler realizes I had nothing to do with this, or else he'll have BelleClair burned to the ground. That's what he said he'd do to plantations giving refuge to bushwhackers, and if he does, it's all your fault."

When they reached the house, someone shouted to bring a wagon around. Anjele's hands were jerked behind her back and tied with a rope. Officers and their wives, awakened by the commotion, gathered on the veranda to see what was happening.

Anjele listened in angry silence as Claudia embellished her tale, saying she'd been noticing Anjele was behaving strangely lately. And, of course, she hadn't wanted to actually believe her own sister would give refuge to a bushwhacker, but she had started spying on her and was horrified to discover it was true.

"Get her away from here now," someone shouted. "I hope General Butler has her hanged."

"Oh, she won't hang," an officer spoke up. "But I can guarantee she'll be in prison a long, long time. She won't be hiding any more bushwhackers. That's for sure."

From a distance, Kesia wrung her hands, tears streaming down her cheeks as she watched the pitiful sight of Miss Anjele being taken away.

She didn't dare open her mouth to intervene, because she was at Miss Claudia's mercy now, like all the other slaves. Master Sinclair wasn't around to protect them, and Miss Anjele wasn't able to do anything. Still, Kesia felt guilty over not disputing Miss Claudia's lies. She had seen Miss Anjele when she left struggling with that basket, because she'd got up earlier than usual. She'd delivered a baby during the night, and the mother had been too weak to nurse it, so she'd gone to the kitchen to boil some sugar water to feed it. She was about to go after Miss Anjele and ask her what she was doing, but just then she had seen Miss Claudia on the side veranda talking to a Yankee soldier. So Kesia had stepped back so they wouldn't see her. But she had kept on watching and witnessed everything.

And Lord, how she wished she could tell the truth.

That soldier wasn't a Rebel bushwhacker.

He wasn't even a Rebel soldier.

Kesia knew, because she had seen him when he came running down from the cemetery, laughing as he passed the other men on their way up.

He was the same Yankee soldier she'd seen Miss Claudia talking to on the veranda.

Miss Anjele had been tricked.

CHAPTER 23

"YOU DIDN'T HAVE TO COME ALL THE way down here to apologize for your sister again, Claudia," Major Hembree said as he sat behind his desk, wishing she'd hurry up and leave. He had been reading the confidential correspondence from General Walbridge of the Secret Service when she'd arrived and was most anxious to get back to it. "I really am busy this morning," he added.

Oblivious to his haste to end the visit, Claudia admitted, "Elisabeth said the same thing, but I felt I had to come. Really, Major, you just can't know how much this has upset me. I've tried so hard to have a good relationship with the army, because heaven knows, I never wanted to go to war in the first place. I was always trying to get Daddy to free all his slaves and offer to pay them wages. They would've stayed, because the working conditions at BelleClair are far superior to any other plantation in the Delta, and—"

"Yes, yes, I know that," he said impatiently. "Now I really am busy—"

"But there's something you need to know. Something I have to tell you." She smiled, as confident of his sudden interest as she was of the outfit she'd so carefully chosen to wear that morning. The dress was lovely, pink cotton with a dainty shawl collar, fitted bodice, with double puff sleeves and flounced skirt. As a finishing touch, she wore a batiste cap trimmed with ribbon rosettes and lace over her golden curls, with kid gloves and a parasol to accessorize.

Major Hembree hoped she might have the information he was after. "Go on," he urged.

She looked at him demurely through lowered lashes, feigning embarrassment to broach such a delicate subject. Making her voice soft, timid, she began, "I'm afraid this isn't the first time Anjele has brought disgrace to the family. Four years ago, I had the horrible misfortune of happening upon her and one of the Acadian workers, a disreputable man known only as Gator. He didn't even have a proper name, for heaven's sake. Anyway, they were in one of the sugarhouses, and decorum, of course, doesn't permit me as a lady to put what they were doing into words, but I'm sure you know what I'm talking about. Naturally, I had to tell my parents, and it broke their hearts."

Major Hembree noticed how her eyes were glittering, her mouth twitching with a suppressed smile. He knew she was enjoying herself immensely, despite the attempt to appear ashamed to divulge family secrets.

"And," she continued, "to avoid all the shame and disgrace, they sent her away to school in Europe. They didn't intend for her to ever return, wanton and wild as she is, and that's why you caught her sneaking in like she did."

She paused, disconcerted by how he was looking at her sharply, eyes narrowed as though in deep thought, yet his lips were twitching as if he were trying to keep from smiling. Nervously she asked, "Is there something wrong, Major? I didn't mean to make you uncomfortable talking like this, but I thought you should know. I wanted to make my position clear, because I simply can't allow her to continue causing trouble. Frankly, I'm hoping General Butler will do something about her, despite her blindness, especially since it's obvious she's using it to her advantage, pretending to be helpless, expecting everyone to feel sorry for her, and—"

"Yes, yes, that's right." Major Hembree bolted to his feet and swiftly moved from behind his desk to cross the room and open the door as an indication the meeting was over. "You've nothing to worry about."

"Did I embarrass you by speaking of something so despicable?"

"Not at all, not at all. Quite the contrary. I needed to know all that, but as I said, you needn't worry. Your sister had a warning, and now she must pay the price. I'm sure General Butler will agree with me the safest place for her now is prison."

"For a long time?" Claudia's pretense of charm disappeared. It was time to make her intentions known once and for all. "The fact is, I don't want her ever to come back to BelleClair. I want her declared incompetent and title to all the lands held by my father's estate given to me."

"Rest assured . . ." he gave her a gentle push through the door, nodding to the soldier in the foyer to speed her on her way. "Anjele will probably spend the rest of her life in jail."

Claudia felt like singing. "Well, that's best. I mean, she is helpless, and—"

With a murmured "Good day," he gently closed the door in her face.

Returning to his desk, Major Hembree snatched up the folder containing General Walbridge's report. He read again how the Secret Service had learned, from a traitor to the South, the identity of the person believed to have stolen the engraving plates during the takeover of the Mint.

Elton Sinclair.

Smiling, Hembree folded his arms behind his head and leaned back in the leather chair. He had already decided Sinclair's murder had to do with the plates. Somebody else knew about them and had tried to get him to talk but failed. However, he was certain Sinclair would have made sure somebody knew where he hid them. It hadn't been Claudia, for sure.

So it was logical, despite the ugly little story he'd just heard, that Anjele had managed to redeem herself in her father's eyes, resulting in his confiding in her, if only during his final moments of life.

And now she needed assistance in locating them for the Confederacy.

Hembree smiled.

He knew just the person to help her.

By helping her, he'd be helping himself as well—to a promotion to lieutenant colonel.

He went to the door and told the soldier outside to have the prisoner brought to his office. "Keep her hands tied behind her back," he reminded. "She's a feisty one."

"Don't worry about that." The soldier laughed. "I saw 'em bring her in. She landed her foot right between Bailey's legs. He's still cryin' when he pisses."

Hembree wiped away the soldier's grin with a glare of reproach for his crudeness.

The man scurried to obey his order.

A few moments later, Anjele was brought in, defiant, face tight with anger. "What am I being charged with this time?" she asked, as one of the two men with her pushed her down in a chair. "Murder?"

He waved the soldiers out, waited till the door was closed to respond. And when he spoke, she sharply turned her head in the direction of his voice, for she'd been staring at the wall without realizing it. "Not murder, Miss Sinclair, but something quite serious, I can assure you."

"All I did was give a hungry man food," she fired back, stung with fury. "If that's a crime, then shoot me, hang me. I'll not beg for mercy."

"You are being charged with receiving stolen goods. If you cooperate and tell me where they're hidden, I can promise you leniency in your sentence for providing shelter to a bushwhacker, and—"

"That's a lie," she blazed, "I told you—I was giving him food. And I don't know what you're talking about. I don't know anything about stolen goods, for heaven's sake.

"What I'd like to know," she hurried on, "is how you Yankees can even put up a good fight against the South, as stupid as you are! Stolen goods, indeed." She gave an unladylike snort and settled back in the chair.

"We're talking about engraving plates, Miss Sinclair," He had expected her to deny knowing anything but proceeded to refresh her memory to let her know he wasn't making wild guesses but knew what he was talking about.

Anjele listened, incredulous, then told him, "The

truth is, I don't know what you're talking about. My father never told me he was involved in the takeover, and he certainly never told me about any engraving plates. But even if he had, you can be sure I'd die before I'd tell you."

"Have it your way," he said with pretended resolve, "but as I said, if you cooperate, we'll go easy on you. Maybe you'll only be in prison for the duration of the war. If you refuse, I can promise you will die there."

Anjele was quiet for a moment, deliberately trying to make him think she was actually considering giving in. Finally, she sneered, "You bastard! Do you think it really matters to me now where I go? My parents are dead, and my home has been turned into a haven for you dirty Yankees. I've lost my eyesight and probably won't ever get it back. Do you really think I give a damn what happens to me? My life is over, anyway, so why should I care where I spend my final days?

"Do with me what you will," she challenged furiously, "because as far as I'm concerned, all of you can go to hell!"

Hembree reeled, struck by the glow of hatred in her sightless eyes. "Very well, Miss Sinclair. You leave me no choice." He bellowed to the soldier outside, who promptly rushed in to receive the order, "Get a detachment here to take the prisoner to Ship Island. At once."

Anjele felt a wave of panic. "But why there?"

Hembree told her a prison had been established there, near Fort Massachusetts, since the Union was now using the island as a base of operations on the Gulf. "You won't be able to help the Rebs find the plates from there."

"I told you," she said between clenched teeth, "I

don't know anything."

"Maybe a few weeks locked away all by yourself will refresh your memory, but I warn you, don't take too long. Should they be found without your help, General Butler will have no mercy for you. He'll leave you in that prison, locked in solitary confinement."

"I know nothing. As for solitary confinement"—her lips curved in a bitter smile—"I think that's where I already am."

After she was taken away, Hembree opened the drawer of his desk and took out the folder containing the names of recently arrived soldiers and officers. At a party only the night before, some of the officers had been discussing how relieved they were to hear an Acadian had been assigned as a scout in the bayou, and Captain Bishop, Hembree recalled, had an interesting tale to share.

It seemed when one of the new officers came to his camp, some civilians—Cajuns, working for food—had recognized him. Bishop had then listened with interest to the discussion about Brett Cody and how he'd once lived in Bayou Perot.

At the time, Hembree had only been mildly impressed.

Now, however, he was ecstatic.

The man, the Cajuns had said, was known by another name, because of an amazing battle with an alligator some years before.

He'd been known only as Gator.

The similarity could not be coincidence. Bayou Perot, he knew, was adjacent to the Sinclair property. Gator, the Cajuns recalled, had abruptly disappeared about four years ago. From what Claudia said, that was the same time she'd seen Anjele in a sugarhouse with a man also called Gator. It had to be the same person, and Hembree was confident he'd been struck by an idea that could not fail.

First, he went in search of Captain Bishop to share his idea. Bishop agreed it was worth trying, and Hembree promptly sent a dispatcher to find Brett Cody.

It took nearly a week.

Brett was not easy to locate, for he spent most of his time doing what he had been sent to do—leading Union patrols into the swamps of Bayou Vista to search for Reb bushwhackers or Southerners fleeing New Orleans. He did not like being summoned to headquarters and didn't care who knew it.

"What's this about, Major?" he demanded as soon as perfunctory greetings and salutes were exchanged. "As far as I had to come, written communication would have saved me a lot of trouble."

Hembree flushed with irritation over what he considered insolence but reminded himself he needed Cody and it was best to keep things peaceable. "Well, this is something that couldn't be put in writing." He forced a patronizing smile as he went on to comment how he'd seen Cody's records and was quite impressed. "You're highly regarded by every officer who's known you, Cody."

Brett merely stared at him in stone-faced silence, thinking how quickly opinion would change if they knew he'd like just to walk away from it all. No longer did he want revenge on the past by witnessing the destruction of Anjele's world. Hell, he didn't even hate her anymore. She'd become part of the past, and in the horrors of war he'd come to realize that if it happened yesterday, it no longer mattered. All he wanted was to make it through today and do the same tomorrow. And more and more, he found himself wishing he'd stayed out West and out of the war.

"I don't think," Brett finally spoke, "you brought me here to talk about my record."

"You're right. I have a new assignment for you. A very important assignment. I can almost guarantee a citation and promotion if you're successful."

"I don't care about a citation or a promotion if it'll get me back to the Army of the Potomac instead." He didn't like leading whining soldiers who were scared to death of everything from big gray spiders dropping down out of the moss to slithering snakes. Two had fainted at the sight of an alligator. He felt like a guardian instead of a scout.

"Sorry," Hembree said, though he wasn't, and proceeded to get to the point. "I understand you're from this area. A place called Bayou Perot, to be exact."

"I worked there," Brett admitted warily, wondering what the major was leading up to.

"You worked for a planter by the name of Elton Sinclair at a plantation south of the city called BelleClair."

"What the hell are you getting at, Major?"

Hembree calmly continued. "We know that Sinclair was involved in the takeover of the U.S. Mint here last year. We also believe he stole new engraving plates that could be financially disastrous to the Federal government if they fall into the hands of the Confederacy."

Brett didn't care about that. "What does this have to do with me? I wasn't working for him then. I haven't worked for him in over four years. Ask him—"

"He's dead."

Brett drew a breath, let it out slowly before coolly repeating, "Like I asked, where do I fit in?"

"We believe his daughter Anjele knows where the plates are hidden."

"Then ask her." He bolted to his feet. "I don't want any part of this."

Hembree decided it was time to pull rank, and shouted, "I didn't ask if you did, Captain. Now sit down and shut up."

Their eyes locked.

Not wanting to sit the war out in jail, Brett bit back the urge to tell him to go to hell.

Hembree continued. "I understand you were once romantically involved with her, and—"

Brett tensed. "Where the hell did you hear that?"

"It doesn't matter. And if you'll stop interrupting, I'll explain your place in all of this."

Brett gave a curt nod. Inside, he was bristling, knowing he wasn't going to like what he was about to hear.

"As I said, we feel Sinclair told his daughter where the plates were hidden, but she obviously hasn't been able to get them to the right people, because they haven't shown up anywhere. Believe me, we'd know if they had. And it will be even more difficult for her to do so now, because she's been sent to prison on Ship Island for giving refuge to Reb bushwhackers."

"Prison?" Brett reeled. "But—"

"She's been quite a Rebel, herself, Cody. She gave us no choice."

Brett shook his head. Despite everything, goddamn it, the thought of Anjele in prison was too much. "It's not right."

"Well, I'm glad you feel that way, because you're

going to get her out."

"You seem to forget I'm not exactly wearing her favorite color uniform."

"You are to convince her you're actually a spy for the Confederacy. You'll use a false name, and you'll tell her the Rebs know her father took the plates, and you've been assigned to help her escape so she can find them, because they're desperately needed.

"We believe," Hembree rushed to add, noting how Cody suddenly looked amused, "that you're the person for the job, because you know her. You know her people. You know how they think and act, and you should be able to persuade her. You also know your way around the area, and you'll be able to find where the plates are hidden from her directions, and—"

Brett burst out laughing. All of a sudden, the absurdity of the scheme was too much. "You don't know as much as you think you do, Major," he said, still chuckling. "Yes, I was romantically involved, as you call it, with Anjele Sinclair, but evidently your sources didn't have all the facts. The truth is, she accused me of raping her, and that's why I had to leave here. I'd be the last person she'd confide in.

"I think"—the mirth faded, as his eyes became hard and cold with rekindled bitterness—"you'd better get somebody else if you want her to talk."

Hembree solemnly shook his head. "You're the man for the job. You can do it. As I said, you know her, know what she's like. Admit you're a Southerner who only pretended loyalties to the North. Hell, tell her you're Acadian, from Mississippi. I don't really care how you work it as long as you get your job done. Manipulate her, Cody.

"Hell, you did it once before, didn't you?" he finished with a sly wink.

Brett let the sarcasm pass, though he felt like slamming his fist in his face. "That was a long time ago. The memories aren't pleasant. She'll take one look at me and it will all be over."

Hembree chuckled. "But she won't."

Brett was confused. "She won't what?"

Major Hembree reached for a cheroot and took his time lighting it. He leaned back in his chair, watching the smoke spiral upwards, enjoying Cody's suspense. Finally, he said, "She won't know it's you." He grinned in triumph. "You see, Anjele Sinclair is blind."

When Brett left, somewhat in a daze, Major Hembree stood at the window and watched him going down the street. Captain Bishop, seeing him leave, came into the office to ask how everything had gone.

"Fine," Hembree told him. "He was shocked at first, as I knew he would be, when I told him about her blindness, but he'll do the job."

Bishop conveyed his relief, then wanted to know, "Are you going to tell our contact about your plan, how you're going to arrange for her to escape and lead our man to where she hid them?"

"No," Hembree replied without hesitation. "Because I don't care what anybody says, I don't trust these Southerners who claim to be working for the Union. He's served his purpose. We won't be telling him anything else."

CHAPTER 24

NO ONE PAID ANY ATTENTION TO LEO AS he slowly shuffled along Basin Street. Shoulders stooped, head bowed, he looked neither right nor left, for he knew the way well. Each night, he made the pilgrimage to St. Louis cemetery, proud of his disguise as an old, bedraggled man.

At last he saw the gates looming and quickened his pace. He was broke. Dead broke. Had been for nearly a week. He'd been evicted from the boardinghouse, forced to sneak into a livery stable and sleep in a straw-littered stall. Sometimes, when he managed to steal whiskey and drink himself into a stupor, he'd wake up to find he'd rolled in a pile of horse dung. And damn it, he didn't like living that way, and if The Voice didn't return pretty soon, Leo knew he'd have to find a job, which was impossible in New Orleans, unless he was willing to work the fields like a slave, and he sure as hell wasn't. So he would have to leave town, head west, maybe, so's the army wouldn't slap a uniform on him, stick a gun in his hand, and kick his ass right into the goddamn war. But if he did hightail it, The Voice might find out and see him arrested for murder.

Leo gave a soft growl of frustration as he took shuffling steps into the cemetery, appearing drunk if anybody was watching and wondered why he'd dare go in at midnight.

The sight of the impaled white glove evoked an excited gasp. At once, he ran nervous fingers across the cold stone inset about the door, laughing out loud to discover the desperately needed money.

"Be quiet, you fool," The Voice cracked from within. "Some other drunk might be around to hear and wonder what's going on."

Leo stuffed the money in his pocket before crouching in front of the door. "Okay. I'm here, and thank God, you are, because I'm broke."

"Follow my orders, Leo, and you'll never have to worry about money again."

"I'm listening."

"Anjele Sinclair has been arrested and sent to a Federal prison on Ship Island. She's housed in a shed situated next to a swampy area that runs into the ocean. Go to Biloxi. Find a man named Seward, who owns a little fishing boat. He's been paid to take you to the island."

"And do what?" Leo was elated to think it might soon all be over. He could collect the big money and hightail it out of New Orleans, and the South, forever.

"She's inaccessible to us now. We can't watch her every move. She might suddenly remember everything, including you, Leo." The Voice paused to give him time to absorb what that could mean. "I'm afraid I'd have to have you killed. I couldn't risk your implicating me."

"Hell, I don't even know who you are," Leo roared. "Shit, you're just a voice inside a grave, damn it. I couldn't say nothin' about you—"

"I wouldn't be comfortable if you were alive, should

she name you as her father's murderer. No . . ." The Voice sighed in resolution, "The time has come to get rid of her. I have too much at stake. I want you to kill her."

Leo smiled in the darkness. "You gonna pay me good, right?"

"Oh, yes. But only if you succeed. And if you don't, you will keep trying. She's got to die."

Brett studied Anjele's file, then had another session with Major Hembree. He would have liked to question Dr. Duval about her condition and prognosis, but Hembree said Duval, along with several business associates of her father, had requested and been granted permission to visit her in prison to ensure she was being properly cared for. Brett couldn't risk Duval telling her someone had been making personal inquiries. He was going to have a tough enough time winning her confidence, anyway, especially while being careful lest she figure out who he was.

At first he had been puzzled to learn that Claudia was the one to marry Raymond but figured Elton Sinclair probably hadn't been able to keep Anjele's so-called rape a secret. Raymond had found out about it, no doubt from Claudia, and apparently decided Anjele was soiled goods, unfit to be his wife.

Yet, when reading about Anjele's first encounter with the Federal navy, Brett wondered why she'd been coming in from Europe at such a dangerous time and what she'd been doing over there in the first place. Hembree then related Claudia's story but also shared Anjele's tale of wanting to be with her father after hearing of her mother's death.

Brett felt pity but remained impassive as Hembree talked on. The fact was the card shuffle of life had dealt her a losing hand, and no matter how she'd betrayed him, Anjele didn't deserve such misery.

The mission had to be kept secret, Hembree decreed, warning, "You're on your own. If you get caught, it will have to be revealed you were on assignment and not actually working for the Confederacy, so you won't hang. But the risk will be your getting shot if you're discovered helping her escape. You won't have any cover. It's got to look like a guard was actually a Reb spy, helping get another spy out of prison."

Brett agreed, pointing out, "We can't even risk letting the guards in on the setup, in case the Rebs really do have a spy planted."

"Exactly. It's got to be carried out quietly and discreetly."

Brett confidently assured him it would be.

Face set and grim, Hembree issued his final orders. "Once you have her off the island and safely ashore, you have permission to use any means necessary to get her to tell you where the plates are hidden. Understand?"

"And then what?"

Hembree shrugged, lips quirked in a mirthless smile. "There's an insane asylum in New York. We'll have her sent there to get her out of the way."

Brett knew he wasn't going to let that happen. "What if all this is a waste of time?"

"She goes to the insane asylum, and we cross our fingers and hope Sinclair died without telling anyone where he hid them."

Brett swapped uniforms, stepping down to the rank of private. With proper legal orders assigning him to the position of guard at the Federal prison on Ship Island, he reported for duty.

Sgt. Edgar Bodine was in charge.

Brett looked him over and decided the man's eyes reminded him of a wharf rat. A matted beard covered the lower part of his face. He was short, with hamlike arms, stomach protruding to hang over his belt. He did not offer to return a salute when Brett reported to his office, nor did he stand or hold out a hand in greeting. He merely continued to sprawl in the chair behind his littered desk, picking his yellowed teeth with a letter opener.

Gaze flicking over Brett in arrogant scrutiny, he took the folder containing his orders from him, absently tossing it among the rest of the clutter. "So you're the new guard," he said, unimpressed. "Sit down."

Looking around, Brett saw only an overturned crate, and declined, along with Bodine's offer to help himself to a bowl of fried pork rinds.

"Good stuff." Sergeant Bodine shoved a handful into his mouth and talked around crunching. "You'll like it here. Easy assignment. The navy takes care of the water, and we take care of the prisoners. Not many of 'em, thank God, so there ain't a lot to do. We keep 'em in what the Rebs used to use for a barn. They sleep on straw in the stalls and gather in the large area during the day. All we gotta do is post guards outside the door and take food in twice a day. Nothin' to it."

Brett felt his nerves stretch raw to think of Anjele being here. He dared venture, "I hear there's a woman prisoner. She doesn't stay in the barn, too, does she?"

"Are you crazy? Damn it, it's a pain in the ass to

have her here, I'll tell you. We don't have no facilities for a female, especially one that's blind. I told headquarters that, but they wouldn't listen, said for me to do the best I could. So I did. I had a storage shed fixed up for her, put a cot in, a table and a chair. Somebody takes her food out three times a day, and other than that, she's on her own. I locked her in at first and then decided she wasn't going anywhere. She's got a bolt on the inside, makes her feel safe, I guess.

"Frankly," he finished with a yawn, "I don't think I've seen her outside over once or twice. Guess she's scared to walk by herself, after I told her about the swamp behind her place."

Reminding himself to appear nonchalant, Brett probed, "What about medical care? I suppose that's another responsibility."

"Not really. She's been here less than two weeks, and already her family doctor came out here to check on her. Also the family lawyer and some guy who says he's a banker in New Orleans. According to the doc, other than not being able to see, she's okay.

"So go find a place to call home," the sergeant said in dismissal. "Introduce yourself around to the other boys. Not much to do here. We play a lot of poker. Saturday nights I let a few cross over to the mainland for a little fun. You know, find a woman that ain't untouchable." He grinned and squeezed his crotch for emphasis.

Brett turned away, all the more determined to get Anjele out of there for reasons of his own. She wasn't safe. Sooner or later some soldier would have too much to drink and get bold.

And this time, he frowned to think, she wouldn't be lying if she called it rape.

He had left his horse stabled on the Mississippi coast in Biloxi, then sought transport to the island on a gunboat. All he had was a haversack, and he left it on an empty bunk in a forgotten corner of the barracks, then forced himself to take time to meet the other guards.

The others seemed friendly enough, and he saw at once they'd become lazy and overweight from too much food, too little work. They spent all their time gambling. Guard duty was merely a temporary distraction, and it looked as if Brett's assignment was going to be easier than he'd thought.

On the pretense of learning his way around, after sharing a quick lunch with the others he set out to explore the area. The base of operations, he discovered, was at one end of the island, which he guessed to be about ten miles in length, while the area designated for a prison was situated at the other. That, he surmised, was the reason the sergeant and his guards could get away with their drinking and revelry. Until more prisoners were brought in, their responsibilities were few, and no one came around to monitor their activities.

He was determined not to go near the building where Anjele was imprisoned until it was his turn at duty, so as not to arouse suspicion. But God, it was tempting, for it had been so damn long. Yet he had only to remind himself bitterly how those sweet memories had been shadowed by deceit, and the pangs of longing would fade to jolts of anger. He had a job to do. He was also compassionate enough to want to get a blind woman out of prison. That's as far as it would go, as far as he could let it go.

He was forced to wait three days, and during that time he planned the escape route. There was a small cove where a rowboat was kept for emergencies. With a distance of nearly twelve miles to shore, Brett estimated, it would no doubt require a real crisis to make a man take on such a formidable task. Well, if all went according to plan, he had one coming up, for sure. Besides, his experience at sea gave him confidence, for he'd been out in similar craft in rougher waters than the bay between the island and the coastline of Mississippi.

At last it was his turn to take Anjele's trays.

"All you gotta do," said Ramey Stocks, the instructing guard, "is knock on her door, and she'll unlock it from the inside. But it takes awhile, 'cause she's got to find her way. She's blind, remember."

Brett nodded, pained. Since hearing of her loss of eyesight, he could not get out of his mind the sweet memories of the nights they'd shared when he'd pointed out the sights of the bayou. At least, he thought, dispirited, she had those memories indelibly etched in her mind, but wondered if she ever thought of them at all.

Ramey was continuing, "So you hand over the tray. You don't go in unless she asks you to, like if she wants you to take out her bucket and bring her a fresh one. Something like that. She's friendly, though. I guess she gets lonesome. Once she asked me inside"—he boasted grinning—"to get a splinter out of her finger, which I did, and Lord, I was struck by how she's such a pretty thing. Hair like spun gold. And when you look at her, you can't even tell she's blind. Her eyes are a green and yellow color. Reminds me of a cat's eyes. But they don't look like she can't see out of 'em, a'tall. When she keeps on staring straight ahead, though, you can tell she ain't seein' nothin. A shame. Real shame." He shook his head. "But she's a spy, you know. They say she was givin' refuge to Reb soldiers."

Brett didn't comment, feigning disinterest.

He got her breakfast from the kitchen, noting it looked a bit more appetizing than the buckets of slop disguised as food given to the male prisoners. Then he headed toward the shed, which was situated at the edge of a small, swampy area.

Standing before the door, he braced himself before calling, "Breakfast, Miss Sinclair."

He heard the sounds of movement inside, and then the door was opening.

Brett could not speak. Actually, he almost forgot to breathe as he drank in the sight of her. She was even more beautiful than he remembered, despite the tattered dress she wore, her dirty and tangled hair. He stared down at her upturned face, long, silken lashes framing hazel eyes that saw only heartache, sadness. His hands gripped the tray he longed to toss aside so he could grab her, crush her in his arms, and kiss away the years and all the pain. God forgive him for being such a fool, but he was never more sure he loved her still.

"Who's here today?" she asked softly. "Ramey?"

"No," he replied in a tight voice. "Not Ramey. Want me to set your tray down?"

"Inside. On the crate." She moved aside, felt him pass. Having noticed a hint of Southern accent, she remarked, "You must be new. Where are you from, soldier?"

Brett knew he had to gain her confidence from the start. There could be no slipups. If she spooked, it was all over. And he'd probably find himself swinging from the end of a rope before Major Hembree even heard about it and had a chance to intervene. Careful, he reminded himself, watch every word. "Mississippi."

"Oh," she said in a condemning tone. "You're one of them—the traitors who turned against the South."

"Not exactly." Damn, he was off to a bad start.

She lifted her chin in a gesture of scorn. "There's no getting around it, soldier. You're a Southerner. You fight for the North. To me, that spells traitor."

"A man does what he must, Miss Sinclair. Just like you. This isn't exactly the place a Southern belle should call home, you know. And I hear you don't venture out much." Lord, it was all he could do to keep his voice from faltering.

Anjele slowly found her way to the cot and sat down. While she didn't like him being a Yankee, it was nice to have someone to talk to. "I'm afraid I'll fall into the water, though sometimes drowning doesn't seem like a bad idea."

"Someone could walk with you," he said. "Keep you from hurting yourself."

"They don't have time. I can hear them sometimes, hear their drunken revelry. I'm sure you're a part of it."

"Actually, I'm not. I just got here a few days ago, and I see how it is, all right, but I've never cared much for drinking and gambling." He hesitated, then plunged ahead to offer, "I'd be glad to take you for a walk any time you want to go. I'm sure it'd be all right with Sergeant Bodine. He'd probably be relieved to see you getting some fresh air."

Anjele stared into the dark abyss, moved by his gentle voice, his apparent attempt at kindness, yet she was wary. He was still the enemy, and she was helpless. "I'll think about it," she said finally, stiffly. "I don't know you. I don't know if I can trust you."

"I guess it's like having faith, Miss Sinclair. You have to believe in what you don't see." He said it before he thought about it and was astonished by his own proclamation. Maybe some of his mother's earlier teachings had actually been instilled someplace deep within, waiting to be summoned one day.

Anjele was likewise impressed but cynically countered, "And sometimes, soldier, things you *can* see are *not* real."

Unsure of what to say next and deciding he'd tarried long enough for a first visit, he turned to go.

"What's your name?"

"Cody. Private Brett Cody."

"Well, Private Cody," she said pleasantly in dismissal, "I'll just think about your offer to go walking."

He hurried out, anxious to get away and pull himself together.

When he carried out her lunch tray, she greeted him with, "I've decided to take you up on your offer, Private Cody. I realized I'd be a fool not to. After all, I need the exercise and fresh air, and I figure it's daylight. What can you do to me in daylight?"

"You've nothing to fear from me daylight or dark, Miss Sinclair." Brett moved by her to set the bowl of fish stew on the crate by her bed. "I'll come back later after you've eaten—"

"No," she all but shouted and with a shy little smile hastened to explain. "I don't want anything to eat. I'd really like to go for that walk now, if you don't mind. It's been so long. Besides, the stew smells awful." She laughed, wrinkling her nose.

Brett, very controlled, agreed. Then, bracing himself for the sweetness of her touch, reached for her hand.

He would have liked to steer her toward the clump

of sheltering palmettos but knew they would raise fewer eyebrows if observed out in the open. The other guards would, no doubt, mercilessly tease him about honeying up to the pretty prisoner, and he would, of course, let them think they were right. All had to go according to plan. No one could suspect anything.

It was bittersweet delight to witness Anjele's rediscovery of the world around her. He found himself easily becoming her eyes, responding to her eager questions. Yes, he confirmed, it was a sea gull she heard, and he described it for her, the graceful arc of glistening white wings a silver shadow on the rippling turquoise waters.

"Is the sky blue today?" she innocently inquired, turning her face heavenward. "It must be. I can feel the sun, and it's wonderful."

Brett swallowed, coughed, struggling with the sudden rush of emotion. God, it was unbearable seeing her this way, so helpless and lost to the splendor of the world surrounding.

Drifting in happiness for the moment, Anjele paid no attention to his silence and went on to share, "I used to live on a plantation south of New Orleans, right on the Mississippi River, and I had this special place on the bank where I could lie on my back and look up at the sky and wish the world would turn upside down so I could swim in it. And when there were big, puffy clouds, I'd see faces in them, shapes. They came alive to me." She laughed, reveling in backward flight to happier times.

Brett hung onto her every word but sensed her chattering was merely a way of covering up her nervousness. After all, he was a stranger, and the enemy, as well.

After awhile, she confided eagerness to hear of the war, and he accommodated. He told her how most of the fighting seemed concentrated in Virginia, though skirmishes were widespread in many states. England, he advised, was still staying out of the conflict.

But she also wanted to know other things besides battle stories, such as how the South was faring in other areas, food, clothing, and money.

Brett found her curiosity as to finances interesting. Was she wondering whether the engraving plates were sorely needed, and if so, grieving because she couldn't get them to the right people?

He went on to tell her candidly of damages in her parish. Expensive cypress rail fences around plantations were being used for firewood by Yankee soldiers to heat their rations, and he predicted it would get worse as winter came on and there was a need for heat. Racehorses and mules had been confiscated, creating a hardship for planters trying to get their crops in. Furniture and fixtures in abandoned houses were handsome booty, but Northern entrepreneurs, as they called themselves, were flocking South to take over mansions and farms after Congress passed the July confiscation act. It had been decreed that property considered used in aiding the Southern rebellion was to be seized by the Union to dispense any way it wanted.

He also described how partisan activity was drawing the wrath of the Union. In reprisal, Farragut had ordered raiders to attack the steamboat Sumter while it was being loaded with sugar at Bayou Sara, burning it.

And the levees were fast deteriorating, he said, due to shortage of laborers. Malaria was on the increase, because quinine was hard to come by. "As for money"— he watched her face for any reaction—"it's practically disappeared in the South. Folks are having to barter. Of course, those who can get their hands on Federal money, greenbacks in particular, are finding a way to get anything they need."

Anjele shook her head in sympathy but made no comment, gave no clue she might have the means to help her people.

They walked together that day till nearly sunset, and she made him promise to return the next afternoon for another outing.

Brett lay awake a long time that night, aware his quest had begun and realizing it was even more difficult than he'd imagined it would be. How much easier it would be if he'd kept on hating her, if anger still raged. To be so near, yet so far, was anguish untold. But he had no choice except to go through with it. And not because of the damned plates. Hell, he didn't care any more about them than he did the war. If she did know where they were, maybe it was best to let them stay there, of no use to either side. They could decide that later. The task now was to build, little by little, to the point where she would believe his story of being a Confederate spy.

He was concerned Anjele could be in danger from several sources. No doubt one of the vigilantes involved in seizing the U.S. Mint had been a spy and was responsible for the Union finding out. So others had to know. Some of Elton's accomplices might also have been aware of the theft. Both sides would be keeping an eye on Anjele's movements. Then there was the matter of her father's murder. Her memory might be dim for the moment, but no doubt the murderer was sweating over how she could start remembering and point the finger at him.

Brett knew he had to move fast, because Anjele's life might be in his hands.

CHAPTER 25

IN THE DAYS THAT FOLLOWED, ANJELE knew she was inexplicably drawn to Brett Cody. And not because he filled a void in her miserable existence. There was more. Much more. Not only was he kind and gentle, tender and caring, but he seemed to have taken it upon himself to become her window into the world. And why? The question plagued her, kept her awake, haunted her dreams.

And not once, in the hours and days they'd spent together, had he made any improper overtures.

Her laugh was bitter.

Why would he?

No, she decided, he was just passing time. After all, he had told her that first day he had no interest in gambling and drinking, and what else was there to do at the remote prison—except be kind to a blind lady?

She told herself she was being a fool to feel anything for him. After all, she was painfully reminded, once before she'd dared let herself care about a man, be taken in by charm. Never again.

Still, she couldn't help wondering what he looked like. She could tell he was tall, because once when they'd been walking, she'd stumbled, brushing her head against a broad, strong shoulder. He had to be tall. And his hands were large, and . . .

She gave her head a brisk shake to dispel such nonsensical daydreaming. One day, maybe soon, he'd be sent somewhere else, and she'd go back to long, lonely days of staring into the cesspool of darkness, thinking how merciful it might have been had the killer succeeded in also murdering her.

Dear Lord, it wasn't fair, any of it, and it was the reality of the horror of her life that nagged her to reach out for any shred of happiness offered.

And, for the moment, Brett Cody was all she had to cling to.

Brett arrived with her noon meal of fish cakes and cheese and cheerily suggested a picnic on the beach. "It's a nice day, hot, but a good breeze. I'll even take you wading."

Anjele bounced up and down on her toes, clapping her hands in childlike glee. "I'd love it. I used to go wading in the river back home."

He took her hand and led her into the sunshine, urging her to talk. Already she had told him about BelleClair, how happy she'd been growing up there. But he had noted how she declined to discuss anything beyond childhood. It was as though her memories stopped after adolescence. When he had mentioned hearing that her first encounter with the army was upon her return from England, he'd asked what she had been doing over there. Curtly she said she'd been in school, then changed the subject.

They talked about the war, how they both wished the dying and suffering would end. She wanted to know what made him turn against the South and fight for the North. "I didn't turn from it," he hastened to say. "I guess I thought it was more important to preserve the Union."

She shook her head, not understanding how anyone could abandon his heritage. Then, turning her head toward him, as though desperate to see his face, she said with candor, "I like you, Brett Cody. You've been a good friend to me. You remind me of someone I knew a long time ago . . . ." her voice trailed away. She bit her lip, turned away, cursing herself for being so brazen.

Brett's heart slammed into his chest. Did she know it was him? He'd been careful not to let on, watched every word. "What do you mean?" Icy fingers of apprehension clutched at his spine. "You make it sound like it's bad that I do. Who was this person?" He forced a convincing laugh.

Anjele shuddered, shook her head, and murmured, "It doesn't matter. I was young then, and very foolish. He . . . he isn't worth remembering. But there was a time, before I came to my senses, when I found him to be a very gentle man, like you. And no,"—she managed to smile in his direction, assuring—"it's not bad that you remind me of that part of him. I don't mind remembering that at all."

Brett clenched his fists, glad they were not sitting close beside each other lest she feel his tension, the smoldering resentment, the echoes of bitterness to hear her say he wasn't worth remembering.

He stared out at the greenish blue ocean, absently

noticed the lazily drifting fishing boat just offshore.

Damn it, he'd been young. Foolish. She had never loved him. He was a Cajun, looked down on by people like her. He had been nothing more than a lark, tempting her capriciousness. He'd been a fool then. He was a fool now. He told himself to get on with the scheme, fulfill his mission, and get her out of his life once and for always. Yet he dared to probe further, asking, "What happened? You seem bitter?"

"We came from two different worlds. I realized I was a fool ever to get involved with someone like him, and I really don't want to talk about it."

"I think there's a lot you don't want to talk about," he said sharply, without thinking. Seeing her frown, he added, "What I mean is, I don't blame you. You've obviously been through a lot, and there's no need in chewing an old bone."

She didn't respond.

Brett was tempted to get up and walk away and keep on going. But he knew he had a job to do. And despite everything, he intended to see her to safety. Best, he commanded himself, to leave the past alone. Bad memories were like scabs on wounds. Pick at them, and the wound bleeds and takes longer to heal. Leave it alone, and the scab eventually falls off. It leaves a scar, but it happens quicker.

They were sitting on a small stretch of sandy beach. So much of the island was surrounded by bulkheads. Brett had found the isolated spot on one of his explorations and knew they had complete privacy there.

The others knew he was spending all his free time with the female prisoner. He had turned a deaf ear to the ribbing from the other guards. Sergeant Bodine warned him about getting too overzealous in his attentions to his prisoner, saying "You lay one finger on her, and she'll tell those friends of hers from New Orleans, next time they come out here, and you'll find yourself in front of a firing squad for rape. General Butler might take up for his soldiers, but I'll wager even he wouldn't take kindly to a Union soldier forcin' himself on a blind woman."

But Brett had assured the sergeant he only felt sorry for her, all the while knowing he had to move as fast as possible to get her out of there. For the time being, everyone was merely amused by his paying so much attention to her, but sooner or later, they might get suspicious.

Anjele had taken off her shoes and was digging in the sand with her toes. Suddenly she squealed with delight and scrambled to grasp a seashell. Turning in Brett's direction, she pleaded, "Describe it to me."

He told her it was a conch. Large. Spiral-shaped. "Sort of like a twisted horn."

"And the colors," she said, running her fingers over the marblelike texture. "Tell me about them."

As always, Brett felt a wave of pity and obliged. "It's kind of a milky white, with streaks of peach and pink. And the inside is peach but deepens to a pink down inside. Here. Let me show you something." He took it from her and gently pressed it against her ear.

Her sightless eyes widened as she cried, "It sounds like the roar of the ocean. That's amazing."

"It sure is." He laughed with her, glad to see her so happy.

"I want to keep it."

He examined it carefully, explaining that crabs sometimes lived inside, though this one seemed to have been abandoned.

"Maybe it's a Rebel crab," she teased, "and he ran when you Yankees came ashore."

"Here." He pretended gruffness. "Take your shell, Rebel wench."

She could hear the smile in his voice and squeezed his fingertips as he placed the shell in her hands once more. "I'll keep it always," she murmured. "And when I hear the ocean, I'll think of you, and this very special day."

Reaching out, she touched his face.

He did not move.

Slowly, gently, she traced her fingertips along the firm line of his jaw, then trailed to his chin, softly touching his mouth.

Brett could not hold back, pursing his lips in a kiss, touching his tongue ever so lightly to her fingers.

She drew a sharp breath, quickly dancing her caress up to his nose, then across his cheeks, onward to his brows and forehead. "You've a nice face, Brett Cody," she said in a quivering voice. "I can tell. Handsome. Strong. But I wish I could see your eyes. Eyes tell so much about a person, most of the time . . . ." She winced to remember other eyes, warm and laughing, caressing with mirth, then smoldering with the heat of desire. Never had she seen deceit in Gator's eyes, but in her naivete, she had not looked.

Brett caught her hand, pressing it against his lips once more. Damn it, don't do it, his brain pounded, don't grab her and kiss her till she's breathless. It didn't work before. It won't work now. "You've nothing to fear from me," he assured her. "I'm your friend."

"You are, indeed. But I must tell you something." She pulled her hand from his, not liking the way her stomach was starting to feel as if she'd swallowed butterflies. "I have considered the possibility that you may have been sent to try to get information from me."

Brett was jolted, caught off guard. It was only with great effort he was able to coolly, calmly respond, "I don't know what you're talking about."

"Surely you've heard what a desperate criminal I am, haven't you? Why, if I weren't blind, I imagine I'd be locked in a cell with bars, wouldn't I? I mean, after all, I did give food to a starving soldier, and frankly, I probably wouldn't have cared at the time if he *had* been a Yankee.

"And no doubt," she rushed on, "you know about the Yankees accusing my father of breaking into the Mint in New Orleans last winter and stealing engraving plates? That's probably why he was murdered. And now they think I know where they're hidden, so it stands to reason they'd think a pitiful, helpless damsel like me would warm to a charming soldier who'd shown a little kindness."

Brett was only mildly uncomfortable. After all, Anjele Sinclair was an intelligent woman. It was only natural she'd have suspicions, and he was ready for them. "I knew your father was murdered. I knew you were also injured that night, and that's what blinded you. I also knew why you were sent here, but I didn't know about any engraving plates, and my only motive was, whether you believe me or not, to try and bring a little sunshine into your life. You're a beautiful woman, Anjele," He gazed down at her adoringly. "A man would be a fool not to want to make you happy."

"You're kind," she murmured, wondering whether it

was her imagination or could she actually feel the warmth of his eyes upon her. "And I appreciate all you do for me. I dread to think of the time when you're gone. It gets terribly lonely."

"Maybe the guard who takes my place will be the one sent to find out about the plates." He wanted to talk, not only in hopes of learning something but also to steer away from the intimacy that was making him extremely uncomfortable.

"What would you do if I told you where they are?" She taunted. "Would you run to your commander and tell him?"

"Of course I would." He played along with her. "I'd get a nice promotion, for sure."

Her laugh reminded him of little silver bells, caught by a sudden breeze. Delightful. Light. Musical.

"I'm afraid I can't help you get that promotion, Private, because the truth is, I don't know where they are. My father said something to me in his dying breath, but my memory is blocked. When I remember, maybe then I can figure it all out. Till then, it's a waste of time for your government to try and get me to tell them anything."

Brett dared wonder if the time were right to confide his mission. Others might come who would stop at nothing to make her talk. It was imperative to get her off the island. "Anjele," he began, "there's something I have to tell you. About me, about you, and—"

"No!"

The word sliced into the tranquillity of the moment.

"I don't want to speak of serious things. Not ever." She swung her head slowly from side to side, hugging her knees and drawing them up beneath her chin. "I'm safe here, in my dark world, and I feel as though nobody can see me, because I can't see them. Maybe it's best I can't see into your eyes, to your very soul, because I might not like what's there.

"So don't talk of you and me, Brett Cody," she finished, almost angrily, "because there is no *us*. There's just here and now, a soldier being kind to a blind lady. It's today. With no yesterday. No tomorrow."

The sound of a bell clanging was heard in the distance. The day was ending, and it was time to get back, time to get her supper to her and say good-night. "There *is* a tomorrow, and we *will* talk, or maybe I should say, *I'll* talk, and *you*, my dear, will listen."

Anjele wished she'd not been so abrupt. Perhaps he'd been about to confide he cared about her, for she sensed that he did. And maybe if he had, she would have admitted feeling a fondness for him, as well. She could see no harm.

She would have to wait for the tomorrow he believed in.

They did not speak on the way back. He left her at her door, and a short while later, Ramey brought her tray. She dared ask where Private Cody was. He told her Cody had been assigned to duty in the barn for the night.

"We got us a real big game goin' tonight," he confided. "And you probably know, Cody, he ain't no gambler, so he said he'd take the duty. I'll probably be the one to bring your breakfast. He'll be up all night and have to sleep. He said to tell you he'd see you tomorrow afternoon, for sure."

"For sure," she said breathlessly, pleased to anticipate the moment.

"He sure got sweet on you," Ramey chuckled. "Who knows? Maybe when the war is over, the two of you will—"

"Thank you, Private Ramey." Anjele dismissed him, easing the door closed to end the uncomfortable conversation.

She ate her supper, drank the accompanying cup of milk, then lay down to lose herself in her musings. Every nuance, every word spoken between them that afternoon, danced through her mind. If he did, indeed, plan to declare his affections, how was she going to react? Did she dare let him know she was also starting to care for him in a way other than friendship?

There was so much to think about, yet Anjele cynically told herself none of it probably mattered, anyhow, for there were differences between them that might not be overcome.

Long ago, when she'd fancied herself in love with Gator, the contrast in their worlds had been cultural, social, and, suddenly, she could not help comparing the two men. Unlike Brett, with his husky, clipped way of talking, Gator had delighted with his easy drawl. Also, he'd been leaner from hard work in the cane fields. And never would she forget the way he wore his hair, pulled back and tied to hang like a horse's tail. Further, he'd seemed more at ease than Brett, who was always serious, as though worried about something, and . . .

She gave her head a brisk shake to cast out the creeping shadows of the past. As far as she was concerned, Gator did not exist, and she was now undeniably drawn to Brett and forced to acknowledge the barrier between them was one of loyalty. She was allegiant to the South. He was a soldier for the North.

Whether opposing viewpoints would eventually cast a shadow on their growing feelings for each other remained to be seen, and perhaps they could even find a middle ground for understanding.

Still, there was one stark actuality that remained, one that might never change.

She was blind.

Ben Seward told Leo he had no idea who'd paid him to take Leo to Ship Island. "All I know," he had said, "was somebody jerked one of my crew into an alley at gunpoint one night when he was leavin' a saloon. Gave him a hundred in gold to give to me, along with the message you'd be coming looking for me soon, wanting passage out to the island. If I take you, I get another hundred. If I don't, I get my throat cut. The crewman didn't get a look at his face. He stayed in the shadows. Hell, I decided if you showed up, I'd take you. Why gamble on getting killed?"

Leo instructed Seward he wanted to sail around the island first, so he could look it over.

"You gonna break somebody out of prison?" Seward asked, bug-eyed. "Oh, Lord, I hope you don't get me in trouble."

"All you got to do is wait for me when you put me off. I got a job to do. It won't take long. That's all you need to know."

"That's all I want to know. Don't get me involved, please."

Drifting slowly, as though merely fishing the waters, Seward guided the boat around the island. Leo had stood at the bow, pulse starting to race as he saw a man in a blue uniform sitting beside a woman. He saw her hair, blazing like liquid gold in the bright sunshine and knew, beyond a doubt, it was Anjele.

Squinting against the glare of the dazzling water, Leo strained to see everything. They rounded a little bend, and he spotted what looked like a swampy area. "Right there," he advised Seward. "Right there is where I'll jump in tonight, around midnight. Give me an hour. You drift around. Then come close as you dare and drop the anchor. I'll spot you and swim out. All you gotta do is wait.

"If you leave me there," he warned, whipping a knife from his boot in a flash, "then you don't have to worry about that man in the alley killin' you. I'll do it for him when I find you. You understand?"

Seward said he did, wanting only to do what he'd been ordered and get it over with. It was times like this when he hated getting involved outside the law. Obviously, word was out he dealt in contraband—goods that made it through the blockade to be sold at the highest price possible. In the future, he vowed, he'd make sure he was less notorious.

As the hour approached midnight, it began to rain. There was little wind, however, so the ocean was not unduly choppy, and Ben Seward was not concerned by the inclement weather. Nevertheless, he asked Leo if he'd rather wait till the next night, when conditions might be better. He pointed out, "You're going to be heading in through that swampy area. I hear tell it's dangerous. Lots of trees down, roots and branches a man could get hung up on."

Leo laughed long and loud, proudly telling him, "I was born in a swamp. I was swimmin' before you was walkin', and to go in that way is safest for me. Don't worry about it."

Ben wasn't worried. In fact, it would suit him fine if the bastard drowned.

Leo slid off the side of the boat, hardly making a sound. Ben and his six crewmen stood watching at the railing, but he quickly disappeared, swallowed by darkness and foaming swells.

Leo swam in a straight line, finding himself in knee-deep water in only a few moments. He then waded to the edge of the swamp, picking his way over rotting stumps and fallen limbs. He had no difficulty, even though he could scarcely see his hand in front of his face. It didn't matter, for he knew what to feel for, grope for, knew not to step down on something merely because it seemed solid at first touch.

He held his knife between his teeth, ready for anything, but most of all, ready to take care of Anjele Sinclair.

At last he was able to see the outline of the shed. The back of it sank down into the thick, brackish water, the window maybe three feet above the surface. He could easily reach it from where he stood, feet mired in the muddy bottom. It was not surprising to find the shutters closed to keep out bugs, maybe even snakes. Moving very slowly so the splashing wouldn't be heard, Leo stepped to the side onto dry ground, stealthily creeping to the door.

He paused to glance about. Lanterns glowed in the windows of a building not far away. He could hear the sound of men talking and muted laughter. Whatever they were doing, they weren't paying any attention to anything going on outside.

Leo felt for the door, tried to turn the knob but couldn't. It was locked, and he supposed that shouldn't have surprised him. There was nothing to do but go back to the window and work on the shutters and hope the noise didn't wake her up.

He had not taken two steps when he froze at the sound of a sleepy voice softly calling, "Ramey, is that you? Goodness, is it morning already?"

Anjele sat up, yawned and stretched. She hadn't even remembered falling asleep, provoked by thoughts of Brett Cody . . . very *pleasant* thoughts. But now it was morning, and she was glad, because soon he'd be there to tell her what was on his mind. "Let me find my robe. I'll let you in."

Finding it right where she'd left it at the foot of the cot, Anjele wrapped it around her and padded the few feet to the door. She didn't have to feel her way, for well she knew it.

She slid back the bolt, was about to turn the knob and open the door, when suddenly she hesitated.

Since being blind, Anjele had endeavored to develop her other senses. Like her sense of smell. And taste.

And sound!

Something held her paralyzed to listen for—what? What was the sound causing such alarm?

And then it dawned.

What she realized she was hearing were the sounds of night. Tree frogs. Crickets. Even a hoot owl. It wasn't morning, wasn't time for breakfast, and dear God, she realized in panic, hand flying to her throat as fear began to choke her, it wasn't Ramey outside her door.

She fumbled for the bolt but couldn't make her shaking fingers move fast enough.

On the other side of the door, Leo heard her gasp, heard the scraping sounds as she tried to relock the bolt. Quickly he backed up, braced himself to throw all his weight.

The door burst open. Anjele was slung backwards, stumbling and falling. Leo cursed, flinging his arms about wildly, the knife slicing through the air as he said, “Where are you, bitch? I can make it quick, easy, or I can make you hope to die. You don’t give me no trouble, you hear?”

Anjele felt as if her lungs were on fire, as she fought to stay still and hold her breath. With a faint stab of hope, she realized her attacker was, for the moment, as blind as she was. But when his eyes grew used to the darkness, he’d find her. The only advantage she had was knowing the arrangement of the tiny room. Hearing him stumble against the cot, she knew he was mere inches away. She also knew the wooden crate was right at her fingertips. Mustering all her strength, she grabbed it and sent it slamming in the direction she estimated his legs to be. He gave a sharp yelp, and she knew she was right on target.

“I got you now,” he cried, falling back against the cot.

Anjele sprang up and dove for the door, hoping she knew exactly where it was. If she bounced off the wall, it was all over.

But she did know, and when she hit the ground began to roll sideways, as fast and furiously as her body would carry her, straight into the swamp to lie very still amidst the brush and weeds. As she heard the man stumbling around, trying to find his way out of the shed, she dared begin to move, creeping backward, deeper into the slime and seaweed.

Leo decided to get the hell out of there, and fast. He didn’t know his way around the camp, didn’t stand a chance of finding her in the dark. But he damn well knew how to find his way back into the swamp and head for the ocean and Seward's waiting boat.

The Voice was going to have to find a better plan, he thought as he crept silently through the night. He'd have to fix it so he could get into the prison during the day, disguised as a guard, maybe. The Voice would know what to do. So there was no need for him to worry about it. He'd get another chance, for sure, and he'd make Anjele Sinclair pay for putting him to so much trouble, too. He'd just sink the knife a little deeper and twist it a little harder.

Anjele was terrified, afraid to move, afraid to cry out. She had no way of knowing how much time had passed, knew only that every muscle in her body ached, burned. And she was cold. Despite the warmth of the mid-September night, she was submerged in water up to her chin and felt as though she were freezing. But she was helpless to do anything. That man, that fiend who wanted to kill her, was out there somewhere, watching, waiting. Sooner or later, it would be daylight. She wouldn't know, unless she could tell by sounds. The tree frogs would be silent, as well as the other nocturnal creatures that had just saved her life by reminding her it was still night time. Only then would she have any inkling of the hour. But long before then, in that mystical moment between darkness and dawn, he would be able to see her, find her.

And God help her then.

Ramey started from the building housing the small prison kitchen, carrying Anjele's breakfast tray. Whistling, thinking what a nice day it was going to be despite last night's rain, he did not, at first, look toward the shed. Instead, he was gazing at the sparkling ocean bleeding into the horizon.

He turned toward the shed and the whistling stopped, replaced by a startled cry of, "What the hell—"

The door was open. She never left the door open.

Gripping the tray, not caring that the mug of coffee was sloshing over, he began to run, calling out as he did, "Miss Sinclair, Miss Sinclair, are you all right?"

He slowed, set the tray down outside the door before warily peering inside. With a jolt, he saw the cot turned over, and the crate.

There was no sign of Anjele anywhere.

He turned back toward the prison, shouting for help.

Brett was sound asleep. It had been nearly four o'clock when his replacement arrived. Exhausted, he hadn't bothered to return to his bunk, instead bedding down on straw right in the barn. But suddenly he came awake at the sound of Ramey's cries and scrambled down the ladder to rush outside.

Hearing the news, he went at once to the shed to see for himself, silently cursing all the while. He should have already got her out of there, damn it.

"You think she escaped?" one of the other guards cried, running up to him. "She had to have had help. I mean, she couldn't get away by herself, could she?"

Brett gave him an impatient shove to get him out of the way, because he was right in his face, and he had no time for speculation. Anjele hadn't escaped, and he knew it. Stepping inside the shed, his blood ran cold to see the muddy footprints on the worn wooden floor. There was signs of a struggle, but no blood, thank God.

The sound of a bugle split the stillness, signaling the call to formation. A search party was about to be formed.

Brett pressed his fingers against his temples and turned all the way around, eyes straining for some sign, anything to give a clue of what had happened.

And then he heard it.

Like the soft whimper of a kitten.

He raced towards the sound, crashing into the brush and weeds. With a cry of joy, he saw her and knelt to gather her in his arms and anxiously ask, "Are you all right? Did he hurt you?"

Weary, nerves shredded raw by the anguish of the night, Anjele could barely whisper, "No . . . no, but he wanted to kill me."

"You're going to be all right," he vowed, holding her yet tighter. Others were coming, and he knew he had to get his emotions under control but dared press his lips against her ear to whisper, "Nothing's going to happen to you, Angel, I swear it."

She smiled and pressed her head against his strong shoulder as he lifted her into his arms and out of the water. Clutching fingers of sleep were reaching out for her, because now she was no longer afraid. He'd called her Angel, just as her father used to, and someone else she couldn't quite forget. Somehow, she knew she was safe.

Brett looked down at her, saw she'd either fainted or fallen asleep. He breathed a sigh of relief, for she seemed to be all right.

But tonight he was getting her out. There would be no time to confide anything. He'd have to move fast and explain later. That's the way it had to be, because whoever had tried to kill her would doubtless try again.

CHAPTER 26

SERGEANT BODINE WAS LIVID WITH RAGE. "She wasn't any trouble till you came here. I don't know what happened to make her go wandering out by herself last night, and I don't care, just so's it don't happen again. Now, I'll let you keep an eye on her today, 'cause when she wakes up, she's going to be upset and scared, but tomorrow, you're goin' on duty elsewheres. It ain't good, your spending so much time with her. She's gettin' too dependent on you."

"You're right, sir," Brett agreed readily, knowing neither he nor Anjele would be there tomorrow. "She probably had a nightmare."

Bodine ordered her door locked from the outside. "If she gets hurt, I'll be in big trouble."

Brett assured the sergeant he'd take care of it, then hurried to the shed, where Ramey had been sitting beside Anjele's cot, in case she woke up while Bodine was raising hell with him. As best they could tell, she wasn't hurt, except for a few scratches and bruises.

When Ramey left, Brett gave her a gentle shake and softly called her name. She stirred, moaned, then suddenly lunged to sit up, wildly tossing her head about as she gasped in terror, "No, no . . ."

"I'm here. It's okay." He pulled her into his arms and held her till she calmed, continuing to assure her she was safe. "Now tell me," he finally said, "everything you can remember about last night."

As he listened to her horrifying tale of how a man had forced his way in, threatening to kill her, Brett was flooded with hot anger, as well as renewed determination to make the escape that night. Yet he knew he had to tell her a little of what was going on, so she'd understand what was happening and not be scared.

When she had finished talking, her head leaning against his shoulder, he began. "Anjele, listen carefully. I have reason to believe what happened last night has to do with your father's murder and the missing engraving plates."

She tensed, pulled away to cry, "But why? What could any of that have to do with me?"

"Because somebody thinks you do know where they're hidden, and since the plates haven't turned up by now, they figure you're the only one who knows. With you dead, the plates stay hidden and pose no problems by falling into the hands of the Confederacy."

"Dear God. As I told you, I don't know anything about them. And that's the truth. I swear it.

"I believe you, but evidently your enemies aren't taking any chances. That's why I've got to get you out of here. Tonight. Because they may try again."

Panic was mirrored on her face. "But where would you take me? To another prison inland, or up North somewhere? No! They'd find me, but at least here my father's old friends can keep a check on me, and when I tell them about this, they'll see to it a guard is outside that door all the time."

"Anjele, it's too risky. They'll keep on trying till they succeed in killing you. I don't think you realize what a catastrophe it would be to the Union for those plates to be used to make counterfeit greenbacks. They'll stop at nothing to see you dead."

"Even if I knew where they were, I'd never tell the goddamn Yankees!" She struck at the air with her fist, causing him to duck instinctively.

He urged her to keep her voice down lest someone hear, explaining, "You don't understand. I'm not taking you out of here to another prison, Anjele. I'm helping you escape. And the Yankees aren't going to know anything about it till it's too late."

"The Yankees," she sneered, "You make it sound like you aren't one of them, Brett."

"I'm not."

Stunned, she waited for him to continue.

He told the lie, and she listened quietly, thoughtfully, but he could tell she was having difficulty believing him. "Trust me," he urged. "I mean you no harm. I'll get you to safety, I swear."

"How do I know this isn't a trick? I'm no fool, Brett Cody. And besides, how many times do I have to tell you I don't know anything about those damn plates?"

"You might remember later on, but I'm not concerned with any of that now. All I want to do is protect you."

"I don't know," she bit down on her lower lip.

"Hell, Anjele, you don't have any choice." He grabbed her shoulders, gently shook her. "The sergeant has already said he thinks I'm spending too much time with you. Tomorrow he's assigning me to other duties. I won't be able to look out for you. Don't you see? You have to trust me.

"Listen," he rushed on, beginning to feel desperate, "Remember that day you asked me if the sky was blue, and I said it was? Anjele, it could have been gray. It could have even been the middle of the night. You had no way of knowing. You had to trust me. And you did. Because you wanted to. You wanted to believe that sky was blue. It's called blind faith, and it's what you've got to have if I'm going to be able to help you."

Her lips sardonically curved. "Blind faith, Brett Cody? You're asking me to believe because I want to?"

"Angel," he said softly, tenderly tracing his fingertips down her lovely face, "I can't think of a better reason."

She shrugged away his touch, afraid he could feel how she was trembling. "Wanting to believe hasn't got anything to do with it, but like you said, I really don't have a choice, do I?"

"Afraid not." He grinned, relieved, then went on to confide the plans he had made, finishing by saying they should leave shortly after dark.

"But what happens when we reach shore? Where will you take me?"

"Somewhere safe." He wasn't about to tell her of his decision to go home, to Black Bayou. He couldn't take a chance on running into soldiers from either side, and it was the only place he could be certain of refuge. When the time came, he'd worry about encountering people who used to know him all those years ago, who, God forbid, might call him *Gator*.

It started raining around noon, so they couldn't go for their usual walk. Brett knew better than to linger very long in the shed, lest eyebrows be raised. He told her to get some rest. Later he would bring her supper tray and pretend to lock her up for the night as

Sergeant Bodine had ordered. And, as soon as everyone quieted down for the night, he would return.

The afternoon seemed to last forever. Brett tried to keep busy, polishing his boots, cleaning his gun, staying out of the way of the other soldiers lest his nervousness be obvious. He didn't want to answer any questions, didn't want to be bothered talking to anyone. All he wanted was for the infernal clock to move a little bit faster.

He tried to figure out who wanted Anjele dead. Major Hembree wouldn't be involved, and Brett knew he wouldn't be where he was if the army had any hand at all in passing the death sentence. No, it had to be someone not directly connected with the army, and, assuredly, responsible for Elton Sinclair's murder. So he decided to stick to his original theory that it was all tied together. And while he wasn't sure how the pieces fit, he was firmly convinced Anjele was in real danger.

Finally it was time.

"I'm not hungry," Anjele told him when he arrived with her supper. "Just hurry up, lock me in, and come back, and let's go!"

"You'd better try to eat. I can't promise you when you'll have another opportunity. Food is going to be scarce." He planned to skirt around heavily traveled areas, going up the Wolf River into the heart of Mississippi, then going on foot to the Pearl River, which would take them all the way to Vicksburg and the Black Bayou to the west. He would buy a few supplies in Biloxi after hiding Anjele somewhere. But there wouldn't be much time, and they needed to get out of the area as fast as possible.

After he left, Anjele was still too nervous to eat and stuck the biscuits and plums into the pockets of her muslin dress for later. She frowned to think that it wasn't even her dress. Her nice clothes had been stolen. Not that there'd been that much to begin with. Someone, probably Kesia, had sent a trunk to the jail in New Orleans, she'd been told. Upon arrival at the island, someone had said the wife of a fisherman would come ashore once a week to pick up her dirty laundry and deliver clean. She'd known after the second visit that her good things had been replaced by cheap, worn garments. No doubt the fisherman's wife thought because she couldn't see, she wouldn't notice. But she'd said nothing, because what did it matter . . . till now, when she found herself wanting to look nice for Brett.

She told herself she was a fool. What difference did it make how she looked? She was still blind. And what man wanted to be saddled with a blind lover? A blind wife? He was only doing his job as a spy for the Confederacy, as he'd said. And he was a diligent soldier, a kind man, and no matter how she was feeling inside, it didn't matter. She would not let it matter.

She sat on the edge of the cot, poised and ready, every nerve raw, tense. As she waited, she thought back to the trepidation of the night before. She'd been saved not only by her sense of awareness, but now she realized she'd actually smelled the danger. It was as though the monster had exuded an aura of blood and violence.

With a shudder, her thoughts drifted back to another nightmare, and in the darkness that was her existence, she once more saw her father's face, how he begged her to listen to—what? What was it he was trying to say? Would she ever be able to remember or would she forever be haunted because it escaped her?

"Anjele."

She leaped to her feet, ran to the door without hesitation, unbolting it from her side, as sounds told her it was being unlocked from outside, as well.

She flung it open and said excitedly, "I'm ready."

He took her hand and squeezed. "Do as I tell you, and remember, don't be scared. I will be your eyes."

And my heartbeat, as well, she thought, chiding herself for allowing the folly of such fanciful musings.

By the light of a waning moon, Brett led her along the path he had memorized. He stepped cautiously, making sure there wasn't anything she could stumble on, before guiding her to follow. He kept a firm grip on her hand, sometimes putting his arm around her waist when the trail was wide enough to walk side by side. Always, he talked to her, in a quiet but carefully reassuring tone.

Anjele knew she could never truly be afraid of anything as long as Brett was close by. Something about him, and not merely the comforting words he spoke, filled her with a sense of being safe from all harm. Yet, while she reveled in the feeling of security, she prayed he was not lying, that he would take her behind Confederate lines. And, hope against hope, she prayed for the cobwebs in her memory to dissipate, revealing the link, the clue, to finding the all-important plates.

Brett was impressed that Anjele showed no fear during the less-than-comfortable crossing. He continued talking, weary of hearing his own voice but could tell she clung to the sound as tightly as her hands clutched the boat on each side of her.

He described how the moon slipped in and out behind silvery-tipped clouds, sprinkling the dancing ocean with thousands of tiny, shimmering diamonds, only to snatch them away in a passing shadow. All the while he rowed as fast and hard as his burning muscles would allow, careful to glance down at the compass each time the moon afforded enough light. He wanted to come ashore in the sequestered cove, away from the main harbor of Biloxi. He was also anxious to make land before the first creeping fingers of dawn began to erode the camouflage of night. He could discern distant outlines of Federal gunboats and knew there was always a chance, if he was spotted, that they might investigate. These fears he also related to Anjele, so she would be aware of everything going on.

At last, they reached the cove. "Just in time." Brett breathed a sigh of relief as he stepped into the foaming surf to drag the boat onto the beach. "It's almost light. Another fifteen or twenty minutes, and we'd have been spotted."

"Do you think we've been missed by now?" she asked, unable to hold back a yawn. She was exhausted from lack of sleep as well as the mental anxiety of the night just past.

"Probably. And the first thing they'll do is discover this old boat missing, so they'll be trying to communicate with the fleet to start searching the water. We've got to hurry. I know you're tired, but you can rest while I'm getting the things we need to go upriver."

Doggedly, Anjele tried to keep up with him, and this time as he talked, describing everything in their midst, she could tell he was also weary and offered, "You don't have to keep being my eyes, Brett. I know you're tired, too."

He squeezed her hand, and she could feel the warmth of his gaze. "But I want to be your eyes, Anjele. I want . . . ." He caught himself, about to confess that he wanted to be everything to her. Quickly he altered, "I want to make sure you're aware of everything around you, so you won't be scared."

"I won't be, as long as you're with me."

"Well, I'm going to leave you soon. There's an abandoned shack ahead. This is a deserted stretch. I've already made sure of that. I'll be back as soon as I can."

When they reached it, he told her there was nothing around but some scrub palmettos. The blanket he'd left over a month ago was still there, and he spread it on the sand, guided her to it. "Go to sleep. I'll try to be back by the time you wake up."

He turned to go, but she flailed out with frantic hands, touching, grasping his sleeve. "What if you don't come back? What would I do? Please, take me with you."

Pushing back a golden curl from her forehead, he dropped his hand to cup her chin. "I can't. You'd slow me down, and I've got to get in and out of town fast. Besides, I don't want anyone remembering a Union soldier with a blind woman. Now, don't worry. Nothing will stop me from coming back, I promise."

It was as natural as drawing a breath, how he bent slightly to press his mouth against hers. Her response was to twine her arms about his neck, melding against him as his lips began to roam her face, bestowing light kisses to her cheeks, her eyelids, her temples, and the tip of her nose. All the while his hands held her tightly by the waist, finally slipping to her back to pull her ever closer.

Anjele reveled in the delicious feel of his warm mouth against her flesh.

Brett knew he had to end the torture. Stepping back, he sighed in apology, "I didn't mean for that to happen. Forgive me, Anjele."

She traced his mouth with her fingertips and said,

"You don't need to be sorry. I think I've been waiting, wanting this moment. I'm glad it's here."

Brett caught his breath, for all at once it struck him that she might actually be falling in love with him. Dear God, without knowing she'd once felt him not good enough, now, depending on him for survival, she dared to care. He wasn't sure how it made him feel.

He caught her wrist, held it, kissed her fingertips, then stepped away. "I will be back," he promised, a slight tremor of emotion in his tone.

She heard the soft crunching of his boots on the sand, retreating, disappearing. Finally she lay down, curling on her side, a smile on her lips.

Maybe, she dared fantasize, he could love her despite her blindness. But did it really matter, she was pained to wonder? Did she dare think of permanence in any situation in these turbulent times? It was only the here and now that mattered.

And Anjele intended to grasp every second.

Leo wasn't the least bit scared to tell The Voice what had happened. "Hell, what was I supposed to do? She knew her way around in the dark, and I didn't. And I wasn't gonna go stumbling around looking for her and maybe wind up getting shot."

There was only silence, no sound from within the tomb.

Leo gritted his teeth. As soon as he had got back to New Orleans, he had impaled an old glove on the bottom of the fence as a signal of his return just as The Voice had instructed. Every night for five nights, he had come by at midnight, but the glove was always there, burrowed down in autumn leaves, noticeable only to someone looking for it. Tonight, he'd been relieved to see it was gone and immediately crouched down in front of the mausoleum door to recount his failed mission. Only now he was starting to wonder if maybe somebody else had taken the glove, and he was only running his mouth to the corpses in there. He got up to go. "To hell with it—"

"I don't blame you, Cody. Sit down."

With a sigh of relief, he did so.

"It was a quick plan. A desperate plan. Haste and desperation seldom spawn success."

It dawned on Cody then that The Voice didn't sound surprised, and he said as much.

"I'm not," came the matter-of-fact declaration. "When I heard Anjele had escaped from prison, it was obvious you'd failed."

"Escaped?" he cried. "How could she? She's blind."

"She had help. One of the guards is also missing. He had been spending much time with her, I hear. We can only hope he wasn't a spy. We'll know sooner or later, if the Confederacy suddenly starts trading in millions of greenbacks," he sardonically added.

"So what do you want me to do? I'm still gonna be paid, ain't I?

"You will come by here once a week, as you have done in the past. A little money will be left over the door to compensate you for your trouble. If the glove is here, so am I, which means I've succeeded in finding out where she's hiding.

"Which also means," he added, "you will kill her, because I intend to find her for you."

Leo laughed. "Don't worry. You find her, and my knife will find her throat. And this time, she'll be just as dead as her poppa."

CHAPTER 27

"CLAUDIA COULD ONLY STAND THERE, blue eyes fear widened, mouth agape, as Major Hembree read the order from General Butler.

It was early morning. They stood on the columned porch, Claudia still in gown and robe, golden hair flowing loose around her face and shoulders.

Beside her, leaning on his cane, Raymond could scarcely hold back a gloating grin. He had waited for this moment, for Claudia to come crashing down from her smug throne of confidence. He had figured all along the complacency of the owners of plantations south of New Orleans would be short-lived, and once General Butler was prepared to spread out his sphere of operations, he'd grasp the rich section with little effort. Most planters had abandoned anyway, but some, like Claudia, by virtue of patronizing the enemy as well as signing the requisite oath of loyalty to the Union, had blithely and ignorantly thought their lives would be unchanged. So Raymond was glad to see her comeuppance, though distressed to hear the circumstances.

"I tell you, Major, if my father was involved with vigilantes, I don't know anything about it," Claudia declared furiously.

Major Hembree conceded. "We understand you two weren't close, but we believe he did, in fact, confide in Anjele."

"Well, you won't find any stolen government property at BelleClair, I assure you." Claudia leaned over to whisper, lest the others overhear. "I really can't believe any of this, Tyler. You know your wife and I are like sisters. This is an outrage. Why, she'll no doubt have the vapors when she hears of your insulting me by searching my house."

The corners of his mouth twitched with amusement as he, too, lowered his voice. "She does know, Claudia, and she's very upset to hear about all this. She asked me to tell you not to expect her and the other ladies for tea tomorrow afternoon. Wouldn't do, you know, for them to be seen at BelleClair once word spreads your father was a thief."

Raymond was pleasantly surprised to think of Elton having had the mettle to get himself involved with vigilantes, yet concern over Anjele's escape and present whereabouts shadowed his pleasure.

Suddenly, out of the corner of his eye, Raymond saw Claudia raising her hand, knew she was about to slap Major Hembree. Lifting his cane to block her hand, he said, "I don't think that's wise, my dear. You could wind up replacing your sister at Ship Island."

"An astute observation," Hembree said, "but I'm confident Anjele will be recaptured. Meanwhile, we'll proceed with what should've been done long ago—finding out if those plates are hidden around here."

He motioned to his waiting soldiers, who began eagerly

scattering in all directions. A dozen or more rushed across the porch and through the doors and into the house.

Claudia screamed, hands flying to her ears to mask the sounds of furniture being turned over, smashed, paintings torn from the walls, draperies being yanked down. "Bastards! All of you! How could you do this to me after I opened my home to your entire army? You had refuge here, all the comforts BelleClair could provide. And now you destroy it."

"We don't seek to destroy anything, Claudia," Hembree said calmly, "We're merely looking for what's ours. And I can assure you, your hospitality has been appreciated. But be that as it may, the Union army won't be imposing in the future. Like my wife, General Butler feels it's not a good image to patronize the home of a man who would steal from the government."

"And what about my slaves?" Claudia asked. "Everybody knows the slaves in all the parishes below New Orleans are getting more and more rebellious. Why, gangs from other plantations are roaming the countryside, urging rebellion. I've lost count of the numbers slipping away during the night. If you withdraw your men, I'll have no protection. There's no way I can keep BelleClair operating."

Major Hembree was unmoved. "We have our own problems with the Negroes. Just last week, a large group marched into the city, complaining of overwork and short rations. They were armed with clubs, scythe blades, and knives. When we tried to stop them, one was killed and several wounded."

"I'm afraid your situation is of no concern to the Union army, Claudia." He clicked the heels of his polished boots and gave a mock salute, then went down the steps to his waiting horse. Without a backward glance, he mounted and rode away, leaving the soldiers to commit mayhem upon the once glorious plantation.

Turning her fury on Raymond, she yelled, "Oh, you're enjoying all this, aren't you? I can see it in your eyes. You're enjoying every goddamn minute of it. You want to see BelleClair destroyed. You'd like to see me destroyed, too. I know you hate me, but not half as much as I hate you, you spineless ninny."

She slumped into a rocker and began to sob wildly, beating at the wooden arms with her fists and stamping her feet. She did not dare go into the house, for fear of losing control and picking up the first thing she could get her hands on and attacking the soldiers who were tearing her world apart.

Raymond shrugged. He had ceased to be hurt by her vicious tongue because he just didn't care anymore.

Sitting down beside her, he began to rock to and fro, humming absently, knowing he was irritating her, which is what he wanted to do.

"Will you stop it?" She glared at him, eyes bulging. "Goddamn you, Raymond, I was such a fool to think I ever loved you."

He looked at her as though he was sure she'd lost her mind. "You never loved me, and we both know it. The only reason you wanted to marry me was to keep Anjele from having me. You always were a selfish bitch, Claudia," he added with an arrogant sniff.

She was on her feet, towering over him, swinging her hands back and forth across his face, slapping him again and again, till he managed to swing his cane in defense. When it struck her shoulder, she cried out, stumbling backward.

"You worthless, hopeless cripple," she shrieked. "One day you'll pay, and so will Anjele. I'll see her dead if she ever comes back here, and you, too, if you get in my way."

Lifting her skirts, she ran down the steps and disappeared around the corner of the house, angry sobs echoing.

Raymond leaned back, closed his eyes, and slowly began rocking again. His cheeks were smarting. She had slapped him pretty hard. But it wouldn't hurt long. As soon as the Yankees finished what they were doing and got out of the way, he was going to the sugarhouse and find his stash of home-brewed rum.

And then the whole world could go to hell, for all he cared.

Brett moved mostly by night, for two reasons—there was less chance of anyone seeing them and remembering them, but perhaps more importantly, he also wanted to avoid the intimacy of darkness. Awareness since he'd dared kiss Anjele was almost a tangible thing, hovering between them to make them tense, edgy. Despite wanting her so much it hurt, he vowed not to take advantage of either her vulnerability or the precarious situation they were in. Foremost in his mind was the chilling fact that someone was out to kill her, and he wanted to get her to sanctuary.

By day, if the weather was good, he found refuge in the woods and dense growth on the banks of the Wolf River. It had not taken long to realize it would be dangerous to try to navigate a raft blindly so all he could do was follow the river's course north on foot as far as Lumberton. Doing so slowed them considerably, yet it was easier to forage for food.

They happened upon a friendly fisherman, too old and decrepit to be involved in the war but eager to share news he'd heard in Lumberton. General Stonewall Jackson, he was happy to report, had led an attack on Harper's Ferry in Virginia, and it was being said nearly twelve thousand Union soldiers had been captured.

But the old man was sad to have to report a battle in the northeast corner of the state, up at Iuka, near the Tennessee and Alabama lines. Union General Rosecrans had soundly beaten back Confederates and taken control of the town.

Anjele was anxious to hear how things were going in Louisiana, particularly New Orleans, but the fisherman said all he heard from that area were continued horror stories of General Butler's tyranny.

Farther along, they encountered a grief-stricken father taking the body of his Confederate son home for burial. He said there had been intense fighting at Corinth, and even though Rosecrans's Federal troops were hit hard by General Van Dorn,Van Dorn had finally had to retreat.

Brett hated pushing Anjele so hard but knew it was only a matter of time till the war moved deeper into Mississippi.

On a chilly morning in late October, he was grateful to stumble across the remains of a log cabin. Positioning rotting boards, he was able to put together hastily a lean-to for shelter against the cool, brisk wind.

He then built a fire and began to roast the rabbit he'd caught in a snare. Mostly their diet was raw vegetables he managed to scrounge and steal from gardens along the way. Meat was a rare treat. "A few more weeks," he told her. "The Pearl River goes right into Jackson, and once we get there, I'll feel safe enough to get a couple of horses for the rest of the way."

"And then what?"

He knew she was restless, knew how terrible it must be, eternally trapped in darkness, trudging mile after mile, stumbling and falling now and then, despite his best efforts to keep her going. His heart went out to her, and God knows he hated driving her as he did, but he had no choice. "A few more weeks, at least. I wish we could move faster, but—"

"I can't," she was quick to let him know. "In case you haven't noticed, my feet are blistered, and I can't remember the last time we had a decent meal, or . . ." her voice cracked, and she bit back the tears as she apologized, "I'm sorry. I know you're doing the best you can, but why do we have to go on this way? Surely we could find a Confederate patrol, and they'd protect us. Why do we have to keep running like criminals?"

Why, indeed? Brett frowned. Contact with the Rebel army would result in exposure of his lie about being a spy. And he didn't dare risk letting the Union army get hold of Anjele, because he didn't know who was out to kill her, didn't know who to trust, and was taking no chances.

"It's best," he finally told her, once more hedging. "You can rest up without having to answer a lot of questions, and maybe then your memory will come back, and—"

"And maybe it won't!" She suddenly burst into tears.

Brett could only stare, speechless. They'd been through some extremely hard times in the past weeks, and he had marveled over how she never complained, impressed by her fortitude, and when called upon, courage as well. A woman with good eyesight could not have done better, he knew. Yet now it looked like she was finally breaking.

Propping the green stick with the roasting rabbit so it wouldn't burn, he turned to take her in his arms to comfort her.

Feeling his hands upon her arms, Anjele slapped at them, twisting from side to side as she exploded, "No, don't touch me. I don't want your pity, damn it. Just leave me alone . . . ." She scrambled to her feet, ashamed by her weakness. Ever disoriented in the clinging web of darkness, she stumbled, righted herself, cursing her helplessness.

"Anjele, wait. You're going to hurt yourself." Brett was up and right behind her to grab her by her waist and whirl her around to face him. "What the hell is wrong with you? I've never seen you this way."

She laughed, a harsh, ugly sound. "I've never seen you at all, Brett Cody, so you have the advantage."

Bewildered, he gave her a gentle shake. "Damn it, Anjele, what is wrong? Tell me. We've a ways to go, yet. I can't have you giving up now, feeling sorry for yourself."

The tenseness in her face relaxed. "Oh, no, that's not it at all. It's . . . it's . . ." She shook her head, unable to come right out and say she couldn't stand being with him any longer. To be so close to a man, so dependent, loving him more and more with each passing day was unbearable. If only he hadn't kissed her back in Biloxi, perhaps she could have denied what she was starting to feel, but since then, nothing was the same. And she had tried. Oh, dear God in heaven, she had tried. Pretending to be jolly, keeping her chin up, friendly and warm. Yet it had been agony, for so many times she'd wanted to throw herself into his arms and lift her mouth for his wonderful kiss and let the tide of unbridled passion sweep them away. Had he given her any encouragement at all, Anjele was sure that's what she'd have done, tossing propriety aside. But he hadn't, and what stung was how he could pretend it had never happened. That was the final insult.

"Come on," he urged, when she fell silent. "It's cold out here in this wind. Let's get back to the shelter. You're just tired and need some rest."

She allowed him to lead her back, feeling terribly foolish. And when he helped her settle onto the blanket, she waited till she felt him take a place beside her before apologizing, "I'm really sorry. I should have known better. I'm afraid I'm acting like a child. I've been so embarrassed since you kissed me, because I guess I thought . . ." She paused to draw a long, steadying breath, feeling his curious eyes upon her. "I guess I thought there was something romantic growing between us, and I got mad with myself when I realized there wasn't. After all . . ." She gave her long hair a disdainful toss, lifted her chin in a gesture of confidence not truly felt. "I'm blind, and what else could I expect but your friendship, which I'm very grateful for. I was being silly, that's all. It won't happen again." She forced a brave little smile.

For one frozen moment, Brett could not speak, as emotions he'd fought to keep under control were suddenly unleashed. It was not seduction, for he could see desire etched in her face, hear it in her voice.

She wanted him.

And he wanted her.

This time, there was no turning back.

Gently, so as not to startle, he drew her into his arms. He laughed softly, a rich sound from his very soul. "You little fool. Don't you know how much I've wanted this but didn't dare? You're so helpless, and I was afraid you'd think I was taking advantage. But God help me, I do want you, Anjele." He kissed her deeply, pressing his tongue into her mouth. She moaned, arms encircling his neck as she leaned back, gently taking him with her till they were lying down.

Locked in the breathless kiss, he raised himself only enough to afford room for his fingers to find the buttons down the bodice of her dress. She did not resist, arching toward him in eagerness.

When the buttons were undone, he peeled the dress off her shoulders and down her arms. As he moved to lower his mouth, she begged in a suffocated whisper, "Tell me what it's like, Brett. Tell me what you're feeling . . . ."

He caught one nipple between his thumb and forefinger, gently squeezing to hardness. "Like a cherry, my love, sweet and succulent." He touched it with his tongue, then began to roll it between his teeth, softly nibbling, then drawing as much as he could take into his mouth to suckle.

Anjele felt imprisoned upon a sea of velvet, as needles of pleasurable sensation assaulted every nerve of her being. Her own fingers began a delightful dance of exploration, moving down his back to feel the strong, rippling muscles. "I want to take this off," she said, pulling away from his grasp to boldly maneuver out of her dress. "I can't see you, but I can feel you, and I want your naked flesh against my own . . . ."

Brett tore off his own clothes, felt himself hard, throbbing, his loins aching with the intense heat of his desire. Yet he knew he'd find strength to hold back, for he had no intentions of rushing the ultimate pleasure of being inside her. He'd waited too long for the ecstasy and intended to savor every tantalizing second.

He gazed hungrily at her breasts as she lay beckoning. Full, high, rounded, and firm. The nipples were tiny, pointed, and he could not resist devouring them once more in turn.

Anjele gasped at the feel of his hot, probing tongue. Digging her fingers into his thick hair, she held him captive, wrapping her legs around the backs of his to cling yet tighter.

Her own hands became bolder, slipping to cup his buttocks, marveling at the firm contours. He continued to bathe her breasts with honeyed tongue, sharply gasping as her tender fingers trailed around, and down, between his legs to torment and tease.

"Now," she throatily commanded, "Take me now, Brett."

"Not yet, Angel. Not yet."

He maneuvered away from her torturous touch, lest his pleasure come, then and there. Feasting on the wonders of her body, as his hands roamed at will, he was captivated by her incredibly tiny waist, smooth belly, and perfectly curved hips.

"My God," Anjele crooned, on fire with wanting him, "I think I'll die if I don't have you."

"And have me you shall," he huskily assured her, "again and again, till you beg me to stop."

"Never." She laughed recklessly, helplessly, "I'll only beg for more."

He moved his palm from her waist and downward, reveling in the feel of her soft, satiny skin. His mouth was doing crazy, wonderful things to hers, but she reached out to clutch his neck, bringing his face close, her lips singeing his. Anjele knew in that crystalized moment that her body and soul were his for the taking. In the weeks, months, they had been together, he had become her porthole into the world, seeing it through his eyes. There had actually been times when he made it all seem so vivid and real she could forget, for one exhilarating moment, that she was blind. He was part of her now, for always and all times, and she wanted to be a part of him. Boldly, her hand snaked down to find his manhood and cast aside his assaulting, probing fingers and thrust it against her.

Brett could hold back no longer and plunged inside her, as his hands deftly moved to clutch her waist and render her helpless against his assault. Control cast to the winds, he began to pump his hips against hers. She did not resist, did not indicate if there was discomfort, instead raising her legs to lock about his hips and render her all.

He could see the rapture on her face, hear her pleasured sighs and moans, knew she was rapidly approaching her own pinnacle of ecstasy. He held back till he felt the velvet recesses of her begin to quiver against him. He set a slow, tantalizing tempo, then increasing. Her nails digging into the hard flesh of his back were like spurs, urging him onward.

At last, he felt the final zenith approaching, the great, inward shudders, simultaneous with near-agonized cries as she burrowed her face in his neck. He took himself onward to ultimate release, gasping out loud at the sheer wonder, for never, not with any of the women in his past, had it ever been this way.

Dizzily he slumped against her, then abruptly rolled over onto his back to take great gulps of air, for he was breathless. Was it so wonderful before, he dared wonder, all those years ago on that one special night? He knew he'd loved her then, but now loved her more. For there had been a mellowing of heart, of spirit, as he'd come to know her even better. He couldn't bear to think of ever letting her go, but knew he couldn't control the future, could only grasp the here and now.

She rolled on her side, snuggling her head against his shoulder. His arms tightened about her protectively as she teasingly whispered, "I'm not going to let you go, Brett Cody. You might not want to be saddled with a blind woman the rest of your life, but you'll have to hide so I can't find you, because I never want to leave your side, and—"

"You won't," he vowed fervently, fiercely, turning to jerk her roughly into his arms. Hungrily, possessively, he began to rain kisses over her face. His hands moved over her as though wanting to touch all of her, savoring the feel of what he now considered his very own. "You aren't going to lose me, Anjele Sinclair. Forget the war. Forget everything but you and me, and here and now, because I want you for always and ever."

His lips found hers, and they clung together in the cooling breezes, the dying embers of the fire before them merging with their bodies to ignite once again the carnal passion.

CHAPTER 28

THE WAY BECAME INCREASINGLY FAMILIAR to Brett as they left the banks of the Pearl and moved west to the Big Black River.

Crossing by ferry, they continued on to the Mississippi. Moving parallel, they would reach the fringes of Black Bayou a few miles south of Vicksburg.

Pressing her head against Brett's broad back, Anjele was filled by the wondrous feeling of love. He made her feel needed, wanted. Though she hungered to see his face and drink in the precious sight of him from head to toe, she felt no less a woman in his presence. In only a short while, Claudia had made her feel inferior, useless. Yet, despite the arduous journey, wrought with misery, Brett gave her confidence in herself, lifting her spirits. Perhaps most wonderful of all, by painting with words, he had created for her a landscape into the world, and she no longer felt totally trapped by darkness.

He had told her he was taking her to a place of shelter, where she could rest and try to get her memory back. She relished the thought of being with him, but still wished she could return home and attempt to claim what was rightfully hers. But as long as the war went on, it was impossible. To the Yankees, she was a criminal, as well as a fugitive.

Brett was describing the forest around them, laughing over the antics of a chipmunk that seemed to be following them. He would appear every so often to peer curiously out from foliage at the edge of the trail, then scamper away to meet them farther ahead. She told him how she adored animals and found it easy to recount her nights in the bayou and the wondrous sights to behold.

"Raccoons, deer, even a fox. It was wonderful. The person showing me was Cajun and knew the bayou, so he was able to take me to special places."

Brett managed to keep his voice even as he asked, "Was he the one you mentioned back at the prison?"

"Yes," she admitted, with only a twinge of pain to remember, for loving Brett made Gator easier to forget. "Like I said, I was so young, only sixteen. I was just having fun, like girls do. He didn't mean anything," she added with a scornful laugh, lest he suspect she was lying.

When he made no comment, lapsing into a stony silence, she teased, "You're jealous, aren't you? I told you, he didn't mean anything to me, but he was a wonderful guide into the bayou, and—" She fell silent, noticing the horse was slowing, at the same time she could feel his tension. Fearfully, she asked, "Is something wrong? What do you see?"

Brett had promised himself as he got close to the Laubache plantation he would stick to the river trail and avoid the temptation to look around. After all, it had been nearly nine years. Still, he didn't want to risk seeing anyone who might recognize him. He had changed into civilian clothes way back in Biloxi, putting his Union army uniform in a saddlebag.

So it was his intent to keep on going. But then he realized he was passing the spot where the Laubache pier had once been. Riverboats had even tied up there sometimes, when loading or unloading guests. Now, however, all that remained were pilings and rotting boards jutting up out of the muddy water.

"Brett?" Anjele prodded behind him, alarmed by his continued silence.

"Nothing to be afraid of," he murmured.

"But what is it?"

"I'm not sure." He reined the horse away from the bank, cutting towards what used to be a flower-bordered path leading beyond rows of meticulously pruned evergreens. Now he saw the flowers were choked by the grasp of rank weeds, the passage tangled and overrun by wild honeysuckle.

He could not believe what he was seeing. Once, a carpet of green velvet had spread up the gentle slope to the mansion. Now, like the path, the lawn was overgrown with stirrup-high weeds. Ahead, he blinked in pained bewilderment at the sight of the once-grand house—doors swung from jambs, one section of roof was caving in, windows broken.

And then he saw the gazebo, or what was left of it. Once trailing with fragrant roses and wisteria, it was now barely held together by briars and bramble vines. He stared at the floor with its gaping, rotting holes and smiled sardonically to envision Margette and him in the throes of the passion he so stupidly thought was never-ending love.

Gone were the endless lines of whitewashed fences with prize horses grazing beyond. In the distance, he could see what looked like the burned remains of the barn.

He told Anjele what he was seeing as he rode on toward the sugarhouses. He merely said he'd known the folks who lived there when he was a boy, not about to divulge the truth.

Peering through a broken window, he could see huge vats, half-filled with soured and crusted molasses. Beyond, he saw the fields of rotting cane.

What had happened? True, the Yankees were pushing up the river, but slowly. Hell, he'd heard only a few days ago about the battle at Labadieville, down at Bayou Lafourche. That was way south of New Orleans, almost to the Gulf at a point between the mouths of the Mississippi and the Atchafalaya. So the Union didn't have total control of Louisiana, and sure as hell hadn't made a serious assault on the Vicksburg, Mississippi area—yet. So what in thunderation had happened to Haskill Laubache's once-splendorous plantation?

He rode past deserted slave cabins, stretching in parallel rows behind the main house. He recalled how, at the time he had worked the fields, Laubache had already replaced the old clay-between-posts structures with new ones of solid brick. Now nature was creeping out from the swamp beyond to devour with tongues of weeds and vines.

Moving back to the house, Brett dismounted at the foot of the marble stairs leading up to the dilapidated porch. He carefully guided Anjele inside. He'd never been in there, had no idea what it had looked like in its day of grandeur. Now the walls were bare, stripped of curtains and adornment.

He led her throughout the house, describing devastation. "It was plundered. Totally. I don't see anything left. Not a piece of crockery, not a chandelier, not even a candle." He took her upstairs to find the same abandonment there, as well.

He paused in what had once been Margette's room, and he knew that, because she'd pointed out the French doors leading to it one night when they were in the gazebo. Where the other rooms had merely been stripped, he noted this one bore evidence of destruction, vandalism. Holes had been knocked in the walls, all windows and the French doors smashed. Bits and pieces of furniture shattered beyond repair. It was as though someone had gone berserk, bent on committing absolute ruin. He described the pathetic scene to Anjele, but of course gave no indication he had known the former inhabitant.

The upstairs hallway formed a gallery, which opened to the entrance foyer below. Brett was about to descend the stairway when he noticed how the rear of the gallery hooked back to a hallway almost hidden from view. Steps there went down to what looked like the service wing of the house, but he also discovered a small bedroom still containing furniture—a bed, a small chiffonier. In one corner, there was a dumbwaiter, which, he decided after opening the door and peering down the narrow shaft, went into a service pantry below. Obviously, a slave had slept there, probably in service to the Laubache children. He recalled that Margette had two young brothers, twins. Whoever had plundered the house had failed to notice the room, or perhaps they weren't interested in what had been provided for a slave.

Brett was mystified but knew they needed to be on their way. Soon it would be dark, and he hoped to reach Black Bayou before then so there'd be time to check out the area while it was still light.

Returning to the river trail, they hadn't gone far when Brett saw the Negro man sitting on the bank with a cane pole, fishing. Three nice-sized catfish, secured by a line, desperately flip-flopped at the water's edge. Startled, the man dropped his pole and scrambled to his feet as fast as his decrepit old bones would allow. "Please, massah, please don't hurt me. I ain't doin' nothin' wrong."

Quickly explaining to Anjele what was going on, Brett assured the man he meant him no harm. "We're just passing through."

"Oh, praise the Lord." The old man's head bobbed up and down. Patting his shirt pocket, he offered a toothless grin to say, "But I was ready for you, for sure."

Brett laughed. "You got a gun in that pocket? Must not be a big one."

"Oh, naw sir, I ain't got no gun. I got my papers in here, so's you'd know I ain't no runaway slave."

"What's your name?"

"It be Rufus. That's the name what's on my papers Mastah Laubache give me. He gimme that name, too."

Brett, jolted, wanted to verify. "You were a slave of Haskill Laubache's? And he freed you?"

"Yassuh. He freed all his slaves, and they all took off up North, afraid somebody would tear up their papers and put 'em right back on the block and auction 'em off to a new owner. But me, I stayed, 'cause I is too old to be making treks like that. Besides"—he lowered himself to the riverbank once more, confident everything was now all right—"Mastah Laubache, he also give me permission to fish this river all I wants, so I ain't goin' nowhere."

"And where is Mr. Laubache, Rufus? The house is falling down. The entire plantation has gone to seed. What happened here?"

Anjele, arms about Brett's waist, was listening intently, not about to ask questions, though she was puzzled by his apparent deep concern.

Rufus saw no harm in telling what everybody around knew, anyway, and said bluntly, "Terrible things happened, that's what. Mastah Laubache, he's dead. Killed himself. Reckon he figured he didn't have nothin' to live for, once them boys o' his got in all that trouble.

"And I knows all this," he proudly declared, " 'cause I was house help. I was Mastah Laubache's butler, and I knowed ever'thing what went on in that family."

As Brett listened, stunned, Rufus proceeded to recount the tragedies leading to Laubache's downfall. Margette had run away with a married man. When the twins took exception to a wisecracking drunk in a Vicksburg saloon, they were both gunned down. Edythe Laubache died of a broken heart, and Haskill Laubache had then freed his slaves, shut down all operations of the plantation, and finally committed suicide.

Rufus shook his head in disgust and said, "Within a week, the place had been stripped faster than vultures on a stillborn calf."

"Does anybody ever come around here?" Brett wanted to know.

"Soldiers sometimes. Passin' by. Ain't seen no Yankees, yet," he added, frowning. "And I hope they don't come this way. Don't want no fightin' around here. No Sir. I just wants to spend the rest o' my life fishin', not dodgin' bullets."

They rode on, and Anjele couldn't resist asking, "Did

you know those people?"

"Not very well," he said, which was not far from the truth. When it came down to it, he hadn't known Margette at all or he'd never have believed her when she swore to love him. And he should have learned his lesson then, damn it, and he wouldn't be in the mess he was in now. It was hell being able to love a woman only because she was blind, and he wondered how long he could go on living a lie.

Anjele did not pursue it. Brett had lapsed into an uncharacteristic silence. Something was wrong, but she didn't want to ask. Maybe, she thought warily, it was best she didn't know.

When they entered the fringes of Black Bayou, Brett was dismayed to find no trace of the old path leading in. The weeds and undergrowth were nearly saddle high. Above, gray moss rained down as though still grieving over the Cajuns' departure. No doubt they had moved on when Laubache and his plantation crumbled, probably heading farther downriver, as his family had done so many years ago.

He reined the horse about. There was no point in looking for shelter within, for if any of the pirogues or huts remained, they'd be in worse condition than Laubache's mansion.

The idea struck.

Laubache's mansion was the perfect hideout. They could remain indefinitely. He could forage for food, slip into Vicksburg now and then to hear news.

Anjele, unable to stand the suspense any longer, asked, "Will you please tell me what's going on? Why are you turning around? I thought you said we were almost there."

"Well, 'there' isn't there anymore, honey." He

reached to pat her thigh. "So we're going back to that house we just went through."

Anjele had felt the weeds slapping at her just before they'd turned around and figured the house had to be more comfortable than whatever he'd intended, but she was so tired of it all and protested, "I don't want to stay there. I think we should try to go all the way to Richmond. We'd be safe there, and if I ever do remember anything about those engraving plates, I could go straight to the government, and they'd find a way to get them."

"It's not that simple. Not since we found out somebody is out to kill you, Anjele. We don't know who to trust, because you can bet the Yankees have spies among the Rebs. Besides, from all the war news we've heard, Richmond isn't all that secure. We'd be heading straight into the war."

Wearily, impatiently, she asked, "So how long do we have to hide?"

He told her had no idea, not ready to confide his plan. Sooner or later, he figured, the Yankees would forget about them, the way the war was heating up. When he felt the time was right, he planned to ask her to go away with him, out West, to make a new life. But he wouldn't propose the idea to her till he felt she'd agree.

He couldn't bear the thought of her rejection—again.

They settled into the little room in the far corner of the upstairs. Brett caught game, or fish, helping Anjele prepare it in what was left of the kitchen building out back. Rufus came around now and then, bringing catfish and crayfish, never needing persuasion to stay and share the feast.

By day, they walked hand in hand across the land. It was November, and Brett described the fading colors of autumn as nature prepared for winter's arrival.

And by night, they made bold, breathtaking love, and Anjele never ceased to be awed by the wonder of it all.

Still, despite the peace and serenity of the world they'd created, she knew it could not last. They would either be found or have to return to civilization. They couldn't hide forever. Yet when she broached the subject with Brett, he refused to discuss it.

"We take one day at a time," was all he would say.

"But what about your assignment?" she wanted to know. "The Confederate government is going to wonder what happened to us."

"Perhaps," he hedged, "but they'll probably think we got killed somewhere."

"And you're hoping the Yankees will think the same thing."

"Exactly."

"And then what?" she cried, exasperated. They were lying in bed in the secluded, out-of-the-way room. It was a chilly night. There was only one thin blanket, but they lay close together, as always, for Anjele felt safest when he held her.

He ran loving fingertips across her face, absently asked what she'd like to do, as he thought how much he adored her.

"Sometimes I think I want to go home. Then again, I wonder if the bad memories don't really overshadow the good, and how maybe I'd be better off to start anew somewhere else."

Brett's heart gave a leap. He'd been waiting for her to say something like that, for it meant the time might be near when he could actually suggest she do just that—with him. The fact was, he didn't really feel he had a stake in the war, never had. He'd been bitter about her, bitter about the prejudice of those who looked down on the Acadians. And while he'd always hated slavery, he just didn't feel as if it was his fight.

"I think about it most of all when I'm standing on the riverbank," she whispered, loving the feel of his hand moving downward to squeeze her breasts. His lips, warm and sensuous, nuzzled hers as she arched against him, pressing yet closer. "I can hear the water, and I think how all I've got to do is float right down that river and in no time at all I'll be right in front of my weeping willow tree. I used to call it my dreaming tree, where all wishes would come true as long as I stayed wrapped up in the long, draping branches. And it was always so sad to come out from under it and find nothing in my life was as I wanted to be.

"With you, Brett"—she boldly reached to encircle his manhood with her hand, delighting in the swollen hardness, evidence of his desire—"I feel as if I'm always beneath my willow tree, and instead of the soft fronds, it's your arms holding me. And then I start believing dreams could really come true, if I could just see you . . ."

"Look at me with the eyes of your mind," he said huskily. "Let your vision be driven by memory . . . and desire . . ."

He kissed her hard, fiercely, as though to seal absolute possession. Gathering her close, he reveled in the feel of naked flesh. His tongue moved inside her mouth, deliciously probing. Anjele could feel the tightening way deep inside her belly, moving on down into her loins as his fingers ever so gently pinched at her nipples. They leaped to hardness, her breasts aching, swelling against his chest.

With a moan, Brett assaulted her neck with his mouth, nuzzling, tickling with his tongue as he moved ever downward. Slowly, he began to trace hot, wet circles around her nipples. She gasped, reaching to entwine her fingers in his thick hair, holding him captive as he divinely assaulted.

"Take me, Brett, please," she begged. "Give me all of you and stay inside me all night long . . . ."

He positioned himself on top of her, the tips of her nipples brushing against the soft mat of hair on his chest. Yet he did not yield to the hunger to enter her, holding back to tease and touch, laughing softly as she squirmed beneath him, wantonly begging him to drive himself inside her.

At last, he could hold back no longer, and she buried her face in the hollow between his shoulder and neck, whimpering with delight as he thrust to and fro. She tilted her hips closer, clinging to him as wildfire raced through her veins. His hips ground into her mercilessly, and she welcomed every jab, willing him to push so deeply they fused together into one being, forever and always.

He felt the fever boiling forth from his loins, at the same instant she began to quiver against him, saw how her neck arched back, pressing her head into the pillow, flinging from side to side in wild throes of rapture beyond equal.

In the afterglow, Anjele lay once more with her head on his shoulder. "It's times like this, when I'm content to stay here forever, in this room you tell me is so small, in this house you describe as falling down."

"Suits me," he agreed, turning to kiss her cheek. "The condition this place is in, it's no Garden of Eden, but I'm in no hurry to leave."

"You've forgotten your assignment, soldier?" she charged with mock severity. "All you do is ravish your prisoner."

"Mmmmm." He smiled, playfully patting her bottom as she turned on her side to snuggle. "I think I like it better this way."

"Ahh, but what if I do one day remember?" She sought and found his cheek, pressing her finger against it. "And what if I get my eyesight back? What happens to us then? We can't stay here. We'll have to return to the world."

He had instinctively tensed at the thought of her being able to see him, recognize him.

Nothing had really changed, he was pained to remember. Instead of dreaming beneath the weeping willow tree, grasping fantasies and pretending they were real, she was doing the same thing under a cloak of blindness.

None of it was real or ever could be, for when the day ultimately came that she guessed who he was, they'd be right back in the sugarhouse at BelleClair, from two different worlds, forbidden to love.

Till then, he could only seize the day, the moment . . . .

He froze, instinctively tightening his arm about her, at the same time using his free hand to press against her lips for silence.

"Someone is in the house," he whispered, mouth against her ear. "Don't move. Don't make a sound. Stay right here."

She obeyed, silently screaming in protest as she felt him move away, but he made no noise once he was off the bed, and she was terrified to be alone.

But he returned swiftly to guide her up and to her feet. "They're coming up the stairs. I'm hiding you in the dumbwaiter, in case they notice this room. Whatever happens, you stay in there, understand?"

"But what if you get hurt?" she whispered in response.

"No matter what, stay there." He squeezed her arms for emphasis, then helped her up and inside.

She felt his parting kiss, then heard the soft click as he closed the door.

Then she could only wait, crouched in fear, desperate to know what was going on.

Finally, when she could stand it no longer, she heard voices, but curiously realized the sound came from below, where the dumbwaiter opened into the service pantry.

"Nobody in here."

"Nobody any place."

"I'd say this is a perfect place for a command post," one of them was saying. "It looks deserted. Our dispatchers can slip in and out to rendezvous when the time comes. Nobody will know. We'll be able to gather information about what's going on in Vicksburg and get word to General Grant."

Anjele's hands flew to her mouth to stifle a gasp of horror. Yankees! And they were spying on the Confederate troops defending Vicksburg. She pressed her ear to the wooden platform, desperate to hear more.

"General Grant's up at Grand Junction. He's got

troops moving in from Corinth and Bolivar, Tennessee. We can get a line of communication going as they move south."

"Yeah," came the response of the other soldier, "but right now I got to get some sleep. Can't hardly keep my eyes open. Let's bed down in the front hallway."

"Yeah, sounds good. Nobody will come in. We're safe . . . ."

The voices faded away, and Anjele began to tremble, anxious for Brett to come and get her out of the dumbwaiter.

He was there in moments, and she understood the need to continue to be quiet as he helped her down. He then gathered her in his arms to tell her what she'd already figured out. General Grant was planning to attack Vicksburg, was gathering troops, and the soldiers downstairs were advance scouts. Their job was to learn the strength of Vicksburg's defense and get word back to Grant.

"We'll wait till they leave in the morning," he said, "then find another place to hide."

She stared in into the black ocean in which she eternally swam, wishing for perhaps the thousandth time she could gaze into his face and read his expression when she asked, "Why would you want to leave? This is wonderful, Brett. We can hide here, in the dumbwaiter, when they come, and listen to them and report to the troops in Vicksburg. We can let them know what's going on."

He didn't respond, because he didn't know what to say just then. Good Lord, she was asking him to spy on the Union but was forced to remember she believed he was part of the Confederacy. "It would be risky," he began. "They might find out we're here, find out who you are, and I've told you over and over, we don't know who to trust."

"We have to take that chance. We don't have any choice."

Brett grimly, silently, knew it was so.

CHAPTER 29

THE CONFEDERATE PICKET STARED AT THE bedraggled man and the blind woman beside him. He'd been told not to let anybody through without proper papers. "I don't care what kind of news you got. You'll have to wait till I send word to the General. And say . . ." His eyes narrowed as he addressed Brett. "How come you ain't in uniform? Ain't you heard about conscription? Law says if you're between eighteen and thirty-five, and fit, you gotta fight. You ain't seventeen, and you don't look thirty-six. And I'd say you're real fit, mister."

Brett had been prepared for censure. "As you can see, my wife is blind. She has no one to look after her except me. I scraped up the five hundred dollars to pay somebody to take my place. That's allowed, you know." The soldier relaxed a little. "So tell me what's so danged important?"

Brett hedged. "It's best we speak to an officer—"

"We have news of advance scouts for General Grant," Anjele burst in, anxious to let someone, anyone, in the Confederate army know of the danger. She was exhausted, had been unable to sleep the night before, knowing the Yankees were on the porch. And the minute they rode away, she'd insisted on starting for Vicksburg.

She had the picket's attention, and he turned from Brett to her. "What're you talkin' about, lady? Where'd you see Yankee scouts?"

Nervously, Brett glanced about to see other soldiers curiously moving toward them. The last thing he wanted was to draw attention. Attention meant questions, and all he wanted to do was get the information to someone in authority, and then find a new place to hide out. Maybe get out of Mississippi. Head west. Anywhere Anjele would be safe from whoever was out to kill her. There could be Union spies, right there in the encampment, and they would waste no time in getting word out that she had been located.

He grabbed Anjele's arm and squeezed, at the same time leaning to whisper, "Please. Let me handle this."

"I'm sorry," she mumbled, hearing sounds of people pressing closer. It was unnerving, and, like Brett, she didn't want to linger longer than necessary.

Brett straightened and looked the picket squarely in the eye as he resolutely declared, "We talk to the officer in charge, or not at all."

Motioning to one of the other guards to take over, the picket led the way.

Anjele could feel curious eyes upon her as they walked. "Talk to me," she pleaded nervously. "Tell me what's going on."

He described the camp, an endless sea of tents. Soldiers sat around, cleaning guns, polishing boots. Horses munched on hay in a corral.

Outside the hospital tent, the wounded lay on stretchers. He didn't tell her about the small pile of amputated limbs, awaiting burial in a pit somewhere—

the gangrenous aftermath of the battle up in Corinth a few weeks earlier.

At last, they reached the heart of the command post. Brett told her it was bigger than any of the others. A large Confederate flag was flying outside. There were also two guards, who stepped to cross their rifles, barring their going any further. The picket almost apologetically proceeded to recount Anjele's startling outburst. The guards exchanged skeptical glances. Brett was losing patience, about to turn and leave, when the flap of the tent flew open.

General John Pemberton, double rows of brass buttons gleaming down the front of his gray tunic, stepped out. Thick gold epaulets of his rank adorned his shoulders. "Well?" He glared about him, finally raking Brett and Anjele with annoyance. "What's going on out here? What are these civilians doing in my camp? And why aren't you in uniform?" he demanded of Brett.

Repeating his lie of having paid someone to take his place in combat, again reminding it was legal to do so, Brett then suggested, "Could we talk in private? What we have to tell you is very important."

"No." General Pemberton said. "Talk to one of my officers. I'm busy. Sergeant Crenshaw," he called out, snapping his fingers.

Brett saw a potbellied soldier step from the crowd that had gathered.

The general waved his hand in dismissal. "Take them somewhere and find out what they want." With a scowl of warning, he snapped at the picket, "And don't be bringing any more civilians in here, understand?" He disappeared inside the tent.

Sergeant Crenshaw motioned for Brett to follow him, leading the way to a nearby tent. Inside, after they were seated, he ordered in a bored tone, "Okay, let's hear it."

Anjele couldn't resist blurting, "I think your general is rude. And besides," she added scornfully, "he has a Yankee accent."

Brett, ignoring the sergeant's annoyed frown, told her, "That's because he is a Yankee, by birth, anyway. I've heard he's from Pennsylvania, but his wife is a Southerner, from Virginia, I believe. He graduated from West Point but went with the South, because he supports states' rights. That explains his accent. It also explains"—he looked pointedly at the sergeant—"why his background causes a lot of Southerners to mistrust him. I have my own doubts now, after he didn't care to hear us out."

"Yes, well, he's a busy man. So am I. You got something to say, say it," Sergeant Crenshaw impatiently snapped.

Brett proceeded to confide what had happened the night before.

The sergeant listened, and the more he heard, the more interested he became. Still, suspicion needled. "You say you-all was camped out in a deserted house. What were you doing there?"

"Seeking shelter," Brett responded. "We've nowhere else to go. We lost our home." That was no lie, he thought resentfully.

"Let's see now . . ." Sergeant Crenshaw scratched his chin thoughtfully, leaning back to gaze up at the roof of the tent. "We hear Grant is up at LaGrange. Damn bastards took the railroad at Holly Springs.

"Yes," he went on, talking to himself, "it stands to

reason Grant would send out reconnaissance forces to try and find out our strength here, and damn it . . ."

He suddenly pounded the desk and turned to glare at them, "What better way to do it than sending a couple of civilians right into our camp, pretending they overheard Yankee spies, so they can count heads and report back to Grant?"

Brett tensed, fearing any minute the man was going to yell for guards to throw them in jail as spies. "Wait a minute, Crenshaw, you're fixing to mess up real bad here."

It was Crenshaw's turn to be uneasy. Somehow, he knew he was looking at a man who could be quite dangerous. "Now, see here," he began, starting to rise from his chair.

"No, *you* see here," Brett leaned toward him, eyes shooting angry sparks, the nerves in his jaw tensing.

Anjele caught her breath, held it, fearing something terrible was about to happen. Maybe Brett was right, and they were wrong to come here, and . . .

Brett proceeded to inform the sergeant, "Now, we've come here to do the Confederate army a favor and report that the house where we're staying may be used as a meeting place for Yankee reconnaissance. If you-all don't care, then neither do we, damn it."

Crenshaw swallowed hard, apprehension a lump in his throat. Maybe the man was telling the truth. He reached for a pen and a piece of paper. "All right. Exactly where is this house?"

"Oh, to hell with it." Brett got up so fast his chair tipped over. He grabbed Anjele's hand and pulled her with him.

Sergeant Crenshaw was right behind them. "Wait a minute. We can ride out, take a look around. We can even station a patrol there, in case they come back, and—"

"And scare them away, is that it?" Brett couldn't believe what he was hearing.

"Well, I really doubt—"

Brett snapped, "Forget it. If we see them again, we'll let you know," he lied, heading out of the tent, wanting to get as far from the camp, and Vicksburg, as possible.

That night, he tried to convince Anjele they should move on.

"Where would we go?"

"It doesn't matter. I just don't feel you're safe here."

"We're not going to be safe anywhere," she argued. "The fact is, you're a deserter, because you didn't do what you were supposed to do, which was take me to the Confederates. But at least we've got the chance now to help the South."

He laughed shortly. "I'd like to know how. You heard what happened today. All that fat sergeant wanted to do was find the way out here so he could capture a few Yankees to show off for General Pemberton. He didn't give a damn that there might be a chance we could turn the tables, spy on them, and—" Brett caught himself, realizing he actually sounded indignant. Good Lord, he was an officer in the Union army. What was happening to him?

They had gone to bed for warmth, because it was a chilly night, and Anjele snuggled closer to plead, "Let's do it, anyway. Let's stay a little while longer. I feel so useless, Brett, but this way I've got a chance to do something for my people."

Brett knew he could force her to go with him. Helpless, she wouldn't dare stay behind without him. True, she and Rufus had got to be good friends, and he knew the old man would probably lie down and die for her, if need be. Still, she wouldn't want to depend on a decrepit ex-slave. She would go with him, all right, and part of him wanted to tell her that's how it was going to be.

Yet another part of him wanted to stay.

In the days and weeks following, Brett wandered about the plantation and the countryside. Reminded of his past, he came to realize how more good memories were being evoked than bad. After all, he had grown up there, and till Margette came into his life, times had been pleasant—except when his father went on one of his drinking binges. Brett learned to stay out of his way, and that's how he came to spend so much time in the swamps, learning his way around—and also learning to hunt alligators.

He ventured deep into the swamp and found the place where he'd once lived. There wasn't much left as evidence there'd ever been a village there. Rufus told him the Cajuns who'd lived there had moved north of Vicksburg. Working for plantations along the Yazoo River, most had settled in the Chickasaw Bayou. It was just as well, Brett decided. He didn't have to worry Anjele would hear someone call him by the name that would lose her to him forever.

Sometimes he was embittered to think how his background now made no difference to her. Dependent on him, she didn't care whether he was rich or poor, so long as he took care of her. But maybe, he brooded, it wasn't right to think that way. After all, her parents weren't alive to censure, and she was no longer engaged to marry someone else. Maybe, under similar circumstances back then, she might have loved him then as she loved him now. At least, he liked to think that's how it would have been.

November faded into December. They were ever alert for any sign of Yankee scouts, but no one came around.

Rufus learned more about what was going on in the war than Brett, due to his daily vigil on the riverbank. Folks got to know him, and fishermen, too old to have to fight, would stop and share the latest news with him.

They learned that Grenada, around a hundred miles northeast, had fallen to the Federals, but not before the Confederates were able to destroy a large number of locomotives and wagons to keep the enemy from using them.

Brett was content to exist in a state of limbo, taking one day at a time. He was confused, because he finally came to realize he didn't want to return to fight for the North, not when he was becoming increasingly stirred with feelings of loyalty to his homeland.

With each passing day, he loved Anjele more and more, but felt guilty to think that he'd rather have her blind, if her regaining her vision and discovering who he really was, meant losing her. Painfully, he knew that could happen, which made him shy away from her hints of marriage. He couldn't do that to her. It would be one thing for her one day to open her eyes wide and see him and instantly hate him and be able to just run away. But to look at him and realize he'd tricked her into marrying him, well, he didn't want to think about that.

Rufus asked him one day when they were alone if he thought she'd get her eyesight back. Brett had to tell him nobody knew. "Well, she's got such pretty eyes," Rufus remarked. "Sho is a shame she can't see with 'em."

And Brett felt another stab of guilt.

* * *

Anjele tried to content herself but became increasingly restless. She was desperate to know what was going on in the world. Travel along the river had come to almost a complete stop since word spread that the daring Confederate Brigadier General Nathan Bedford Forrest was on his way from Tennessee with nearly three thousand cavalrymen. They were after General Grant, who, it was said, was headed for Vicksburg, and they intended to attack his lines of communication.

Brett had told her all they could do was dig in for the winter but warned that if the fighting got too close, they were getting out.

One chilly day in mid-December, Brett had asked her if she minded his going hunting with Rufus. He was short on ammunition, but they had made themselves bows and arrows and both were drooling at the thought of fresh venison. She told him to go ahead, but he insisted she stay in their room. He didn't like her wandering around when he wasn't there, afraid she might get hurt, and also hesitant to believe no one would ever pass by.

Reluctantly, she had agreed, crawling beneath the covers to keep warm and thinking how bored she was. But what was there for a blind person to do? Then she chided herself for allowing self-pity, and thought maybe Brett was right, after all. Maybe they should leave. He had hinted a few times he would like to go out West, and she wasn't opposed. She just wanted a little more time to make sure she was ready to turn her back on the past forever. After all, the war wouldn't last forever, and when it ended, maybe the North would let the Southerners reclaim their homes. But did she really want to go back to BelleClair? Increasingly, she found herself dwelling more on bad memories than good. Perhaps it was time to put it all behind her and think only of the future—with Brett.

She drifted away to awaken with a start, for even in slumber, her senses had become keen, alert for any sound. She could hear voices coming from the dumb-waiter shaft, and she carefully got out of bed and made her way closer. Putting her head inside, she could hear them almost as clearly as though they were right in the next room. One had a nasal inflection, the other was gruff, gravelly.

They were talking about how they'd rendezvoused a few miles downriver and were beginning to think they were lost when finally they'd found the house. Nasal voice said he didn't think it was such a great meeting place, and his gravel-voiced cohort agreed.

At first they said nothing of interest, each expressing fatigue, hunger. There were other sounds, as if they were looking around. Brett had told Anjele he made sure the other rooms in the house were kept bare, so there'd be no evidence anyone was staying there. Even in the kitchen out back, all traces of their food preparation were cleaned away the instant they were finished.

She could also be confident Brett would not walk in on them. Always, when coming or going, he scouted about to make sure there were no surprise visitors.

Abruptly their conversation shifted to something she found interesting. Nasal voice asked sympathetically, "Did those sons of bitches really get as much as we heard they did?"

"Yes," came gravel voice's angry reply. "Maybe a

million in supplies, and they probably burned a couple thousand bales of cotton. Only six companies from the Second Illinois Cavalry were able to cut their way out of the trap. We figure they took around a thousand prisoners."

Nasal voice muttered an oath Anjele couldn't make out.

"Grant's had to postpone taking part in the attack, but Sherman is moving out of Memphis, anyway. I was sent to see if you'd managed to find out what's waiting on him."

A snicker from nasal voice, and then, "I managed to eavesdrop on a conversation just two days ago between two drunken Rebs with loose tongues. I think one of them was a dispatcher, because he knew all about Jeff Davis sending word to Pemberton he's worried he can't hold Vicksburg against Grant."

"That's good. If the Reb president is worried, that means Sherman might be able to do some damage without Grant. What else have you got?"

Anjele was petrified to hear the spy describe plans to destroy the Vicksburg and Shreveport railroad to cut Confederate supply lines into Vicksburg, and how Federal gunboats were about to start shelling batteries at a place called Haine's Bluff. Next came the startling advice for Sherman to cross the Yazoo River at Chickasaw Bayou, because the Rebels anticipated he would come in at the Big Black River and had most of their defense waiting there.

At that, the scout gleefully proclaimed, "Then the Yazoo River it will be, and I'm heading out to tell Sherman as soon as I get some food in my belly."

"I got some bacon in my saddlebag," the other

offered, fading away as they left the pantry, "and I saw an old frying pan in the kitchen out back."

Anjele pulled from the dumbwaiter, dizzily backed across the room to slump down on the bed. Her head was spinning, and she felt absolutely petrified as she endeavored to absorb what she had just learned. Vicksburg was going to be attacked.

"Dear God," she whispered out loud, hands fluttering to her throat as she began to rock to and fro in horror. Brett would have to get word to General Pemberton, but he couldn't even return so she could tell him about it, till the Yankees cooked their food and ate it. He'd see the smoke from the kitchen chimney and be forced to stay away, no doubt worried about her.

With a resigned sigh, she told herself there was nothing to do but wait.

She got back in bed and pulled the covers up to her chin, not about to fall asleep, nervous that the Yankees might return.

At first she didn't really notice what was happening. So used to being in complete darkness, she did not discern how black was slowly melting to dark gray.

Only when gray begin to shimmer with silver was she startled.

Blinking her eyes, her breath caught and held.

It was true.

Light was actually appearing at the fringes of the curtain that blinded. Although it was pale, it was there, by God!

She began to tremble, nervously wondering if it could possibly mean her vision was returning. But as long moments passed, turning into perhaps an hour, she started thinking maybe it would not happen all at once. It might be a gradual process, taking days, even weeks. Yet there was no denying it wasn't quite as dark as before.

She decided not to share this startling revelation with Brett, not wanting to disappoint him as she would be, if it didn't mean anything. She would force herself to wait.

At last he burst through the door to grab her in his arms and cry, "Thank God, you're all right. Jesus, you don't know how worried I've been. Rufus and I saw the smoke and came running, and all we could do was hide in the bushes and wait for those bastards to eat and leave. Did you get in the dumbwaiter like I told you to?"

"Brett, you've got to listen." Quickly she related all she'd heard, and could tell by the way he sharply drew in his breath, he was equally disturbed.

When she finished, he wasted no time in deciding. "You'll stay here. Rufus will look after you. I'm leaving now."

"Good. You need to get to General Pemberton as fast as you can."

"He didn't want to listen last time we had information for him. Neither did his fat sergeant. Why should it be any different now? Besides, I don't have time to try and convince them it's true. I've got to do this my way."

Anjele felt a wave of apprehension, reached out for him, but he was already on his feet. "Where are you going?"

"To Chickasaw Bayou," he told her with a confident smile she could not see, but could hear in his tone. "I've got some friends there who aren't going to like Yankees marching through their territory."

It was only later Brett thought about how, in that moment, he had finally crossed sides.

The Yankees were in his world now, and that made them his enemy, also.

CHAPTER 30

BRETT SKILLFULLY ROWED THE FLAT-BOTtom boat into the slough winding from the Yazoo River into the Chickasaw Bayou. He had hunted in the area in his youth, and as the river narrowed, felt that he was coming home.

All seemed peaceful in the world of snakelike vines, their clutching fingers wrapped around everything in sight. Now and then a sound would split the stillness—the hoot of an owl, the roar of a bull gator, or the screeching of a startled bird.

The water looked darker, thicker, and he knew it was becoming shallow. Laying down the oars, he picked up the steering pole and began to push his way along.

He had done a bit of scouting on land before taking to the river. Slipping around Yankee pickets had been easy, because he kept to the swamps and forest. He could move at night, for he knew the way well. And he had seen General Sherman's troops, only a few miles north, marching towards Vicksburg and planning to cross the Yazoo, just as Anjele had heard.

He began to move faster. He didn't have much time.

He had sent a message to Pemberton but couldn't be

sure it would get to him. After all, Brett grinned to remember, he hadn't wanted to take any chances on getting shot, so he'd jumped the picket from behind and scared him half to death.

The picket had listened, of course. He had no choice with a knife held to his throat. Brett gave him the message, then melted back into the brush as silently as he'd come. He watched the picket take off running, clutching his throat even though it hadn't been nicked.

So Brett could only hope the frightened soldier ran straight to his headquarters and didn't just keep on going.

The reeds were getting taller, thicker, and Brett dug mightily with the pole to make his way through, also struggling to maneuver about the clumps of cypress roots. He saw no sign of life but knew the Cajuns took a different route in and out, one more accessible. He had deliberately chosen the most forbidding way, in case he was spotted out in the river and had to escape. Fortunately he was able to slip through in the darkness.

He had left Christmas Day, in time to witness, from a distance, the railroad being destroyed. Anjele had obviously heard right again, and he wished he could have done something to prevent it happening, but was too late. All he could do was go on with his plan to try to slow Sherman down and give the Confederates time to realize what was happening and send in reinforcements.

Because he had never forgotten what he learned about the bayou, Brett knew survival depended on being ready for anything. In the vague early-morning light filtering down through the cascades of moss, he could tell the log up ahead wasn't a log at all. It was a large alligator, and Brett gave him a sound whack on his head with the pole. With a mighty roar, the deadly jaws opened to reveal razor-sharp teeth before snapping shut. With a swish of his tail, he retreated, too lazy to fight back and not hungry enough to care.

Any other time, Brett would also have been alert to the man stepping from behind a tree only a few feet away, but his attention had been on the gator, lest it change its mind about attacking. But he recovered quickly, because he had rapidly drawn his knife from his boot by the time it came over him that the man had called him by the name he'd like to forget.

"Gator. By God, is it really you, boy?"

Brett grinned when he recognized him. "Bel Talouse. I thought you'd be dead by now, you old swamp rat."

Bel stood with hands on his hips, legs apart, and threw his head back to laugh gustily. "Hey, I not be the one who couldn't leave the ladies alone. How come you not dead?"

How come, indeed, Brett grimly reflected, then hoisted himself from the boat and onto the bank to grasp Bel's hand and begin, "I'd really like to tell you all about the past years, my friend, but right now, there's something more important. Where're the rest of your people?"

Bel Talouse knew something was wrong. He turned and started through the reeds, motioning Gator to follow quickly.

The Acadian settlement was larger than the old one had been. Brett saw they had done well for themselves, because there were adequate shacks up on stilts, rather than make-do huts and pirogues.

The women took their children to one side, allowing the men to gather around the fire and talk.

They all remembered him, but there was little time to

exchange pleasantries. He got straight to the point and told them the Yankees were marching towards Vicksburg by way of crossing the Yazoo. "And we've got to slow them down so the Confederates can rally."

He saw the way they exchanged uncomfortable glances, knew they didn't want to get involved. They weren't slave owners and didn't care whether the farmers and planters they worked for were from North or South.

Finally, Bel Talouse took it upon himself to speak for all of them and said uneasily, "The fight isn't ours, Gator, and we ain't willing to die for it."

Gator was ready to fire back, "The fight becomes yours when your children cry with hunger, Bel, and you've got nothing to feed them, because the enemy takes all the food and puts a torch to the fields.

"And you can all believe"—he swept them with a fiery glare of warning—"when Vicksburg falls, you fall with it. Life as you know it will be over. Now you've got a chance to help save it."

The Cajuns exchanged nervous glances again, and Bel gave a resigned sigh and wanted to know exactly what Gator had in mind.

Gator told them he knew where Sherman planned to cross and didn't think he'd have any trouble doing so. Once Sherman made it, though, the Confederates would no doubt have rallied to confront him with a force nearly the size of his own. They would be fighting from nearly impregnable defenses at the base of a high bluff.

"Sherman will attack, of course," Brett went on to theorize, "but his approach will be blocked here, by Chickasaw Bayou. We all know there are only two favorable crossing places."

"And?" Bel prodded suspiciously.

Brett swept the crowd again, this time with a confident smile. "We're going to show them how damn good Cajuns can fight. We're going to cover one of those crossings."

They gathered weapons—pistols, shotguns, knives and axes. Then, with Brett shouting encouragement, they set about hastily constructing crude rafts, which they packed with oil-soaked tree limbs.

All day they worked. Scouts went out and returned to report Sherman was almost to the river and predicted a crossing at dawn. A few men made the eight-mile or so trip into Vicksburg to ensure Pemberton was alerted. He was moving, they said, but slowly, and, just as Brett had predicted, Sherman would make it across with relative ease. The real battle would come when he attempted to make it through Chickasaw Bayou.

The firing began with the first light of day, December 28. The air was thick with the smell of sulphur. Screams of the wounded and dying rang out amidst the bursting explosions of the Parrott guns. In the narrow river, battles were waged between gunships. The Confederates were holding, but if Sherman succeeded in breaking through the Bayou, they'd be overrun.

Brett and the Cajuns boarded their crude rafts, poling them through the inlet to the most vulnerable point of crossing. Then, one by one, they torched the oil-soaked cargo and all joined in to push each raft into the current.

Slowly the burning barges made their way to cluster as one giant wall of flame, blocking the path of the invading soldiers.

There were a few skirmishes as several Union soldiers were able to break through. Brett was anguished to see Bel gunned down. Dragging him to shelter, he was relieved it was only a flesh wound. Two other Cajuns, however, were not so fortunate and died where they fell in the first moments of fighting.

At last, a cry went up from someone who had scrambled up a tree to watch the warfare in the river. "They be pullin' back!"

Jubilation was as wild as the flames from the rafts, stretching toward heaven. They had held off Sherman, and he was caught by fire from the base of the bluff while Union gunboats were under heavy assault in the river. But Brett warned against optimism, told his men to dig in, for the Yankees weren't about to withdraw.

The fighting continued all night, and on into the next day and the next, as Sherman made repeated attacks on the Confederate positions. Again and again he was pushed back, to the delight of the Cajuns and repeated warnings by Brett against early optimism.

Finally, aided by a fleet of mortar boats, Sherman made one more attempt to take both the bayou and the bluffs. As Brett saw the bodies piling up, he wondered how he could have thought the deaths that first day were so significant. Bel sadly reported they had lost twelve of their number.

At last, mercifully, it was over. General Sherman ordered his troops to withdraw, and everyone was shouting victory. Brett retained his pessimism to warn, "He's not through. He's only retreating to wait for Grant and regroup. Then he'll be back. Probably in the spring."

Bel happily assured him, "And we'll be ready." Then, on a somber note, he placed his hands on Brett's shoulders and told him, "Thank you, my friend, for making us see it is our war, too."

"I'm afraid it eventually becomes everybody's war. Whether they like it or not."

"And you are gonna stay and help us fight it, no?"

Brett told him there was something he had to do but declined to go into details. In the past days, when he'd come so close to being killed himself a couple of times, he had realized he'd been wrong to leave Anjele as he had. If anything happened to him, she was helpless. So he had made up his mind to do what he should have done a long time ago—turn her over to the Confederate government for protection.

Then he had a war to worry about.

And when it ended, he'd find her and see what the future held.

"A woman," Bel teased. "I bet the Gator has another woman."

"Not another woman." He grinned. "She's the same one, only she doesn't know it."

Bel blinked. "I don't understand."

Brett turned away, thinking how it wasn't important that he did.

It had happened over a period of days.

At first, the silver blanket turned to one of smoky white. Then came pale pink, and finally, miraculously, came the morning when she awoke to the world in all its glory.

She could only lie there, slowly looking about the

room, fearing that if she moved too much the curtain would fall again, returning her to the pit of eternal darkness.

But the curtain did not come down, and after a few moments, she slowly got out of bed and walked about. Deciding movement would not harm, she padded from the room and out into the gallery leading around the stairway. Then she began to skip about, finally running, giggling with delight at everything she saw.

Remembering she was barefoot and wearing only a thin nightgown Brett had stolen from someone's clothesline they'd passed along the way, she hurried to dress.

Finally she ran all the way downstairs and burst out the front door. Arms spread wide, face lifted skyward in thanksgiving, she ran across the brown lawn. It was the first of January, though unseasonably warm, but after all it was Mississippi, and the Southland, and praise God, she could see, and oh, how she wished Brett were there so she could share her joy, and—

Brett.

She stopped running, stopped dancing about, suddenly sobered to realize that at long last she'd be able to look into the eyes of her beloved. What did he look like? Oh, she yearned to know but knew it didn't matter. He could be the ugliest creature God ever put on earth, and she'd love him no less. Her heart was his, for always and always, and now that she had her eyesight back, they could really make plans and start to live.

Rufus had come upon her, scared to see her out and roaming about by herself. When she shared the miracle, he leaned very close and stared into her eyes, then cried, "Glory be! Praise God! You can see, Miss

Anjele! You can sho' enuff see!"

Two days passed. Anjele was getting nervous, anxious for Brett to return. By day, she walked about, drinking in the sights of the place that had been her home the past months. By night, she lay awake, reveling to think that it really was just night and, best of all, only temporary.

It was almost pitch dark when Rufus came running to tell her he'd spotted Brett coming around the bend in the river. He could tell it was him, because he was moving slowly, close to the bank, avoiding being seen by one of the many gunboats cruising up and down the Mississippi.

"He's gonna sho' be happy when he finds out you ain't blind no more," Rufus cried.

Anjele wanted the time to be special. She didn't want to just run to meet him yelling she could see him, at last. No, that wasn't the way she wanted him to find out, and had planned the moment carefully.

It would be at dawn, becasuse there was no moon this night. Wanting him to be able to see the love mirrored in her eyes, she would force herself to wait till the first light of day fell across them.

Rufus understood she wanted to be alone when Brett got there, so he grinned and bid her good-night.

Anjele made her way to the pier, using a walking stick to probe the way. In the pitch darkness, it didn't matter her sight had returned. It was impossible to see anything, but she could hear the sounds of his boat bumping against the pier as he groped to tie it. She called softly, "Brett, is that you?"

"Anjele, honey, what are you doing out here?" He leaped to grab her and crush her in his arms, showering her face with kisses. "God, I've missed you so . . . ."

"And I've been crazy with worry," she cried, pressing close against him. "Are you really all right?"

He assured her he was fine and took her hand, leading her away from the river. "Come on. I'll tell you all about it."

She continued to pretend she was still blind. They sat down, and after a soul-searing kiss that left both of them breathless, he recounted the battle.

"Thank God," she whispered, relieved that, for the time being, the Union had been forced to withdraw. "But what happens next?" She smiled in the darkness, confident that any plans he had made could only be enriched when he learned her vision had returned. But when he didn't answer, she felt a shiver of apprehension. Something told her whatever he had in mind he was reluctant to discuss.

He reached for her, whispering, "We'll talk in the morning, Angel, because here and now, I want you. It's all I've dreamed about." He pulled her almost roughly down beside him. Her breasts squeezed against his chest, and his hands moved to cup her buttocks and crush her tighter still. Immediately she felt his hardness between her thighs as his mouth found hers, warm, hungry, fierce with passion.

His tongue touched hers possessively, and he then moved to devour her face and neck, all the while nimbly unfastening the bodice of her dress, jerking it almost savagely away to free her breasts.

Anjele was licked with flames of desire. Spreading her thighs to receive his probing fingers, she cried out as the fire burned brighter. Shamelessly, raggedly, she begged him to take her.

A great roaring began, and she felt herself being

swept away as molten waves of pleasure washed over her writhing, twisting body. She felt his hot, ragged breath against her ear, the thunderous pounding of his wildly beating heart against her naked breasts. Then he was pulling away from her, but only long enough to strip off his clothes before once more savagely, but sweetly, assaulting.

She gasped to feel the delight of his entry. Almost furiously, he hammered into her. The explosive thrusts charged through her loins, upwards into her belly, and deeper, still, to the very depths of her enraptured soul. Mercilessly, her nails dug into the rock-hard flesh of his back as she sought to bring him yet closer.

At last, when she thought she would surely die if he didn't end the ecstatic torture, they came simultaneously. It rocked them both with wonder, and they clung together for long moments afterward, naked flesh drenched by the sweat of near-savage consummation.

He rolled away to lie on his back, keeping her close beside him, her head upon his shoulder. As always, they shared whispered vows of love for all eternity.

Brett was exhausted but so grateful to be back and holding her close. Dreamily he told her, "In the spring, I hope we make love outside all the time. Maybe on a spot like this hillock. I remember it used to be covered in flowers. All colors." He turned to hold her close once more, nuzzling his chin in her soft hair. "Oh, Angel, darling, I can't wait for spring. Making love to you is like holding heaven in my hand, like finding heaven in a wildflower."

He closed his eyes. Unable to stay awake any longer, weariness took him away.

Anjele was drifting herself, so at peace in his arms.

* * *

She was awakened with a jolt and sat upright. The cool breeze from the river brought her to instant alertness. This time, it was not a sound just heard but the echo of Brett's words of the night before.

She had been dreaming, in the throes of the same, recurring nightmare. She was kneeling beside her father, straining to listen to what he seemed so desperate to tell her. Only this time, she could hear him.

Wildflowers.

The door had been opened, and now she knew—the last word her father had spoken had been *wildflowers.*

Another memory came flashing back.

The day they had been to the family mausoleum, he had been touched by the sight of wildflowers growing out of her mother's crypt. "Life growing out of the aperture of death," he'd said.

And now she knew what he had been trying to tell her in his last breath—the plates were hidden in the family crypt.

The first light of dawn was streaking the sky, and she turned excitedly to Brett. He lay with his back to her, and she touched his shoulder, anxious to share two exciting miracles, instead of one.

He sleepily grumbled, rolled over on his back, but did not awaken.

Anjele's hands flew to her gaping mouth.

Dear God, she realized with a slamming jolt of her heart that left her struggling to breathe, *she was looking at Gator.*

CHAPTER 31

ANJELE FOLLOWED THE COURSE OF THE river.

In its constant turning and twisting, the Mississippi relentlessly ate into the banks, making undercuts on one side, new points on the other. Riding Brett's horse, she had to be ever alert, for the way was treacherous, and what appeared to be solid ground could actually be eroded beneath.

She rode doggedly, wanting to get as far away as possible before Brett woke up to find her gone.

Brett . . .

She bristled, burning with white-hot rage.

Gator . . .

She cursed herself for not realizing the truth but how could she? He'd had the advantage, because she could not see him, and he had successfully endeavored to mask other ways he might be recognized. He had changed his voice, his personality and mannerisms, and, blast him, even the way he'd made love to her.

Anjele also reminded herself that Gator had been out of her life for over four years.

Oh, she was furious. To think it had all been a trick,

a scheme, from the very start. Brett was a Yankee soldier. Somehow, someone had discovered she had once made a fool of herself over him and figured, given her blindness, he could use the same guile to bewitch her again. Of course, the motive was for her to eventually lead him to the lost plates.

Perhaps some things did change, she thought with a grimace, but not Brett's ability to deceive.

The pieces began to fall together. Now she knew why he hadn't taken her to the Confederates. He wasn't worried about someone trying to kill her. He just wanted to make sure he was the only one around when her memory returned. The attempt on her life had no doubt been staged to make her look to him for protection, willing to believe anything he said.

In that frozen moment, when she saw the truth, the scream of indignant rage had mercifully locked in her throat, allowing time for shock to melt into seething anger and force her to realize she had to flee. Once he discovered she knew of the ruse, there was no telling what he might do. But one thing was certain—he'd never let her go.

Anjele knew she had to get to New Orleans as quickly as possible to find out if she was right about the meaning of her father's last word. If so, if the plates were indeed hidden in her mother's coffin, she would retrieve them and then make her way to Richmond and turn them over to the Confederacy. Brett would come after her. She had no doubt about that. Once he found out from Rufus she could see, he'd know she had recognized him at first light and quickly left in a rage. He would also conclude she'd head back to New Orleans to try and find the plates, suspecting she had known all along where they were, and the fact that she was considered an escaped prisoner by the Union would not stop her from returning.

She had taken his horse, and that would slow him down a bit. He would lose time having to find another, because he couldn't take the small boat all the way downriver to New Orleans, and there was no other means of water transportation. Steamers and paddle wheelers were, of course, no longer operating for passengers.

She passed a few cabins along the way but waited till almost dark to stop at a small farmhouse. A friendly elderly couple, who introduced themselves as Jasper and Daisy Kinston, kindly gave her shelter, especially when she told her hastily contrived lie about being on her way to New Orleans in hopes of reaching her ailing mother before she died.

Jasper, however, was very vocal about the dangers she faced. "You ain't got no business travelin' by yourself. And you not only have to worry about Yankee raiders and foragers, but Rebel deserters, too. Lots of meanness goin' on out there now, missy, and it'll be suicide when you get to Natchez Trace. Ain't even safe there during daylight hours, but at night it's terrible, the haunt of the worse scourges of Mississippi and Louisiana—murderers, renegades. You'd never make it."

Anjele knew he spoke the truth and wasn't just attempting to frighten her. "I've got to try," she said with firm resolution. "No matter what, I've got to try to reach New Orleans as fast as possible."

Daisy thought of her daughter, who'd died at the age of four. Perhaps she would have grown up to be as pretty as Anjele. Her hair had also been the color of a March sunrise, and she had a little dimple in her cheek, too. Daisy couldn't bear the thought of someone not helping her daughter, if she were trying to get to her as she lay dying. Reaching to cover Jasper's hand with her own, she asked hopefully, "What about your brother in Baton Rouge?"

"What about him?" Jasper sharply asked, suspicious as to what she had in mind.

With an embarrassed smile in Anjele's direction, Daisy informed him, "I happen to know a few things that go on in your family, Jasper, and I've known for some time how Luther and those friends of his sneak into New Orleans every week to sell home brew to some of the soldiers.

"They make good money off them Yankees, too," she remarked gleefully before asking, "so why can't they take Anjele with them next time they go? Nobody searches their boat, 'cause they know what they're hauling—sin in a jar, that's what." She frowned with disapproval.

Anjele leaped at the idea. "Yes, that would be perfect. All they have to do is get me to the outskirts of the city, and I can make it the rest of the way."

Jasper pursed his lips, scratched his head, thoughtfully looking from one to the other as he tried to convince himself it could work. Finally he announced, "If it's all right with Luther, why should I care?"

Both Daisy and Anjele hugged him with grateful joy.

Within three days, Jasper delivered her to his brother, who agreed to smuggle her into New Orleans in exchange for the fine horse she was riding. Anjele didn't bat an eye at turning over the stallion. It was a kind of redemption, she felt, since the horse belonged to Brett, as though *he* were the one financing her journey home.

Luther's partners, Hollis and Edwin, were, like Luther, too old to go to war. Anjele liked them at once, finding them to be kind and polite and felt at ease around them.

They smuggled her on board, where she hid in the smelly bait well below deck, along with the bottles and jars of their homemade whiskey. Once they were safely out of port, they invited her topside, where she would remain, sleeping on deck, for the two-day journey into New Orleans.

They confided that they were making quite a bit of money, explaining how Federal officers had access to alcohol, but the common soldiers had to scrounge for theirs. Since Baton Rouge had fallen to the Union after fierce fighting last August, the trio had been slowly getting rich off thirsty Yankees.

Anjele was grateful for their company, as well as shared news of the war. Engaging in conversation kept her from thinking about the smoldering rage within.

"Rains and high winds," Luther grumbled as they reached the outskirts of New Orleans. "Weather's been like this for weeks now. One of the soldiers said the streets in the Vieux Carré look like canals."

Hollis spoke up to add, "Colder than normal, too. And lots of pneumonia and not enough doctors. Them that didn't go off with the Confederates 'cause they were too old, like us, ain't allowed to work nowhere 'cept the Union hospital, and then they ain't allowed to treat anybody that ain't took the oath."

Edwin joined in the conversation to share, "There's a

terrible shortage of everything. "No candles. Folks either make their own or do without. And no kerosene. Gas is turned off at dark, so there's no streetlights, and everybody's scared to go out after dark."

"Who wants to?" Hollis said with a derisive snort. "I got a cousin who still lives there, and she says the Yankees just march in any time they want to, lookin' for contraband, like gray wool, anything with Confederate colors. Even sheet music of Southern songs. If they find anything, they just run the people out of their house and confiscate it.

"Jelsie," he went on, "my cousin, she was bound and determined she wasn't gonna take the oath. Said she'd die and go to hell first. But then she realized those what didn't could expect to be raided every night, so she said hell, she'd sign it. Didn't mean nothing, no how. Said it was like a young'un promisin' he wouldn't steal no more cookies. Like me, she said why not use the sons of bitches? We keep 'em in rotgut whiskey and grin when we take their money."

By the time they arrived, Anjele was in a very foul condition. Her clothes were filthy, tattered, and torn. Her hair hung limp and loose about her face. But her spirits were high, and she knew that was all that mattered. She had her precious eyesight, and she was nearly home.

They put her ashore about a mile out of town just before daylight. They took turns bidding her farewell and wishing her good luck the rest of the way.

Hollis pressed money into her hand as he hugged her, saying, "Rent you a buggy to get where you're going. A pretty girl like you don't need to be out alone around them damn Yankees."

Edwin also gave her a few Federal greenbacks and told her to buy a new dress.

Luther's donation was for a bath, as he apologized to have to tell her, "You're going to scare folks to death, the way you look and smell, missy."

With tears of gratitude and a heart filled with love for all their kindness, she gave them each a warm hug and a fond kiss on their whiskered cheeks.

Waving them away, she hurried into the woods to get her bearings and try to figure out what to do next. The only people at BelleClair she felt she could trust were Raymond and Mammy Kesia, but she didn't intend even to encounter them if it proved possible to slip in and out without doing so. Even so, looking as she did, she wasn't about to be seen by anyone. Then she thought of Melora Rabine. If she was still there, Anjelc knew she would help.

She headed into the city, moving at the edge of the woods, unnoticed by anyone traveling on the road. Head bowed against the chilling, slicing wind, she absently thought how it had been so unseasonably warm only a few hundred miles north, warm enough to—

She gave herself a vicious shake.

Never, she vowed, would she allow herself to think of that warm night in Brett Cody's arms. She would force herself never to think of any time with him at all.

It was the only way she could cope with the nightmare of the past.

Reaching New Orleans, she went directly to Melora Rabine's house, praying to find her there. Creeping in by a back alley, she felt a hopeful jolt at the familiar sight of the old carriage in the rear yard.

She moved quickly, not wanting the neighbors to see and wonder why such a wretched-looking woman was in Melora's yard.

After a few rapid knocks, the door opened and Melora's mouth dropped open at the sight of her. "Oh, dear God, child, come in," she cried, reaching out for her, and then the miracle dawned, "You can see! Oh, praise God, you can see, Anjele!" She burst into tears.

Worn out, exhausted physically and mentally, Anjele gratefully collapsed in her arms.

Melora clucked over her, insisting she lie down while she fixed something for her to eat and heated a tub of hot water. "Then you can tell me everything. I heard how you'd been sent to prison for harboring bushwhackers, and it made me so mad, especially when I heard that little witch Claudia was responsible for your getting caught. Then I heard you'd escaped, and I've been worried sick ever since that something terrible had happened to you.

"At least," she rattled on, "I've got something to feed you. I signed their stupid oath, and while it's not much, I do get a ration of potatoes and little beef to boil now and then, and I'm glad to share it with you, darlin', so glad . . . ." Her eyes sparkled with tears as she paused to hug Anjele again.

Finally, clean and fed, Anjele told Melora part of the truth—that she had escaped from prison and was on her way to BelleClair to get some things that belonged to her. "I don't intend to stay long, and I know I'll have to sneak in. Otherwise, with my luck, Major Hembree would meet me at the door and take me straight back to Ship Island."

Melora grinned and told her, "Oh, no, he won't. He left when Butler did, back in November. General Banks is in charge now. Conditions are some better, but not a lot." She went on to describe some of the horrors, how planters who refused to sign the oath of loyalty had been rounded up, along with refugee slaves, and made to work on fortifications of the city. "Even old men and children are prodded by soldiers with bayonets. Why, anybody going out on the streets is in danger of being hauled away at any time. The only reason I've fared as well as I have is that I agreed to teach music to the officers' children."

"What about others I used to know?" Anjele asked. "Poppa's lawyer, Mr. DuBose? What about Dr. Duval? And did the Maxwells get their house back when the Hembrees left?"

Melora told her Hardy Maxwell did indeed regain possession of his house, and he and Millard DuBose had both signed the oath and now worked in the Federal bank. Dr. Duval was one of the head doctors at the Union hospital. "I don't suppose they're any prouder of themselves than I am," she was sad to point out, "but we did what we had to do to survive. Still, the Yankees haven't had as easy a time as they thought they would, because we haven't groveled at their feet. We've let them know we hold them in contempt."

She went on to express sympathy for the Negroes who thought they would be better off once the Union took control. No distinction had been made between freemen and slaves, and all were rounded up either to labor in the city or be carted off to plantations and warned not to return to New Orleans. Women whose duties had never been harder than caring for their mistresses' wardrobes, or wet-nursing their babies, had found themselves at hard labor.

Anjele could only shake her head with sadness.

"The Union wives have behaved the ugliest," Melora angrily continued. "Our women have to stand back and wait in the shops while they push their way to the front. And we're supposed to step off the banquettes into the gutters, in mud if need be, to let them swish by, three or four abreast, noses up in the air like we're just dogs. And they ride along in carriages or horse-cars, while we have to walk. I got to keep my buggy, as you may have noticed, because I go to their homes to teach music, but they've told me if I'm caught using it for any other reason, it will be taken away."

"I suppose Claudia is smug to have been among the first to grovel at their feet, and . . ." Her voice trailed as she saw the mysterious way Melora was smiling at her. "What is it? Why are you looking at me like that?"

"Well, it's bad news for your home place, of course, child," she said, "but I have to say, I'm glad it happened."

Anjele was even more confused. "What are you talking about?"

"BelleClair. Major Hembree not only declared it off-limits for officers but withdrew the protection of the army, as well. He said it wasn't proper to socialize at the home of a man who'd steal from the Union. And here it is sugar-making time, and your daddy's cane is just rotting in the fields."

Anjele guiltily realized she didn't care, not if it meant Claudia getting her comeuppance. "But what happened to the slaves? Did they all run away? I wouldn't be surprised, the way she treated them."

"I heard most of them did, according to Ida. But she hasn't been out there in a long time. Nobody ever sees Claudia anymore. She got so mad when the Yankees tore the place up that she had a big fight with Major

Hembree's wife, and the major told her not to show her face in New Orleans again, or he'd send her to Ship Island, too."

"And why did they tear it up?"

"They were trying to find whatever it was they claim your father stole from the government."

It was Anjele's turn to smile. She was becoming even more confident her suspicion as to where the plates were hidden was correct. Her father had cleverly assumed no one would enter the mausoleum, much less open a coffin. With BelleClair no longer crawling with Yankees, she wasn't worried about going there long enough to look for them.

Melora went on to relate how she saw Ida Duval from time to time in the market. "She worries so over Raymond. I understand he practically lives in a drunken stupor now."

It was a life of his own choosing, Anjele felt like saying, but held her tongue. He should have been stronger, because *his* blindness had come from his mind. He could, at least, have seen the person who was beguiling him.

Melora said she was going to make some tea. "It won't be very tasty, I'm afraid. The leaves have been used several times, but I suppose it's better than nothing."

They were sitting in the parlor, for it was the only warm place in the house. With wood so scarce, Melora could only afford to have a fire in one room. Outside, the wind howled, and Anjele pulled the wool afghan tighter about her. Leaning her head back on the sofa, she closed her eyes and let exhaustion take her.

When Melora returned with the tea, she drank it all herself, deciding it was best to let Anjele sleep the afternoon away.

* * *

Brett was almost to Louisiana. He rode like a man possessed, which he was, and driven by one burning thought. *He had to get to New Orleans and find Anjele before whoever wanted her dead found her first.*

It had been midmorning when he had finally awakened, there on the hillock. He hadn't realized how tired he was, having had only snatches of sleep in the past week. Still groggy, he had instinctively reached out for Anjele, and was jolted to discover she wasn't there.

He had leaped to his feet, snatched up his clothes, jerking them on as he ran. First he went to the riverbank to look anxiously for some sign, God forbid, that she'd fallen into the water. Then he had turned and run to the house, rushing upstairs to the room they used.

And that was when he saw it—the peach and coral conch shell she had treasured, smashed on the floor in bits and pieces.

He went in search of Rufus, whose first words had been, "Ain't it wonderful Miss Anjele got her eyesight back?"

And then he knew.

She had seen him, probably in the early morning light, wanting to surprise him with the miracle. But in that instant, love had dissolved and hate was born, and now it was all over.

So be it.

Brett had always known it could end this way, and though it hurt like hell and he felt as if his heart had been broken in more pieces than the conch, he knew he still had a job to do.

No doubt she was headed back to New Orleans.

Maybe to get the plates. Maybe she had always known where they were but never quite trusted him enough to tell him. He didn't give a damn about any of that. The only thing he cared about was that she was headed straight into the clutches of whoever it was that was out to kill her.

And he had to stop it.

Then, and only then, would his quest be finished.

It didn't matter about his heart.

Like the delicate conch, it could never be mended.

Anjele awoke to the sound of excited voices. Struggling to escape the cobwebs of sleep still clinging, she sat up and rubbed her eyes, trying to remember where she was. Then, with a terrified lurch, it all came rushing back.

New Orleans. Melora Rabine's house. But dear Lord, who were those people coming in?

She did not have long to wonder.

Ida Duval ran to embrace her, sobbing, "Anjele, darling, you're home, and you're safe, and thank God you can see."

Dr. Duval was right behind her, carrying his leather bag and excitedly wanting to examine her, but he was having to contend with Drusilla and Hardy Maxwell, along with Millard DuBose. All were eager to greet her and hear where she had been since escaping.

Anjele couldn't help being glad to see them but shot Melora an annoyed glance.

Melora shrugged. "They would never have forgiven me if I hadn't told them you were here, and you said you weren't staying long. Besides, they won't tell."

Ida was quick to assure her, "Of course we won't. We've all got to stick together, dear."

"That's right," Drusilla chimed in, along with her husband.

Vinson Duval succeeded in getting them to move so he could quickly look into her eyes. "You're safe now," he was saying, leaning closer as he examined her.

Finally, to everyone's delight, he declared, "By God, your eyes look perfect. Evidently, when you took that blow on the head, there was bruising and swelling, and it took a long time for it to go away. And when it did, you got your vision back." He moved then to let the women crowd about her.

The men all agreed Anjele was taking a chance on returning to BelleClair, but she assured them she'd not be there long enough for the Yankees to find out she was back. "I just need to get a few things, that's all. Then I'm leaving."

"Where will you go?" Ida anxiously wanted to know.

"Straight to Richmond," she replied with firm resolve.

Melora pressed, "But why? It's so far, and so dangerous, and—"

"Oh, I'll have an escort once I make it to our lines," Anjele said confidently. "I'll be safe."

Hardy wanted to know, "But why? Why are you so desperate to get to the capital?"

Anjele's smile was mysterious. "I just think it's time I went to war, too."

CHAPTER 32

"ARE YOU GOING TO BE WARM enough?" Melora fretted as Anjele took the reins. "Heavens, if I didn't know better, I'd swear we were going to have snow. I've never known it to be so cold."

"I'll be fine. I'm so bundled up I can hardly move, thanks to you." She was wearing one of Melora's wool dresses with matching cape, too large, but it didn't matter. A heavy carriage robe was tucked about her from the waist down, and she wore a bonnet and scarf and heavy gloves. "You won't forget where I said I'd leave the buggy?" she asked.

"Hardy said he and Millard would go get it late this afternoon. But how will you get back? Are you sure you don't want to set a time for them to pick you up?" Melora rubbed her shivering hands together, teeth chattering in the early-morning chill.

Anjele repeated that she had no idea how long she would be at BelleClair and pointed out it was best she not return to New Orleans. "I'm going to have to go by sea. Surely I can find a fisherman willing to smuggle me through the blockade and get me to a Confederate ship somewhere." Noticing Melora was cold, she urged,

"You'd better get back inside, before you freeze."

"I think I'm going to cry," Melora said, "because I've a feeling I'll never see you again."

Anjele swallowed against the lump in her throat. "I know, but I'll never forget you. To think how I used to dread seeing your buggy coming down the road"—she shook her head and laughed—"but what would I have done without you now? I'll always be grateful."

"I was glad to do it. I always loved your momma, and I thought the world of your daddy, and . . ." She began to blink furiously, stepping back to wave Anjele away. "Be gone with you, before I *do* cry. The tears would freeze on my cheeks, and wouldn't that be a sight?" With a sob, she turned toward the house.

Anjele popped the reins and set the horse into a fast trot down the alley and into the cobblestone street, not looking back.

Because of the early hour and the unseasonably cold weather, few people were out. Skies were gray and overcast, and a smoky mist crept out of the rivers and swamps to swirl about the carriage, making her barely visible as she headed out of town.

She was glad for the concealing fog, not wanting to see the desolation of the plantations she passed. She could almost hear the long-ago echoes of slaves singing as they worked the hardest season of the year—sugar making. But now, misery and gloom silently whispered throughout the bleak, spiritless lands of the delta.

She was grateful not to have to go on foot through the woods, and Miss Melora had provided her with papers that would make the Union soldiers, should she be stopped, think Anjele was her, instead.

As she rode, thoughts of Brett crept into her mind.

She wanted to hate him but had to acknowledge she did care. Oh, yes, despite the anguish of knowing he'd only used her, there was no denying the wondrous moments forever embedded upon her soul. But he had been clever, able to manipulate her into trusting and believing in him. From the start, she'd been entranced, felt herself strangely drawn to him. Tender and compassionate, he had been her eyes. He had made her *feel* the world, rather than *see* it. Brett had, with words and touch, taught her to absorb life, taste it, hold it, and it was an experience she would forever remember and hold dear.

Being in his arms had been ecstasy untold. It had been glorious, and he had taken her on a journey to the stars, whisking her away amidst silver-tinged clouds of bliss and rapture. Fused together in the consummation of their passion, they had become one. Anjele had started truly believing they would find a way to be together always. Never once had he given her cause to doubt he cared.

He had also given her confidence in herself, in her ability to cope with her blindness. He had made her think it didn't matter, for they would be together despite any obstacle or handicap.

Again and again, she desperately tried to think of any clue that would indicate he had merely been using her. But there was none. Obviously, the man was a master of deceit, and knowing that made the anger boil once again.

She wished she did not love him. That was what hurt the most. True, she'd loved the part of him that was Gator, and perhaps that made it all so much worse. It was like loving one person twice as much as was meant to be, resulting in double anguish when the dream so cruelly died.

Anjele left the horse and buggy in a grove of palmettos, where they would not be seen by anyone passing by. There was little chance of people being about, anyway, for she'd not seen a soul during the ride from New Orleans. Still, she hurried along, wanting to get off the road.

At last she could see the driveway, the great house looming in the distance, and was struck by the dismal aura surrounding it. She could see the cane fields beyond, brown with rot as Melora had said, bending toward the ground as though weeping with sorrow. Cotton fields exposed yellowing buds, unpicked and left to die like the cane. All about was the evidence of how the once proud and grand plantation was falling to ultimate ruin.

A stiff breeze from the river rattled the bare limbs of the great oaks, the sound like skeletons stamping their feet in protest. Perhaps, Anjele glumly mused, she was actually hearing her father and grandfather angrily tossing about in their coffins, for it was a desolate sight to behold.

Entering the house through the rear, the overpowering silence was actually like a great, disturbing roar, almost deafening in its haunting vibrations of sadness and despair.

Surveying the service pantry, she saw signs of use. But where was everyone? Melora had said Claudia and Raymond still lived here, and a few slaves, she'd heard. Yet Anjele had not seen a soul.

A sound from the yard made her whip about in hope, and she cried out in relief to see Mammy Kesia crossing the yard from the kitchen.

Mammy broke into tears and raced toward her, arms outstretched and sobbing, "Miss Anjele, Miss Anjele, praise be to God, is it really you, child?"

"It's me," Anjele laughed, her own eyes moist as she welcomed the embrace. "Oh, am I glad to see you."

Mammy held her at arm's length, blinked in surprise as she realized, "Why, you can *see*! Lord, Jesus, child, you can see!"And then she did break into wild sobs.

Anjele urged her to calm down, drawing her inside, though the house was freezing cold. She then explained she would not be staying long. "I'm a fugitive, Mammy. If the Yankees find me here, they'll take me away and lock me up again. Now, where is everyone?"

Sniffing, wiping her nose with the corner of her apron, Mammy tearfully began, "Well, Miss Claudia, she don't never come downstairs till nearly noon, and then it's just to scream and complain about somethin'. 'Bout time fo' her, too. And Master Raymond, he's either sick drunk in the bed, or sleepin' in your daddy's study, or off in the sugarhouse, where he makes his rum.

"And there ain't nobody here but me and a few of the hands," she continued, "and they don't do nothin', no how, 'cause they hates Miss Claudia, and they knows she can't make 'em do nothin'."

Something told Anjele she didn't want to hear the answer but was driven to ask, "What about your boy, Mammy? What about William?"

Mammy burst into fresh tears as she sank down on a nearby stool. Painfully she described how William had been stricken with the ague only two months earlier. With no medicine, death came quickly. "I ain't got nobody else and nowhere to go, and I is old, Miss Anjele, too old to go traipsin' around the country lookin' for a home. At least here, I got shelter, and Miss Claudia, she does give me food. The soldiers, they took all the cows and pigs. And the horses, too, 'cept one, and they only left it, and a buggy, 'cause of Master Raymond, him bein' Dr. Duval's son. Dr. Duval, he works at their hospital, you see, so he's taken care of. And the only time we gets food is when Master Raymond sobers up long enough to ride into town and beg some from his poppa."

"Dear Lord," Anjele whispered brokenly, to think how desperate and miserable times had become.

Mammy rocked to and fro, swung her head from side to side as she moaned, "It's bad around here, real bad, and you shouldn't of even come back, 'cause if the soldiers catch you, they'll take you away. I knows they will. Oh Lordy, Miss Anjele, why'd you even come back? There just ain't nothin' to come back to."

Glancing about, Anjele repeated, "I'm not staying long, and I had my reasons for returning."

"What about when Miss Claudia finds out? She might go screamin' to the Yankees . . . ."

"I hope I'll be out of here before that happens." She started out of the room but turned to plead, "Don't say a word about me being here, Mammy, understand? Not to Claudia *or* Raymond. I'm going to hurry and get out of here as fast as I can."

"You ain't got to worry, but you better get movin', 'cause I told you, Miss Claudia, she comes downstairs every day around this time, and if she sees you, there's gonna be big trouble."

Anjele hurried on her way, heading in the direction of the study and hoping she would not find Raymond there.

The door was closed, and she reached to open it

but froze as torturous memories flashed. She remembered the last time she had gone in there. The horrible sight of her father's body, and how she'd rushed to kneel beside him. The sudden movement that caused her to turn her head, but too late. The brief, fleeting glimpse of a vaguely familiar face. And finally, a sharp, crashing pain . . . and merciful oblivion.

She took a deep breath, held it, then let it out slowly as she commanded herself to enter the room. There was no time for haunting nightmares. The past was dead, the present was bleak, and she had to take care of the task at hand and get on with her life.

Opening the door, she peered inside, flooded with relief to see the room was empty. Quickly she went to the fireplace and knelt at the hearth. On the second row of bricks, to the left, her fingers danced their way to feel for the loose bar. One, two, and according to her father, it should be the third one, and . . .

The brick shook beneath her touch.

With an excited lurch of her heart, she saw the key right where her father had said it would be. She put it in her pocket and replaced the brick. She was tingling with happiness over how everything was going so smoothly. All she had to do was get up to the crypt and look for the plates. Once found, she could be on her way.

Maybe, she mused with a mischievous grin, she'd steal Claudia's horse as she'd stolen Brett's, which would mean more sweet revenge.

She stood, pausing to take one last look around the room. Melora Rabine had sensed it was the last time the two of them would ever meet, and now Anjele had the same feeling about this house. It was doubtful she would ever return. What reason did she have?

BelleClair, as she had known it, lived it, was dead. Were it revived, it could never be the same. Perhaps it was just as well. A new life awaited her, somewhere, and even though she was all alone in the world now, she was not afraid to walk into the future.

She moved slowly around the room, touching things, reminiscing over happier days. Finally it was time to commit it all to memory.

With a wistful sigh of farewell, she turned to leave... then froze at the sight of Claudia.

She was standing in the doorway, a wretched sight to behold. Her once meticulously coiffed golden curls hung limp about her gaunt face. Her morning robe was stained, and despite the chill, she was barefoot. With a shrill giggle, she observed, "So, you can see again. Well, well." She took another sip from the glass of whiskey she held before furiously demanding, "Why'd you come back? What are you doing here, you little bitch?"

"I'm leaving now," Anjele said carefully, not wanting a scene, anxious to be on her way. "I shouldn't have come. I'm sorry."

"You're sorry?" Claudia echoed shrilly, hiccupping.

Anjele could tell she'd had too much to drink. "Yes. And I'm going—"

Claudia flung the glass at her, and Anjele ducked just before it smashed against the wall. "How dare you come back here?" she screamed, "All of this is your fault. If it hadn't been for you, BelleClair wouldn't be in ruins now . . ."

"I told you," Anjele repeated, "I'm going. There's no need for you to be upset."

Her upper lip curling back in a snarl of contempt, Claudia cried, "I was going to have what I wanted at last—you out of the way and me in control of BelleClair. I thought I had it all figured out, to have you arrested for harboring bushwhackers, and then I'd be rid of you forever, but no, the Yankees had to find out your goddamn daddy was a thief and I was the one to suffer.

"And when you escaped from prison," she raged on, "they came back, and they tore up everything again, looking for you. I told them they didn't have to worry, that I'd kill you if you came back." She started into the room.

Anjele warily backed away toward the wall separating the study from the dining room.

Reaching the fireplace, Claudia snatched up the poker, and Anjele was struck with horror to think it was the same weapon used to nearly kill her. "No, listen to me," she pleaded, "just let me leave. You can have BelleClair, and I'll never come back, I promise."

Claudia began to swing the poker, slicing it through the air back and forth, sneering as she taunted, "Oh, really, dear *sister*? You say I can have all this? I find that very generous of you, after you caused its destruction. Tell me, are you planning to give me my husband, too? Are you going to crawl out of his mind, so he'll stop trying to drown his brain to keep from thinking about you day and night? Even when I told him how I saw you in the sugarhouse that night, rutting like an animal with that Cajun, it didn't matter. Oh, he was anxious to marry me then, all right, thinking it'd make him forget you, but it didn't work. He turned into a spineless ninny, grieving for you, and then you dared come back and drove him to become a worthless sot. But now you'll pay . . . ."

From the corner of her eye, Anjele saw the door to the dining room and realized she could escape through the connecting closet. She lunged for it, flinging it open and dashing inside. Crossing the small passageway, she reached for the knob and twisted, horrified to find it locked.

At the same instant, she was plunged into darkness as the door behind her slammed shut. There was an ominous clicking sound, and she knew she was locked in . . . trapped.

Claudia laughed shrilly. "I've got you now, bitch. Did you think you could outsmart me? I saw you going down the hall, heading in here, when I was coming down the stairs, you little fool. I slipped around to lock the other door so I could drive you in there, and that's where you'll stay till the soldiers get here to take you back to prison. I'm going after them now.

"And thank you, Anjele," she crowed, pounding on the door in triumph. "Thank you for making it possible for me to get back in their good graces. Turning you in will prove my loyalty, and I hope this time they hang you."

Claudia rushed out of the study and up to her room, trembling with excitement over what she had done. She dressed quickly, grabbed her warmest cape and bonnet, and headed back downstairs.

Mammy Kesia was waiting in the foyer, and Claudia could tell by the worried look on her face she knew what was going on. She walked right up to her and slapped her face, hard. Mammy cried out, stumbled away, eyes widening in fright.

"Yes, the bitch is locked in the closet, Mammy," Claudia said between clenched teeth, "and I've a feeling you knew she was here, and if I weren't in a hurry, I'd beat you till you bleed for not coming and telling me. If you've got any ideas about letting her out once I leave, you'd better think again. I'm going into New Orleans to tell the authorities she's here, and if they come back and find her gone, they'll arrest you for helping her. They will shoot you, Mammy. Do you understand?"

Trembling from head to toe, hands clenched over her quaking bosom, Mammy fearfully whispered, "Yassum, yassum, I hear you. I won't let her out. I promise."

Claudia pushed by her and out the door, heading for the stable.

Anjele once more found herself locked in a world of darkness.

She sank to the floor in dismal defeat, and for the first time, knew it would have been better had her eyesight not returned.

She would not be here, about to be turned over to the enemy, for God only knew what fate.

She would still be with Brett, blissfully oblivious to his treachery.

He had spoken of love, a new life together, and even if it had all been a part of the deception and the scheme, at least the happiness would have lasted awhile longer.

Perhaps, she thought in bitter defeat, blindness to the cruelties of life was merciful.

Leo shuffled into the storage room and took out the broom. Damn Yankees, he fumed, they wouldn't let him alone. He had signed their stinking oath, even though he'd told them he didn't give a hoot about the war. But that wasn't good enough for them. They wanted him to work. So he had faked a limp and said he wasn't able. Then they argued that he and all the other derelicts had to be good for something, so they gave him the job of sweeping up, emptying trash, doing small chores. But last night he had forgot, because he'd managed to steal some whiskey out of one of the officer's desks and he'd got himself real drunk and passed out in his favorite alley, oblivious to the cold. The soldiers had found him and kicked him right in his butt and told him if he didn't want to find himself digging ditches, he'd better get those floors swept.

It was hard to remember to limp, because it was awkward, and his head was pounding, but he managed. Hardly anybody was around, anyway, and the place was practically deserted. Leo had heard some soldiers talking about how the officers were gathered at the navy's headquarters on the waterfront, because all hell was said to be fixing to break loose in Bayou Teche.

He didn't care. He didn't care about a damn thing but getting through and finding some more whiskey. Every week, he found a little money above the door of the tomb, but it wasn't much, and it didn't last long. He just wished he'd find that blasted glove impaled one of these nights, which would mean The Voice had found out where Anjele Sinclair was, and he could then take care of her, collect his money, and leave these parts.

It was nearly three o'clock when he finished, and he was cursing because he hadn't found any liquor in any of the drawers he'd searched. That meant he'd have to roam the alleys in hopes of finding somebody passed out with a bottle that wasn't quite empty.

He went back to the basement storage room. A lantern

on the wall provided light to see the way. Opening the door, he started to put away the broom, and that's when he saw it and cried out loud with joy.

A glove was hanging on the broom nail.

It could mean only one thing, he realized, breath coming in quick, excited gasps—The Voice wanted him at the cemetery right away, not at the usual time.

And that could also mean but one thing.

He ran from the building and headed for the cemetery and the tomb, anxious to hear The Voice tell him where Anjele Sinclair was.

CHAPTER

ANJELE POUNDED ON THE CLOSET DOOR, calling for Mammy, for anyone, to let her out. Finally, wearily, she sank to the floor in defeat.

It was over.

The soldiers would come and take her away, and all her efforts would be for naught. Yet, angered by the futility of it all, she knew she wouldn't give up. Let them take her away. This time she had her eyesight, and she'd never stop trying to escape. She was wiser now, and never again would a man be able to trick her, for she'd learned her lesson, and . . .

She lifted her head. "Who's there?" She held her breath.

Mammy's agonized voice was barely audible. "It's me, missy, and I just had to come tell you how sorry I am I can't let you out. Miz Claudia, she said if I did, the soldiers, they'd shoot me. And I's scared, missy, so scared. . . ."

Anjele sprang to her feet, jiggling the door knob as she pleaded, "Mammy, listen to me. You've got to let me out. The soldiers won't shoot you, because I'll take you with me—"

"No, I can't do that," Mammy cried, "I can't leave here, Miz Anjele. Don't you see? I ain't got no place to go, and I can't leave my baby. He's buried here, and I feel close to him, and—"

"Mammy, stop it!" Anjele was losing patience and nearing hysteria in her determination to get out before the Yankees got there. "Unlock this door and let me out. You can't do this to me, do you hear me? Claudia is lying. They won't shoot you. *Now open this door . . . .*"

Suddenly all was silent.

"Mammy, do you hear me?"

When there was no response, Anjele knew she had gone away. With all hope lost, there was nothing to do but wait for the inevitable. She sank to the floor again in desolation.

The afternoon wore on. Anjele began to wish they'd hurry up and get there so she could start making plans to escape. Maybe on the ride back to New Orleans she'd have a chance. If they put her on a horse by herself, even with her hands tied behind her back, she might be able to get away by lunging into the swamp when they crossed the bridge just down the road. They'd never be able to follow her once she reached one of the old trails, and maybe one of the Cajuns would still be in Bayou Perot to help her, and—

Again she was alert to a sound outside the door, only this time it was a scraping noise amidst muted curses.

Slowly she got to her feet, groping along one of the shelves behind her in search of some kind of weapon. Obviously the Yankees had smashed all the dishes, for she touched a piece of broken crockery. It would have to do. If she could slash out at the first soldier to enter, they might all be caught off guard, and she could dash by, and—

"Damn this lock!" a masculine voice bellowed.

The door burst open at the same instant Anjele recognized Raymond's voice.

With a shriek of joy, she tumbled into his arms, seeing Mammy standing to one side, nervously wringing her hands. She reached out to her and whispered, "Bless you, Mammy, bless you."

"Took me awhile to find him," Mammy said. "Had to look all over. He changed hidin' places. Guess Miz Claudia found all the old ones."

Raymond was clinging to Anjele like a child, head resting on her shoulder as he wept. He reeked with the sickening sweet smell of his homemade rum. She looked at Mammy with brows raised in question.

"He's like that most of the time," Mammy said with a helpless shrug. "Only time he sobers is when the food runs out, and he has to go into town to see his poppa."

Carefully, Anjele pulled from his embrace. He looked at her then with bloodshot eyes, a mellow smile on his lips as he said, "I'm not too terribly drunk at this moment, dearest. I was able to save you from Claudia's clutches, wasn't I?"

"And I'm grateful," Anjele assured but was quick to add, "You have to save Mammy and say you let me out, say you heard someone screaming and opened the door to see who it was."

He chuckled, hiccupped, then reached in his pocket for his flask and took a long swallow before replying, "Don't worry, my dear. I'm quite adept at dodging Claudia now, but oh, sweet Jesus, I wish I'd learned how to do so long ago. I'd have waited on you to come back, because"—he closed his eyes momentarily, swayed, then looked at her and grinned to vow—"you're the only woman I could ever love, Anjele."

"Thank you for saving me, Raymond," was all she could think of to say. She stepped from his embrace and watched with pity as he staggered to a chair and sat down and lifted his flask to take another drink. She turned to Mammy and explained, "I've got to get out of here. Fast. They'll be here soon. Take care of him, please, and yourself, too." She hugged her, biting back the sorrow of having to leave them, but a glance out the window told her it was nearly twilight. There was not a moment to spare.

Bleary eyed, Raymond held out a beseeching hand, calling, "Wait, Anjele. We'll run away together, you and I, and we'll make a new life. I've always loved you, Anjele . . . I always will . . . ."

She winced with regret to have to hurt him by leaving him behind, but there was no way they could travel together. She had a mission to complete, and only when it was done could she even begin to think about a new life. And, sadly, it did not include Raymond . . . or any man. She would go to her destiny alone.

She hurried to the cemetery. The first clutches of night did battle with the clinging gray vestige of the gloomy day, and the mausoleum struggled to rise above the shadows. In the months she'd been away, vines had begun to cover it but had turned brown and now drooped toward the ground. From the way the weeds had grown up in the past month, it was obvious no one had been around.

She started for the gate but paused as something in the bushes nearby caught her eye. With a stab of bitter anger, she saw it was the cane she'd dropped that fateful morning and went to pick it up. She did not see the man rushing up behind her, did not realize what was happening till he grabbed her and threw her roughly to the ground. With a cry of terror, her hands closed about the cane, swinging it wildly as she twisted about to face her attacker.

Leo was crouched over her, reaching for her throat, but the cane struck him on the side of his head, just above his ear. With a yelp of pain, he staggered backward, struggling to regain his balance.

Anjele bounced to her feet and swung again, just as he ducked, taking the blow on his shoulder. At the same instant, she saw his face, and the nightmare came flooding back with the petrifying realization that it was the same face she'd seen that night in the study. "You!" She choked out the words. "You killed my father, and I know you—I saw you that day in the field. You're Gator's father. Oh, dear God . . ."

Leo took advantage of her shock and reached out to jerk the cane from her hand. "Yes, it was me," he gloated, "and it's too bad I didn't finish you off that night, 'cause now it's gonna be real messy . . . ."

Anjele watched in frozen horror as Leo slipped the knife from his boot and started toward her.

Suddenly Brett stepped out of the shadows, gun in hand, his voice cracking through the silence like a death knell. "That's far enough, Pa."

Anjele gasped, reeled in disbelief, could not speak.

With his free hand, Brett beckoned to her, but she was too stunned to move.

Leo, mouth agape, struggled from his own stupor to cry, "Get the hell outta here, boy. I got no quarrel with you."

Brett kept the gun pointed straight at him as he attempted to convince Anjele, "You've nothing to fear from me. I was waiting outside, and when you came out of the house, I was going to follow you, but I saw him and held back. I won't hurt you," he assured her, keeping an eye on his father. "I love you. That's why I followed you from Mississippi, to tell you that, to tell you everything."

Anjele was starting to recover and rage was fast overcoming fright. "Bastard," she said, fists clenched at her sides. "Do you really think I'd believe anything you said? I know now it was all a scheme to get your hands on the plates, you goddamn traitor! Get away from me, and take your murdering father with you."

"Listen to me, damn it." Brett knew there wasn't time to argue but tried to make her understand, "Don't you see? If my father was the one out to kill you, he had orders. He wouldn't have done it on his own, and whoever is behind all this won't stop till you're dead. We've got to get out of here."

With a wild shake of her head, Anjele snapped, "No. I'm not going anywhere with you, and he's going to tell me why he killed my father . . . why he tried to kill me . . . ." She turned blazing eyes on Leo, hot tears of fury streaming down her cheeks. "Why, you devil? Why did you do it?"

Leo snickered. "He paid me. Damn good, too. But I didn't mean to kill your pa, though it don't bother me that I did. He made me do it, tried to jump me. All I wanted was them goddamn plates he stole. Then you came along, and I had to take care of you, 'cause I was afraid you'd remember me."

"And that's why you went to Ship Island to make another attempt?" Brett slowly, evenly asked. "She was blind then, remember? And she'd lost her memory. Why didn't you just leave town and forget about it?"

Leo said that's what he'd intended to do but was told that if he tried to run away without finishing the job, he'd be turned in for murdering Elton Sinclair. "And I told you, I got paid good. And I'll get paid even more when I take care of her. So get on out of my way, 'cause I'm gonna finish this job once and for all." His eyes narrowed to evil slits as he went on to taunt, "And what do you care, anyhow? You ain't so stupid as to really be in love with a little bitch who'd scream rape, are you? She made me lose the best damn job I ever had, got us both chased off, and—"

"What are you talking about?" Anjele said, whirling on Brett to admonish, "You even lied to your father? You told him you ran away, because I accused you of rape? Didn't he know you were running from a husband out to kill you for bedding his wife? You blamed *me*?"

Brett was looking at her quietly, calmly, as though peering into her very soul. After all their months together, he felt he knew her well, and he knew, somehow, in that shattering moment, she wasn't making anything up. He continued to study her in impassive silence, then turned contemptuous eyes on his father. "Tell her, damn you, tell her everything her father said to you that day."

Leo obliged, enjoying himself, sure that Brett was going to be riled when he heard it again and would go on and get out of his way.

With each word, Anjele felt the chill of abhorrence creeping. With a vicious shake of her head, she turned to Brett once more and cried, "No! That's a lie. All a lie. I never told my parents you raped me. I found out later Claudia spied on us, but at the time, I thought she'd just tattled on me for sneaking down the trellis. When they asked me who I went to meet, I wouldn't tell them."

Brett was bewildered. "Then why did your father say you claimed I raped you?"

Miserably blinking back fresh tears as the pieces all began to come together, Anjele could only whisper, "I don't know, unless he and my mother wanted to get rid of you, to keep us apart." She swallowed hard before daring to ask, "You weren't trifling with me? You weren't bedding a married woman?"

Brett had to laugh at that. "No. Where'd you get that ridiculous idea?"

She told him. About Simona and Emalee. And how she was so crushed she'd agreed to go away to England, hating him with every beat of her heart.

"Dear God," Brett whispered, realizing they had been the victims of such treachery. "All this time, I was thinking you got caught and claimed it was rape to save yourself, because I meant nothing to you."

"Oh, that's not true." Anjele was overcome with feelings she'd tried to bury, then remembered and was stung with bitterness again as she challenged, "But why did you trick me and not let me know who you were?"

"Would you have gone away with me?" His lips curved in a teasing smile. "No, you wouldn't. The truth is, I was a Union soldier, sent to New Orleans to be a bayou scout, but I was given the assignment to get you out of prison and make you think I was a spy, so you'd lead me to the plates. Somehow, they found out we'd once known each other."

"Claudia!" Anjele said. "Somehow, she was involved."

"So there was no way I could tell you who I was. After

all, you haven't held me in fond memory all these years."

She started toward him then, but Leo sliced the air with his knife in menace and roared, "I told you, I aim to kill the bitch—"

"No." There was an ominous click as Brett pulled the hammer back on his gun. "I'm not going to let you hurt her."

"And you're going to hang for murdering my father, damn you,"Anjele avowed.

Leo's eyes widened. "No, I ain't. It won't my fault, and The Voice told me to do it, anyhow."

"The Voice?" Brett echoed. "What are you talking about? Who told you to do all this?"

Nervously, daring to hope that by confiding everything he might be allowed just to take his leave and get out of their lives forever, Leo told of his mysterious encounters with the man hiding inside the crypt. "He gave me all my orders, left money for me above the door, left a glove in the closet this morning," he babbled on. "I knew to go to the grave right then, and he was waitin' inside, and he told me to get out here as fast as I could. Said she was back. Even had a horse hid out for me to ride. Said for me to kill her."

Anjele had slowly moved to stand beside Brett, all fears dissolving at the feel of his strong arm pulling her close against him. She sensed Leo was going to try to bargain for his freedom, and she listened carefully, anxious to learn the identity of the fiend who had sentenced her father to death, and her, as well.

Brett, making his voice soft and coaxing, continued, "Then nobody can really blame you, Pa. But who was it? Who was hiding inside that crypt? Did you ever see him?"

Leo realized how he didn't really want to kill the girl,

and if what she'd said was so, that she hadn't accused Brett of raping her, and Brett really did love her, then maybe they deserved to be together. He would just have to forget about the money The Voice had promised him when the job was done. He would get out of town and never look back. "I never knew till today. I never dared hang around to wait for him to come out, but I figured today would be my last chance, and I wanted to find out who it was, anyway, in case I went back and my money wasn't there. I wanted to know who to go lookin' for, so I hid and waited for him to come out, and he did."

Brett tensed, felt Anjele also stiffen. "Go on. Who was it?"

"Don't know his name," Leo said nervously, the hand holding the knife dropping to his side. "But I've seen him before. I know who he is. He—"

A shot rang out, and with a look of panic frozen on his face, Leo fell to the ground. Blood poured from the bullet hole in the back of his head.

Instinctively, at the sound of gunfire, Brett had shoved Anjele to the ground, intending to fall on top of her to shield her. At the same instant, terrified, she had lunged for him, knocking the gun from his hand without meaning to. As he reached out for it, a voice warned, "Don't try it."

Anjele whipped her head about, astounded to see Dr. Duval. "No," she whispered in denial, "it can't be. Not you . . ."

"Now you both have to die," he said, eyes cold with resolve. "I didn't mean for it to end this way, but I was afraid Leo would make another blunder, so I decided to follow him in case I had to take over. A good thing, too. I had no idea he had hidden to watch me leave the crypt."

Fright was dominated by the anguish of discovering a lifelong friend was responsible for such tragedy. "Why?" she could only ask. "Why, Dr. Duval?"

"Simple. Your father, and myself, along with some of our other friends, were involved in the takeover of the Mint. Your father took the plates, but I believe he must have become suspicious of me, because he didn't let anyone in our group know he had them."

"What he didn't know," he continued with a gloating smile, "was that I saw him take them. I knew he was just waiting for the right time to get them to the Confederacy. I made it my business to get my hands on them, and you know the rest of the story."

"You're a traitor," Anjele breathed in wonder, thinking he looked like a demon from hell, face bathed in the strange grayish glow of the creeping night shadows. "The whole time, you were actually working for the Yankees."

"I'm no fool. I made sure when New Orleans fell, I didn't fall with it. I'm not poor and starving like all those too ignorant and stubborn to act in their own best interest.

"But now it's over. All of it," he declared, raising the gun.

"Daddy, don't!" Raymond yelled, suddenly stepping from the shadows behind his father. He sounded sad, defeated, spirit broken as he pleaded, "Don't make it worse. I heard it all. I followed Anjele and saw you and heard the shot, and oh, God, don't kill them . . . ." He collapsed to his knees sobbing, covered his face in his hands so he wouldn't have to watch.

Anjele had time for one quick glimpse of Dr. Duval's stricken face before he turned the gun on himself.

* * *

For long, seemingly endless moments, no one moved or made a sound. And then Raymond began to crawl toward his father's body. Reaching him, he pulled him into his arms and began to croon, "Oh, Daddy, you didn't have to do it. I would've loved you just the same. And so would Momma. We would've forgiven you . . . ."

Brett gathered Anjele close. "It's over, Angel. He couldn't face his family finding out he was a traitor. Maybe it's best this way. But one thing is for certain—we've got to get out of here, now," he emphasized.

"The plates . . ." she whispered above the roaring within. Reaching into her pocket, she brought out the key and pointed to the crypt. "In there. In my mother's coffin.

"*Life*," she choked on a heart-wrenching sob, "*growing out of the aperture of death . . .*"

Brett had no idea what she was talking about, was concerned only with getting the plates so they could be on their way. Taking the key, he went to open the door. "You'd better wait out here," he advised as she hovered beside him. He didn't want her there when he opened the casket.

Once inside, he gathered all his strength to shove aside the heavy slab covering her mother's tomb. Holding his breath, steeling himself, glad for the faint light, he slowly raised the lid of the coffin. Avoiding the grisly sight of the decaying corpse, he ran his fingers down the side of the casket. At her feet, he felt a burlap bag, and knew he had what he was after.

He wasted no time in closing it all up again.

Outside, he handed the bag to Anjele and triumphantly told her, "Let's go."

"Not yet," she said, moving to where Raymond still held his father in his arms. "Raymond," she attempted to comfort, "If you want to come with us—"

"No." He shook his head vehemently. "No, I've got to take him home and bury him. Then I'll leave. I'll convince my mother there's nothing left for us to do. You go ahead. And hurry. Mammy said Claudia had gone to get the Yankees."

Just then, Brett saw Claudia running up the hill. "She's here," he warned. "And the soldiers won't be far behind."

Anjele gave Raymond a quick hug in parting and ran to Brett.

Raymond reached to pick up his father's gun, which was lying close by. "Get going," he ordered. "I'll hold them back. Head for the bayou. They won't dare go in after you."

Brett didn't argue, though he heard Anjele's soft cry of protest. Holding tight to her hand, he rapidly led the way, and in seconds they were swallowed by the swamp, by the night.

Claudia burst on the scene, looked from Dr. Duval's body to Leo's and shrieked, "What happened? She's killed them both. Where did she go? We've got to stop her, keep her here till the soldiers come."

Raymond, still holding the gun, gently removed his arms from around his father. He got to his feet and calmly asked, "Where are the soldiers, Claudia? Why aren't they with you? You did go to town to get them, didn't you?"

"Of course I did." She strained to see him in the semi-darkness, puzzled by his composure in the wake of the carnage, the death of his own father. Reproachfully she admitted, "They didn't think an escaped prisoner was important, said they'd be out soon, but they were all excited about a battle going on in Bayou Teche.

Rage returned to remind her how she'd found the closet empty, then heard the gunfire. "Who let her out? Mammy swore she didn't do it, so it had to be you, you stupid bastard! Don't you know you'll hang? And maybe it's for the best. You can't forget her, can you?"

Raymond knew she was nearing hysteria but easily soothed her with the lie, "She said if I'd let her out, she'd lead me to the engraving plates. I thought that was more important. It gives us something better to offer them, doesn't it? The Federal government will reward us handsomely, don't you think?"

Claudia was overcome with joy. "Of course, you ninny. We'll have soldiers to help us rebuild BelleClair, all the food and supplies we need. Where are they?" She glanced about wildly, excitedly. "I want to be waiting with them in my hands when they get here."

He pointed to the crypt. The door was still open. "In there. Elton didn't think anyone would think to look in there."

"Of course they wouldn't. What a wonderful hiding place."

"They're lying on the top of Twyla's casket."

She blew him a kiss, suddenly cheered and buoyant to think everything was going to be all right, after all. To hell with Anjele. Let her go. As long as she didn't come back, Claudia didn't care.

She ran inside the crypt.

Raymond swiftly moved to slam and lock the heavy door behind her.

He could hear her screaming as he lifted his father's body in his arms and started down the hill.

By the time he got to the bottom, he couldn't hear any sound at all coming from the cemetery.

He figured in a few days, it would be real quiet up there.

Real quiet, indeed.

Safely in the bowels of the bayou, Brett took Anjele in his arms and kissed her till they were both breathless.

When at last he released her, she gazed up at him in the scant light and murmured, "I love you, Gator, believe that."

"Oh, it's Gator now, is it?" he responded huskily, then murmured, "I do believe you, *ma chère*, and know that I love you, too. I always have. I always will."

"What waits for us out there?" she asked timorously. "Where do we go from here?"

"We've got a war waiting, and when it's over, we've got the rest of our lives—together."

"That's all we'll have, but it's all that counts, my darling. As long as I have you," she promised, "I won't look back to what I've had to leave behind."

"If we can find it, we've got a gold mine waiting," he told her with a mysterious grin, "but we've got something more important to look for than that."

"And what might that be?" she pressed closer, lifting her face for his kiss.

"Springtime, Angel," he whispered. "We've got to go find springtime, and flowers, so I can hold heaven in my hand, my heart, for always."

And his lips claimed hers in promise of spring eternal . . . and *heaven in a wildflower.*

New York Times bestselling author, Patricia Hagan, has published 21 books with over eleven million copies in print. A former award-winning motorsport journalist, she resides in the western North Carolina mountains with her husband, Erik.